DAYS OF WHINE AND VOLLEYBALL

R. Paul Fry

For Susan, Hannah and Natalie,
My joy and inspiration

PUBLISHER'S NOTE
This is a work of fiction. Names, characters, places, business establishments, and incidents either are the product of the author's imagination or are used fictiously.

PART ONE

FINDING A SPORT

CHAPTER ONE

DREAMS OF THE EVERYDAY SPORTS DAD

Let's face it, Saul thought. Every dad's dream is to have a son.

When that son turns out to be a daughter, everything still works out. The dad ends up loving the daughter just as much and probably more given his natural instinct to protect said daughter from the untrusting boy scum that stains the earth, the kind that festers inside the walls of high schools, shopping malls, movie theaters, dance clubs, chat rooms, or any other nefarious place that facilitates contact with the female kind.

Before that daughter exists, however, or even before the subtly disguised admissions to friends and family that go something like: "Oh, I'm just happy we have a healthy baby. I really didn't care if it was a boy or a girl. I always wanted to have a little daddy's girl in the family." Yes, before those sugarcoated lines of regurgitated BS, a dad still secretly yearns for that son.

He can't help himself. It's part of his DNA. He's driven by the simplest, most cliched of images: throwing a perfect spiral to his son's outstretched hands on a cool, crisp November afternoon, mimicking the Boys of Summer by shagging fly-balls on a freshly mown baseball diamond, or trading shots in a game of Horse on a smoothly-paved driveway with the basketball goal perched high atop the garage door. These are all natural longings for a dad to have.

Saul Bryson had these longings. He had thought about them for quite a while. For his boy, academics and other important life lessons of society, business, and industry could wait. He wanted his son to have every opportunity to be the athlete he couldn't be. He had it all mapped out in his head, his so-called Master Athletic Plan, or MAP for short. It had been ruminating in his cluttered subconscious for years in various states of alteration, but it could be summed up in three basic steps.

Step One: find a sport.

Find a sport that will showcase his boy's amazingly-gifted attributes, attributes that obviously were passed down to him from his devoted and attentive father.

Step Two: outwork the competition and out-father the other fathers.

Practice and train everyday and be there for support always. Whether his boy needs mental or physical encouragement, JUST BE THERE.

Step Three: bask in the fruits of their labor.

This would manifest itself in winning, lots of winning, along with lots of championships and trophies and accolades such as all-district and all-state honors that would adorn the shelves of their home, looking like a decadent metallic shrine to some obscure cult or religion.

Yes, his son would accomplish things Saul never dreamed of accomplishing. And it didn't have to end in high school. There was the college scholarship to consider--from a prestigious university no doubt. Saul envisioned envious dads looking on in awe at HIS boy, the one with the full ride to the University of

Texas or UCLA or North Carolina. And it never would have happened if it weren't for the time and commitment put into training and teaching him everything there was to know about the game, not to mention all the talent and prowess his boy was simply born with, a natural byproduct from his dad's outstanding gene pool.

After college, he could attempt a pro career. He could be that good. Sure the odds are tough, but not every athlete has the upbringing, desire and mental toughness instilled in him by the kind of loving, caring father that didn't leave anything to chance. You make your own destiny in this world and Saul could certainly help in making his boy's. Saul recalled reading an article once that said the odds of an athlete making it to the NFL or NBA were low, somewhere between zero and one percent. Pretty tough odds, he reasoned. But that's why we dream and why we have to dream big. Start the boy on a course early and get him ahead of everyone else and the sky's the limit.

Saul was sorting through these paternal aspirations as he was cruising along Interstate 90 near downtown Seattle on a typical silver and gray evening. He wasn't asleep at the wheel, per se, but he was guilty of daydreaming while he drove his nine-months pregnant wife, Veronica, to the hospital. Veronica's water hadn't broke so there was no need to rush, which meant Saul felt perfectly fine imagining his new son's future during the twenty minute ride to Washington Medical.

His Master Athletic Plan was never something to be put to paper. It resided solely in his head where it was free to be edited at a moment's notice. It also meant his dreams could be grand and untethered, even a tad overzealous at times, but no one else needed to know that as far as he was concerned.

Veronica was a week past her due date and her doctor had recommended inducing the labor if it reached that point. She was fine with the decision. The same thing had happened with their first child, Brianna. There were some risks with inducing labor but Veronica didn't mind them since it made the delivery less stressful and, more importantly, narrowed the pain threshold by preventing a prolonged labor.

Brianna had been the ideal first child, a beautiful baby with curly blond hair, blue eyes and a great smile. Saul used to joke that they should have named her Marilyn, because she favored Marilyn Monroe. Both Saul and Veronica were amazed at how beautiful she was. Saul's adoring mother called her the baby to end all babies because she was so perfect.

Saul had always said that most babies weren't cute even though that's the first compliment that comes out of everyone's mouth when seeing a baby for the first time. But both Saul and Veronica, being as objective as parents could be, agreed that Brianna was especially beautiful. To top it off, her behavior and personality were almost angelic. They had very few problems with Brianna when she was a baby. She slept through the night religiously and during the day she had a delightful and happy countenance.

Saul was a little disappointed when he discovered Brianna wasn't going to be Harper, which was the name they were prepared to give their child if Brianna was a boy, but he hid his disappointment well and got over it quickly. Yes, he said the aforementioned obligatory remarks to friends and family: "I'm just happy we have a healthy baby. I didn't care it if was a boy or a girl. Truth be told, I always wanted a little daddy's girl in the family." But the longer he held Brianna and discovered how easy it was to make her laugh, a simple pleasure he enjoyed immensely, the more he became at peace with it all. Besides, there would be more babies to come. Saul and Veronica had agreed they wanted a big family with three or four kids. And the odds were high that the next one would be a boy.

Ever the statistician, which came about naturally from his love of sports, Saul had calculated the odds of having a boy based on the siblings of their immediate family. He had two brothers and a sister and Veronica was the only sister to two brothers. That meant, based on his very crude attempt at statistical analysis, that the odds of having a boy this time were greater than ninety percent. Veronica knew his calculation was crazy and challenged it internally, but went along with it because she didn't want to take away from his excitement. She also truly felt, deep down, through whatever innate sense a mother has regarding the sex of her baby, that she was carrying a boy.

With Brianna, they didn't find out her sex until she was born. They were doing the same thing with baby number two. They both believed in being surprised at the time of birth, that there were very few miracles in life and this was an event that shouldn't be spoiled by the benefit of today's technology.

Whatever urge Saul might have had to know the baby's sex was alleviated by one certain fact. He knew it was a boy. At least, he was 99 percent sure. How did he know this? It wasn't because of Veronica's natural maternal instinct or his crude statistical calculation. It was because of what he saw and heard at Veronica's final sonogram.

He could see his son's private parts on the screen with his own eyes. He was sure he made them out. There it was, the skinny little thing jutting out like a little golf tee. He had never seen this image before in previous sonograms, but it made sense that he would notice it this time because the baby was further along in his development.

To add to his certainty, when the sonogram was over, the doctor accidentally said the following: "Everything looks good, he is . . . sorry, I mean, IT is going to be one healthy baby."

The doctor corrected herself in mid-sentence! It was an obvious mistake on the doctor's part. Veronica didn't catch it or didn't think anything of it, but Saul did. He had put it all together. He was going to have a son.

It hadn't been sixty minutes after the epidural was administered when Veronica was dilated to a point where they were ready to begin the heavy breathing and pushing part of what has been falsely labeled the miracle of childbirth. Pacing back and forth in the room waiting for something to happen, Saul didn't enjoy this part of the birthing process, having to give his beloved wife moral support while re-educating her on how to breathe. The more he thought about it, there was no part of the birthing process he enjoyed.

During said miracle, he would have much rather been transported to the 1960s when real men with real cigars lounged in the waiting room biding their time until the big news came. They then simply walked down the hall to the nursery and proudly inspected their child for the first time, wrapped all clean in swaddling cloth not unlike the baby Jesus in His manger.

When Brianna came into the world, Saul witnessed first hand the utter horror of childbirth. It wasn't pretty. Watching horses or cows give birth in those old educational nature films was less horrific than watching Brianna pass through Veronica's vaginal canal.

So as he anxiously awaited the arrival of his new son, he couldn't help but turn away from most of the gross stuff. He had a weak gag reflex and the sight of blood, vomit, feces or even amniotic fluid made him extremely nauseous.

"I see the crown!" the doctor said frantically.

Saul, forgetting all the gross stuff for a split second, released Veronica's hand and ran over to see his new baby son.

The doctor looked at Saul. "Mr. Bryson, would you like to help bring your baby into the world?"

"No sir, doctor. You're doing fine. That's what we're paying you for, right?"

The doctor looked at him strangely. "Okay, if that's what you want."

Veronica pushed ferociously a couple of times until the baby slid out quickly into the doctor's arms. It came out so fast Saul couldn't make out the sex. Shouldn't he have at least seen the little golf tee? Before he could get a second view, they had slapped the baby on Veronica's stomach.

Veronica squeezed the baby with all the love a mother can muster. "Welcome to this world, sweet Harper," she said adoringly.

Right name, Saul thought. Before he even had time to ask if it was a boy, the doctor blurted out, "Congratulations, Mr. and Mrs. Bryson, you have a healthy baby girl."

"Baby what?" Saul shouted. He then looked at Veronica. "But you said Harper."

"I wanted that name whether it was a boy or a girl, dear," she said, looking at him with such warm, happy eyes. "Remember?"

"Oh, that's right," he said, trying to gather himself. "That's great. That's fantastic."

"Is everything okay?" She asked.

"Sure, no problem. There are millions of other names for the next one. I love Harper."

Saul was still in a state of shock but he was disguising it well. Nothing against the new baby but all the signs had pointed to a boy. Harper was supposed to be a boy. That was his father's name and his father was a boy the last time he checked. In his head, he started recalculating his 90 percent probability scenario trying to figure out what had happened."

"Scissors, Mr. Bryson?"

"Huh?" He grunted as the doctor was handing him the severing tool.

"You can cut the umbilical cord, Mr. Bryson."

Saul was still trying to do the calculation in his head. Dazed, he barely noticed when the doctor guided Saul's hand and helped him squeeze the scissors, separating Harper's cord from Veronica. He didn't cut Bree's cord. His gag reflex wouldn't permit it. But in the mass confusion of mathematical improbability and shocking gender surprise, his gag reflex must have disengaged temporarily.

"Thank you, Mr. Bryson. Would you two like to keep the cord and placenta?"

"Huh?" Saul asked, coming back from the void. "Oh, God no. We don't have any need for organic souvenirs. My stomach couldn't take it knowing that was in our freezer."

The doctor turned to Veronica. "Mrs. Bryson, we are going to begin cleaning you up. Just so you know, the labor did cause some minor tearing and you will require some suturing. We will begin that process now."

Veronica nodded to the doctor. "Thank you." Then she looked at Saul. "Honey?"

"Yes, dear."

"You want to hold our new baby?"

"Of course I do," Saul said, now back in reality and remembering the reverence of the moment. He walked over and cradled little Harper in his arms. Her face was a bright little red ball of scrunched-up skin. She wasn't the prettiest baby he had ever seen. He was just being as honest and objective as a parent could be, but he didn't relay this to Veronica, of course.

"Everything okay, sweetie?" Veronica whispered.

"Of course everything is okay." He sat down on the bed beside her. "We have a beautiful, healthy baby girl." Minor fib on the beautiful.

"I know you wanted a boy. We'll have one next time," Veronica assured him, looking more tired and sleep-deprived by the moment.

"Of course we will. I'm not worried. I love you, Very. Very, very much." Then he whispered, "But you need to get some rest now. We really don't need to be discussing our family's future while vaginal stitching is going on."

Veronica laughed and closed her eyes, slightly dozing off.

He was lucky to have her. Very was Veronica's nickname which he had given her at a time when their passion for each other was young and flourishing. Sure, it was corny, but the word "very" seemed to aptly match all the overabundance of love he was feeling for her at the time. Plus, he just liked nicknames. Brianna had become Bree (spelt in honor of Saints quarterback Drew Brees) just like Harper would soon become Harp.

He never had a nickname and that bothered him, but it's hard to create a nickname from just a one-syllable name. His son will have a two-syllable name for sure. And his nickname will be cool. How great an athlete he would be would have to remain in the thoughts and dreams of Saul's mind for a while longer.

In the meantime, he stared at his new daughter and kissed her on the cheek. He tried to etch the moment into his memory. "God has given us another angel, little Harper," he said admiringly. Little did he know that this would be the last time he'd use the words Harper and angel in the same sentence.

As perfect a baby as Bree had been to raise, Harper was the exact opposite. It all started with the yellow jaundice that required weeks of phototherapy. That was the easy part. Harper then developed a case of colic for the ages. Usually lasting for just a few weeks, Harper's condition ran on for months. Endless days and nights of crying fueled endless days and nights of no sleep. All the love, warmth, caring and reassurance Harper's parents provided were useless. Harper cried on.

Amid the days, weeks and months of chaos, Saul and Veronica were never able to tell exactly when the colic actually ended because at some point Harper's diagnosis transitioned from colic to night terrors. It's uncommon for babies to have night terrors at such a young age but Harper, as her parents were discovering, was an uncommon baby.

Night terrors are not nightmares. Nightmares are a walk in the park compared to night terrors. Night after night, Harper would wake up screaming uncontrollably like she was possessed. Veronica would try to hold her and Harper would resist all attempts at cuddling. She wanted to be left alone, but yet she wailed at the top of her lungs for something.

Saul and Veronica could never figure out why Harper was crying. Was she wanting comfort? Was she wanting to tell them something like I just saw Freddy Krueger in my room and please don't leave me here alone for Gods' sake? They never knew.

Saul blamed it on sleep deprivation, but one night when the night terrors began again, it was his turn to go tend to Harper. He came running back into their bedroom aghast.

"Very, wake up!"

"I am awake, dear. You can't sleep when your baby's crying next door."

"I swear I just saw Harper's head spin around."

"What?"

"Like in that movie *The Exorcist*, you know?"

"Oh, Saul, get back in bed. I will go tend to her."

Evidently, Saul was experiencing his own night terror but after that evening, he never looked at Harper in quite the same way. It didn't help that her eyes were a deep green and at times stood out so much they resembled Linda Blair's eyes when the devil was inside of her. He had a new nickname for Harp now, Exorcist Baby. He only said it aloud jokingly a few times but Veronica would quickly rebuke him for it. He promised her the nickname would only last until the night terrors subsided.

During Harper's second year, another problem began. There was no name for it. It was not a diagnosed condition. It was another parental challenge sent from God above, Saul mused, or from below depending on how much you believe *The Exorcist*. Saul termed it "Swollen Colon Syndrome." All of the sudden, Harper had trouble pooping.

The doctors said the problem would go away eventually as Harper's bowel muscles developed and got used to pushing out the stool. In the meantime, taking care of Harper's condition required dedicated parents willing to do anything for their little girl, including sticking their fingers up her butt to loosen the feces so she could defecate properly.

Veronica became an expert at this; Saul, not so much. His weak gag reflex kicked in every time he tried to help. This was not surprising given the same thing occurred when he tried to change a diaper. The number of times he changed a diaper you could count on both hands. They usually happened in emergency situations when Veronica was out of town and Bree was unavailable.

Thankfully, Bree had become pretty reliable with changing diapers. He could manage her from afar and make sure she was

11

doing it properly. As long as he didn't have to smell or see the poop, he was okay.

Bree was only three years older than Harper but was astutely aware of the inherent obligations that come with being a big sister. She was ecstatic to find out Harper was a girl and not a boy. She now had a real playmate and she cherished the time playing mother, friend and big sister to baby Harper.

The problems the parents were experiencing with Harper didn't register with Bree. She thought Harper was no trouble at all. She thought the scenes of Harper crying uncontrollably and the parents pulling poop out of her rear-end were hysterical. They were just part of the joys of sisterhood. It also helped that Bree had no trouble sleeping through every colic or night terror episode. She was always well-rested and ready to go the next day.

This actually helped Veronica. With Bree's readiness to play with Harper and keep her occupied, Veronica could take little catnaps during the day and catch up on housework that she was always behind on.

Saul went to work sleep-deprived most days. He would come home exhausted, unobservant as to how poorly the house was being kept. Veronica was glad he was oblivious to those things. They were a good team. They both managed to do their part. What he lacked in changing diapers he made up for in other things. Together, they would find a way to get through the days of whine and constant constipation.

Veronica hoped that the news she had to tell Saul that evening wouldn't overwhelm him. They hadn't had much time in their life of late to discuss important things, like the future. The last couple of years had flown by as Harper's issues consumed their days and Saul's job took him places both geographically and mentally. At times, Veronica would wonder what was going through his head. She always assumed it was the pressures at work but sometimes she thought it might be something else, like thoughts of his father. Saul had unresolved issues with his dad and she could tell at times, he struggled with it.

He came home that evening tired as usual. She had learned to give him space when he got home. He needed the time to go to his decompression chamber, otherwise known as a closet, take off his uniform, otherwise known as a suit and tie, and change into something relaxing, which usually featured an elastic waist band. He was then ready to catch up on the events of the day with her and the family.

After dinner that night, the girls went upstairs to play. Veronica asked Saul out to the patio to drink a glass of wine. Their patio was lushly landscaped and featured a great view of the Seattle skyline and the Olympic mountain range. It was a great place to relax and unwind. It was also a great place to talk about all things family-or-work-related in a quiet, undisturbed setting. Saul termed it their Conference Room for Private Family Discussions and it was ideal for the news that Veronica was about to relay.

"Whenever I want to enjoy our view, there are always clouds," Saul said in a forlorn tone looking up at the sky. "It would be nice to see the stars, the moon or the sun for a change."

"It's been a nasty winter," Veronica said in agreement. "We knew we couldn't change the weather when we moved here."

They had lived in the great Northwest for the past six years. They transferred from their home in Dallas with the hope that a willingness to relocate would move Saul up the corporate ladder more quickly. Unfortunately, for six years now they had been on the same rung. The natural beauty of Seattle was starting to wear thin, especially during winter when the gray, misty days hid the spectacular scenery you knew was there.

"You ever feel like moving back to Texas?" Saul asked.

Veronica was a little surprised by the question. "Occasionally, especially on days like this."

"We're in the seafood capital of the world and we don't like seafood. We're in the coffee capital of the world and we don't like coffee. You find that strange?"

"We knew that when we came here, Saul. We wanted the adventure. Remember?"

He chuckled. "True. But right now all I want is a big plate of greasy Tex-Mex. This Northwest-Mex sucks. How can you prepare food that looks so pretty yet tastes so bland? You've got to work at making Mexican food bland, don't you?"

Veronica raised her hands in defense." You're preaching to the choir."

He let out a long sigh. "I just wonder where this job will take me next, you know? I've been here a little longer than I expected."

"It will work out. It always does." Veronica said, sensing an opening. "Besides, maybe we're meant to be here for a little longer."

"Why would you say that?" Saul asked curiously.

Veronica hesitated a bit, then said, "Because I'm late."

"Late for what?"

"My period."

Saul looked at her strangely. "You're kidding, right?"

Veronica shook her head no. Saul looked up at the overcast darkness.

"Are you sure we are ready for this?" He asked.

"I don't know. It's not the best timing that's for sure."

"Are you sure it's mine?" Saul asked, while doing a lousy job of keeping a straight face. "After all, our rate of doing the nasty has slowed substantially with Harper and all?"

Veronica laughed. "I'm pretty sure it's yours, although Rock the gardener was here about five weeks ago so . . .

"Rock?" Saul blurted out.

"Great nickname, huh?" Veronica teased. Then she got a little more serious. "Listen Saul, let's not worry about this right now. It may be a false alarm. If nothing changes in a few days, I'll go see the doctor, okay?"

"Sounds good, Hon," he said, trying to act as if he were calm and settled down.

She could tell he wasn't.

As Saul drove to work the next day, he had still not settled down. He spent his time and energy considering the possibility of baby number three, but spent more time and energy thinking about baby number two, the one that had worn his ass out. Did he really have the strength and stamina for a third baby? Did he have the time to commit to a third baby? Yes, he still wanted a boy and all the wonderful things that went with that, but did he want a boy if it meant he had to go through the jaundice and the colic and the night terrors and the Swollen Colon Syndrome?

Two parents and two kids was a good size for a family. You could ride most amusement park rides together. You could sit in most booths and tables at restaurants without having to get a special setup. You could get normal-sized cars without having to go the mini-van route, which was so beneath his urban professional status.

He then started thinking about a conversation he had a few weeks ago with Charlie, his boss and fellow partner-in-crime at the work place. Charlie was the father of four girls, which meant he was also the father of four college tuitions and the future financier of four weddings. Even with all that, he said he never missed not having a boy. He loved his girls and also loved the fact they were all athletes. Each played a different sport in school. He reminded Saul of Title IX and what that did for women's athletics several years ago; how it opened up equal opportunities for women to compete in college sports. Charlie thought girls today still had a better shot at getting an athletic scholarship than boys did.

Amid all the pondering, Saul began to ask himself some hard questions like, did he really have to have a son? Couldn't he throw a baseball to Bree or Harper just as easily as he could throw a baseball to Tyson? (Tyson was his current favorite boy name and he loved the rhyming potential it had with Bryson, plus the nickname Ty.) Couldn't the joy and satisfaction be the same if he raised a female athlete? Girls can play basketball and a host of other sports. They can't play football but who wants to deal with their kid getting their head bashed in everyday.

Saul spent most of the day considering these questions and going through the pros and cons of baby number three. A lot of his decision would be based on what Veronica wanted. After all, they agreed before they were married that four kids would be a great number for their big family. And there may not be any point in reconsidering, especially if she was already pregnant.

He arrived home a little earlier than normal because he wanted to talk with Veronica about the thoughts he had that day. Also, it was Monday Night Football night and when you lived in Seattle, that meant that the game started at 5:30 p.m., Pacific Standard Time, not late at night like it did on the East Coast. After his daily decompression routine, he came to the kitchen in his relaxed evening attire, a Dallas Cowboys sweatshirt and elastic-waisted sweatpants.

"I guess you're not going to the parent meeting at the pre-school tonight?" Veronica deduced after looking at his clothing.

"What? That was tonight?"

"Yes. I reminded you this morning."

"But the game's tonight, Cowboys and Seahawks," Saul pleaded.

"I'm fine if you want to stay home. Bree and I can do this on our own. That way you can keep Harper."

Saul's CODE RED antenna immediately went up. He had to quickly compute the probability of Harper having a fecal crisis during the football game versus going to the parent meeting and having Veronica there to handle any emergency.

"How is Harper feeling today?" He carefully inquired.

"She's had a very good day. She actually had a nice big drop this morning."

That was encouraging, he quickly thought to himself. Usually that meant she wouldn't have her second drop until late at night.

"And how long do you think the meeting will last?"

"We should be back by eight at the latest."

Perfect. He estimated the odds were below ten percent for a possible CODE RED before 8 p.m. "Ok, Hon. I think I will stay here with Harp and enjoy the game."

"All right. You guys have fun. There are some leftovers in the fridge you can warm up."

Around 6 p.m., when the football game was still in the first quarter, Harper started getting hungry. Uh-oh. Sometimes eating could stir up her digestive system and wake up the intestinal tract. Saul didn't want that to happen on his watch. He tried to keep her mind off food by playing some games with her. During commercial breaks, he would also turn the channel to cartoons to divert her attention.

He was able to delay dinner until halftime. The kitchen clock read 7:05 p.m. In less than an hour, the cavalry would be home. For the next fifty-five minutes, he kept his eyes on the game clock and the kitchen clock. As the game moved to the fourth quarter, he began to get nervous. His beloved Cowboys were losing by four points. He had been talking his Cowboys up all week at the office and had put a little money on the game. He didn't want to hear any trash talk about how great the Seahawks were from his native office mates.

The Cowboys were driving for the go-ahead score with just under seven minutes left in the game. Romo completed a 35-yard pass to tight-end Jason Witten and Saul jumped up and screamed.

"Way to go! Come on, Cowboys!"

Harper cracked up laughing at her father's antics. She started clapping her hands. "Way to go, Cowboys!" She shouted.

Saul looked at her smiling face and grinned. He then looked at the kitchen clock. 7:45 p.m. "Come on, Mommy," he muttered through his teeth.

Romo threw another pass that moved the ball inside the Seahawks' twenty-yard line. The game clock ticked below five minutes. Saul was beginning to get worried they might score with too much time on the clock. A running play was next and it moved the Cowboys to the eight-yard line.

"Yes!" Saul cheered.

"Yes!" Harper echoed.

"Eight more yards, Harper. Here we go."

The next play was a pass play. Romo stepped back in the pocket to find a receiver. He threw a perfect spiral to the end zone. There was only one problem. No Cowboy receiver was there. He threw it right into the hands of a Seahawks defender who began returning the ball 100 yards for a touchdown.

"NOOOO!" Saul shouted.

"NOOOO!!" Harper began crying in unison.

Saul knew the game was over and slumped in the couch. He thought Harper was sharing in his disappointment.

"Ouch, Daddy, tummy! Harper cried.

Saul turned his head slowly from the game to his daughter. Uh-oh. He looked at the kitchen clock. 7:50 p.m. Harper's face was turning red. Tears were starting to pour down her cheeks. She had that look of utter unpleasantness.

"Tummy hurts, Daddy," she wailed.

Looks like I've lost twice tonight, Saul thought, as he bent over to pick her up. "You have poopy?" He asked her.

Harper nodded.

"Okay, let's see what we can do." Saul rushed her upstairs to her changing area.

"Are you sure you have poopy?" Saul asked, hoping it might be a false alarm.

She nodded again. Saul looked at his watch. 7:53 p.m. He took two deep breaths and then opened up her diaper. He was relieved there was no poopy in the diaper.

"There's no poopy there," he told her.

Harper screamed in pain, "Yes, poopy."

Saul then lifted her legs up and tried to look more closely. There it was and Saul's gag reflex took over. He immediately started convulsing and vomiting on the carpet.

"Oh, my God. Sorry Harper," he said trying to compose himself.

Saul had seen a huge round boulder of stool compacted in Harper's anal cavity. It was not coming out. "Harper, can you try pushing a little harder?"

She continued to bawl her eyes out, those same green Exorcist-Baby eyes from the night terrors.

"Okay, okay, Daddy is going to help," his voice sounding nasally now as he tried to hold his breath and not smell the odor. Saul reached for some latex gloves and put them on. He positioned her legs so that he could try to reach in and dislodge some of the black matter. As he reached in, Harper let out another scream just as Saul started gagging up more of his dinner. He had to reposition fast so his vomit didn't hit Harper. He then made the mistake of looking at his own vomit on the carpet and that induced further convulsions.

"It's okay, Harper. Daddy's back," Saul assured her as he neared the table again.

He positioned her legs again for another approach. His watch now read 7:56 p.m. He moved his right index finger into position. He started gagging again but there was nothing left to come out of his stomach. He continued to gag off and on as he steered his finger into a crevice that enabled him to loosen some of the stool. Saul sensed victory.

"I think I've done it, Harper. Now let's start to push again."

But she had already pushed. Suddenly, all of her load came flooding out onto Saul's hands, his face just inches away from the pile.

"Hello, we're home," shouted Veronica from downstairs. "Right on time."

Saul looked at his wrist. Some of the defecation was on the face of his watch. He tried to wipe it away. Straight up eight o'clock the watch read. Very had beaten the buzzer. He couldn't even scold her for being late.

"Up here, Very, and hurry," Saul pleaded, panting heavily from still trying to hold his breath.

Veronica rushed upstairs and viewed the mess. "Oh my," was all she could say.

"Everything's okay except the carpet's a little messy," Saul panted.

"I see that. Why don't you head downstairs and decompress again while I contact the HazMat team."

"Very funny," Saul said, not wasting any time to exit from the disaster zone.

"Go, Cowboys!" Harper shouted as he left the room. Saul looked back at Harper who was all smiling and aglow again. She had pushed out her poopy and Mommy was home. What could be better when you were a two-year old.

Outside on the patio, Saul was staring out at another cloudy evening. No stars and no moon to admire. Veronica brought out a can of beer for him to drink.

"You think your tummy can stomach this?" She teasingly asked.

"I think so." He reached for the can but noticed he still had his latex gloves on.

"Take those off and use this," Veronica said. She was also holding a bottle of Purell.

"Thank you," Saul complied. "How was the parent meeting?"

"Uneventful. Unlike your evening," she laughed. "But something eventful did happen today."

"What's that?"

"I got my period."

"Oh, thank God," Saul immediately blurted out in relief. He then realized the weight of what he had just said. "I'm sorry, I didn't mean . . ."

"Don't worry about it. I'm relieved, too," she interrupted.

"Really?"

She pulled out her own can of beer from her pants pocket. "You want to celebrate?" She asked.

"Definitely," he said, touching his can to hers.

"I can't deal with another kid right now," she said.

"I know what you mean. Heck, I can't deal with another bowel movement."

"I know how badly you want a boy and all, but . . ."

"That's not necessarily the case," Saul interrupted.

"What? You've always wanted a boy, especially with the relationship with your dad and all."

"Trust me, I've been doing a lot of thinking about this." Saul proceeded to tell her about his conversations with Charlie and Title IX and how Charlie's daughters had all been great athletes in school and about everything else that had been flowing through his mind since Veronica's surprise announcement the previous night.

"But what about you?" Saul asked Veronica. "You've always wanted a big family."

Veronica paused for a moment. "I love the size of our family as it is."

"Very, I love you baby. Great minds think alike." He leaned over and kissed her and then started to laugh at something.

"What is it?" Veronica asked.

"My mother thought Bree was the baby to end all babies," he said. "Guess she was wrong."

Veronica laughed at the remark and said, "I guess Harp has that distinction now."

They headed back in the house and Saul noticed Bree standing in the kitchen holding a kickball in her hands. Saul thought this might be an omen of athletic wonders to come.

"Hey, there's my little athlete. What have you been up to?" Saul inquired.

"Oh, just bouncing the ball off Harper's head," Bree said laughingly.

"Let me see that."

Bree handed him the ball. "You know how to play catch?" He asked.

"No, Daddy."

"It's time your old Dad showed you." Saul told her to stand back a few feet and to hold out her hands. "Get ready. Here it comes." He tossed the ball gently in the air and watched it slowly approach her arms and then pass right through them, hitting the ground with a thud. There was no effort by Bree to even attempt to catch the ball.

Bree giggled, "That was fun, Daddy, let's do it again."

While not the result Saul was striving for, he was at least pleased with her enthusiasm. Little did Bree know that this night was the beginning of her and Harper's path to a professional athletic career, all dreamt up in the mind of their devotedly proud father. His MAP was nearing activation, although it needed some minor modifications since a girl would now be catching the spiral and shagging fly-balls and shooting baskets.

As Saul continued to bounce the ball with Bree, he couldn't help but harbor some doubt about their decision. Were they choking away their dreams of a large family because they weren't tough enough to handle a little adversity? Was his gag reflex making him choke away his dream of having a son? Or were they just being practical in an ever more practical world. Love was love, whether it was for a son or a daughter, he surmised. Bree and Harper had proven that. But it would take some time before he would truly be at peace with their decision.

CHAPTER TWO

THE OBSESSIVE SEARCH FOR SPORT

Veronica was a little nervous.

Her husband was gearing up for the big sports push. According to Saul, Bree had finally come of age to begin her competitive sports career. Veronica had no problem with her daughters playing sports. She just didn't want them getting annihilated. Bree still seemed so fragile in her frail seven year-old body and Veronica could only envision nightmarish thoughts of broken legs and fractured arms. She knew when she married Saul that his intense sports drive was something she would have to live with. She knew it was a byproduct of the relationship he had with his father and, in some weird way, that attracted her to him even more. She had never been a sportswoman herself; never swung a bat, never shot a basketball, never had the desire. She was a band nerd at heart.

Her formative days were spent battling for first chair in the school orchestra, flirting with boy band nerds at band camp, and sweating out days on the football field practicing for the marching band. The flute was her sport, she would tell Saul, while he would correct her and call it her art. But even as a band nerd, she was still attracted to the stud football, basketball and baseball players like most girls were, as long as they looked somewhat intelligent. She thought Saul looked somewhat intelligent when they first met but was a little concerned when she later learned he thought, at first glance, she looked flaming hot. She expected something a little more romantic and Mensa-esque.

She hoped that Saul's intelligence would kick in when it came to finding a sport for Bree and that he would modulate his intensity based on his daughter's age and physical ability. For example, she didn't want Bree playing basketball. It looked too dangerous and, since it was Saul's sport, she worried about a dad's overzealous expectations.

As they entered this new phase in their lives, she couldn't help but feel she was flying blind a bit. She didn't have any real first-hand knowledge of playing sports. She didn't have any real advice to give. She told herself repeatedly all she could do now as mother to her two daughters was do everything in her power to keep their bodies safe from physical injury, ensure they were enjoying themselves in what ever physical activity they undertook, and make sure her testosterone-fueled husband didn't expect them to be the second coming of Michael Jordan before they graduated from elementary school.

To her pleasant surprise, she was relieved when Saul told her that the first sport they were going to try was soccer. It seemed like an intelligent decision and quieted her nerves just a bit. Not a lot, mind you, but just a bit.

Saul wished Veronica would give him a little more credit when he saw the look of relief on her face when he mentioned Bree would play soccer. He knew better than to start Bree with basketball. It required too much skill and coordination for her age. Plus, basketball was his sport and he didn't want to be the kind of father that forces his own sport down his kid's throat. His own father had done that with mixed results.

Saul ended up having a respectful basketball career. He was a one-year varsity player in high school and went to a small NAIA school in Fort Worth on a scholarship. The step up in talent from high school to college was significant for Saul. The dream of transferring to a major college or playing professionally was quickly stamped out in his freshman year when he experienced first hand just how good the talent was in the lowly NAIA college ranks. He remained thankful though that his better-than-average talent and 6'5" frame were good enough to pay for his college degree. That degree had given him a good job and a good enough life to support his wonderful family.

As for soccer, he was happy with the decision. It didn't seem like it required a ton of coordination. You just had to use your feet. No hands were involved. Soccer was a sport that was still growing in America. Everywhere you looked, the parks were being consumed by soccer fields. Saul didn't know much about the game but it didn't look too complicated. Kick a ball in a net and you're done. The newness and uniqueness of the game also attracted him because it reminded him of his younger days with his dad.

Harper Sr. loved all sports, even the unusual ones. Starting at the age of six, he would play a different game with Saul every weekend. It was rare for a Texas boy to play a game like cricket or lacrosse or ice hockey, but his dad exposed him to all kinds of sports and activities. The variety was infectious and forged a special bond between them that lasted the better part of Saul's youth.

Saul wanted to forge that same bond with his girls, but he soon learned it was not going to be as easy. Bree wasn't that excited about learning a new sport. Saul was admittedly at fault for Bree's lack of interest because, until now, he had never really tried to provide Bree a physical education. He was just waiting for his boy to come along.

Bree was totally satisfied with playing Barbie or Webkinz or Bratz or whatever was the girl toy of the day. She was also involved in arts and crafts. She loved to color and create things and had a good talent for drawing at a very young age. She was also totally enamored with being a big sister and was one hundred percent invested in making Harper happy.

So when Saul decided it was time to separate Bree from the crafts table and her little sister and move outdoors to the playing field, she provided some resistance. She demanded that Harper come with them to watch. He didn't like this compromise because Harper could be a distraction, but it did make Bree more willing to buy-in to whatever it was her dad was trying to get her to do.

Every weekend Saul and Bree got in the habit of going to a soccer field to practice. Harper would be there at Bree's insistence. Harper would sit and watch on the sidelines, playing with her red little Elmo. Elmo was the stuffed animal that got Harper through the colic and the night terrors and the Swollen Colon Syndrome. It wasn't the sleepless nights and tireless attention of her parents. It was the love and loyalty and security of Elmo. Thank you, *Sesame Street*.

Saul watched helplessly as Bree would try to simultaneously run and kick the ball, but she could never get the hang of it. She would step on the ball by mistake and fall down, or swing at the ball with her leg and totally whiff and fall down, or just stand there at times and fall down because she was laughing so hard when she did something silly. It didn't help matters that the sound of Harper giggling in the background made Bree want to display her silliness even more.

Saul patiently acknowledged to her that, while it was fun falling down, falling down was not the point of soccer. So Saul decided to keep the soccer ball stationery and just have Bree stand there and kick it. This she got the hang of. It wasn't pretty at first but she eventually could kick the ball a few yards. Saul made her kick with both her right leg and left leg. He thought it odd that she could kick the ball farther with her left leg than right, her being right-handed and all, but he felt that was a good thing. Switch-hitters were valuable in baseball, maybe switch-kickers were valuable in soccer.

He knew he had to get her to where she could simultaneously run and kick the ball or her soccer career would be short-lived. There were no penalty kicks in little league recreational soccer and that's about all she could do at this point. Even if they were allowed, she still couldn't kick the stationery ball hard enough to reach the goal.

At the end of their practice session one day, Harper's amusement was running low. She left Elmo on the sideline and walked up to Bree and Saul and asked if she could try.

Saul told her to go back to the sidelines, but she resisted.

Bree butted in, "Oh, come on, Daddy. Let her try."

Saul gave in and placed the ball on the ground. "Okay, let me tell you what you have to do," Saul began saying.

Harper didn't listen. She instinctively took a few steps toward the ball (albeit awkwardly for a retired toddler) and planted her left foot in the sod and swung her right foot into the ball's belly. Saul and Bree watched as the ball hopped along and into the goal. It was hit harder and further than Bree's attempts had ever gone. Saul couldn't deny he was a little impressed, but he didn't want to take attention away from Bree. This was her practice session.

Bree began clapping her hands and excitedly said, "Harper, that was fantastic. Daddy, did you see that?"

"Yes, I saw it. Lucky kick, Harper."

"Can I do it again, Daddy?"

"Not right now, Harp, I'm working with Bree. Go back over and give Elmo a hug for me, will you?"

Harper thought that was a great suggestion. Elmo had been alone for a few minutes and he needed a hug. She quickly ran to be with him.

Later that evening Saul began to think, given that his younger daughter who was half the size and half the age of Bree had just out-kicked the older daughter on one try, he might be failing as a soccer coach. He admitted he didn't know the game that well and that it might be time for Bree to play in a recreational league. She needed someone that could give her better instruction. Plus, she didn't need Harper distracting her at all times from the sideline.

"Are you sure she is ready to be on a team?" Veronica asked Saul with some concern. "You haven't even taught her the rules yet."

"That's because I don't know the rules, Very," Saul confessed. Soccer is a strange and weird sport. It's very European. I've never gotten it from watching it on TV. I'm usually asleep before something happens. Besides, that's what we pay the coach for. He will teach her the rules. It's just like riding a bike. You fall down a few times and keep getting back on until you learn."

Veronica relented. "I guess there has to be some good reason I see thousands of kids playing that sport."

Saul did his research and found a team Bree could play for in the spring. Bree did not want to do it. She didn't know any of the girls. She didn't know what the game was about. She didn't like running around and kicking a ball. She didn't want to go to practice when she could stay home and play with her sister.

"Mom," Bree pleaded. "Do I have to?"

Saul could see Veronica fighting her maternal instincts of protection.

"Bree, it's important to your dad that you do this. Plus, it's good exercise for you."

Thankful that he had Very's support, Saul continued to work on Bree. "Mom's right, Bree. It is good exercise. And remember, don't say no to things you don't really know about. Try it first because you might actually like it."

Saul could tell Bree didn't have a response for his well-thought-out comments. She surrendered and agreed to give the team a try. On reflection, Saul thought in another eight years or so he might have to adjust his well-thought-out comments. Try it, you might like it sounded like something out of the flower-power sixties. Those comments may not get the desired results when discussing teen drinking, teen sex or teen drug-use with his teen-age daughters.

Bree's first and only soccer season was a sight to behold. Watching young seven-year olds running (or walking in some cases) around wet and muddy Seattle fields in search of a round ball provided, at times, some laughter but the laughter paled in comparison to the extreme boredom that set in after a few short minutes of action, or inaction. Parents spend more time watching the coaches (and other parents who think they are coaches) yell at their daughters to run, kick, pass or do anything that resembles movement. Because it happened so rarely, scoring a goal was a monumental occasion followed by shouts of pure ecstasy from the parents on the sideline.

Saul couldn't understand how a bunch of girls could just stare at a ball and do nothing. Bree was the guiltiest of the bunch. She would run away from the ball like it was an object from outer space and couldn't be trusted. It took him a few games to realize that she wasn't afraid of the ball at all. She was just being nice. She didn't want to step in to kick the ball if it meant little Judy or little Belinda didn't get a turn. When Bree finally decided to take a turn, she kicked the ball with all the force of a baby snail. The ball would trickle a few feet and then she would let someone else kick it next, instead of trying to control the ball herself downfield.

Following each game, Saul would instruct her that she needed to be more aggressive and not worry about taking turns hitting the ball. Bree would nod her head in agreement as if she fully understood what he was saying. But when the next game came around, she would do exactly the same thing.

Another thing that drove Saul crazy was that Bree would cheer every time there was a goal scored, even if it was the other team that scored. She would jump up and down clapping her hands and give the other team's players high fives. On rainy days of which there were many, Saul would put his head in his umbrella and act like he didn't notice. He couldn't bare the strange stares from the other fathers.

This habit Bree had of congratulating the other team, Saul had seen coming for a while. Whenever Bree played games with Harper or the four of them played as a family, Bree would always go out of her way to congratulate the winner. When Bree herself won, she was always remorseful and apologized to the rest of the players. This annoyed Saul to no end. Being a good sport was one thing, but good sports don't apologize for winning. He was obviously concerned how this kind-natured attitude of Bree's would translate to the world of youth sports. His concern was justified for it had translated all right--to a soccer field in West Seattle.

Did Bree improve that season? In Saul's mind, no. The coach was somewhat at fault. He knew very little about the game of soccer which was still a lot more than Saul knew, but the coach tended to play favorites, primarily his own daughter. He had very little patience with Bree and other girls who were still learning the game.

31

It's an amazing coincidence how, in youth sports, coach's kids always seem to lead the team in playing time, scoring, and in playing the most important position on the field. Saul admitted maybe it was their right as a coach since they were sacrificing their personal time. But heck, somebody that has the time and commitment to be a little league coach probably means they have the time to come to all the practices and games anyway so maybe they aren't sacrificing much. Screw him, Saul thought. He was a bad coach.

Did Saul want to commit to a second year of soccer? Heavens no. And it wasn't just due to the bad coach. It also wasn't due to the fact that Bree didn't improve or that she appeared to have no knack whatsoever for the game. The real reason was Saul and Veronica couldn't bare another season of watching sloppy soccer games played in the muddy outdoors on a typical misty-gray 40 degree Seattle day, where you couldn't tell the difference between cloud and fog.

"Let's search for something indoors," Veronica begged.

"Very, I am totally on board with that," Saul said. "There are a lot of indoor options out there."

"And maybe soccer was too demanding a sport for her to start with. Maybe we need to try something that will better prepare her to play a sport like soccer, but that isn't soccer."

Saul nodded in agreement. What could they try next? If Bree wasn't ready for soccer, she sure wasn't ready for basketball. And he didn't want to play that card yet anyway being that it was HIS sport and all.

"How about gymnastics?" Veronica asked.

"Gymnastics," Saul pondered. Where the F did that come from?

He was a little taken aback that Veronica wanted a voice in the decision. This was dad stuff, after all. She was not a sports person. Never had been, never would be. And she had never shown any inclination to get in the way of Saul's Master Athletic Plan. In fact, it was her lack of athletic genes that made Saul fear for his children's athletic future. He could only pray that his athletic DNA won out in the end.

"What kind of gymnastics?" Saul wondered. "Do you mean stuff like in the Olympics?"

"I don't know for sure," Veronica admitted. "It could be tumbling, cart wheels, somersaults, or balance beam. A number of Bree's schoolmates are doing it. It helps them get stronger and improve their coordination."

Bree could definitely use help in that department. She was in the ninetieth percentile in height and tripping over her own big feet became a regular occurrence.

"Well, she could definitely benefit from improved coordination," Saul said. "She doesn't need a soccer ball to make herself fall down anymore. She can do it on her own."

"Don't be mean," Veronica said, while laughing with him.

"Well, let's research it and see what we can find out about it. I'm willing to try it. But please, no rhythmic gymnastics. I saw it once and it's just so . . ."

"So what?"

"So feminine."

"Okay. No rhythmic gymnastics," Veronica said. "I will look into the non-rhythmic kind."

Veronica was amazed Saul heeded the suggestion. She just knew the next sport would be basketball, but she was wrong. She had to give him some credit. Even with her limited knowledge of sports, she knew Bree wasn't ready for basketball. The suggestion of gymnastics was a way of protecting her. Veronica was hopeful gymnastics would be something that Bree could enjoy, while developing her athletic prowess over time. It was also something they could get Harper involved with, too. She was excited about researching gymnastics training centers and even more excited that Saul was letting her participate in his athletic aspirations for the girls.

Saul always prided himself on being a reasonable and patient man. Gymnastics required all the reason and patience a dad with ambitious athletic goals for his children could bare. While he always respectfully enjoyed watching a few gymnastic events during the Olympics, which was a once-in-every-four-year occurrence (God help us if it was more regular than that), watching eight-year olds in a gym doing somersaults on a cushioned blue mat tested the definitional limits of calling gymnastics a sport.

There was no competition here. There were no winners and losers here. There was no danger here. The balance beam was six inches high, for crying out loud. Saul became extremely bored with the process very quickly. It didn't take him too long to tell that this was nothing more than glorified baby-sitting for his two girls. Yes, Harper was included, too, which was still a distraction for Bree. They had a laugh-riot losing their balance and making silly mistakes, collapsing on the mat without a care if proper technique was being applied.

Saul didn't waste any time questioning whether they had made the right decision. He didn't see any improvement in Bree's coordination, which is what he was hoping for. It didn't help matters that Bree had experienced another growth spurt, which made her tall skinny, lanky frame even more pronounced. Her height made it harder for her to do the most basic of gymnastic moves. She couldn't do a proper somersault because her neck was too long, forcing her to roll over side ways. Her long arms didn't have the strength to do a proper cartwheel so she relied instead on some kind of twisted side-winder orbit for her legs that ultimately ended up in a dizzying tumble on the mat. Tumbling, whatever that meant in gymnastics, was the proper adjective to describe Bree's talent in the sport. She could tumble with the best of them alright, always landing flat on her tush.

Veronica could see her husband losing patience in the sport and she could also see Bree's lack of progress. She felt the lessons had been good for Harper. Even though Harper was still too young, she showed a pretty good talent for balancing herself on the balance beam and her arm strength was evident when she tried to do headstands. Saul didn't pay any attention to this because priority one was Bree. He would tell Veronica that Harper was not old enough yet to seriously compete in anything athletic. But Veronica remained encouraged by Harper's early abilities.

That being said, Veronica knew it was time for a change. She approached Saul one evening with a new idea while he was sitting outside on the back porch looking up at the night sky. He had moved his telescope outside and was trying to focus on something in the vast and expansive galaxy.

"What are you looking at?" She asked.

"Well, I heard on the radio that there was supposed to be a spectacular meteor shower tonight, but guess what?"

"Too many clouds?"

"You guessed it. Remind me if I take up a career as an astronomer that we move to a place where you can actually see stars."

"Will do," Veronica said.

"I might become an expert at cloud formations, though," Saul added. "If the depression doesn't get to me first."

"Oh, stop being so down in the dumps."

"What do you think this telescope trades for on eBay?"

"You are not going to sell your telescope," implored Veronica. "Sit down for a moment. I've got something I want to run by you."

Saul complied. "What's up?"

"I'm tired of gymnastics," she bluntly blurted out. She could see Saul's ears perk up at the comment.

"I thought you were loving the gymnastics."

"Yes and no. It's nice to see the girls having fun and all, but I can also tell it's been a waste of time . . . and money."

"But they are such good tumblers," Saul said wryly, still managing to keep a straight face.

Veronica laughed. "They can tumble and bumble and crash and burn like no other. It's a wonder they haven't hurt themselves."

"So what are you thinking?" Saul asked.

Veronica could swear he had his fingers crossed as he awaited her answer. This caused her to pause a bit before responding. "I was thinking Dance."

Saul stared at her for a moment looking as if there was another word she needed to utter, like baseball or basketball. "I'm sorry but what do you mean exactly? I'm confused. Has a new sport been created combining the skill of dance and some athletic movement like swinging a tennis racket?"

"Saul, I'm serious about this. Dance would be great for their coordination at this age. It's something else they seem to be into. You see them playing their dance games upstairs and they love watching *Dancing With the Stars*."

"Gymnastics was supposed to be great for their coordination, too, but they ended up being great . . . " Saul searched for the word ". . . tumblers, which isn't synonymous with coordination in my opinion."

"Saul, we have to take our time with them. They are growing girls. They are still so very young and fragile."

Saul nodded his head reluctantly in agreement and said, "I know. I guess I need to remember what Charlie told me, too."

"What's that?" Veronica asked curiously.

"He preached the importance of patience when it came to daughters and sports. He should know. He has four of them." Saul sighed, then asked, "So what kind of dancing are we talking about?"

Veronica shrugged somewhat in disbelief that he even posed the question. "I don't know yet. There are many kinds of dance that might interest them."

"Well, do the research and let me know what you find out."

She was amazed. He was still letting her contribute to the process and the basketball word was never even brought up. "I'll start looking into it," she said, while having to ever reevaluate this kind, sensitive and caring man she called a husband.

Veronica looked into it and six months later, Saul found himself sitting in a cavernous 2,000 seat theater with an audience of maybe just a hundred parents who were there for their daughters' first dance recital.

It wasn't hard for Veronica to find the right kind of dance for her young girls because, ultimately, it wasn't about the rhythm or the music or even about the steps or moves. It wasn't about dance at all. It was about what kind of clothes they got to wear.

As soon as Bree and Harper saw the pink tutus, they immediately knew whatever dance was danced in that cool get-up was for them. Saul insisted to Veronica they didn't have a clue what a ballerina was or what ballet was for that matter, but because the tutu was pink, it must be associated with something a Disney princess might wear. So ballet it was. Veronica didn't disagree with his assessment. She was just happy they found something they liked.

For Saul, sitting in the auditorium watching little girls dance around on their tip toes acting like ballerinas, fluttering their arms in the air, while running into each other or forgetting where to go was the ultimate in humiliation and futility. He only thought soccer was excruciating. He only thought gymnastics was a waste of time. He couldn't believe that with ballet dancing, you could get both of what soccer and gymnastics had to offer, but in one five-minute performance.

Bree, bless her heart, was out there trying so hard without a dance move in her body. She stood a head taller than anybody else and they kept her in the back of the stage behind all the other girls. Saul didn't know if that was due to her height or due to the fact that she was just plain awful. She didn't really do anything until the very end, or the Big Finish as Bree liked to call it, when she got to move to center stage with all the other girls swarming around her. Bree then got to twirl awkwardly on her toes a few times holding her arms in a pirouette, her head and arms sticking out above the others like a spindle top.

And then it was finally over. Saul thanked God for his infinite mercy in making the performance only five minutes long. Before he could finish his prayer, Veronica yanked him up. Everyone in the audience was giving their daughters a standing ovation.

"Bravo!" one parent yelled.

"Encore!" another parent screamed.

Saul could only think to himself, really? You have to be kidding me. But then he came to his senses and realized this was not really a sport. This was not a competition. This was not *Dancing With the Stars*. This ovation was their reward. There was no trophy to be presented. So he started clapping his hands politely and then couldn't wait to get in the car.

Later that night Saul was sitting out on the back patio daydreaming. Veronica walked out and handed him a glass of wine.

"Maybe this will take the edge off," she said.

"The edge off of what?"

"I don't know. You seem in deep thought."

"I'm just waiting in suspense for Harper's first recital," he joked.

Veronica laughed.

"What did you think of the performance today?" Saul asked.

"I thought it was cute. But Bree is upstairs in her room complaining that she doesn't think she's good enough."

"She isn't good enough," Saul jumped in.

"Saul, we can't hurt her confidence at this age."

"I know we can't, but we have to be realists, too. We need to find her something to feel confident about," Saul implored. "She's going to be a big girl. Gymnastics and Dance are for small, svelte little people like the elves in *Lord of the Rings*. Bree is going to be pushing six feet when it's all over."

"All she thinks right now is that she is the worst soccer player, the worst gymnast and the worst dancer in the world. Maybe we need to give the extracurricular activities a break."

"Nonsense. We will find something," he assured her.

"But not basketball," she demanded.

"What's wrong with basketball?"

"She is just not ready for that," Veronica said worryingly.

"Hey, you know my feelings about basketball. I don't want to put undue pressure on her." Saul quickly snuck in, "Even though she may be the greatest basketball player that ever lived."

"I heard that," Veronica smiled.

"Okay. No basketball it is. I know exactly the sport to try. It's not too demanding physically. In fact, the ball is even called soft!"

That weekend, Saul took Bree and Harper to a nearby park and began the process of teaching them the game of softball, or baseball for girls. Baseball, America's Past-time, was definitely past its time, Saul thought. While he loved the game growing up and thrilled at all the great play of the 70s with Cincy's Big Red Machine, Reggie Jackson's heroics with the A's and Yankees, and the Dodgers' rock-solid infield of Cey, Russell, Lopes and Garvey, the game had drifted away from him.

Free agency started it. He could never keep up with what player was playing on what team. Cable television hurt it. The added commercials made the game move at a snail's pace. Middle relief pitchers made it worse. Gone were the dominant pitchers that could throw a complete game in two hours. Aces these days were only expected to last six innings. And whenever there was a pitching change, that was now what Saul termed "nap time".

But Saul was sure the game was still fun for kids so he eagerly took his daughters to the field and began throwing, catching, swinging, running, and hitting, i.e the fun stuff. He also began teaching them the rules: the balls, strikes, outs, double plays, foul balls, passed balls, home runs, wild pitches, sac flies, infield fly rules, ground rule doubles, balks, stolen bases, pick off throws, squeeze plays, singles, triples, errors, running to first base on a third strike that was dropped by the catcher, etc. Or the not so fun stuff (especially if you are pre-adolescent.)

Saul quickly found out there was only so much teaching his now ten-year old and seven-year old girls could absorb. They seemed to enjoy the fun stuff (which to them also included picking dandelions in the field) but the rules of the game were beyond their mental capacity. He soon decided the only way for them to really learn was to get them on a team so they could play. Saul thought this was a great idea but he was quick to recall he had this great idea before, with soccer.

Harper was still too young to play, which annoyed her because she was hitting the softball harder than Bree and throwing the ball further as well, but she was relegated to the stands where she got to watch her big sister in action. Saul was impressed with Harper's strength but with Bree, he surmised that she was growing so fast that her arms and legs hadn't caught up with her body. The longer your arms, the harder it is to do a push up or throw a baseball or swing a bat. He had learned that with his own tall and lanky frame back in the day. Her strength would come eventually.

Bree had enjoyed the trips to the park with her father and sister, but when Saul told her it was time to join a team, she flatly refused.

"No. I don't want to do it," she pleaded.

"Bree," Saul said calmly. "Don't say no to something you don't know anything about."

She let out a frustrated sigh when he said this. Saul knew she didn't have an answer for it.

"But I am not any good at softball, Daddy."

"Bree, you will never know unless you try. You might be the greatest softball player in the world. But you won't know that unless you try."

Bree thought about it for a few grueling seconds, her face wearing a pained look of surrender. "Okay," she sighed reluctantly. But Daddy, I will know enough about something some day."

Saul chuckled. "I have no doubt."

Veronica had overheard the conversation Saul had with Bree about joining a softball team and she could sense the frustration building in Bree. She had an idea of how Bree could release some of the tension boiling inside of her. She went to the Fred Meyer store near their house and purchased a pink Disney Princess diary.

"What's this?" Bree asked, staring at her unexpected gift.

"It's a diary. I had one when I was your age. It's fun. You can write down important thoughts or interesting things that happen to you each day." Veronica neglected to tell her she logged in maybe all of three entries in her own diary, which was eventually relegated to the bottom of her pile of miscellaneous nothings in her closet.

"The cover's pretty," Bree said. "Why all the blank pages?"

"That's where you put down your thoughts and other things."

"Hmmm," Bree grunted. "Thanks, Mom." And she quickly walked upstairs to her room.

BREE'S DIARY
July 26
Dear Diary, my mom got me a stupid diary today. Doesn't she know I don't like to write? I like to read, but I don't like to write. The princesses are pretty, tho.
    The End.

Bree's softball team was called the Patriots. They were decked out in uniforms of red, white and blue. They looked good. But that was the only thing good about the team or that softball season. They were the worst team in the league and they were in a league of very bad teams. The play was so poor it was hard for the kids to learn anything. The kids would swing their bats at air 99 percent of the time. When there was contact, a loud gasp of joy was heard from the stands even if it was a foul ball.

A few times, though, an infield hit would occur that maybe travelled all of eight feet. The batter, once she remembered to run to first, ran with the frantic hope of beating the throw just in the nick of time. But there was no need to worry because the fielder couldn't throw the ball far enough to reach first base. Most of the batters either walked to first because the pitching was so bad or struck out swinging because the hitting was so bad.

Bree never made contact with the ball the whole season. She did walk a few times and got to experience the joy of base-running. She made it around home a couple of times, too, thanks to the endless array of wild pitches. But it was a very stupid game to her.

She first started at right field, then moved to left field and by the end of the season, she was in center field. Why the changes? Who knows. It was probably to keep her awake because not one ground ball ever left the infield.

When she told her dad it was a stupid game, Saul couldn't disagree with her. It was a huge disappointment for him and, again, a seemingly waste of time. The players didn't get a chance to learn much about the game or enjoy what there was to enjoy about the game. Plus, the flurry of cancelled games due to rain didn't help either. This was Seattle, after all. Saul and Veronica kicked themselves for not following their mantra after soccer, NO MORE OUTSIDE SPORTS.

Sadly, it would be a few more years before girls Bree's age would get the hang of the game. Saul knew Bree wouldn't have the patience to endure it, and neither would he. Bree's games were timed for 75 minutes. In that timespan, you were lucky if you got forty-five seconds of action. The game had gotten more boring at the little league level than at the major league level. If only he could transport Bree to the 1970s when baseball was at its most exciting, maybe the game wouldn't seem so stupid to her.

The evening following Bree's last softball game, Veronica was on the back porch looking up at the clouds like her husband normally did. Saul walked out to hand her a soda.

"Do you see Saturn or Venus?" He asked.

"You're so funny," she said, acknowledging his bad joke. "But I do see one cloud up there that's shaped like a star."

"Really." He looked up curiously.

"No, it's not a star. It's something round, though," she said continuing to gaze at it. "I think it looks like a basketball."

"I can't see it." Saul kept staring at the clouds looking for it until he realized his wife was giving him a green light. He looked over at her.

"It's time to see if there's any of your basketball DNA embedded in our offspring," she said.

Saul was speechless for a moment. He knew this was a big concession for her. It just amplified how bad the softball must have been. For her, of little sports background or knowledge, to have come to this deduction was prolific.

"Are you sure?" Saul asked, trying not to seem too excited for he had been thinking the exact same thing.

"I don't care what my daughters play as long as it is indoors, with ample heat and air conditioning. No more sitting out in cold, rainy weather freezing our asses off."

Saul nodded. "I get it, Very. I get it."

BREE'S DIARY
September 2
Dear Diary, I hate softball and all sports. They are stupid and not fun. My dad needs a boy and I need a brother. I really wanted to be a dancer.

The End.

That next Saturday morning Saul was at the Sports Authority store when the doors opened. He purchased a couple of basketballs and a backboard and all the necessary tools and materials to mount and center the backboard above the garage.

Bree and Harper were jolted out of their beds by the loud hammering noises coming from outside. They walked out to see what their father was doing.

"I'm building a basketball court for us," Saul responded to Harper's inquiry.

"Is that the sport you used to play, Daddy?" Bree asked, her eyes squinting from the morning sun, a rarity in Seattle for a Saturday.

"Yes, it is."

"So you can teach us to be good basketball players?"

"I think so," Saul said.

"So no more softball?" Bree continued.

"I was thinking we would try something else."

"Thank God," Bree blurted. "I hated softball. I'm going inside. My eyes hurt."

Saul was screwing a bolt into the mount when he noticed Harper still outside watching him.

"So you put that ball in that hoop, right?" She asked.

"That's right, Harp."

"Let me know when you're ready to play," she said.

"Will do, Harp." She then rambled off to find Bree.

As Saul was building his new basketball court, he did have some reservations. Here he was teaching his daughters HIS sport. Maybe it was unavoidable, but his memories of playing basketball were not all colored with fairy tales. Yes, he loved the sport but the sport also symbolized a falling out of sorts with his father, a bending of their strong bond. His dad, who had played a different game with him every weekend for years shocked him one day when he was just shy of his fifteenth birthday. Harper Sr. told him he needed to pick a sport and stick with it.

"But I don't want to pick a sport, Dad. I like playing all kinds of games."

"But you're not getting good at any one thing," his father would implore.

"I like being good at a lot of things," Saul would counter.

"But you're not good at a lot of things, son." You know a lot of different games but your skill level isn't strong enough to play them competitively. You need to focus on a sport you can excel in."

Young Saul was hurt by the comments and didn't understand his new rationale. It seemed to go against everything his dad taught him about athletics. A few weeks later, when Saul entered high school as a freshman, he went to the gym for his first day of P.E. class. He was startled to see his father there talking to the basketball coach. He soon discovered that his dad had signed him up to play basketball. Saul was furious that his dad did this without his approval. Yes, things worked out and he went on to have a decent basketball career, and he eventually realized his father was just pushing him to get out of his comfort zone. But their bond was never the same after that. And that memory, etched in his mind, of his dad talking to the coach behind his back, was another reason Saul had been hesitant to cram basketball down his daughters' throats.

BREE'S DIARY
September 10
Dear Diary, my dad wants me and Harp to play basketball now. I'm better at drawing a basketball but my dad doesn't know this. It's his sport and he is smart so maybe I will learn something. I still believe all sports are dumb. I don't know why we stopped dancing.

The End.

Saul had the basketball goal ready that afternoon and 3 p.m. was the first official practice time scheduled for the newly christened Bryson Court. Over the next few weeks, the girls enjoyed themselves as Saul taught them the game. He first taught them how to dribble with both hands and to try and dribble by feel, without looking for the ball after every bounce. They had a blast playing Keep Away from each other as one girl would dribble while the other tried to steal the ball.

He then had them start learning to shoot. This was more of a challenge because he set the goal at regulation height, which was ten feet. They rarely made a shot because they didn't have quite the strength to get it to the rim. They still had fun watching where the ball would land and chasing after rebounds or airballs with wild abandon. Saul was pleased with how much they were enjoying it, but it was hard for him to gauge how good they were getting.

He thought his coaching techniques were solid and that both girls had come a long way in a short time. But their practices on Bryson Court didn't really do an effective job of simulating five-on-five basketball and all the passing and cutting and offense and defense you had to learn. He knew he would have to find a team for Bree soon.

Harper was still probably a year away from team action but she was in a good spot. Athletically and physically, she was miles ahead of Bree when Bree was her age. But Bree still had a lot of awkwardness to work out. Saul was still frustrated she couldn't seem to learn how to do a basic layup. She always kept jumping off the wrong foot, which drove Saul crazy.

After the disasters of soccer and softball, he dreaded having the conversation with Bree. He knew asking her to join a basketball team would be like making her simultaneously eat spinach and squash, while getting a flu shot. Tears and screaming would be the result. He would have to muster up all his manipulative powers for this one.

Veronica recommended taking her to get ice cream to soften the blow. Saul thought that was a great idea. He and Bree went to Baskin-Robbins and sat down at the table to eat their cones.

"Why didn't Harper get to come?" Bree asked.

"I had something I wanted to talk to you about alone."

"What is it?" Bree asked, indulging in cookies and cream, her favorite flavor. She also appeared very interested in why this conversation applied only to her.

"Well, your basketball playing is getting really good."

"I know it is. I love dribbling the ball and taking the ball away from Harper. And I think I'm really close to having a breakthrough on making all my shots."

Saul was taken aback by her spontaneous confidence and enthusiasm. "That's great, Bree. That's all great. I agree. And I think . . ."

Bree interrupted him suddenly. "And I want to play on a basketball team! Can I play on a team, Daddy? When can I play on a basketball team?"

Saul couldn't believe what he had just heard. The sugar rush from the ice cream was working wonders. "That's fantastic,

Bree. I think you are ready. We will definitely find you a team to play on."

"Thanks, Daddy. I can't wait to show people what I can do," she boasted.

As they finished their cones, Saul didn't know exactly what to think. He was relieved the conversation went so easily, but he was a little nervous about this newfound confidence she had.

"What was up with that?" He asked Veronica later that evening.

"It's nice she is feeling good about herself," Veronica exclaimed. "She knows she's got the best basketball coach in the business."

"She still has a lot to learn, though," Saul cautioned. "I'm a little worried she thinks she'll be good just because I was good."

"You should be happy about this, dear. For once, you don't have to drag your daughter to a practice kicking and screaming."

Veronica was right, he thought. Just let this play out and what happens, happens.

BREE'S DIARY
September 25
Dear Diary, okay I was wrong. Basketball is a little fun and my dad is a pretty good teacher. I am better than Harper at it and she does not like this. I hate to beat her all the time but she is so hilarious when she loses. She gets SOOOOOOO mad. Ha ha. Oh, and I made a new friend at school today. I really like her.
P.S. I sort of like my new diary, too.
    The End.

Saul soon found Bree a local recreational team to play on. It was a higher level of competition than he wanted, but he felt Bree was probably ready for it. He was wrong.

The first practice with her new team, the Panthers, was a struggle for her. Bree's teammates were all pretty good. They were all more fundamentally sound and they knew a lot of the drills, while Bree had to be shown what to do. Saul quickly evaluated that Bree had to get a lot more work in if she wanted to catch up with her teammates.

When they did a layup drill, Bree continued to struggle jumping off the wrong foot. The coach would try to work with her footwork but Bree wasn't adapting to his instruction. When the girls started playing five-on-five, Bree didn't know where to go or how to get open and call for the ball. Bree still had to learn how to mix it up with the girls, throw her weight around, get her nose dirty and fight for the ball. This was all to be expected being her first practice, Saul knew, but the key was keeping Bree's enthusiasm and confidence up. At some point, though, Bree had to start generating some natural instinct for the sport. Saul hoped it would start immediately, but he knew he had to be patient.

The car ride home was tough.

"They are all better than me," Bree moaned.

"They are not," Saul assured her. "They just have a little more experience with the game. Once you get a few practices under your belt, you will get the hang of it."

"You think so?"

"I know so."

"But the girls are all so rough and mean. They push and shove a lot."

"That's part of the game, Bree. You have to learn how to use your body for positioning."

Saul had to admit he was surprised at how physical the game was at Bree's age. He didn't expect that. He was happy though, that he was able to keep Bree in a positive state of mind. After their ride home, she was still willing to go back for a second practice, which was encouraging.

He was also impressed with how good the girls were and he immediately blamed himself for not getting Bree involved soon enough. Evidently, there were other fathers out there that were being more aggressive in preparing their daughters for the great game. This was Saul's game and he was not going to be out-coached. He decided he would increase the number of practices on Bryson Court to speed up Bree's learning curve. The next day he was able to get off work early and he was prepared to start practice as soon as Bree got home from school.

"Home so soon?" Veronica asked, surprised to see him.

"Yeah, I thought I would get the girls out on the court and work with them, especially Bree. She needs the work."

"Sorry. Wish you would have checked with me. Bree's not here."

"Where is she?"

"Off with her friend, Callie."

"Who's Callie? Never heard of her."

"They've been hanging out together during recess the last couple of weeks. They seem to be hitting it off."

"Glad to hear she's made a friend, although it's interfering with my basketball practice," Saul said.

"I'm sorry. I didn't know you were slacking off on the job to-day."

"That's okay. We can get some work in tonight, I guess."

Bree's first game was coming Saturday, and Saul had only a few days to work his magic. Her team had practice on Thursday night, and Saul wanted her to show the coach some improve-ment from the last practice. They continued to work on her footwork for a basic layup, but she continued to struggle. He didn't understand why this was such a problem for her. It was a very easy two-step maneuver that everyone should be able to master. They also worked on guarding each other with the ball. Saul was getting a little more physical with her so she could get acclimated to the pushing and shoving that comes with the game.

Unfortunately, Thursday's practice didn't produce the improvement Saul had hoped for. Bree actually took a step backward. She seemed afraid of the ball. She didn't want to go near another player. She was good at one thing, though, scampering back on defense. When the other team rebounded the ball, Bree would race back to her spot before the coach had a chance to yell, "Get back on D!"

They played a zone defense and the coach had Bree defending the high post area, which meant Bree's spot was at the top right corner of the free throw line. Once she was in position, she still didn't know where to go or who to guard, but she was always the first one to reach her defensive position. Saul had to at least admire her hustle.

At the end of practice, Bree's coach motioned for Saul to come over and talk with him. He had no idea what this could be about.

"Mr. Bryson, is it?"

"Yes," Saul replied as they shook hands.

"Listen, I just call it like I see it and I mean no disrespect by this, but your daughter has a lot of work to do. We will try and work her into the game on Saturday but don't be surprised if she doesn't see the court much. She still has to learn the offense. "

Saul nodded. "I understand."

"Plus another thing. Did you know she was left-footed?"

Saul looked at him strangely. "Left-footed. What do you mean?"

"She can't shoot a basic lay-up. Keeps going off the wrong foot which means she favors her left side. Is she left-handed?"

"No."

"Well, you might want to teach her to shoot left-handed. She might have a better chance at playing the game. If not, she's gonna have a tough time teaching that right leg what to do. This may not be the game for her." The coach reached over and patted him on the shoulder. "We'll see you on Saturday, okay?"

Saul nodded to him as he walked away. He wanted to tell him he was a smart-ass and he didn't know what he was talking about. This was HIS game and Bree was HIS daughter. He knew what his girl could do. Don't tell me this isn't the game for her. The nerve of that guy. Although, the left-footed thing troubled him a bit. The coach made it sound like a disease with no cure. It did make some sense though, why she couldn't make a basic lay-up, and come to think about it, why she couldn't kick a soccer ball.

Driving home from practice, Bree was more upset. "I stink at this game. And the girls are mean, too. I don't like it."

"Bree, we need to be patient, okay. You're making progress. The more you play, the more you will understand what you need to do."

"Daddy, I can't make a basket. I can't dribble. They steal the ball away from me all the time. How were you so good at this game?"

Saul wanted to answer but he knew Bree wouldn't understand. He wanted to talk about what it was like growing up and watching Bill Walton and Lew Alcindor play for the UCLA Bruins or John Havlicek play for the Boston Celtics. How they executed the basic beauty of the game so flawlessly. How great John Wooden was in coaching the Bruins to twelve NCAA titles. How many hours he spent watching the game on television, both college and pro. How it felt to shoot a ball that you just knew was going in, watching it with the perfect arc, and that great sound it made zipping through the net. How fun it was to outsmart a defender on a fake jump shot or back-door him for an easy lay-up. He knew she wouldn't understand these things so he didn't bother trying. He gave her a simple answer instead.

"It was the one game I found I could do well in. I was always super tall for my age and super tall people were usually pretty good at basketball. Plus my dad was a good teacher."

"Well, I'm tall," Bree countered.

"Yes, you are."

"But I'm not super tall."

"No, but you are just as tall as the other girls out there. And you have great quickness. I'm happy to see that you're the first one back on defense. That's great hustle."

"Thanks, Daddy," Bree said. "And I've got a pretty good teacher, too."

"Yes, you do," Saul smiled.

Then she steered the conversation in a totally different direction. "What did the coach talk to you about after practice?"

Saul had to think quick. He wasn't prepared for the question. "He just said you needed more game time under your belt, that's all. That you're a quick learner and he looks forward to seeing you improve the rest of the season."

"That's good, I guess," Bree said, seeming satisfied with the answer. "Do you really think I'm ready to play in a game?"

"Sure, you are," Saul said. "Just stay ready and when you get the call, go out there and show 'em what you can do."

BREE'S DIARY
October 18
Dear Diary, why do I start every note with Dear Diary? That is stupid. You know you're a diary. I'm not going to do that anymore. I don't want to play basketball anymore either. My dad says everything will be okay but I don't know what I am doing. I don't want to make him mad at me tho. He will feel bad because it's his sport.
 The End.

Game day came that Saturday. Tip off was noon. Saul was startled by the level of nervousness and uneasiness he was feeling that morning. He went up to Bree's room at about 9:30 to make sure she was awake.

"Get moving, Bree. We need to leave here in an hour or so."

"Daddy, I'm not feeling good," she moaned.

"What's wrong?"

"I don't know. I just don't feel good."

Saul reached over and touched her forehead. "I don't feel any fever. You'll feel better when you get up and move around. Mom's making a nice breakfast for you."

"Daddy," Bree said in her most weak and pitiful voice. "Do I have to play today?"

"Of course, you have to play. Your team expects you to be there. I expect you to be there."

"But I'm not ready. I don't know all the rules."

"Bree, you'll do fine. You will learn the rules as you play. Now get moving."

Bree covered her face in her Disney princess sheets and started pouting. Saul closed the door and walked downstairs. A few minutes later, Bree entered the kitchen. Her game uniform was on but her game face wasn't. She was still sulking.

"What's wrong, Bree?" Veronica asked.

"Daddy's making me play and I don't want to."

"Why don't you want to?"

"Because I'm not ready and I'm not any good."

Saul watched as Bree tried to sway Veronica to her side.

"I don't think Daddy would let you play if you weren't ready. Isn't that right, Saul?" Veronica asked.

"Of course not," Saul responded. "She will do fine. She just has some opening game jitters. Now stop your sulking, Bree, and start eating your breakfast."

Bree plopped down in her seat as loudly as she could, trying to make a statement with her movement. She looked meanly into her dad's eyes. "These aren't jitters," she said. "These are serious doubts I'm having."

Saul moved closer to her and looked her firmly in the eyes. "Then let's go play and remove those doubts. Okay?"

Bree didn't like the answer. She got out of her chair and ran back upstairs.

"Bree?" Veronica shouted. She looked at Saul with a look of what do we do next.

"Should we make her go?"

"Yes, we need to make her go," Saul insisted. We've made a commitment to do this. We just need to get through this first game and everything will be fine. She's just nervous."

The car ride to the gym was an agonizing experience. Bree was in the back seat in tears the entire time. It wasn't a big, howling obnoxious cry. It was the quiet kind with little moans and sniffs that could just break your heart and make you feel like you were the worst parent in the world.

Harper would put her arm around Bree trying to give her some assurance, even though she didn't understand what the big fuss was about.

"Daddy," Harper said.

"Yes, Harp."

"Maybe I should play in Bree's place. I don't think she's ready."

"That's sweet of you, Harp, but this is Bree's team. She needs to play."

Bree let out another loud moan after hearing this, sounding as if she was gasping for air. Saul rolled his eyes at the dramatics. Veronica saw this and looked at him like he should be ashamed of himself.

When they pulled into the parking lot, Bree's crying subsided and she started getting herself together emotionally. She saw some of her teammates and ran over to be with them. During most of the game, Bree couldn't have been happier. The Panthers were up 12 to 10 at halftime and Bree never entered the game. She seemed thrilled with this, Saul noticed from the bleachers. She cheered enthusiastically without worry of going in because the coach probably assured her she wasn't good enough to go in.

As thrilled as she was, Saul was just as irate. The coach had played everyone except Bree. Yes, she had things to learn but she wasn't going to learn them on the bench. It wouldn't hurt to give her a few minutes.

The third quarter went by and it was more of the same. No Bree. The game was tied at 18 and Saul knew the coach wouldn't put her in now with the game being so tight. But then something unusual started to happen in the fourth quarter. A few of Bree's teammates began getting into foul trouble. There were only eight girls on her team and three girls suddenly had four fouls. Five fouls was the limit.

At the six minute mark, one girl fouled out. Saul sensed a bit of hope. At the five minute mark, another girl fouled out. Saul was liking his odds more and more as he watched the coach become more and more concerned. Bree continued cheering on her teammates from the safety of the sidelines, obviously oblivious to what was happening.

Then, like clockwork, at the four minute mark the miracle occurred. Another player fouled out. The coach didn't have any choice. He yelled over to Bree to get in the game. Bree had that startled look of 'Who me?' on her face. He yelled at her a second time and she responded, hopping up and running onto the court. She began talking with her teammates frantically about where she needed to be. The game was tied at 24 and there was chaotic tension filling the air.

"Oh, my God." Veronica whispered with worry.

"Let's go, Bree," Saul yelled.

Veronica turned to look at her husband. Saul noticed the look she was giving him out of the corner of his eye. It was her patented stare of death, the look she gives when she warns him he better know what the hell he's doing. Only she possessed such a stare. Saul pretended not to notice.

Bree's team had the ball and they were looking for a shot. Bree was staying as far away from the ball as possible. One of her teammates went up for a shot but the ball was blocked and started bouncing in Bree's direction. Bree picked the ball up and didn't know what to do.

"Lay it up!" Saul shouted.

She did have an open lane to the basket, but she never heard her dad's shout. She finally figured it out on her own. She dribbled the ball to the goal and jumped off the wrong foot as usual, while tossing the ball high up on the backboard. The only problem was the ball went too high. It sailed over the backboard and out of bounds.

Saul felt like hiding from the other parents who were mumbling unpleasantries under their breaths.

The coach kept his composure and told Bree that everything was okay. Bree sprinted down the court to get back on defense and, just like in practice, she was the first one back. Her defensive posture looked good, although she didn't bother guarding the player with the ball or anybody else for that matter. She was totally confused.

The game went back and forth for the next few minutes with no points being scored. Saul was amazed at the chorus of coaches in the stands, i.e. parents, yelling at their daughters to 'Go for the ball!', 'Shoot it!', 'Don't pick up your dribble!', 'That was a stupid foul!', 'Don't get beat again!', etc.

With a minute left to play and the game still tied, Bree's team had the ball on offense. Bree was making sure to steer clear of any action. She was in her own safe spot far away from where the ball was. As one of her teammates began driving to the basket, a defender stole the ball and gained possession. Bree followed her natural instinct and began running to get back on defense. The girl who had stolen the ball immediately made an outlet pass to a teammate that was wide open at mid-court.

Saul could see that a one-on-one situation was quickly developing with the opponent driving for the basket and Bree the only player that could stop her. Bree was hustling back on defense and was there in plenty of time to challenge the defender, or at least foul her and make her shoot free throws.

"Oh, no," Saul moaned, sensing what was about to happen.

As the dribbler was making her move past the free throw line, Bree suddenly stopped running. She had run to her defensive spot, planted her feet, and got into her defensive posture, just like she was told to do in practice. In the process, she let the opposing player have an uncontested lay-up, not knowing she was supposed to guard the player all the way to the basket. Panther parents were going crazy with anger. "What are you doing!?" some yelled in disbelief. The opposing team's parents were laughing with joy. Saul, on the other hand, wanted a cave to crawl into.

In all this hysteria, there were still thirty seconds left and Bree's team was only down by two. They brought the ball up the court and were trying to run some semblance of an offense. Bree, unaware that she had done anything wrong on the previous play, stood in her usual place safely away from the action as her other teammates scrambled for position.

Ten seconds remained. The ball was swatted out of somebody's hand and there was a scramble for the ball. One of Bree's teammates came up with it but didn't have a shot. Seven seconds were left. She saw Bree open all alone at the top of the key, standing there with her hands on her hips like a spectator. Six seconds. Bree saw the ball coming her way and noticed it had a lot of velocity. Five seconds. Her instincts told her to catch it, but unfortunately her hands didn't respond to her instincts in time. Four seconds. The ball flew right between her hands and smacked her dead in the face. Three seconds. The ball bounced into the hands of the opposing team. Two seconds. Saul and Veronica covered their eyes like ostriches hiding their heads in the dirt. One second. Blood started streaming out of Bree's nose. Zero seconds. The buzzer sounded and the game was over.

Needless to say, the car ride home was worse than the car ride that morning. Bree was in the back seat sobbing with bloody tissues stuck up both her nostrils. Harper was consoling her as best she could. Bree's nose wasn't broken, just her pride. Her crying was the loud, obnoxious kind with the sole intent being to let everyone know she was in agony.

"Daddy," Harper said, while patting Bree lovingly on the head.

"Yes, Harp."

"I told you I should have played."

This made Bree whine even louder. "I don't want to play that game anymore," she wailed.

Saul felt Veronica's eyes on him as she waited for him to respond. At first, he wanted to rebuke Harper for her comment. But except for bad timing, it did have some element of truth to it. He ended up not saying anything amid the chaos. He had more important things to consider, like why his Master Athletic Plan was taking so long to take root.

It had been three years since he first walked the girls out to the soccer field. He couldn't believe where the time had gone, but it was gone and there was very little to show for it. For a fleeting moment, he wondered if it would have been this difficult if Bree or Harper had been a boy, but he refused to dwell on it. He was determined to have a breakthrough this time. He was determined to stick with HIS sport. He wasn't going to give up on basketball like he did with soccer and softball. He gave up on those sports too early. But before he could continue their basketball journey, he had to put the MAP on hold and focus on the problem at hand, the unbearable wailing coming from the back seat of the car.

How was he going to get Bree back in the gym?

CHAPTER THREE

LIKE DAUGHTER, LIKE FATHER

Bree did get back in the gym. It just didn't go quite as Saul had planned.

Following the infamous basketball game, he went up to tuck Bree in bed that night. She was worn out from all the events and emotions of the day and he was not surprised to see her already asleep. He leaned over to kiss her on the forehead and whispered "Good night" and "I love you." As he was leaving, he heard Bree stir.

"Daddy," Bree said.

Saul turned around. "I thought you were sleeping. What's up?"

"I can't get to sleep."

"Just keep those eyes shut and you will nod off soon enough," Saul said, now sitting beside her on the bed.

"I'm sorry I'm not a good basketball player."

The way she said it broke Saul's heart. It was like the weight of a thousand failed sports dads had smashed his gut in two. He moved quickly to dispel her notion. "You are a very good basketball player, Bree. I'm very proud of the progress you've made."

"I thought I would be good like you, though."

Another piece of his gut shredded, Saul responded assuringly. "You will be someday, Bree. It just takes practice."

"But I don't like practicing with the team. I like practicing with you, Daddy."

"I like practicing with you, too, Bree, but don't you want to get better?"

Bree nodded. "I think so."

"Then you need to practice with girls that are good. That's how you will get better."

"Even if they are mean?"

"They are not all mean, are they"?

"I guess not. They hurt me when they push and shove me, though."

"That's just part of the game. You need to do some pushing and shoving yourself."

"But it's not nice to push and shove."

Saul didn't know where to go at this point of the conversation. Bree was gentle and kind-hearted and Saul wasn't ready to get into the dynamics of sport being a metaphor for life and sometimes you've got to fight for what is yours, like pushing and shoving for position to gain an edge in basketball.

"We can talk about this more tomorrow. And we will practice some pushing and shoving. I'll show you how it can be fun, okay?"

"Okay," Bree smiled.

Saul left the room thinking that things were in a good place. She seemed satisfied with the conversation and open to practicing on Bryson Court at least.

He had been planning on what they needed to work on in preparation for next Thursday's practice. The number one priority would be catching more passes to prevent future bloody noses. He had his workouts for Monday, Tuesday and Wednesday evening set and then remembered one important detail. He was traveling to Dallas on business that week. He wouldn't be around to host any practice on Monday, Tuesday or Wednesday. He wouldn't be back until Friday, which meant he wouldn't be there for Thursday's team practice, either.

Saul was bummed. Reluctantly, he had to go to Plan V.

They spent the Sunday afternoon before he left practicing on Bryson Court, and they included Veronica. That was his Plan V. He wanted Veronica to see all the drills he had the girls doing so she could conduct their practices while he was away. Saul knew they wouldn't be at the same intensity level, but at least it would keep Bree active and focused for Thursday's team practice.

Veronica wasn't crazy about playing coach. One, she didn't know what she was doing and two, she didn't think this was the game for Bree, especially after her memorable debut. But she went along with it to keep Saul happy. The girls thought it was fun to have their mom out on the court, too.

When Saul was away that week, he would call to check up on things. Monday's call was a disappointment. It had been raining all day and they couldn't go out to practice. Tuesday's call also wasn't good. When he asked Veronica about practice, she said Bree wasn't home.

"Where is she?" he asked.

"Playing with her friend, Callie."

Saul sighed disappointingly. "Well, when will she be home?"

"After dinner sometime. Guess what they are doing?"

"I have no idea," Saul said losing patience.

"She's at a volleyball camp."

"A volleyball camp?"

"Yes, Callie got her to go. Evidently, Callie is a pretty good player."

"I didn't even know they still played that sport."

"At least she's doing something active."

"I guess. But do you still plan on practicing with her tonight?"

"Yes. I will do my best."

BREE'S DIARY

November 5

I love Callie. We like the same toys. She is my best friend. I want to tell her this soon. She is also a great volleyball player. She is trying to teach me. Volleyball is my favorite sport now. She is a much better teacher than Mommy. Mommy is trying to teach us basketball. Ha Ha. She's only good at playing the flute. And that's not a sport according to my dad. I need basketball to go away. I wish I had a brother.

The End.

Saul still didn't feel good after his conversation with Very. If Bree had a lot of homework, the basketball practice would be sacrificed which meant two nights in a row of no practice.

He was happy to hear Bree might be developing a real friendship. Bree had many friends but they weren't close friends. Veronica would tell him it was because of Harper, and Bree's determination to be a good Big Sister to her. Harper always took precedent over any outing with a friend. Part of it, too, Saul thought, was their age. When Bree got older, she would move on to other things that interested her. Right now though, Harper was her primary interest.

The next night when Saul called he was pleased to hear that they got out and practiced the night before. They didn't practice for very long but at least they got out.

"And what about today's practice?" he asked.

"Still waiting for her to get home," Veronica replied.

"Is she out with Callie again?" Saul asked, somewhat annoyed.

"Yes, they are at camp. It goes on all week after school. They seem to be having a great time."

"I'm glad they are having a great time but we need to get her focused and ready for practice tomorrow night."

"I understand. I will call you later and let you know how our workout goes tonight. Will you still be awake?"

"Yes, I'll be awake. I will be in my hotel room all evening." With the two hour time difference, it would be late for Saul's body clock but this was too important. He wouldn't get to sleep anyway without knowing how the evening went.

He picked up the television remote and started surfing channels going back and forth between sports and news. He ordered some room service and it arrived within thirty minutes. He got hooked on a *Seinfeld* marathon and watched a few episodes. He then started wondering why Very hadn't called. It was 11:30 p.m. Dallas time, 9:30 p.m. Seattle time. Practice should be over by now. The girls should be showered and getting ready for bed. He watched one more *Seinfeld* episode and then decided it was time to pick up the phone and call.

"Hello?"

Saul barely recognized the voice. "Who is this?"

"It's Harper, Daddy."

"Harp, what are you doing answering the phone?"

"Mommy told me to."

"Where is Mommy?"

"In Bree's room."

"Can you get her?"

Harper dropped the phone on the kitchen counter, the loud thud hurt Saul's ear. A few seconds later Harper was back. "She can't come to the phone now. She said she would call you tomorrow."

"What's going on, Harper?"

"Bree is being a baby and crying."

"Over what?" Saul knew over what but wanted to be sure.

"Basketball. She hates that game."

"Did you guys practice tonight?"

"Yes. I beat her in H-O-R-S-E again."

"Is that why she is crying?"

"No. She loves when I win."

Saul knew that was true given Bree's penchant for always being happy for the victor and feeling guilty whenever she won. She would much rather forfeit her win and give it to somebody else. Harper, on the other hand, would lie and cheat and scheme for a win. While playing cards, she would draw a card and if she didn't like it, she would blatantly put it back on the deck and draw another card, hoping no one would take notice or dare to call her on it. If you did call her on it, she would look you in the eye and flat out deny it.

"She's crying about practice tomorrow night, isn't she?" Saul asked.

"Yes. You think I should go in her place?"

"No, Harper, and don't bring that up to her. That will just make her more upset," Saul said, always amazed how mischievous Harper could be. Exorcist Baby still resurfaced from time to time.

Saul told her to tell Mommy that he would talk to her tomorrow. They said their good nights and Saul hung up the phone. He tossed and turned in his bed all night, and did not get much sleep. Tomorrow would be a hectic day for him with little time for phone calls. His schedule was crammed with meeting after meeting, including a working lunch.

It was at lunch the next day that he decided to make the call. He excused himself to go to the bathroom. He found an open stall and sat on the toilet. He figured he had a few minutes to talk. Luckily, there was no one else in the restroom when Veronica answered.

"I've only got a few minutes. Give me an update on things," Saul said, with matter-of -fact abruptness.

Veronica let out a sigh before beginning. Saul knew that wasn't a good sign.

"We practiced last night. Everything was fine. The girls were happy. We go inside and Bree asks me if she had to go to the team practice. I said yes and then all hell broke loose. She starts crying her eyes out saying I don't want to go."

"And what did you say?"

"I told her she had to go. That she was on a team and we don't let our teammates down."

"Good comeback, Very. I'm impressed."

"I'm trying here, but it's not easy. I think she really doesn't want to go."

"She's got to go," Saul implored. "You've got to get her there. Then everything will be fine."

"You really think so?"

"Yes."

"She keeps saying she hates basketball. That volleyball is the game for her."

"She doesn't hate basketball," Saul implored. "My God, after two days of volleyball, she's ready to claim her passion for the game? Give me a break."

The bathroom door opened and Saul heard a couple of men walk inside.

Saul whispered, "Hey, Very, I've got to go. Just get her to practice, okay? Love you."

Saul hung up and put the phone in his shirt pocket. While he hadn't the need to use the toilet for its normal purpose, with two men now in the bathroom he thought it proper to flush. They didn't know he was there just to make a phone call. He bent over to flush the commode when suddenly, his phone slipped out of his pocket at warp speed and into the toilet.

"Oh, crap," Saul panicked.

To make matters worse, he now noticed someone had used the toilet before him and forgot to flush. Saul wasn't so quick to put his hand in. He decided to go ahead and flush the toilet before he retrieved the phone. He pushed the lever and waited for the waste to spin around and disappear, all the while cursing himself for his rotten luck.

The rest of the day he was ill-at-ease. His phone was out, broken, kaput. He couldn't call, text, email, stream, read a book, listen to music. He was helpless until he got back to the hotel and that didn't end up being until midnight. There was the obligatory cocktail reception followed by a dinner banquet followed by drinks at the nearby sports pub. Saul didn't want to go but his boss was going so he felt he better mingle and brownnose with the rest of his peers. He didn't want to be known as the loser who goes to bed early and doesn't party. It could cost him a promotion. Even though that probably wasn't true, you could never be quite sure with the political games played at Corporate headquarters. Plus, after ten years in the same job, some level of paranoia does start to creep in.

He finally tried calling Veronica from his hotel phone at midnight, 10 p.m. her time, but there was no answer. He tried calling again but no answer. She rarely answered the landline because of all the unwanted calls you get. Saul was annoyed but he was also exhausted and he had a little bit of a buzz from the liquor he drank. He had virtually no sleep the night before and today's full day was a killer. Plus, he had an 8:30 a.m. flight back home. As much as he wanted to get the practice recap, it would have to wait until tomorrow. He drifted off very quickly.

Saul showed up at the house the next day around 1 p.m. Veronica was making herself a sandwich and was surprised to see Saul back so early.

"I thought you were going to the office once you landed," she said before kissing him on the cheek.

"I'm tired. I decided the office can wait until Monday."

"Good for you. I missed you."

"I missed you, too."

"You want a sandwich?"

"Sure." That's not what he really wanted. He wanted the recap from last night's practice STAT! "So . . .," he began somewhat calmly. "Give me the recap from last night."

"Do you really want to have that conversation now?" Veronica forewarned.

"Sure. How did she do?"

"Not good."

"What happened?"

Veronica grimaced and said, "We didn't go to practice."

Saul felt a slow-building rage develop inside him but tried to remain calm. He let out a long simmering sigh. "Why not?"

"She was hysterical all evening, dreading it from the moment she got home from school. I didn't have the heart to make her go."

"You mean you didn't have the will to make her go," Saul said, with disappointed agitation in his voice.

"If that's what you want to call it."

"I can't believe you let her get her way with this, Very. This is important. We can't let her quit everything she doesn't want to do. She's got to at least try things first."

"I'm sorry you're upset, but I did what I thought was right. She was in no shape to go to practice last night. All she wants to do now is play volleyball and what's wrong with that?"

"You don't think she is just using that as a crutch to get out of playing basketball?"

"I don't know but if she is, then let's congratulate her on showing a little cunning. Why are you pushing the basketball anyway? Because it's your sport?"

"Of course, not. I'm not pushing it. We went through three years of trying everything before we got to basketball. It's only been a couple of months. She still has a lot of developing to do. She can get better."

"She won't get better if she doesn't want to."

"She's eleven-years old," Saul pleaded. "Do you think she knows what she wants?"

"I know she doesn't want to look ridiculous on a basketball court again."

"Fine," Saul said. "Now, I've got to be the bad guy and figure out a way to get her to the game tomorrow. It would be helpful if we were both on the same page here." Saul took a big angry bite out of his sandwich and began munching loudly.

"Saul, maybe she's just not meant to be an athlete. You see her with Harper and how she lets Harper win all the time. You see her awkwardness out there. And maybe she's just not competitive enough. Maybe she's the intellectual type."

"Is this coming from your years of experience in marching band?" Saul knew the minute he said it, it was the wrong thing to say.

Veronica stared at him in disbelief. "Would you listen to yourself?"

Saul was tired of the conversation. He didn't want to entertain any dialogue that could result in his daughter being labeled the class nerd. He was focused on how to get her to the game tomorrow without drama. He also wanted to find out when practice could begin that evening on Bryson Court. "When does she get home?"

"I'm picking her up today. The camp ends at 5:30 p.m. and I've got to take Callie home, too."

"I will pick her up."

"You sure?"

"Yes, I will pick her up. Let's plan on eating around six and then we can get some playing in after dinner. I'm going to go into the office for a couple of hours first."

"I thought you were tired."

"I've found some renewed energy." He left his sandwich on the table half-eaten and got in his car and drove off.

After Saul's abrupt departure, Veronica sulked at the kitchen table and finished her lunch. She didn't know what was going on in his mind. Did he need to blow off some steam? Did he really need to get some work done? Did he need the friendly confines of his office to put together a practice plan for the evening? She didn't know. She only knew that the impending evening was shaping up to be a disaster.

Saul did go to the office but he didn't do any work. He had too much on his mind. He stayed for about an hour and then left to grab some much-deserved comfort food, a Big Mac and fries. He sat in his car eating his calories and fat grams while listening to sports radio, a guilty pleasure of his. It helped him get his mind off things.

He had to pick Bree up at 5:30 p.m. but it was only four o'clock. He decided to drive to the gym where the volleyball camp was being held. He wanted to see what was actually happening. He put a golf cap on that he always kept in the car and some sunglasses. He wanted to remain out of view from Bree and anyone else for that matter. Luckily, the outside doors to the lobby of the gymnasium were unlocked. The inside doors to the gym itself had glass windows, which were perfect for him to view the action.

There were probably 25 girls at the camp. They were bouncing the ball off their arms back and forth to each other in pairs. He spotted Bree laughing and chatting with her partner, who he guessed was Callie. They went from drill to drill and Callie was the one that was always helping to lead the drill or describe what needed to be done. One drill had the coach tossing them a ball from the other side of the net and the player would have to direct the ball with her arms to a target area.

Saul assumed this was the volleying part of the game but he didn't know for sure. What he did know was that Bree was very adept at hitting the target area on a consistent basis. The ball seemed to come off her arms softly, but with the right kind of firmness, if that made any sense. Whatever she was doing, she made it look quite easy and, dare he say, natural.

Was she the best one there? Of course not. Callie was clearly the best one there. But Bree was definitely in the top five. Most of the other girls watched their volleys go off in a variety of directions. Left, right, even backwards. But not Bree's.

Saul was impressed. He was even more taken by the joy on his daughter's face. He also admired the playful bond she and Callie had while volleying together. As the practice ended, Saul went to get his car to pick them up.

"Hi, Daddy," Bree said excitedly as they jumped in the car.

"Hi, Sweetie, good to see you."

"Where's Mom"?

"Back at the house making dinner. I got home early and thought I'd pick you up."

"Daddy, this is my friend, Callie."

"Hi, Callie."

"Hi, Mr. Bryson."

"So how was practice?" Saul asked.

"It was so fun, Daddy," Bree began. "Me and Callie got to be on the same team and we won a lot of games."

"Yeah," Callie agreed. "Bree's getting really good."

Bree was gleaming after the comment. "We also worked a lot on passing today," Bree continued. "And I think that's probably what I'm best at."

Saul deduced that the drills he was watching must have been passing drills, even though it still looked like a form of volleying to him.

"Hey, Mr. Bryson, can Bree try out for one of the teams in our league this season?" Callie asked assertively.

"Can I Daddy?" Bree jumped in.

"I don't know, Callie. We will have to talk about it."

"I think she would be one of the better players," Callie added. "I think my team is filled up but there are other teams she could be on."

"We will have to see if it fits in with our schedule," Saul said. "She's on a basketball team right now."

Saul could see Bree cringe in the backseat through the rear-view mirror when he said this.

"Whatever," Callie said. "Just thought I would let you know."

Bree mouthed the words 'Thank You' to Callie so her father wouldn't hear, but Saul could see that, too.

That evening at dinner, the talk was all about volleyball camp and how much Bree enjoyed it. Saul kept waiting for the right time to bring up basketball practice and tomorrow's game but he knew no time would be the right time. As they transitioned to dessert, Saul figured it was time to segue.

"Don't eat too much girls, we are going out to practice in a few minutes."

"Oh, Daddy, do we have to?" Bree moaned.

"Yes. I heard you missed last night's practice so we especially need to play tonight to get ready for the game tomorrow."

"The game!" Bree shouted. "You're going to make me go to the game?" She looked at Veronica for help. "Mommy."

"This is between you and your dad, Bree."

"Daddy, I don't want to do it. I want to play volleyball."

"You can do both," Saul said.

"But I don't like basketball. I like playing volleyball. Daddy please, I've finally found a game I like."

The tension at the table was getting tight. Saul could see the expression on Veronica's face that said we are such bad parents. He could see the look on Bree's face that said he was the worst father in the world. And he could see the look on Harper's face that said I can't wait to see what happens next. They didn't know that Saul had made up his mind while watching Bree at the volleyball camp. He still wanted to see how she responded when he brought up the basketball game though, hoping there still might be some ray of hope for his sport. The tears welling up in her big blue eyes were also pretty persuasive, but he didn't want her to know that.

"Tonight, girls, we are going to play . . . ," Saul spoke slowly to draw out the suspense.

"No, Daddy," Bree begged.

" . . . a game of Uno."

Harper looked at Bree and Bree looked at Harper. They were both confused.

"And no cheating, Harper," Saul added.

"I don't cheat," Harper said, immediately defending herself.

"But tomorrow," Saul stated authoritatively, continuing the suspense. "We will go . . . "

Saul saw Bree looking on edge, holding her breath.

" . . . buy us a volleyball net and put it up in the backyard."

"Yes!" Bree celebrated, breathing a sigh of relief. She ran over to give her dad a hug.

"But only on one condition," Saul added, staring at Bree. "You won't miss any volleyball practices and you will not quit any volleyball team you end up being a part of."

"I promise, Daddy. Thank you."

As Bree hugged her father, Veronica also breathed a sigh of relief. Saul looked over at her and smiled. She mouthed the words *I Love You* to him. He mouthed the words back.

"I'll go get the cards," Harper said, oblivious to all the drama. She had the appearance of someone who was ready to win Uno at any cost.

Saul remained at the table pondering if he had made the right decision. His Master Athletic Plan kept taking unexpected detours and Bree was growing up fast. There weren't too many younger years left. He had been searching for the right sport for her and maybe they had found it. And if they did, it wasn't even his doing. It was due to a new friend of Bree's.

Veronica broke his train of thought. "I don't know what you're thinking right now but look on the bright side. She's still playing an indoor sport. No cold weather or rain to deal with. I love it."

Saul smiled. After their afternoon argument, he was glad Veronica was happy. Parenting sometimes comes down to instinct and Veronica had great instincts. She was probably right letting Bree miss practice. As for the game of basketball, he could set it aside for a while to see what happens with this other sport. Besides, basketball still had some old wounds that didn't need to be reopened. And volleyball sounded fresh and new. It was one sport his dad never taught him to play. Saul liked the uniqueness of it. Maybe this would help forge his own special bond between him and his daughters. And the more he thought about their newfound sport, the more he started looking on the bright side.

Bree was back in the gym.

CHAPTER FOUR

BLESS YOU, ST. PIUS

On Saturday morning Saul was the first in line at the Sports Authority when their doors opened. A sales representative recognized him from his last visit.

"You're the guy that bought all the basketball equipment," the sales rep said.

Don't remind me, Saul wanted to say. Instead, he purchased the finest volleyball net and volleyballs he could fine. He decided the best location for the Bryson Volleyball Court would be right smack in the middle of the backyard. That would give them plenty of room to pass and hit balls and the fence line would be far enough away to keep the occasional shank or miss-hit inside the yard.

The girls awoke and walked outside to see their dad driving stakes in the ground to anchor the poles. Saul enjoyed their excitement and as he began attaching the net to the poles, he could tell they couldn't wait to play. Bree and Harper began volleying with the new ball and Bree started showing Harper how to bounce the ball up and down with her arms.

"Ouch," Bree suddenly cried.

"What's wrong?" Saul wondered.

"This ball hurts."

"It's a regulation volleyball. I made sure I checked when I was at the store."

Bree continued to bounce it and then quickly stopped. "Daddy, this ball is too heavy. It hurts my arms."

"Nonsense, Bree. Harper, does it hurt your arms?"

Harper shrugged, not providing an answer. He could tell she was caught in a Catch-22. She didn't want to answer yes and hurt her father's feelings and she didn't want to answer no and hurt her sister's feelings.

Saul put the finishing touches on the net and announced that Bryson Court was officially open for play. He ran inside to get Veronica who was making breakfast. She came outside to inspect the court and was satisfied that it passed her safety inspection.

"Let's have a quick game," Saul said. "It's the parents against the girls. You two get on that side of the net. Me and Mommy will stay on this side."

They began trying to volley the ball back and forth and none of them were very good at it. Bree tried to serve underhanded and kept hitting the ball into the net. The parents were winning, but winning ugly.

"This net is too tall," Bree complained.

"Bree, I checked at the store. This is a regulation net," Saul said, getting a little annoyed at Bree's complaining.

"It's still too tall," she exclaimed. "I don't like it."

"You'll get used to it," Saul assured her.

They continued to try and play a game but the girls continued to struggle getting the ball back over the net.

"Ouch," Bree cried again. "This ball hurts too much."

"I agree," said Harper, suddenly forming an opinion on the matter.

Saul guessed Harper was siding with Bree because they were losing and she was looking for an excuse to start a new game.

Bree tried serving the ball, but again it hit the top of the net and plopped down on her side. Her enthusiasm was gone. "I'm hungry. Can we go in and eat?"

"I'm hungry, too," Harper added.

79

Veronica looked at Saul who was obviously agitated.

"I think it's time for breakfast," Veronica said.

The girls ran inside ahead of them.

"It's never easy," Saul sighed under his breath.

"No it's not," Veronica sympathized. "But good job on the court. It looks nice."

The volleyball league Callie was referring to on the ride home from camp was a recreational Catholic school league. Callie had played in the league last season. Saul could find no other recreational leagues in the area. Callie's league was open to anyone, not just Catholic school students. There were six teams in the league and no tryouts were necessary, which relieved Bree.

Unfortunately, when it came time to sign up for a team, Callie's team was already full. They had managed to keep all the players from last year's team. Bree was disappointed but kept her resolve and commitment to her father and signed up with another team.

They ended up signing with a school called St. Pius. The good news for Bree was that they practiced at the same time and in the same gym as Callie's team. This made her feel better knowing her best friend was nearby. Plus, they could chat before and after practice and during water breaks. Callie played for a school named Jesuit and they were the defending champions from last season.

When Saul drove Bree to her first practice, he could tell she was nervous. He could see some tears welling up in her eyes as if she wanted to beg her father not to make her go. To her credit though, she didn't unleash the water mains and kept her composure. He didn't have to remind her that she had sworn to him she would see this through.

They arrived at the gym and Bree was introduced to her teammates. Most of her teammates knew each other from school because most went to St. Pius. Bree was the only non-Catholic student on the team, but that didn't matter. Her teammates gathered around her and introduced themselves and welcomed her with open arms. They immediately made her feel a part of the team without her feeling awkward at all.

The coach got them organized and they started working through some drills. Saul took a seat on the bleachers and watched as Bree blended in. She actually was doing quite well and the teammates seemed to be impressed with her skills, especially her passing skills. Bree seemed to be enjoying it and smiled when she did something especially good. Bree never complained about the ball hurting her arms like she did at home and she managed to get most of her serves over.

Saul began studying the net and comparing it to his net at home. It was hard to tell from his perspective but the net did appear to be shorter than the one he erected on Bryson Court. Later, an errant ball bounced over to him and he bent over to pick it up. As he tossed it to one of the players, he noticed that it felt different than the one he had bought for the girls. It felt softer and lighter.

After the practice, he asked the coach about the volleyball and the height of the net. The coach relayed to him that for this age group and up to the age of 12, the height of the net was shortened by four inches.

"And the ball?" Saul asked the coach.

"It's called a Volley-Lite. It's a lighter ball for younger girls to play with. They play with it through the age of twelve as well," he confirmed. "They have some adjusting to do when they reach thirteen. Both the net and ball change."

Huh, Saul thought. Bree was right. She knew the equipment he had bought was the wrong kind.

"I told you so," Bree blurted out in the car ride home.

This ride home was a breeze. Saul couldn't get a word in. Bree rambled on about how she loved her teammates and how they were all so nice to her. And she also bragged on herself a bit, too. "I don't feel like I'm the worst player on the team. I think I did pretty good. What do you think, Daddy?"

Finally able to say something, Saul said, "Bree, I think you were one of the best players out there."

"Do you really think so?"

"Of course I do," he said.

Saul always wanted to remain encouraging, while at the same time maintain some truth and integrity when discussing Bree's physical talents. The nice thing about his answer was that he truly believed it. Bree was one of the best players on her team. He could be both encouraging and truthful at the same time, which was a nice feeling.

BREE'S DIARY
November 30
I finally found a sport that not's stupid. Volleyball is a lot of fun. I'm so glad my dad didn't make me play basketball. He is a good dad. I just wish he would make Harper stick with basketball. She is becoming a pest around me and Callie. Now I know what an Exorcist Baby means.

The End.

Everything was going well that season. They had a few more weeks of practices before the first game. Saul began driving both Bree and Callie to practice, which the girls loved because they could continue their chatter from school that day. The girls spent a lot of time together, much to the dismay of Harper. Harper continued to play basketball with her dad but was continually distracted when she would hear Bree and Callie playing volleyball together in the backyard.

"Daddy can I go watch them, please?" Harper begged.

Saul would eventually give in. Harper was becoming a pretty good basketball player but her enthusiasm for the game was dwindling as her big sister excelled in a new sport. Harper wanted to show her big sister she could play volleyball, too.

After Saul released her from basketball practice, she would run to the backyard and sit beside the court and watch the two girls pass the ball back and forth. Saul had adjusted the height of the net and bought two new Volley-Lites for Bryson Court. Harper kept waiting for an invite to play but it would never come. She finally asked one day if she could play.

"No, Harper, you are too young. Besides, me and Callie are practicing," Bree insisted.

"No, you're not. You're just goofing around," Harper blurted out.

"Harper, go back and play basketball," Bree demanded.

Harper didn't move. She frowned in disappointment but kept watching them play. Saul watched as Bree would get annoyed when Harper didn't leave. Harper was infringing on her friend time with Callie. Saul knew Bree and Callie had a lot to talk about and they didn't want to be bothered with little Harper. He had overheard some of these conversations in the car ride to practice and was amused. They had to discuss teachers they liked and disliked, boys they thought were cute or ugly, teammates they thought were good or bad, siblings they thought were pushy and demanding (thus the need for Harper to disappear) and parents they thought were nice but too biased toward their other siblings. Callie had two brothers who were the center of her parents' devotion, at least according to Callie.

It was gratifying to hear Bree offering up opinions about things and speaking more freely and independently. Then suddenly, a switch was flipped and the girls would suddenly turn from conversation mode into little girl mode and start playing with their Littlest Pet Shop pets. Saul thought this was so corny but the girls loved it. They collected and traded their pets and gave them special names and voices. They could play with them for hours building stories around each pet's imaginary personality. They were at such a fun age, when you could be both a little girl and a little lady and get away with it; such was life with adolescence knocking at the door.

Harper's jealousy continued to build and Veronica had a front row seat to it everyday. Harper would complain to her time and again about Callie and how she was interfering with everything, mainly her play time with her big sister. She would tell Veronica how she couldn't believe Bree had changed, that funny things she used to joke about that would make Bree laugh were now stupid to Bree, that she was in a total other world now and didn't care about her. When Harper wanted to play with their Littlest Pets, Bree didn't want to. But when Callie wanted to play with them, Bree couldn't wait to get them out. Harper's tirades tested Veronica's empathy and patience.

One day when basketball was cancelled because Saul was working late, Harper decided to go down to the volleyball court and pass the ball to herself. Veronica watched out the window as Harper staked out her turf. She knew Harper was doing this deliberately, knowing that Bree and Callie would be coming any minute to play. When the two arrived, Bree asked Harper to leave. Harper said no.

"Mom!" Bree shouted.

Veronica heard the shout but didn't want to get involved. She was hoping they could settle the dispute themselves.

"Mom!!" Bree shouted louder.

Veronica knew she had to arbitrate, especially with a guest visiting. She didn't want it to get too ugly. She opened the back door and feigned ignorance as to the problem. "What is it?"

"Harper won't get off the court."

"Who was there first?" Veronica asked.

"Harper was but that's not the point. She knew me and Callie were coming to play. We always play now."

"Just let her play with you for a bit."

"But Mom, she's not . . ." Bree decided not to finish her sentence.

"She's not what?" Veronica asked, knowing that Bree was probably going to say something like Harper wasn't good enough.

"Never mind," Bree sighed.

Veronica was relieved that Bree showed restraint. "Harper, you can play with them for fifteen minutes and then you need to let them have the court," Veronica ordered.

"Ok, Mommy," Harper said innocently.

Veronica walked back into the house glad that the dispute was resolved. Harper would get to play with them for a little while, at least, and show them she was worthy. Bree, on the other hand, would be furious and barely acknowledge Harper while the three volleyed together. Sisterly love at its most intense.

Saturday came, or Game Day as it was now referred to in the Bryson household, and Saul was eager to see how Bree would do in her first game. It wouldn't be easy because Bree's team, St. Pius, had to play Callie's team, Jesuit, in the opener. The good news was Bree wasn't crying or screaming or dreading the thought of going. She had some nervous energy but she was mostly looking forward to getting there and seeing Callie.

"Callie is the enemy," Harper interjected at the breakfast table.

"She is not," Bree shot back. "We are just going to have a lot of fun. We aren't going to win anyway."

"Why not?" Harper asked.

"Because they are just better than us. They have better players."

"Don't be so sure," Saul stated. "You guys have looked pretty good in practice."

"Are you going to get to play this time?" Harper said, a subtle reminder of her last time on the court as a basketball player.

"Of course, she is going to play," Saul interjected. "Harper, shush, and eat your pancakes."

"I was just curious, Daddy," Harper said, smiling both innocently and mischievously.

Game time was upon them. The two teams had gone through their warmups. Saul was gratified to see that Bree was one of the six starters on the court. He looked at the other team and saw Callie was starting as well. No surprise there. She had the ball and was ready to serve. One of the things that set Callie apart from the other girls was her strong serve. At this young age, if you could master a good serve the opposing team would have a hard time handling it. Callie was one of the few girls her age that had mastered an overhand serve. She put a lot of power and top-spin behind it, which made it difficult to return.

The referee blew his whistle and the game began. Saul noticed again, just as in other sports Bree had tried to compete in, his nerves had somehow been automatically activated inside his body, that eternal impulse all dads have of wanting their kids to do well and keep mistakes to an absolute minimum. "Here we go," he said to both Very and Harper, feeling a tad helpless and insecure.

Callie's first serve was a laser of an ace. It whizzed right between two defenders who looked at each other like it was the other's fault. Callie served the second ball in the same direction. Another ace. On the third serve, one of the defenders managed to get her arm on the ball but shanked it sharply out of bounds.

Bree, who started on the front row, felt helpless as she watched her teammates on the back row try to return Callie's passes. Bree wanted a chance but would have to wait until she rotated around to the back row. Before she knew it, they were down 12 to 0 and they had barely touched the ball. Thankfully, on Callie's thirteenth serve, she got a little too aggressive and the ball sailed out of bounds. St. Pius was on the scoreboard.

The rest of the game continued in similar fashion. Jesuit had some really good servers and St. Pius had passers that were used to returning underhand serves, not overhand serves. The underhand serves would travel higher in the air and give them more time to react. When Bree finally rotated around to the back row, she had some success in returning some of the serves. Her teammates congratulated her on some great passes, even if they didn't win the point. The final score of the first game was 25 to 5. It was brutal to watch and there wasn't much volleying to be had.

In the Catholic league, you played two out of three games, all of them to 25 points. Saul hoped they could make a better showing in game two. He knew a win was out of the question. The coach decided to start Bree on the back row for game two since she passed very well in game one, Saul deduced.

Bree was the first to serve and she lobbed one of her underhand serves into the air. She had miss-hit the ball and she was afraid it would fall short of the net, but the ball had just enough oomph to clear the net and drop for an ace, fooling the Jesuit girls. The serve was so bad it was good, Saul chuckled to himself. St. Pius led 1 to 0 and Bree's teammates ran over to give her multiple high fives and celebrate actually being in the lead. Unfortunately, the game wasn't over.

Bree's next serve was hit almost exactly the same way, except it didn't quite have the loft of the previous serve. The ball hit the tape on the top of the net and dropped to the ground on the St. Pius side. Their lead was gone.

Callie was the first to serve for her team again and she drilled her first few serves away from Bree. Again, they were too hard for Bree's teammates to handle. Bree stayed ready waiting to see if one would be hit her direction. Finally, one came. Whether it was intentional or not, Callie hit one of her topspin specials that was baring down in Bree's direction. After the ball cleared the net, it began dropping sharply. It looked like it would hit the ground but Bree quickly lurched forward and dropped to her knees, reaching her arms out as far as they could go. She contacted the ball before it hit the ground, popping the ball up into the air, which was a great play in its own right. The ball came off of Bree's arms with enough velocity that it sailed back over to the Jesuit side and fell right in the middle of three teammates for a St. Pius point.

The Jesuit defenders looked at each other wondering what just happened. They weren't ready to make a play on the ball. Callie's serve was never returned like that. It was almost always an ace.

The St. Pius players cheered Bree's great play as did all the parents, especially Saul and Veronica. They both jumped out of their seats with elation. Saul was pumped, but he knew he needed to keep his composure. They were still getting throttled by a much better team.

Bree continued her strong play on the back row but most of Jesuit's servers would avoid serving the ball in her direction. With the score 24 to 11 Jesuit, Callie had one more serve left to finish off the game. Saul was satisfied with the 11 points. He calculated it to be a 120 percent improvement from game one.

Callie then rifled her serve over the net right at a St. Pius defender. The ball caromed off her arms sideways over to where Bree was standing. Bree had little time to react. It was all she could do to just safely pass the ball over the net and keep it in play. Her pass barely cleared the net and went straight to a Jesuit front row player who raised her right arm and swung at the ball as hard as she could.

The ball would have sailed thirty feet out of bounds if it wasn't for Bree's face being in the way. All the players and parents gasped with concern. Poor Bree was caught in a helpless position. She didn't have enough time to gain a defensive position to be ready for the player's attack.

Saul couldn't remember the sound the ball made when it hit her. He only could hear pain. He and Veronica both looked away when it happened, then immediately looked back to check on Bree's reaction. She had her hands covering her nose. They were waiting for the blood to begin pouring on the floor. They were waiting for the tears to come streaming out. They were waiting to see if she might even lose consciousness. For a second, Saul thought this was probably the end of her volleyball career. Bree would be walking off the court in shame and embarrassment just like she did in her first and only basketball game.

But Bree seemed to be okay. She took her hands down from her nose. There was no blood. The coach looked at her face. There was no broken nose. She told her teammates she was fine and then, to Saul's astonishment, she began laughing it off like it was no big deal. Her face was beet red and her eyes were watery from the impact but she was smiling and got in line with her teammates to shake hands with the other team. Callie made a special attempt to reach out to her and make sure she was okay.

Saul looked at Veronica with amazement. "I think we've turned a corner here," he said.

"Our little girl is toughening up," Veronica agreed.

Even though they lost, the ride home from the game was a pleasant one. Bree was excited at some of the plays she pulled off. She bragged on Callie and how well she played and what a great player she was. She was happy they came back in the second game and made it a little more challenging. She was proud of the way she handled the ball in the face.

"It didn't hurt at all, Daddy, it really didn't," she said.

"It looked painful to me," Saul countered.

"It happened so fast it really just stunned me. My face felt numb but it didn't really hurt."

"Bree, why are you so happy after you lost, and lost badly," Harper blurted out, as if resenting the attention her big sister was receiving.

"Harper, hush. That's not nice," Veronica cautioned.

Meanwhile, Saul barely heard the remark. He was beaming with satisfaction inside. He was pleased with his daughter's play and he was pleased with how well she handled the facial attack. There was no talk of hating the game or wanting to quit. There was excitement in Bree's voice.

As the season progressed, Saul didn't have to do much personal practicing with Bree. Bree and Callie would spend a lot of time playing together in the yard. Saul would encourage her to work on her serve so it got stronger. He also wanted her to try an overhand serve, although he knew it would be a while before Bree had the strength to do it consistently.

He continued to play with Harper on the basketball court but Harper continued to lose interest in the sport. They would play for a while and then Harper would make him go to the backyard to play volleyball. Saul had to be her playing buddy since Bree was always with Callie. Occasionally, Saul would bring up the idea of playing for a basketball team but Harper was not excited about it. She wanted to play on a volleyball team. And that desire only increased as Bree's season went on.

After losing to Jesuit, Bree's coach knew they had a lot of work to do in the serve-receive game if they were going to compete better with Jesuit. The good news for St. Pius was that no other team in the league had Jesuit's serving talent. When it came to pure volleying, St. Pius was pretty strong. Bree's serve-receive and overall passing skills were slowly making her a leader on the team. Her teammates knew they could rely on her to make a play when one was needed.

St. Pius only lost one other game that season, a tough three setter to a school called St. Christopher. Saul was encouraged by their play and he continued to be encouraged by Bree's ability to stand out. She was gaining more and more confidence on the court.

When it came time for the playoffs, it was no surprise that Jesuit was the number one seed. They had won all six of their games with hardly a challenge. St. Pius finished the season with four wins and two losses and was tied with St. Christopher for second place. The playoffs would be played in Jesuit's gym. The last thing they needed was home court advantage, Saul moaned internally.

The playoffs were a simple one day affair. St. Pius would have to win two matches to make the final. While Saul was excited for the tournament, he was a little saddened that the season was coming to an end. The season had been tremendous fun for Bree, and Saul enjoyed watching as she developed a great rapport with her teammates.

Their first game of the tournament that day was against a team from St. Paul's Academy. They were the worst team in the league. Bree's team had beaten them easily during the regular season so Saul didn't expect too much trouble. While St. Pius got off to a bit of a slow start, they were able to rally during the middle of the first game and win 25 to 20. The second game went more as Saul had anticipated. St. Pius won handily 25 to 12. That set up a rematch with St. Christopher.

Saul and Bree talked about a possible rematch with St. Christopher on the way to the tournament. Both of them knew they were beatable. When St. Pius played them the first time, the match could have gone either way. St. Pius made a few clumsy errors in the third game that they couldn't recover from.

Bree believed they were a much better team now. A couple of her teammates had taken their passing game to a new level and that helped their defense a great deal. Plus, her team had become much more consistent in their serving with fewer misses, which meant they weren't giving up the cheap points.

St. Pius started the game like they had something to prove. They won the first six points and never looked back. Led by Bree, the team's passing was strong. They also served aggressively by hitting long and deep serves which put more pressure on St. Christopher's back row players. St. Pius won the first game 25 to 18.

The second game didn't start out as well. St. Christopher went on a serving run and held a 10 to 4 lead. Bree's coach called a timeout and whatever he said, it was effective. St. Pius returned to their aggressive play from the first game and tied the game up at 18.

The game went back and forth for the next few points when Bree saw a hole in the back left side of the court and perfectly passed the ball to the open zone for an easy point. That put St. Pius up 24 to 23. The St. Pius parents erupted with elation. Bree was next to serve and Saul and Veronica clutched hands. A rush of nerves passed through both of them.

"Oh, my God, I can't watch this," Veronica said.

Saul couldn't believe how on edge he was. Bree had only missed one serve that day but every serve at this age was still an adventure. Saul was amazed you could get this rattled from watching a bunch of little league girls play in a recreational volleyball tournament. Bree retrieved the ball and was ready. The ref blew his whistle giving her the okay to serve. She took a couple of deep breaths, which she normally didn't do.

"Come on, Bree, let's go!" shouted Harper suddenly.

Saul looked at Harper who was intensely into the game. She had been quiet all day but had been zealously studying the matches. This was the first time he had heard her cheer for her sister. It was nice to see because she certainly hadn't been cheering for her since Callie came along. Bree must have heard the cheer, too, because Saul noticed her break a little smile.

Bree took one more breath, then tossed the ball in the air. She swooped her arm under the ball and it sailed high and deep into the right back corner. Saul thought it was sailing out and it might have been sailing out, but the back defender decided to reach up to play the ball. The defender tried her best to keep the ball in play but it deflected off her arms and bounced way out of bounds into her own coach's hands, who frowned at his player's weak attempt. The match was over and the girls celebrated with Bree in the middle of the court. Saul and Veronica gave each other a hug and let out sighs of relief. Bree ran over to see her parents.

"How was that serve, Daddy?"

"It was great, Bree. Great job."

Harper raced over to give her sister a hug. "Good job," Harper said, as if she was giving her seal of approval.

"Bree, what did the coach tell you that made you guys play better?" Saul asked curiously.

"He said we were playing like crap and if we didn't win we would have to do crap-walks after the game."

Saul looked puzzled. "You mean crab-walks?"

"No. Crap-walks," Bree confirmed.

Whatever, Saul thought. It worked. He didn't want to get into the definition of a crap-walk at this particular time.

"I can't wait. We get to play Callie's team again," Bree exclaimed, running off quickly to be with her teammates.

Jesuit had made it to the finals with ease. Saul didn't expect much from the rematch. He was glad that St. Pius had claimed revenge over St. Christopher and had won the fight for second place. That was the real highlight of the day's competition since the first place team was unbeatable. He was interested to see how much they had improved from their 25 to 5, 25 to 11 thrashing at the hands of Jesuit at the start of the season.

Not much improvement, Saul felt, when the game started. Not much improvement at all. It played out like a carbon copy of their first match. Callie's unstoppable overhand serve led the way to an 11-0 lead. Any thought of a miracle win was quickly quashed. Saul was disappointed because even Bree was shanking balls left and right. The only thing that seemed to stop Callie's serve was if she missed one. Thankfully, she missed the next one.

The teams traded points for the rest of the game, which Saul considered a moral victory. Jesuit, once they got the early lead, seemed disinterested. The final score of game one was 25 to 12, which was noteworthy to Saul, always the statistician. He remarked to Veronica that they had managed to score one more point than their last game against Jesuit and six more points than the first game from their last match. Veronica shrugged, never one to care much for stats.

The second game got off to a much better start. Bree served first and led them on a three point run before missing her fourth serve. Callie was next up to serve for Jesuit, but she rifled her first serve into the net. That was a big momentum swing for St. Pius. The two teams then continued to trade points back and forth similar to the last half of the previous game. Saul was starting to get a little excited, especially when they reached point 13, which meant they had improved upon the last game's total. Their positive trend was continuing.

Before he realized it, the score was 19 to 17 St. Pius. Jesuit called a time-out and Saul watched as their coach tried to get his girls fired up. The St. Pius sideline didn't need any firing up. All the girls and parents were pumped. They came out of the huddle focused and ready.

Callie was again at the service line. She rifled a serve right at Bree's direction. Bree made a perfect pass to one of her teammates who bumped a soft pass to the middle of Jesuit's side of the court. The ball dropped for a point as the Jesuit defenders looked at each other befuddled. Seizing the momentum, St. Pius went on a surprising serving run. The Jesuit players continued to look more confused and frustrated. They weren't used to being behind. They weren't used to shanking passes. They weren't used to the opposing team playing so well.

With every point won, the St. Pius parents were going crazy and the players were jumping up and down in a frenzy. When they won game point, Saul was so euphoric he was ready to host a victory party at his house. St. Pius had won the final six points in a row winning the game 25 to 17, but the St. Pius fans soon remembered there was a game three to be played. The match wasn't over.

Saul and Veronica regrouped and tried to be more calm, cool and collected. Bree and her teammates surely weren't. They were high-fiving and celebrating well into the start of game three.

Jesuit won the coin toss and elected to serve first, which meant Callie was leading off. She immediately reminded every-one who the better team was. Jesuit took a 6 to 0 lead before Bree's teammates came down to earth and realized another game was being played. Bree stopped Callie's seventh serve with a great pass, which ultimately translated into a point for St. Pius and they were on the board.

The rest of the game was well-played with long rallies and few errors being made. Jesuit, playing like champions, stayed in control throughout leading by four or five points all the way through. Saul was pleased that St. Pius was hanging tough and not giving up.

Callie was at the service line again, this time to finish the game. Jesuit was up 24 to 20. One good serve from her and the game was likely over. She fired her serve crosscourt to where Bree was positioned. Bree made a move for the ball but at the angle the ball was coming she decided it was going out. Luckily she was right--by about two inches. Bree breathed a sigh of relief before remembering it was her turn to serve.

"Oh, great," Veronica said. "I can't watch."

"Let's go, Bree," Harper shouted encouragingly.

Saul placed his hands on his face so he could immediately cover his eyes, if needed. They were down 24 to 21 and a missed serve meant the game was over. Bree stood at the line, took a deep breath, and was ready. She swung at the ball and Saul knew instantly that she didn't hit it well. The ball flew lower than it normally did.

"It's going to be short," Saul told Veronica, as he covered his eyes.

When the ball began it's downward flight, Veronica thought it still had a chance. As if in slow motion, the ball came down and landed right on top of the net. It bounced up a few inches and fell on top of the net again before trickling over and landing on the Jesuit side. St. Pius's parents were again cheering as loudly as they were at the end of the second game.

"What happened?" Saul asked, looking up to see Bree being hugged by her teammates.

"It was an ace," Veronica shouted.

Bree headed back to the service line.

"Oh, my God, here we go again," Veronica warned.

Saul insisted to himself he would watch this time. With St. Pius now trailing by two, Bree's next serve had much more force behind it and it sailed to the back row. Two Jesuit teammates called for the ball but they both ran into each other and the ball dropped for another ace. The Jesuit players were suddenly experiencing some déjà vu from the last game.

"Yes!" Saul screamed. "One more, Bree."

"Oh, my God," Veronica said again, the only three words she seemed to now know. She was digging her nails into Saul's forearm, but Saul was oblivious to the pain.

Suddenly, the excitement died down. The Jesuit coach had called a timeout. With the score 24 to 23, St. Pius needed one point to tie the game.

"They are trying to ice her," Saul said.

"What does that mean?" Harper asked.

"I'll tell you later," Saul said.

The players came back on the court. The fans began raising their voices cheering for both teams. Bree had the ball in her hands ready to serve. The whistle blew and it was time.

Bree didn't hesitate. She hit a very solid, but safe serve to the middle of the Jesuit court. Callie was the first to react to the ball. She came charging in and passed the ball in the direction of one of her front row players who quickly jumped up and calmly tapped the ball over the outstretched arms of a St. Pius player. The ball hit the floor and just like that, the game was over. Jesuit won 25 to 23. Cinderella had left the building.

Jesuit fans were cheering raucously. The Jesuit team was huddled together celebrating when Saul saw Bree walk under the net and give Callie a hug. Bree was clapping and jumping up and down with happiness for Callie and the rest of her team-mates. Just like in UNO, she was always happy for the winner.

Saul tried to pretend he didn't notice and he was hoping the other dads didn't notice either. The moms would consider it a generous act of sportsmanship. The dads would consider it im-proper, giving undo praise to the opponent and not showing enough disappointment in the loss. Saul still had to teach Bree about that killer instinct.

For now, though, he was totally gratified. She played well and she got her serves in when it counted. She had a great sea-son and became a better player. More importantly, she felt great about herself.

Saul went over to shake the coach's hand and thank him for the work he had done with the team and his daughter. He then quickly noticed that the tournament officials were handing out second place medals to Bree's team. As Bree bent over to receive her medal, Saul was actually overcome with a rush of emotion. There was his daughter, his athlete, receiving an award for the very first time. He quickly thought about the journey to this point and what it took to get here. He thought of the bloody nose at basketball and the undersized pink tutu at dance and the horrid somersaults in gymnastics and the dreadful rainy days on the soccer field and the utter boredom of softball and all he could feel at this very point in time, was pure thankfulness.

He searched for Veronica and spotted her taking pictures of the girls, tears running down her cheeks. It was all Saul could do to act manly and hold in his own tears. Get yourself together, man. This is just a meaningless rec league game.

But the moment did have meaning. He couldn't deny it. As he watched Bree posing for the cameras and blushing with pride with her teammates, Saul couldn't help but be overcome with pride, too. His daughter was a volleyball player. And a very good one.

They had finally found her sport.

PART TWO

MAP INTERRUPTED

CHAPTER FIVE

THE CALL

Saul sat in his office staring out the window. He had gone from the euphoric highs of a surprising second place finish on Saturday to the plundering lows of a boring business conference call on Monday. He had forgotten what the call was about as he mindlessly watched seagulls circling around in the distance from his office window.

It was one of those unnecessary calls executive management would host from time to time to update second tier management on the company's strategy. Saul had the call on mute. No input was needed from him because executive management wouldn't solicit input from second tier management in a public forum like this. He was in a listen-only mode but that had quickly transitioned to a daydream-only mode.

With Bree's debut volleyball season behind them, Saul was thinking Bree needed a little free time away from the sport, maybe two or three days would be sufficient, and then it would be back to work improving her as a player. Saul didn't want her to fall into a false sense of complacency. There were still many things for her to work on.

The Catholic league only played one season a year. Saul had to figure out how to keep her engaged in the game and make sure she was better when next season rolled around. A few of the parents from Bree's team were talking about joining a volleyball club. Saul didn't know what that was. Evidently, per the parents, there were a few clubs in the Seattle area that had opened up in the past year or two and were focused on developing young volleyball athletes. They told him joining a volleyball club was imperative now if you wanted your girl to play in college.

Saul didn't fully understand that reasoning. He had gotten a basketball scholarship without the need of a club, but the comment still got his attention. After all, a college scholarship was a significant step in his MAP. The only major problem he could see with joining a club was their location. They were not near his house and would require a bit of a commute for Very.

As Saul sat there not listening to the conference call, he decided to pick up his cell phone and call a couple of these clubs to see what they had to offer. Both calls that he made ended up in voice mail. These days you either got voice mail or a polite-speaking person from India. As he leaned back in his chair waiting for a return call, his office phone suddenly rang. Saul picked up the phone quickly thinking it might be one of the volleyball clubs but he soon remembered he left them his cell number, not his office number.

"Saul Bryson," he answered.

It was a voice he hadn't heard in a while. It was Phil Anderson, the Chief Financial Officer from the corporate office. What the hell could he want, Saul wondered.

"What did you think of the conference call, Bryson?" Anderson asked.

Saul looked at the other line on his phone. The conference call had ended and he wasn't even aware of it. He had to ad-lib some BS ASAP. "Uh, It was a great call, sir. The company seems on the right track with its strategic objectives," Saul said, using the best company-speak he could muster on such short notice.

"Well, let me tell you why I'm calling," Anderson continued. "It has to do with some of the restructuring we mentioned on the call."

Restructuring? Saul thought. He had missed that. He had missed most of the call's agenda after going into daydream-mode so early in the call. Anderson went on to convey to Saul the reason he was calling and Saul was speechless during most of the conversation.

This was it.

This was the call he had been waiting for. This was the call that was so big that it would forever live in infamy as "THE CALL" in the Bryson household. This was the promotion he had been wanting. This was the move away from from the rainy Northwest and bland Northwest-Mex and back home to the southern comforts of Dallas and Tex-Mex cooking. He could smell the chicken fried steak frying. This was the call he had been prepared to receive for the last seven years and now, to his surprise, he didn't know how to receive it.

He thanked Anderson for the offer and told him he would go home and talk about it with the family and get back to him with an answer tomorrow. Corporate did not like it if answers to offers extended beyond a 24-hour period. That would show weakness or concern that the employee wasn't fully committed to the team. You either took the job or you didn't. If you didn't, good luck on getting another call in the future.

"You have to take it," Veronica said, without hesitation.

Saul was taken aback at her prompt decision. He had left work early and they were sitting outside in their Conference Room for Private Family Discussions. Saul knew he had to take it, too, but the thought of moving was now more challenging than it was a few years ago. The girls were more entrenched. Bree had a best friend. Bree was part of a volleyball team. Harper was probably still too young to care, but the magnitude of the decision weighed on Saul. In reality, maybe it wasn't the magnitude of the decision. Maybe it was the magnitude of telling the girls that weighed on him more.

"When do we tell them?" Saul asked.

"Let's wait a little while until this deal is firmed up," Veronica suggested. "You will tell Anderson yes tomorrow and then once you get your start date confirmed, we will figure out when to tell the girls."

Saul felt that made sense. Procrastination deduced from rational thought. Saul then looked up at the sky. A big roar of laughter followed.

"What's so funny?" Veronica inquired.

"The sky is clear."

Veronica laughed with him. "Maybe that's the sign we've been waiting for."

"Maybe," Saul said, with a twinge of doubt. It could be a sign to stay, but he didn't tell Very that.

The next day Anderson was thrilled to hear Bryson had accepted the job. They talked start dates as Anderson wanted Saul in Dallas as soon as possible. Saul's soon-to-be former boss, Charlie, wanted more time to help with the transition of Saul's replacement, but Charlie knew he was negotiating with the CFO. He didn't have much leverage. Saul would be starting in Dallas in two weeks.

"That's quick," Veronica said.

Saul had come home early to celebrate and to also plot with Veronica on when to tell the kids. Bree was playing volleyball in the yard with both Callie and Harper. Their world was in perfect harmony right now. And he was about to destroy it.

"How did Harper work her way into the trio?" Saul asked.

"Weeks of cunning and manipulation," Veronica said.

"I need some of that for our conversation."

The two decided that it was better to go ahead and tell the girls the news than wait any longer. They would bring it up at dinner that night.

Naturally, the girls were in ideal moods; cheerful, done with homework, looking forward to playing Webkinz later. Ice cream was served for dessert, making their spirits even higher. Saul was hoping the ice cream effect would help like it helped at Baskin-Robbins that day he told Bree about playing on a basketball team. But it wouldn't. No sugar high could offset the bomb he was about to drop.

"I've got some big news for you, girls," he decided to begin.

"What's that, Daddy?" Bree said excitedly.

Saul hesitated. Look at their innocent smiling faces, he thought. Did he really want to have this conversation now? He turned to Veronica.

"Your Dad got a big promotion today at work," Veronica blurted out.

So much for hesitating.

"That's great, Daddy. Congratulations," Bree exclaimed.

"Thanks, Bree. It's going to be great for us. You know how we have always talked about moving back home and being close again to our relatives?"

The girls nodded in agreement but the news had yet to register.

"Well, this is our chance to do just that. We are moving back to Dallas."

The word Dallas caught Bree's attention. She still had a smile on her face but it was slowly fading into a controlled look of concern.

"That's cool, Daddy," shouted Harper.

"And guess what girls, we'll be able to get that swimming pool we always talked about," Saul added, trying to sweeten the ante.

"Awesome," Harper said. She was all in, but Bree, as expected, was all out. Her reaction was nervously silent.

Saul looked at Bree who's eyes had begun to moisten. "What do you think, Bree?" Saul asked, trying to break the tension.

"That's great, Daddy. I'm happy for you," Bree said, trying her best to hide her disappointment

Veronica reached over to put her arm around Bree. "Are you okay, sweetie?"

"But I just made a friend, Mommy," Bree said, burying her face in Veronica's arms. She was doing her best not to cry but she couldn't help it. Veronica looked at Saul as if her own heart was breaking as she held Bree close.

"We understand that," Saul empathized, trying to remain in charge emotionally. "But you will make new friends in Dallas. And anytime you want to fly back and spend a few days with Callie, we can make that happen." Saul didn't know how that would work and they had yet to talk to Callie's parents about it, but he wanted to keep a positive spin on things. "And Callie is welcome to come visit you anytime, too," he added.

"Really," Bree said through the sniffles.

"You bet," Saul assured her.

That seemed to perk her up a little. "When are we moving?" Bree asked.

"We don't know yet. We still have to sell the house and we have to find a new house in Dallas. It will be months."

This news seemed to put Bree more at ease. Months were like years to a young girl her age. The move wasn't going to happen right away and she and Callie would have a lot more playing time together. The sisters excused themselves and ran upstairs to play and possibly discuss their new future. Saul and Veronica immediately moved to the patio to decompress.

"Boy, that was tough," Saul sighed.

"Oh, the look on Bree's face. It was agonizing to watch," Veronica added.

"Tell me about it."

"So are you really going to pay her way to visit Callie?" Veronica asked.

"I've got to," Saul said. "I just said I would. Let's just hope she meets some friends quickly in Dallas and this will all pass."

Saul's cell phone then rang. "Hello," he answered.

It was one of the volleyball clubs he had tried calling the day before.

"I'm sorry, but we are no longer interested. Thank you."

He quickly hung up and made a mental note to locate some clubs in Dallas when he got there. Hopefully, there would be something similar.

"Who was that?" Veronica asked.

"Oh, nothing important. Just a work issue."

It was a little lie and Saul didn't know why he said it. Maybe he didn't want to bring it up because it spoke to the change they were all experiencing. Or maybe he just didn't have the emotional energy to talk about it. He would be gone in two weeks, leaving Veronica to deal with the kids and all the issues surrounding getting the house ready for sale. That was enough change, transition and upheaval to deal with. At this particular moment, his Master Athletic Plan wasn't the highest thing on his priority list.

BREE'S DIARY
April 28
I told Callie today we were moving. I know what a heart feels like now. Because mine broke. We had just told each other we would be best friends forever. We are still going to be best friends. She said we could spend a lot of face time on her mom's computer. I don't really know what that means. I'm going to miss volleyball, too. It is so fun and exciting with Callie around.

The End.

CHAPTER SIX

THE BLUR

In life, in career and in family you have to make sacrifices at times with the hope that those hard choices eventually pay off and lead to a better life, career and family. Saul and Veronica had moved a few times in their married life but this was the hardest move yet. As much as they hated the rain and cold and seafood and coffee of the Northwest, and longed for the warmth and family and tasteful Tex-Mex of home, they slowly realized that they had become entrenched in Seattle. They had been there for ten years and Bree had lived most of her life there and Harper all of her life. They had collected a houseful of things that years of staying in the same place bring you. More importantly, they had collected a houseful of memories.

This was more apparent to Veronica as she stayed on to deal with prepping the house for sale and deciding what goes and what stays and what is thrown away. She also was there to witness the close friendship and bond that Callie and Bree swore to uphold regardless of the distance between them. And she was there to walk Harper to the local park so she could swing or see-saw or climb the monkey bars, the same play area Harper had used since she was old enough to walk.

Saul, on the other hand, was consumed with work and trying to make a great impression in his new job. A great impression meant working weekends and long hours to show your dedication and your ability to get up to speed as quickly as possible. He was at Corporate headquarters now and if you made a poor impression there, your future could be short-lived. You could be banished to Boise or Tucson, which weren't bad places per se, but in the company he worked for, those markets were where failed executives were put out to pasture. As Siberia is to Russia, Boise and Tucson were to his company.

Whenever Saul took a new job, he always felt the first six months were the most important. And for him and the rest of his family, those six months were a blur. He flew back home every few weeks to stay with the family for a condensed weekend. Veronica flew down a couple of times to look for houses with him. He would soon be called away leaving her to make the rounds with the realtor alone. They would only talk late at night when he got home. The questions were routine and to the point. How was your day? How are the kids? How are their grades? Are they playing volleyball in the backyard? Any offers on the house yet? I'm tired. I love you. Good night.

The house sold after being on the market for three months and the new buyers wanted to move in two months after the contract was signed. This gave Veronica ample time to locate their own movers and ample time to find a house in Dallas. It also pleased Saul because he would be nearing the end of his six-month Great Impression period at work and would be able to focus a little more time on the family when they arrived.

They ended up buying a house in Plano, a large well-established community about twenty miles north of Dallas and known for their good schools. They had lived in Plano before. They bought their first house there a year after they got married so they knew the area well, although they were surprised how much it had grown.

The good-byes were tough but not as bad as Veronica thought they would be. Callie and Bree had a lot of quality time together and were confident they could keep their friendship in tact with the assistance of modern technology. Callie surprised Bree when they were saying their final good-byes by giving her a picture of the two of them. It was from the volleyball tournament. They both had their arms around each other, smiling proudly, with their medals draped around their necks. Bree kept the picture close to her at all times.

The Seattle house was now empty. The moving truck was closing its doors. Veronica loaded the girls in the airport shuttle and she promised herself she wouldn't look back. But she did. She needed one more memory to stow away. It had been such a great house for them. As the shuttle turned the corner, the house was suddenly out of view and that provided a little closure for her, which she needed. She turned around in her seat and looked forward, waiting for the next chapter in their life to begin.

While they were happy they got the house sold in a reasonable time frame, they weren't happy about the timing as it pertained to the girls. They were hoping they could move in time for the girls to be in school at the start of the fall term, but that didn't work out. Harper and Bree's first day was November 1st, a good two months into the fall term.

Saul picked them up at the airport on a Saturday. Halloween was on a Sunday and they started school that Monday. In addition, the movers would be arriving on Tuesday. There was a lot to do that weekend. They immediately drove to the new house for the girls to see. Bree, being the oldest, got to select her bedroom, much to the disappointment of Harper, but Harper's mood quickly changed when she saw the swimming pool for the first time.

Saul thought it would be fun to spend the night in the new house instead of staying in a hotel so he purchased sleeping bags for everyone. They bought Halloween costumes for the girls but, since they were new to the neighborhood, they had to force their shy girls to trick or treat against their will. The holiday provided Saul and Veronica a chance to introduce themselves to the neighbors. They were hoping to find girls their daughters' age that lived near their house but had no luck. Most of the nearby neighbors had kids in high school or even in college. Probably a product of Plano being so well-established now, Saul deduced. But there had to be potential friends somewhere due to the sheer number of schools in the area.

The first day at a new school is always a challenge. The girls were mopey and nervous and a bit jet-lagged from the busy weekend. They didn't want to go, but they knew they had to so there wasn't much whining or complaining. Kids, deep down, know that going to school is like their civic duty so they have to grin and bear it. So they marched inside the school doors together determined to make a go of it; Bree and Harper continuing their sixth grade and third grade educations, respectively.

Saul had planned to stay home from work for a few days to help when the movers arrived. His first task was to figure out where Bryson Court would go. For whatever reason, when they were looking at houses, the location of Bryson Court was never considered in their decision. Maybe he had too much going on with work and all, or maybe he was too infatuated with finding a house with a great swimming pool. Who knows. He blamed it on the blur.

They did find a house with a great swimming pool. The only problem was the current November weather was too cold to enjoy it. As he scoped out the back yard while admiring the first pool he had ever owned, which he sadly estimated wouldn't be of use until next May, he realized there wasn't room for a volleyball court in the back yard.

He was mystified. How did he not think of this? When they toured the house, the back yard seemed huge. Check that. It was huge, but that was because most of the yard was filled with a huge swimming pool with related pool equipment and decorative landscaping and shrubbery designed to enhance the pool's beauty and hugeness. When he walked around behind the pool area, there was only about five feet of green space between the pool and the fence-line. Bryson Court would not be in the back yard. The pool was perfectly designed to host a game of water volleyball though, Saul surmised, but again that first game wouldn't be until May.

Saul then wandered aimlessly around to the front yard looking for possible options.

Veronica opened the front door and asked curiously, "Are you looking for something? You look lost, like you're in need of a home."

Saul decided to give it a shot. "How would you feel about a volleyball court in the front yard?" He said wincingly, knowing what the answer would be.

She laughed. "Don't even go there."

"But we had a basketball goal out front in our last house."

"You can have a volleyball court in the front yard as long as you put it up when you're ready to play and take it down when you're done," Veronica instructed as she walked back inside.

Saul knew he would not win this one. But the thought of having to put up a net every time they wanted to play was not going to work. He didn't want to have to dig holes and put stakes in the ground every time he wanted to play with the girls. His mind was now focused on the cul-de-sac at the end of their street. There was a basketball goal at the end of the cul-de-sac that a neighbor had put up. Which neighbor, you couldn't really tell. It looked like it was there for public use. He was trying to figure out a way to put up a volleyball net in that same area without it being too obtrusive. This was going to take some careful deliberation and planning.

The girls survived their first day of school. No friends were made but no enemies were made, either. As the next few weeks passed, they got settled into their new home and adapted to a new routine. Harper looked forward to getting home from school because she had Bree all to herself again. There was no Callie to share except for later in the evening when Bree would spend her time e-mailing and face-timing with her on the computer. This became a nightly occurrence which annoyed Saul a bit because he wanted to use the computer, but if this helped Bree adapt to her new setting a little more easily, than he was okay with it.

One day at work, Saul decided it was time to try and locate a volleyball league or club. He felt guilty for not doing this sooner but he blamed it on the blur, plus the fact that the girls had really just gotten settled in. He was now secure enough in his new job that he could take the occasional fifteen minutes to goof off and tend to some personal matters. God knows, his boss was doing it every time he knocked on his office door. Solitaire was his CFO's favorite game.

Saul's search led him to a surprising number of clubs, definitely more clubs than he saw in the Seattle area. He called a few but his eagerness to find out more information was quickly dampened by the fact that the club season had already started. They had tryouts a month ago and all the teams were set. He could try to find a team that had an open spot but he knew that wouldn't play well with Bree. While she was forced to join her new school in mid-season, that was her civic duty. Forcing her to join a club team in mid-season might make her hitchhike all the way back to Seattle. Saul would not be that cruel.

He did subtly bring the topic up at the dinner table but Bree quickly shot it down. So did Veronica. He knew this was not the time to push Bree into an uncomfortable situation. Saul hated the fact that Bree had been missing out on getting better at volleyball but this was all part of the sacrifices you make when relocating. He did get a commitment from Bree to play some recreational volleyball in the spring. And he also committed to her that Bryson Court would be open for business soon and he would do every thing he could to help improve her game.

"I can't wait to see the new court, Daddy," Bree said.

"Me, too," Harper chimed in.

"Me three," Veronica said, eyeing him curiously.

"I have a plan," Saul assured her.

That weekend, Saul unveiled his plan and Veronica had a bird's eye view. After running a few errands in the morning, he was in the driveway most of the day constructing something. Veronica saw a long aluminum pole, two car tires which disturbed her, and some concrete, which was even more disturbing because Saul was not the handyman type and had never dealt with pouring concrete as long as she knew him.

She wanted to ask him about his project, but he was so focused she didn't want to be a pest. The real question she wanted to know was, from where did he get the two tires? She quietly opened the trunk of her car to make sure the spare was still there and it was. She also made sure all four tires were still on her car. After satisfying herself that her car was still operational, she went back inside but was unable to get any work done. She sat by the window with a cup of tea and watched amusingly as her husband labored.

She watched as Saul attached both tires to the opposite ends of the aluminum pole, which was about ten feet long, she guessed. He also attached the volleyball net to the pole and wrapped the net around the pole like a spool. She didn't know why there had to be two tires on opposite ends of the pole and she didn't know why there wasn't another pole. A volleyball net had two poles, after all.

Suddenly, it became apparent what he was doing when he started rolling the pole on its two tires like a wheel axle, down the driveway and onto the street. Once on the street, he redirected the tires so they would roll down the street to the end of the cul-de-sac. Once there, he tried to stand the pole up which wasn't easy to do because of the weight of the spare tire at the top. Veronica was worried he would hurt himself, but after wrestling with it for some time, the pole now stood erect.

He then proceeded to unspool the net and attach the net to the mast of the basketball goal. Oh, my God, Veronica thought. What will the neighbors think?

Veronica then noticed Saul rushing back to the house. She immediately went back to the kitchen, so as not to give away her spy chair. Saul yelled at the girls to come outside and they quickly followed him out, while Veronica followed them all the way back to her spy chair. She smiled at the looks on the girls' faces. They were utterly amazed at Saul's genius. They quickly began establishing the boundary lines of the court and started volleying the ball to one another. Saul was proudly soaking up the moment. And he should be, Veronica felt. This was the first time in months he had been able to conduct a practice on Bryson Court.

She walked out on the front porch to feel the cool-crisp winter air. It felt refreshing, just as refreshing as seeing their girls having fun at their favorite game. While she still cringed at Saul's unique and somewhat dilapidated set-up of Bryson Court, it did make their new house feel a little bit more like home.

A few seconds later, however, a car entered the street.

"Uh-oh," Veronica muttered to herself, and quickly went back inside to her spy chair.

The car appeared lost. It drove slowly to the end of the cul-de-sac and didn't know how to proceed with a volleyball net in its way. Saul wisely motioned to the girls to get off the street and Veronica watched as he directed the driver to circle under the net. The car continued slowly making its 180 degree U-turn with Saul raising the net to make sure the car could pass under it. Veronica was glad she was inside the house so she didn't have to endure the embarrassment. But Saul and the girls did not seem phased. They immediately rushed back on the court and started playing again.

Veronica looked at her watch and panicked. Amid all the amusing spy work, she had forgotten to put her casserole in the oven. To the kitchen, she went.

Saul was just in the process of beginning to work with the girls on one of their most important needs, to develop an overhand serve, hopefully similar in effectiveness to that of Callie's. When he went to retrieve a ball that had wandered into a neighbor's driveway, he was startled to see three boys standing on the sidewalk in Dallas Maverick jerseys, with basketballs under their arms.

"Hey, Mister, this isn't cool, man," one of the boys said.

"I'm sorry," Saul walked over to them. "What's the problem?"

"What you've done to our basketball goal. It's not right."

"Don't worry. I will take it down when we're finished. I haven't damaged it in anyway."

"But this is our court, man," another boy interjected. "We are ready to play."

"This is a public street, though," Saul advised. "We will be done pretty soon."

"It's 5 p.m. Saturday. This is our normal time to play," the boy continued.

"I'm sorry. I didn't realize that," Saul said.

From afar, Veronica suddenly yelled, "Time for dinner!"

This took a little bit of the tension out of the air. "That's my wife," Saul said. "I guess we are done here then. Girls, go get ready for dinner."

Saul begrudgingly disconnected the net from the basketball goal, spooled the net around his volleyball pole, pushed the pole down so it was horizontal to the ground, and rolled Bryson Court down the street back to his garage.

"Damn boys," Saul muttered, while taking a big bite of something Italian.

Bree and Harper looked at each other as if they were in shock.

"Saul watch your language at the table, please," Veronica instructed.

"I'm sorry, but we've been here a month now and there has not been one person dribbling a basketball or shooting a basket on that court."

"I know," Veronica said, with mock consolation.

"And the one time I want to use that court to play volleyball, three numb-nuts show up and say it's their time to play," Saul continued to rant.

"What's a numb-nut, Daddy?" Harper asked.

"It's nothing, Harper," Veronica replied quickly. "Saul, please soften your tone around the girls. We will just have to learn to share the court space with the basketball boys. That's the neighborly thing to do."

"But we were there first," Saul whined like a child.

"Daddy's right, Mommy," Bree said.

"I understand that but it was time for dinner anyway and your practice was coming to an end. Can we please change the subject?"

"I just don't want to have to leave the court every time they decide they want to play basketball," Saul chimed back in.

"Saul, don't you think you're being a bit immature?"

He didn't answer. His attention was suddenly consumed by something else. A simple game from his childhood was on the dining room floor for some odd reason.

"Since when have we been playing with Tinker Toys?" Saul asked.

"We haven't been," answered Bree. "But we needed to empty the Tinker Toys out of its can so we could use it to store our Littlest Pets."

That made sense. Tinker Toys was one of the many Christmas gifts Saul had given the girls with the hope they would fall in love with the same toys he loved as a kid. But the love wasn't shared. Tinker Toys ended up in the attic with the Lincoln Logs and the Pickup Sticks and the Marbles and the Ants in the Pants and the Lionel train set and the Hot Wheels cars, the latter of which he knew was a stretch. He walked over and brought a few of the Tinker Toys to the table. A few of the pieces were still connected, probably from the only day they ever played with them on whatever Christmas morning that had been.

"I think I know how we don't have to worry about the basketball boys," Saul said, as if in a trance. "What does this look like to you?" he said, holding up the Tinker Toys.

"A volleyball net," Harper shouted.

"Very good, Harp." He then turned to Veronica. "All we need is one more pole and we don't need to share the basketball goal."

"Duh," Bree added.

"I don't know why I didn't think of this to begin with," Saul continued, ignoring Bree's sarcastic comment. He suddenly placed the ends of two Tinker Toy sticks into two of the round wooden pieces that looked like wheels. When he was finished, he rolled it across the table to Veronica. It looked like both axles of a car connected to the same two tires.

"All I have to do is connect the two poles with the two tires to roll them onto the street and when we get them to the cul-de-sac, we separate each pole from a different tire. And voila, we've got our court!"

Veronica looked at him and tried to offer an encouraging smile, "You're a genius."

Saul was too excited to respond to Veronica's compliment, although he knew by her tone it sounded a lot like Bree's sarcastic remark. After dinner, Saul ran to the hardware store to get the materials he needed. He spent the rest of the evening building the new and enhanced state-of-the-art version of Bryson Court.

Since they didn't need the basketball goal for support anymore, Saul ended up placing the court in the middle of the cul-de-sac. This gave the rude and disrespectful basketball boys plenty of room to play their game while Saul and the girls practiced theirs. The basketball boys didn't like the new set-up at first but they adjusted to it. And in reality, there were not too many times when both groups were out at the same time.

The neighbors adjusted to the new set-up, too. When they would drive toward the cul-de-sac they would make sure to circle carefully around the net. There was no need for a car to go underneath it anymore.

As Saul and the girls got into a regular workout routine, Veronica was getting more used to her new house, and the girls were getting more used to their new school. Life was getting back to a more normal existence and the blur was starting to fade. Saul wasn't working late anymore and the stress on Veronica to take care of everything at home was lessening. It was especially helpful when Saul occupied the girls' time on Bryson Court, which was now occurring almost daily.

Saul was very pleased at how the girls were progressing. Bree's overhand serve was getting more consistent and even Harper, three years younger than Bree, was hitting some overhand serves with enough power to clear the net. Saul did his best to try and keep Bree's passing skills strong and tried to set her balls to hit, but his setting was very poor. He didn't know how setters did it. Having the ability to set a ball that's coming at you with different kinds of spin on each and every occasion was very difficult to do. Saul spent most of his time lobbing balls to the girls because he could never get the hang of setting the ball the right way or at the right height.

As promised, Bree agreed to play in a recreation league that spring. They signed up for a team and when they had their first practice, Saul knew he had made a mistake. The girls were terrible. Not just one or two of them, all of them were terrible, except for Bree. Bree became their assistant coach because the head coach didn't know what he was doing. He was just there to build up some community service hours for his resume. He had no daughter on the team to care about and he had no interest in volleyball.

The head coach ended up relying on Bree to do a lot of the teaching. While Bree was not getting any better, she did feel good about being the best player on the team and she was enjoying the chance to impart her knowledge of the game to the girls. What Bree didn't enjoy were the games. They were a total bore. There was no volleying or passing because the girls were all new at the sport. Bree did work on her serve a lot and they won all their games because the other teams were terrible, too. They couldn't return Bree's serve. While her serve was not yet at Callie's level, it was still good enough to baffle the opposing teams.

While Saul was happy to see Bree gaining in confidence with her serve, he could not gauge how effective it really was because nobody could pass in that league. The passers were not passers, they were more like on-lookers. They watched the ball drop in front of them, beside them or go by them. Saul wondered where all the good players were and was reminded by one of the other parents that club season was still in full swing. That's where they were, he was told.

Saul was happy when the season was over. He felt the practices on Bryson Court were better for Bree than the recreation league they had just endured. He now had the summer to help Bree prepare for making the 7th grade team. He felt he was flying blind though, because he had no idea how good her competition would be. Plus, with the exception of the lousy spring league they had just played in, Bree had no real game experience in over a year. He would need to intensify the practices on Bryson Court and probably look for a summer camp for her to attend. At least he felt his Master Athletic Plan was slowly getting back on track.

Their first summer back in Texas would be a good one. The girls would pass their school classes with flying colors. There would be plenty of warm weather which meant plenty of pool time. Saul had already installed the volleyball net in the pool, which Veronica told him was an eyesore but she let it stand for the good of their marriage. Saul had banked most of his vacation time so he could spend it with the family and enjoy the sunny days. There would also be a 10-day Caribbean cruise in July they had arranged. And the parents had worked it out for Callie to come visit for a week and for Bree to go visit Callie for a week. In addition, Harper had made a new friend at school, which kept her occupied and put less pressure on Bree to entertain her.

Yes, the summer would be a good one. It would move fast and furious and when it was over, Saul would ask Veronica where the summer went.

"I don't know, Dear. It's all a blur to me, now," she would say.

Yes, Saul thought pensively. Sometimes you can't escape the speed of life.

BREE'S DIARY
May 18
I can't wait for the summer. Callie is coming to visit!!! The face-timing is good but I don't get to hug her or play volleyball with her. I can't wait. I told her today I said hi to Bobby again. I told her I don't tell my parents mainly because of my dad. He would be mad if he knew I said hi to one of those bad basketball boys. They aren't bad, tho. They are kind of nice.

PART THREE

OUTWORK THE COMPETITION, OUT-FATHER THE OTHER FATHERS

CHAPTER SEVEN

WHEN BRIBERY BECOMES A WAY OF LIFE

As great as the summer had been, Saul had made one tactical mistake. During all of his effort to work with the girls on Bryson Court, during all of his conversations with the family at the dinner table or by the pool or when they were touring on vacation or when he was on the phone with Bree when she was visiting Callie in Seattle, Saul had never thought to bring up the fact that Bree would be trying out for her 7th grade volleyball team.

He didn't do it deliberately, or at least he didn't think he did. He just assumed it was a given. But during the last weeks of summer, he did start to realize there had been no real dialogue about the issue in some while, maybe even never. Maybe it was deliberate on his part, the more he thought about it. Maybe he was afraid of unleashing a waterfall of tears.

With the first day of school approaching, he thought it prudent to bring up the subject, but how to bring it up was the real question. Surely Bree knew she would be trying out. Why else were they working so hard on Bryson Court?

He would need to bring up the issue in a real cool, casual way, like it was no big deal. Because maybe it was no big deal to her, he rationalized. Maybe she was already mentally prepared for school volleyball. So why make a big deal out of something if it's not necessary?

On the Thursday before school was to start, Saul felt he better put some feelers out in Bree's direction. They were having fun as a family playing two-on-two volleyball in the swimming pool. To Saul, it was really two-on-one because he always felt at a disadvantage when he had Very on his team. The girls were beating them soundly, which always made them extremely happy. Harper loved to be on Bree's team and she tried hard to do well because she wanted Bree to see the benefit of having her as a teammate. As Bree went back to serve, she drilled one that sailed right between Saul and Veronica's outstretched arms for an ace.

"Yes!" Bree yelled.

Harper went over to high-five her. "Yes, Sis!" She cheered.

Saul went to retrieve the ball and as he tossed it back to Bree, he said in a cool, casual kind of way, "You do that in tryouts next week, and you will have no problem."

Bree was preparing to serve again, but suddenly stopped her motion. "What?" She asked. "What tryouts?"

Uh-oh, here we go, Saul feared. This would be a big deal, or rather ordeal. That seemed to be the more appropriate word. "School tryouts. They take place next week," Saul said matter-of-factly.

"I didn't know I was playing school ball," she exclaimed.

"Bree, why do you think we've been working so hard?" Saul replied.

"I don't know. I thought we were having fun. Mom, did you know about this?"

"No. This is the first I've heard about it," Veronica said, with one of her death stares aimed at Saul.

"Oh, come on, Very. We've talked about this, haven't we?" Saul said.

"Not that I can remember. I didn't know they played volleyball in seventh grade."

"Oh, you've got to be kidding me. Of course they do. It's middle school," Saul said, now perplexed.

"I never played sports, remember? You remind me of that all the time. So how should I know if they play sports in middle school."

"We signed her up for this, though."

"We signed her up for physical education," Veronica countered.

"Oh," Saul said, suddenly remembering what had happened.

"What is it, Saul?" She asked with a slight bit of agitation.

"I guess I forgot to tell you," Saul squirmed.

"Tell me what?"

"I changed her schedule and signed her up for volleyball after you had submitted her schedule to the school. I thought it was a no-brainer."

"No-brainer? The no-brainer was you forgetting to tell me, Saul," Veronica said angrily. "And Bree."

"But I don't want to play school ball!" Bree screamed, splashing the ball into the water. She quickly ran out of the pool and back inside the house.

"Here we go again," Harper chimed.

"Harp, please go tend to your sister," Veronica ordered.

Harper obeyed and ran back into the house after Bree.

"What were you thinking, Saul?" Veronica continued.

"I thought we talked about this. I thought that Bree playing in school was a given."

"Don't you know her by now? She doesn't like surprises. Don't you know she needs time for something like this to sink in?"

That was Saul's tactical mistake. He knew it now. "I know. It's my fault. I let the time get away from me. The summer just flew by. I should have brought it up sooner."

Saul was still trying to understand the sensitivities of a twelve-year-old girl. He needed to get better at mind-conditioning Bree, laying the groundwork for what she could expect, and most importantly, not avoid communicating with her because he feared a few tears might pour down her face.

BREE'S DIARY
August 23
I hate my mom and dad. They just don't get me. And they just ruined a great summer. I wish I was back with Callie. We had so much fun together in Seattle. Why can't I find a friend like her here?????

Veronica and Saul would spend the next few days walking on eggshells as Bree's mood swings were volatile. For a few hours, everything would be okay. Bree and Harper would play games and Bree's focus would drift away from the thought of tryouts. Then, Bree would manipulatively cuddle up to her mother and innocently ask, "Are you really going to make me try out?"

"I don't know, Bree. That's for you to work out with your father."

"But Dad doesn't understand."

"What doesn't he understand?"

Bree shrugged. "I just don't want to play."

"But you love playing."

"I love playing with Harper and Daddy. I don't care about playing with other girls. Playing with other girls reminds me of Callie and that makes me sad."

Veronica gave her a hug. "I think Callie would want you to play."

Irritated that Mom was not giving in, she released herself from Veronica's arms and said, "Fine, I will talk to Daddy about it." She stammered off but she didn't stammer off to go see Saul. She went up to her room to pout and let her parents know her agony was real.

Moaning and crying could be heard throughout the house. It didn't make for a pleasant Sunday evening. Tomorrow was the first day of school and the first day of tryouts. Bree was in major meltdown mode raising her theatrics one decibel at a time the closer the clock ticked to Monday. Saul walked into the room where Veronica was lying on the couch, her head in her hands.

"What's wrong with her now?" Saul asked.

"What do you think?"

"You would think we were selling her Littlest Pet collection on eBay or something."

"Don't joke about this. This is serious," Veronica sighed. "Maybe we need to back off this and let her do what she wants."

"That's not going to happen," Saul interjected abruptly. "We did that last year. I didn't make her join a club team because I knew it would be hard for her to join mid-season after the move and all. She's a good volleyball player. She's scared and nervous and we've got to help her get through this. If we waste another year of her not playing, I'm afraid it will be too late for her to keep up with the other girls. I gave in on the basketball. I'm not going to give in on this, a sport I know she likes."

"What if she doesn't make the team?" Veronica asked.

"There are three teams. An A Team, a B Team and a C Team. I know she will make one of them."

"Why are you so sure?"

"Because I know what she can do," Saul said confidently.

"Well, you better go up there and say something to her because she won't do much at tryouts if she's still in tears."

Saul looked over at the stairwell leading up to Bree's room. "Wish me luck." He walked up and knocked on Bree's door and her wailing increased. Bree was crying at a fever pitch to a point where she could barely breathe.

"Bree, you need to calm down," Saul said softly after opening her door.

"O-O-O-Okay," she gasped in between breaths.

"You're not helping yourself by crying like this," Saul assured her.

"I-I-I-I know," Bree said.

"Listen, Bree, I came up here to apologize. I should have talked to you about this long before, I know. I'm mad at my own self for not telling you sooner. You know why?"

"Why?" She said through her sniffles.

"My dad did the same thing to me once and I swore I would never do it to my kid."

"Really? What did he do?" Bree asked curiously, her tears dissipating.

"He signed me up to play for the school basketball team without me knowing it. In fact, he was at the school talking to the coach when I found out."

"OMG, that's terrible."

"I know. I was so angry at him."

"So you won't be at school tomorrow talking to the coach?"

Saul chuckled. "No, I won't. I promise. But I do need to know one thing, Bree. What exactly is your big hang-up about trying out?"

"I just don't want to do it," she answered, her voice somewhat hoarse from a weekend of crying.

"But why?"

"I just don't."

"As a father, Bree, that's just not a good enough answer for me. You know why?"

"Why?"

"Because you enjoy playing the game."

"I know," she cried. "But I just don't want to be out there with other girls."

"Why not? You've done that before."

"But they're going to be a lot better than me. And if I don't make the team, you'll be mad at me."

This struck a chord with Saul, similar to the heartbreak of a thousand failed sports dads his gut had experienced before. He did not think he had ever given Bree any indication he would be mad at her if she didn't make a team. But maybe Bree had the perception he did, or maybe she was just making it up. Who knew for sure. "I won't be mad at you," Saul assured her. "I promise."

"But I'm not that good."

"Bree, you are too good." Saul stopped himself for a moment and decided to go a different direction. "Forget what I just said there."

"See, you don't think I'm any good, either."

"Of course, I think you're good, Bree, but let's be honest with each other. I don't know if you're good enough." He emphasized the word *enough* and this seemed to register with Bree. "I don't know how good all the girls will be at the tryout tomorrow. And you don't either, do you?"

She nodded.

"So don't say no to something you don't know anything about." Saul noticed her roll her eyes at hearing the saying, maybe he had used it one too many times.

"But what if I just don't like playing?" She asked, as if trying to come back with something to change his mind.

"Bree, we are going to find out whether you are good enough together, just you and me. We are going to find out if you like playing school ball together. Okay?"

Bree sighed and nodded her head.

"You are not alone in this," Saul assured her. He felt something was still missing, though. He needed to throw in some motivational support after all the tears of the last three days had drained the color from her face. An idea flashed though his brain. "And whether you make the team or not, do you know what's going to happen?"

"What?"

"You're going to get an iPhone just for trying out."

Bree's eyes widened. "Really?" She gasped.

"Really," Saul confirmed.

"Oh, my gosh. I can't believe it. I can't wait to tell Callie."

And suddenly, the world was back on its axis, spinning smoothly.

BREE'S DIARY
August 26
My dad is so cool!!! He is getting me an iPhone!!! And I don't even have to make a team!! Callie will love this. I can FaceTime her in private now and don't have to use Mom's computer!! YIPPEE!!!

Saul walked downstairs to tell Veronica that everything had been taken care of. She was sitting out on the patio, their new and improved Conference Room for Private Family Discussions, which now featured a beautifully landscaped swimming pool.

"How did you do it?" She asked.

"Lots of mature and honest discussion," Saul began smugly.

"I'm impressed. Please continue."

"I told her we were in this together. I told her she didn't need to worry about me being upset if she didn't make the team."

"She does want to please you so," Veronica said.

"I know she does. I wish she didn't worry about that so much, though."

"Anything else happen?"

"Oh, I almost forgot. I, uh, promised her an iPhone for trying out."

Veronica started laughing. "You bribed her? We were getting her one anyway this year."

"I know," Saul smiled. "But she didn't know that. I needed to tell her something to get her fired up. I considered it more of an incentive than a bribe."

"I don't know if rewarding a kid with an iPhone after three days of crying is the right parenting play here. Do you?"

"I don't know if it is or not. But the crying has stopped and she is trying out tomorrow." And, Saul thought to himself, his Master Athletic Plan lives to fight another day.

"I hope we're doing the right thing, pushing her into this," Veronica said, worryingly.

"Very, did you know what you wanted to do when you were 12?" Saul asked. "We don't know if we're good at anything until we try. She's got to try or she won't get very far in life."

131

Bree's trying started the next day at tryouts. Unfortunately, it wasn't a one-day affair. Tryouts lasted for three days. If you made the team, you started practicing on Thursday, had your first scrimmage on Saturday, and played your first game the following Tuesday. If you didn't make a team, you were moved to P.E. for the rest of the semester.

Saul was amazed how quickly the school season started. There wasn't much practice time at all before their first game. He would worry about that later, though. Bree had to make a team first. Practices were in the afternoons following school and lasted for a couple of hours. Saul made a point of leaving work early so he could pick Bree up at 5:30 p.m. and be the first to get the full report. His personal goal for day one was to make it home without any tears being cried and any shouts of "I hate this" ringing through the car. He pulled into the parking lot about five minutes early and got in line with the other parents, which consisted of all moms. Guess the other dads couldn't get off from work, Saul figured. Advantage Daddy Bryson.

He wanted to get out of the car and go peek through the gym doors but he knew that would be bad form. Parents were not allowed inside for tryouts. He was surprised how nervous he felt. It was almost like being at a game.

Finally, the girls started walking out. He was having a hard time spotting Bree because he was too busy estimating the number of girls that were walking to their moms' cars. He was trying to quickly gauge the competition but there were too many girls to count. This didn't make him feel any better, but he reminded himself that half of the girls were probably there for the 8th grade tryouts. A banging on the car window startled him. It was Bree wanting him to unlock the door.

"Sorry about that," he said, hitting the unlock button.

"Geez, Dad, what were you looking at?" Bree asked.

"Nothing. Just had a hard time spotting you through all the girls." Saul started the engine and they began their drive home. "Well, how did it go?" He asked eagerly, while carefully managing his physical properties so as not to act too eager.

"Okay," she said.

Two hours of tryouts and that was all the elaboration she could muster? He would soon discover this doesn't change at 13, 14, 15, or any age. You have to pull the information out of their mouths with a set of vice grips. But, he conceded, "okay" was a much better answer than "I hate this". Plus, there were no tears. At least not yet.

"What did they have you do?" He asked.

"A lot of drills and stuff."

"What kind of drills?" He patiently asked.

"Mostly passing and defensive stuff. And some serving."

"How did you feel you did?"

"Okay."

He moaned to himself. He got off work early for these kind of answers? "How many girls were there?" He continued.

"I don't know. A lot."

Saul was getting more annoyed but didn't let her see it. "Can you give me an estimate?"

"I don't know, Daddy. I didn't really pay attention to that because we were all in different groups."

The lack of detail was killing him.

"Maybe there was 50 or so," Bree suddenly added.

Finally some vital information, Saul thought. With three teams, let's just say at 10 girls per team, that meant 20 girls would not make it.

"There were a lot of really bad girls, though," Bree added.

This lifted Saul's spirits. "How many?" He asked, hoping for a detailed answer.

"A lot," Bree said emphatically.

Saul sighed under his breath without her hearing. "Like five, ten, fifteen?"

"I would say half of them had never played the game before."

Eureka!! That was music to Saul's ears. She would make a team for sure. If half of the girls were terrible, Bree would definitely be in the top 25. Saul looked over at Bree who was oblivious to his internal calculations. He thought it best not to share his statistical data. He didn't want her to get too overconfident. She obviously hadn't cared enough to do the math. Saul continued his inquisition. "How many girls appeared to be really good?"

"I don't know. It's hard to say since we were just playing defense most of the day. We didn't do any real playing. We're supposed to do a lot of offensive drills tomorrow."

Saul had enough information from day one to satisfy him. He decided to stop the volleyball interrogation and change the subject. "Well, just keep up the good work. I'm sure you will do fine. How were your classes today?"

"Good. All my teachers seemed nice."

"No homework?"

"Yes, I have homework," Bree said with disgust.

Darn teachers today. You don't give homework on the first day of school. A little bit of silence ensued as Saul put the homework out of his mind and enjoyed the rest of the drive home with his little nuggets of tryout data. He then looked over at Bree who was counting something on her fingers. She kept on counting and recounting, perking Saul's curiosity. "What are you doing?" He wondered.

He saw a big grin slowly cover her face. "I'm going to make a team, aren't I?"

"I don't know," Saul cautioned, acting like he didn't know what she was talking about.

"Daddy, come on, just do the math, silly!"

Saul didn't want to increase her expectations and remained calm. "Bree, based on what you have told me, if the information is correct, I think you have a very good chance."

She continued smiling. "Where is my iPhone?"

"Don't worry about your iPhone. Tryouts are not over. Keep working hard and go make a team first."

"Okay," she assured him.

Day two of tryouts came and Saul pulled into the parking lot and got his spot in line with all the other moms. He felt much less nervous today. He did see a few moms strolling outside and a couple of them were getting close to the gym doors. They were getting antsy, Saul could tell. The gym doors opened and the throng of girls came marching out. Saul noticed that many of the girls were crying. He wasn't expecting this on day two. There was a whole other day of tryouts to come. He wondered what was happening. There weren't just one or two girls crying. There were several. He wasn't prepared to handle tears of rejection today. They all looked like zombies with runny mascara pouring down their cheeks, trying to hide their faces to hide the heartbreak they were feeling. This was as pitiful as it gets, Saul had to admit. But what about Bree? He soon saw Bree approaching in the distance and as far as he could tell, there was no moisture on her cheeks. She got in the car and was quick to start the conversation.

"Daddy, guess what!"

"What?" Saul said, wanting to know as soon as possible.

"I made a team," she squealed.

"That's great, Bree. Which one?"

"I don't know yet. They let all the girls know today who wouldn't be on a team. Tomorrow we will find out what team we're on."

"So that's why all the tears."

"Yeah, I feel bad for them, but a lot of them were just trying out for fun. They hadn't played volleyball before. They do other sports."

"So what was practice like today?" Saul asked.

"It was okay. We did a lot of serving again and did some hitting drills. I'm not very good at hitting but I did pretty good at serving."

"What team do you think you will make?"

"I don't know. I hope I'm on the B team because there are still a lot of girls left that aren't that good."

"How many girls do you think are really good?"

Bree thought a moment. "There are six or seven really good girls, I would say."

Saul was glad to hear this. He figured she might have a shot at the A team. "Well, I'm happy for you. Congratulations."

"Thanks, Daddy. How about that iPhone?"

"Tryouts aren't over yet, Bree. Stay focused and do the best you can tomorrow."

"Okay, Daddy," she said rather cockily.

That's good, Saul reasoned. Confidence is a good thing to have right now.

Day three came and Saul was bummed. He couldn't leave work to pick up Bree at school. He had a meeting that ended at 5 p.m. and there was no way he could get there in time with rush hour traffic. Veronica was in charge of picking her up and Saul kept waiting in his office for a phone call. It was now ten minutes past 5:30 p.m. so they should have called him by now. He kept fidgeting in his chair watching the clock. He finally tried to call Veronica but she didn't answer.

Why did he feel so much tension over a lousy 7th grade A team, B, team or C team? Probably because he knew if she made the C team, that wasn't a good thing. The C team sounded like Boise or Tucson to Saul, where they put the old executive has-beens out to pasture. But maybe that's what happened. Maybe Bree made the C team and she is devastated and can't talk to him through her sobbing. She did sound a little too overconfident yesterday. Suddenly, his cell phone rang. This is it, he thought, but it wasn't. It was a strange number he hadn't seen before. He answered it anyway.

"Hello."

"Daddy?"

It sounded like his daughter. "Bree, is that you?"

"Thanks for the iPhone."

Saul smiled in relief. Bree was calling from her new phone. He didn't know Veronica would have her all set up by now. "I'm glad you like it. But why haven't you called me? I've been waiting for some news."

"I wanted to call you on my new phone and it took a few minutes for Mommy to teach me."

"Enough about the new phone, what team did you make?"

"Let's just say I got straight A's today. I got an A on my history test and I got an A in tryouts!"

She did it, Saul cheered to himself. He was pumped. "That's fantastic, Bree. I'm so proud of you. Great job."

"Thanks, Daddy. I can't believe I made it."

"I can't wait to get home and talk to you about it. I'll see you soon. Have fun playing with your new phone."

"Okay, Daddy."

He hung up and immediately jumped out of his chair and threw his fist in the air, his body flush with pent up emotion. Then came a familiar voice from the hallway.

"Celebrating a triumphant work day, Saul?"

Saul, startled, turned around and saw his boss, Mr. Anderson, the Chief Financial Officer, standing there.

"Oh, sorry, sir. Just got some good news."

"Can you share it with me?"

"My daughter just made the 7th grade volleyball A team. With each word he uttered, Saul realized how meaningless this probably was to him."

"I was hoping you were going to tell me we met our plan for the month. But congratulations anyway."

"Thank you, sir. We're still working on making that plan, too," he said as Anderson had already turned to leave. Saul couldn't believe the unfortunate timing. This was the first time he had ever seen the man on his floor but there he was, in time to watch Saul do his victory dance.

Despite the awkward episode, Saul felt the need to stop at the grocery store and pick up some beer to celebrate. This felt like a major victory, almost like winning a state championship. Through the changing of jobs, the move to Texas, the lack of playing any competitive volleyball for a year, the numerous practices on Bryson Court, things had actually worked out. Bree was good enough to make the A Team of Plano Wilson Middle School.

"You were right," Veronica said, after taking a sip of the cold beer Saul had purchased. "She needed to be pushed. She hasn't stopped talking about it all evening. It's amazing how all those tears can turn into all that excitement."

Saul was soaking up the warmth of the patio's outside air, along with the accomplishment of a significant step in his Master Athletic Plan.

"It's nice to see her confidence get a boost," Saul said.

"It's nice she has a father that works with her so much."

"Thanks, Very." Saul finished off his beer with a long, satisfying gulp. "Life gives you good days and bad days, and today was a good day."

The next day was not so good as Bree took part in her first practice. The pace of the drills was much faster than at tryouts. She had a hard time keeping up with some of the girls. This was the price you paid for making the A Team, Saul told her afterwards.

"I don't know what I'm doing half the time," Bree exclaimed.

"You will get there. The coach wouldn't have put you on the team if she didn't think you could handle it."

"I wish I was on the darn C Team. At least I would look better," Bree pouted. "And the coach is a lot easier."

"Do you want to get better or not?" Saul asked.

Bree nodded.

"Then give this some time. Playing with these A team girls will help you," he assured her.

Tuesday night, or Game Night, as it was now referred to in the Bryson household, suddenly arrived. Saul got off work early to make sure he was there in time. They were playing another middle school from Plano, which would be the case every Game Night. The Plano school system was so huge, they had enough middle schools to make up their own conference.

Saul arrived from work and saw Veronica and Harper already seated in the stands. He looked around and saw parents scattered throughout the bleachers. He did see one group of parents nestled together donned in Plano Wilson spirit wear.

Maybe their daughters were playing with Bree. It was hard to say. He figured he would try to introduce himself later after the game. The B Team had just finished their match and Saul got goosebumps when Bree's team took the court to warm up.

When the game started, Saul was a little deflated. Bree was not on the court. The team had nine girls on it and Bree must be one of three bench warmers, he figured. Bree's team, known as the Wilson Wranglers, got off to a quick start. Saul soon picked up on who the really good girls were. There were three girls that could hit the ball really well, far better than Bree could. None of them were very tall. To Saul, it looked like Bree was the tallest girl on the team, not that it mattered much. Her skill set still didn't yet match the level of her height. The Wranglers were up 8 to 2 when Saul was relieved to see Bree get up and enter the game. Thank goodness, she's not a bench warmer.

"Daddy, Bree's in," Harper said excitedly.

"I see that."

When Bree was in, she didn't do much. They didn't set her the ball at all. They only set the really good hitters. Bree was positioned at the middle of the net and looked like she was lost half the time. It was almost like she was there just to fill up space. She did get to serve but she served underhand which bothered Saul because they had worked so hard on her overhand serve. Her serves were high lobs in the air, which made it easy for the other team to pass the ball. When she was done serving, she was substituted out and went back and sat on the bench.

School ball was different from the Catholic league and the spring league she played in. He didn't fully understand the substitution rules and why Bree would go in at times and out at others. But at least she got to play. The Wranglers won the match easily in two games and Bree seemed happy with her play when she debriefed Saul on the match later that night.

"I'm a middle blocker, Daddy."

"What's that?"

"They play at the middle of the net and try to block all the balls that come over. They are usually the tallest girls on the team."

"Interesting," Saul said. "Do middle blockers get set much?"

"They get set some. Not a lot, though. We have too many other good hitters on the team."

"And how do you know when you come in the game and when you go out?"

"Middle blockers rotate across the front row. So when it comes time for me to go to the back row, they substitute in a player for me that rotates across the back row. Back row players are usually better passers."

Saul was impressed with how she was picking up the rules of the game. "You're a good passer. Why don't they keep you on the back row?" Saul asked.

"Thanks, Daddy, but I think they have better passers than me. Or at least the coach thinks so. Can I go finish my homework now?"

"Before you go, I have one critique I want you to work on."

"What's that?" Bree asked.

"You need to serve overhand."

"Oh, that. I'm sorry. I just got too nervous. I don't feel confident doing it right now."

"You will gain confidence by trying it. So continue to work on it at practice and I want to see an overhand serve next game."

"But what if I miss?" Bree said anxiously. "I don't want to make a mistake!"

"Every player misses serves. It's part of the game. How many misses did you see tonight?"

"A lot," Bree admitted.

"So will you please work on it?"

She nodded with some uncertainty and Saul felt the urge to add a little motivation to improve her attitude. "And if you make one during a game, there's a $10 iTunes gift card in it for you."

Bree's eyes lit up. "Cool, Daddy. I will work on it." She kissed him on the cheek and ran upstairs.

"So now do we need to add bribes to our yearly volleyball budget?" Veronica said with a noted tinge of disapproval.

Saul frowned when he heard her voice from behind. "You weren't supposed to hear that. It's just ten bucks."

"I know it's just ten bucks but perhaps she needs to demonstrate a little self-motivation, too."

"I agree," Saul said. "This is just a little boost to get her going. I won't do it all the time," he assured her.

It was Game Night again, a new opponent, which meant another Plano middle school. The opponent was Renner Middle School and according to Bree, they were always good. They had a lot of club girls, i.e. girls that played club volleyball. Saul soon learned that the quality of play at the middle school level was dependent upon how many quality club girls lived in your school district. While Bree's team had four club girls, Renner had nine. It seemed there was a sort of socioeconomic effect at play here. The districts with more affluent families that could afford to pay for club volleyball usually were home to the most successful middle school teams.

As Saul, Veronica and Harper found a spot to sit, he looked around for any parents that might seem recognizable from the last game. Most of the parents were scattered about again, but he did notice that same group of parents from the last game. They must be parents of daughters on Bree's team, Saul guessed. He didn't get a chance to meet them after the last match. He nodded toward them but failed to get their attention. He sensed they were avoiding him on purpose but he was probably just imagining things.

Saul turned his attention back to the court. He was eager to see how good this Renner team was. In warm ups, he could tell they definitely had a few girls that were taller or as tall as Bree. They had several players that could hit the ball with a lot of velocity. They were probably the strongest hitters he had ever seen for Bree's age.

The game began and Bree again started on the bench. Surprised, Saul noticed that the Wranglers now had ten players on their team. A new girl had been added. He didn't know if she was absent the last game or had been moved up from the B Team. He didn't think much of it once he saw Bree get substituted in just like the last game.

Again, Bree didn't get to do much. She jumped up at the net whenever the opposing team hit a ball but Bree rarely got her hands high enough to block a ball. She never got set, either, which bummed Saul out. Renner had started to take a sizable lead and some of Bree's teammates were getting irritable, bickering at each other.

During one point, a ball approached the center of the court and Bree started to go for it but stopped abruptly. She let the ball drop and suddenly there were moans permeating the gymnasium. Bree had made a boneheaded mistake, evidently. Saul didn't know if it was Bree's fault or not but by the reaction of the crowd, it appeared to be all on Bree.

"Get her out of there. She doesn't know what she's doing," said a whispered voice that still managed to reach Saul's ears. Saul turned around to see where the voice came from. He looked at the small group of parents. They weren't looking at him but he knew, deep down in his gut, it was them. Saul was simmering inside.

"What's wrong, honey?" Veronica asked.

"Did you not hear that?"

"Hear what?" Veronica said, bewildered.

"Never mind. I'll tell you later." Saul said, blowing off some steam. He tried to refocus his energy back on the game. He noticed a couple of Bree's teammates griping at her for the mistake. He also noticed the setter, a girl named Savannah, tell Bree not to worry about it, which was nice to see. Bree had told him Savannah was the sweetest girl on the team.

Renner led 14 to 8 when it was time for Bree to serve. Here we go, Saul thought. Would Bree serve underhand or overhand? Bree grabbed the ball and Saul, for a moment, thought Bree looked up at him as if needing advice as to what to do. To Saul's disappointment, Bree served underhand, the safe play. Down six points, that was the perfect time for her to try the overhand serve. She had nothing to lose. They ended up losing the point and Bree headed to the bench. Saul tried to get her attention. He started waving his hands when he thought she was looking his way. A couple of parents behind him were getting annoyed at his distracting limb movements.

Finally, Bree spotted him. Saul raised his right arm and started swinging it repeatedly in an overhand hitting motion, emphasizing to her what she should have done. Bree quickly nodded her head in agreement looking somewhat humiliated by his actions.

The teams traded points for the remaining part of the game. Bree was subbed back in and continued to take up space, Saul cynically observed. She was not a relevant part of the team. When it came time for Bree to serve, however, Saul suddenly panicked. The score was 24 to 18. Renner had game point. This was not the time for an overhand serve. If she missed, the game was over. Saul was hoping she would look up at him for advice. She didn't. Saul stood up and began running down the bleacher stairs swinging his arm in an underhand hitting motion. Bree was not looking his way. She was standing at the end-line, ball in hand, and was ready to serve.

"Sit down," a few parents yelled to Saul, angry he was blocking their view.

Saul didn't hear them. He was focused on Bree. She tossed the ball into the air. It was a high toss, the kind of toss for an overhand serve. Heeding her knowledgeable father's advice, she raised her right arm and powered her hand through the ball. Her form wasn't bad but her contact with the ball was and the ball traveled with a very low trajectory. Saul thought it was in the net but the ball didn't reach the net. It clunked off the head of one of Bree's teammates and fell to the floor. Game one went to Renner.

"Sit down," the parent yelled again and this time Saul obeyed. He sat down, trying like a mole in a hole to hide himself from his daughter's disappointment and the scorn from the snooty parent group above.

Saul eventually got back up and walked out of the gym like he had to go to the bathroom. He didn't have to go but it looked better than having to immediately walk back up the stands to Veronica and Harper.

"Feel better?" Veronica asked as he came back a few minutes later.

Saul didn't answer.

"Well, I'm glad you're here because maybe you can stop me from attacking those parents," Veronica said, referring to the parent group that had annoyed Saul.

"What did they do now?" Saul asked.

"I heard one of them say *she sucks* after Bree missed her serve. I wanted to go over there and kick their obnoxious asses."

Saul was shocked, but pleased with Veronica's sudden viciousness. Maybe there was a killer instinct inherent in Bree's DNA, after all. They both settled down and prepared themselves for game two. Saul was trying to get a sense of how Bree was doing on the sidelines. She didn't look too concerned at costing her team a game point. The second game began and again Renner leapt to an early lead. The team had too much talent, Saul surmised, especially one hitter that could hit the ball with such powerful top spin it was hard for the Wrangler defenders to adjust to the ball in time to pass it. To make matters worse, when it came time for Bree to be subbed in, she wasn't. The new girl he had noticed on the bench was subbed in.

"Oh, great," Saul sighed.

"What's wrong?" Veronica asked.

"She's not going in," Harper bluntly blurted out.

Saul looked over at Harper. For someone that could be so quiet at times, she always knew what was going on. He turned back to the court because he wanted to focus on the new girl. As he watched her play, he wasn't that impressed. She seemed more lost on the court than Bree did. She also served it into the net a couple of times, too. He was relieved she wasn't a ringer. That was the one good takeaway from an evening that was filled with bad moments. The team lost the second game by ten points. Hopefully, the coach would put Bree back for next week's match since the new girl didn't do anything to merit more playing time.

In the meantime, Coach Bryson was prepping his debrief of the game for his daughter. Number one, don't let a ball drop when it's right next to you. Number two, don't worry about being benched in the second game. It's early in the season and the coach is trying to get a feel for all the players. Number three, don't serve underhand when you should be serving overhand. And number four, don't serve overhand when you should be serving underhand.

"But you told me to serve overhand!" Bree shouted, as she listened to her father's comments on the game.

"I know I did," Saul confessed.

"I told you I wasn't ready to start serving overhand," Bree fumed.

"Bree, calm down," Saul said quietly. "You are ready to serve overhand. You are very good at serving overhand."

"I am not," Bree said defiantly.

"Yes, you are," Saul assured her. "You just need to work yourself into it in game situations so you can get your confidence up. Eventually it will become second nature to you. Okay?"

Bree nodded reluctantly but Saul could tell she still didn't agree.

"When you were serving the first time and your team was down 14 to 8, that was the perfect time to try your overhand. There wasn't much to lose at that point. The team was down six. They needed a spark. If your overhand serve worked, it might have helped the team. Understand?"

Bree didn't show any reaction or acknowledgement.

"And at game point, it might have been better to go with your underhand serve since you lacked some confidence with your overhand. That way you don't lose the game like you did. Make sense?"

"No!" She said defiantly. "So I'm the one that lost the game?"

"No, of course not. Everyone contributed to the loss. It's just on game point, you've got to be smarter."

"So I'm not smart now?"

"No, of course you're smart," Saul said, kicking himself for his poor choice of words. "It's more about game situations and doing the right thing at the right time. You'll learn these things in time."

"Whatever," Bree conceded. "So what do I do next time?"

"You're going to serve overhand. You're going to put that last serve behind you and move forward. And when you make one, the next serve after that will be that much easier."

"And I'll still get an iTunes card?"

Saul laughed. "Yes. But only when you make one."

Bree was at least glad to know the bribe was still in play. She wouldn't let him forget.

"And another thing," Saul continued. "Don't let a ball drop if it's in your area."

"But that wasn't my ball, that was the back row's ball," Bree shot back.

"Are you sure?" Saul asked.

"I don't know for sure, Daddy. I mean I'm still learning where I'm supposed to be. I don't know this game like the other girls do. These club girls know what they're doing and I don't. I get confused at times out there."

"Bree, you're doing fine," Saul assured her. "Here's what I suggest. Anytime a ball is in your area or close to your area, go for it. Don't let it drop. That way, you won't look foolish and if the other girl is making the mistake by not going for it, you're showing a great deal of hustle by covering for her mistake."

"Ok," she said. "But Daddy?"

"Yes, Bree."

"Don't coach from the bleachers anymore. It's pretty shameful."

"That's my bad. I agree. I'll try not to, but I can't promise anything. Your dad gets too excited sometimes, you know?"

"I know," Bree heartily agreed.

"So who is the new girl?" Saul asked, thinking this was the proper time to segue into why she sat out game two.

"Oh, that's Pamela. She just moved into town. She's nice."

"She didn't appear to be very good," Saul commented.

"She's not. She's never played the game before. She plays other sports."

"Like what," Saul asked curiously.

"I think she plays basketball and soccer. She's supposed to be real good at both."

Saul was glad to hear that volleyball wasn't her primary focus, that this must be just an amusing side-trip on her way to lettering in other sports. The fewer serious volleyball players to compete against, the better. "Did the coach tell you why you didn't play the second game?"

"No. But we have three middles now so we will all play," Bree said.

She didn't seem too worried about being benched, Saul discerned. Perhaps, she didn't know that this was real competition now. Bree and her good nature probably thought it only fair that all three middles get equal playing time throughout the season. He would need to address this later. For the time being, Saul felt good about the debrief. Bree took it all very well and the box of Kleenex remained on the bathroom counter.

BREE'S DIARY
September 6
My dad was over the top crazy tonight. He was yelling and waving his hands at me from the bleachers. I couldn't ignore him because Savannah thought he was crazy, too. She asked me who the retard was. I had to admit it was my dad. What an embarrassing night!!! I later told Savannah I didn't think retard was a great word to use. Mentally challenged might be better. Either way, they both describe my dad. Savannah is nice and I hope she likes me as a friend.

As the season progressed, the coach played all three middles pretty consistently. The middle that played ahead of Bree was not a true middle. She was an outside hitter but was only playing the position because she knew the responsibilities and the coach already had too many outside hitters on the team. Bree and Pamela managed along in their roles. Neither improved much because, as Saul eventually realized, the middle school coaches didn't know anything about the game. Bree's coach was a softball coach and math teacher that coached volleyball as a secondary assignment. She was just there for the paycheck, not to impart vital knowledge of the sport.

Saul thought Bree was slightly better than Pamela because Bree's serve was much better and Bree had better instincts around the ball. Bree served overhand in the match following their debrief and made all her serves. It soon became routine after that and Saul was extremely satisfied that he never had to see her serve underhand again. It was worth every penny of the $10 iTunes card he gave to Bree.

Saul did see Pamela's basketball and soccer expertise show itself from time to time. Pam could jump higher which allowed her to block a little better and she had an uncanny knack for saving balls with her feet. While other players would dive for a ball with their hands, Pamela would kick them before they hit the ground, popping them back up in the air and keeping the ball in play. To Saul's surprise, touching the ball with your foot was allowed in volleyball. Pamela did have a very strong athletic build which probably suited her well for basketball and soccer. Bree was still tall, thin and very lanky and had yet to fill out. Pamela had thighs that were sculpted like an Olympic track star.

By the end of the season Bree did start getting set a little bit during games. She and her friend, Savannah the setter, would spend a little time after practice working on their timing together. While Bree wasn't able to make full contact with the ball, she started to become proficient at tipping the ball to open spaces which would catch the defense by surprise. Savannah might set her once or twice a match but at least it made Bree feel a little more like she was a part of the offense. Saul encouraged her to hit the ball harder but Bree was insistent on staying with the more safer tip.

Thanks to Bree, Saul became more educated about who her teammates were and more importantly, where they played club ball. For instance, Savannah the setter played club ball at Premier. There was Millie, an outside hitter that played club ball at SkyHi. There was Tracy, another outside hitter that played club ball at MadDogs. There was Amanda, a right side hitter that played club ball at Advantage. It was like their identity was tied to where they played club.

Saul came to the realization that club ball was more greatly embedded in the Plano community than it was in Seattle as the list of available clubs was substantial. This also explained the snooty parent group that sat together at every game and scoffed at every mistake Bree would make. Those parents, Saul soon found out, were all club parents and they hung around together flaunting their aristocracy over the parent minions that had daughters that were playing middle school ball, dare he say, just for fun.

Club season began soon after the school season ended and Saul knew that if Bree wanted to get better, she would have to join a club. He just didn't know when to bring it up. He had made the mistake of not communicating with her about trying out for 7th grade. He didn't want to make the same mistake with club tryouts. Bree needed a certain amount of mind-conditioning for her willingness to kick in. He decided he would tell her soon after the coming weekend's 7th grade championship tournament, the final event of the season.

The Wilson Wranglers had managed to finish fourth in the highly-competitive Plano district. They ended up losing to Renner twice, which was not a surprise. They also lost one match to Robinson Middle School and one to Schimelpfinig Middle School. In Saul's mind, no one should ever lose to a school named Schimelpfinig and no one should ever have to attend a school with that name either.

The top eight teams made the tournament. The team that won all three of its matches would be named Plano District Champions. The tournament was being hosted by Wilson so there was no annoying bus ride for the Wrangler players. Wilson won their first match easily and then Saul and the Wranglers got sweet redemption with a three set win over Schimelpfinig. This put them in the finals against Renner, of course, who hadn't lost all season.

Renner, with their army of club girls, marched through the first game of the finals in championship fashion winning 25 to 14. Saul wanted to believe it was because Bree was not in the game. It was her turn to sit the bench. In reality though, Renner had a superstar club girl that was unstoppable. Bree's teammates couldn't find an answer to her topspin attacks, which were always placed where the defense wasn't. Saul expected more of the same in game two, especially since he knew they would not get any coaching advice from their figurehead of a coach. Bree was inserted into the lineup for the next game, Saul was gratified to see.

Saul was impressed with the start of the second game because it appeared that Wilson was actually showing some backbone. Millie and Tracy, their two outside hitters started finding holes in the defense and hitting the ball with authority. They jumped to an early lead and the team started getting excited. Bree actually blocked the Renner superstar on a couple of occasions and that really got the team fired up. Savannah set Bree once and she tipped the ball to an open zone and it fell for a point. Wilson was able to keep Renner off balance for the entire game. Sure enough, with Wilson clinging to a 24 to 22 lead, it was Bree's turn to serve.

"Oh, my God, I can't watch," Veronica said, turning away.

"Positive thoughts," Saul said.

"Don't look, Mommy," Harper said, patting her on the back. "I'll tell you what happens."

Bree prepared to serve and with no hesitation whatsoever, rifled a serve that barely cleared the net. The ball found an open seam between two defenders and landed for an ace. The Wranglers had pulled even at one game apiece. The girls swarmed Bree congratulating her on the great serve. Even the snooty Parent Group were clapping and cheering with joy. Saul looked back to make sure his hearing was working correctly. He saw one of the snooty men staring at him. He was actually giving Saul the thumbs up sign. It was the first time any of the snooty parents had acknowledged him.

The third game was also to 25 points. Saul was eager to see if Bree would be in the lineup. The coach inserted Pamela as the lead-off middle, much to the chagrin of Saul. Pamela played well starting out, though. She got her hands on a few blocks which helped counter the hitting display by the Renner superstar. Wilson kept the momentum it had from the previous game, building a 9 to 7 lead, as their cocky opponent was still a little shocked from losing a game. Saul thought the match paralleled that classic final confrontation between Jesuit and St. Pius in the Catholic League. But maybe we might win this one, he hoped.

Bree rotated in after Pamela, which Saul was relieved to see. She played well even though she still acted at times like she didn't know where to go. She wasn't letting balls drop to the ground which was a good thing. If there was a ball near her, she would take it even if it meant pissing off one of her sassy club girl teammates.

The game was getting intense and the excitement level in the gym was rising on every point. Savannah set Bree again and she tipped another ball for a point, which cut Renner's lead to 13 to 12. Saul was amazed at how such a benign play could trick the other team.

It was Bree's turn to serve again and, while she didn't get any aces, she served very effectively and left the court with her team up by two. At that point, Renner suddenly began to toughen up and raise the level of their game. Their defense started getting to every ball. Nothing was hitting the floor. They worked their way to an 18 to 17 lead.

On the next point, Savannah received a perfect pass and, to everyone's surprise, set it to Pamela. Maybe she forgot Bree wasn't in, Saul considered. Pamela hadn't had a successful tip or hit all year. Nevertheless, the set was in the air and Saul watched as Pamela jumped with all the athleticism she could muster, sailing through the air like she had done it a thousand times, whipping her right arm through the ball, and spiking it to the ground.

The crowd exploded with enthusiasm. The Wrangler parents were on their feet with joy. Bree and her teammates were hopping up and and down on the sidelines. It was the first time Pamela demonstrated any potential for the sport and, Saul had to admit, it was very impressive. He was quite glad this was not going to be her main sport.

It was now Pamela's turn to serve and Saul noticed that Bree had forgotten to rotate in due to the excitement. Thankfully, Savannah ran and pulled her onto the court. The score was tied at 18 and Pamela was ready to serve. This was always a squeamish moment. Saul was more nervous when Pamela served because she was so darned inconsistent. His nickname for her was Fitty-Fitty. She had a fifty percent chance of making a serve and a fifty percent chance of missing.

She took a deep breath to calm herself down, then tossed the ball into the air and made solid contact with the ball. There was only one problem. She hit the ball harder than she did on her incredible spike. Her adrenaline sent the ball sailing at least forty feet long out of bounds. After the game, parents would try to estimate how far the ball sailed because the gym wall was the only thing that stopped it at forty feet. Pamela walked off the court with disgust. She had cost her team a point and now they were down one again.

Good teams take advantage of opponents' mistakes and Renner did just that. They fed their superstar repeatedly and she reeled off five consecutive points to help Renner build a 24 to 19 lead. Their talent was rising to the top. There would be no miracle win this time either, Saul assessed. On game point, Savannah handled a perfect pass that she decided to set to Bree. Bree had more sets this match than she had all season. Saul gripped Veronica's knee with anxiety.

"Ouch," Veronica whined.

Bree went up with a determination Saul hadn't seen before. It was unlike her previous attempts which were just meant to feebly tip the ball across the net. Bree went up with a purpose and it was to hit the ball hard. Pamela's play must have inspired her. Saul watched as she jumped as high as she could. She sailed as far as she could go. She swung her arm as hard as she could swing. And in the process, totally forgot to hit the ball.

She whiffed.

The sound of the ball bouncing on the floor painfully echoed throughout the gym. The season was over.

"Oops," Harper uttered.

Saul closed his eyes with disappointment. Murmurs from the snooty Parent Group could be heard, but they weren't too bad and they didn't last too long. The murmurs soon turned to applause as all the parents began praising such an outstanding effort. Savannah helped console Bree as the girls shook hands with Renner. The parents took pictures of the girls standing together with the second place trophy. The dad who gave Saul the thumbs up sign actually came up to Saul to introduce himself, catching Saul off guard.

"Stan Mason," he said, extending his hand. "I'm Savannah's dad."

"Oh," Saul said, shaking his hand. "Nice to meet you, Stan. Bree's said a lot of good things about your daughter."

"Is Bree playing club ball this season?" Stan asked directly, not too concerned with idle chitchat.

"I think so, but we haven't really talked about it yet."

"If she wants to keep playing this sport, get her in a club. Tryouts are next week. There's a clinic tonight if she wants to come to it. Here's the address," Stan said, handing him a card.

"Okay. Thanks. Appreciate the advice," Saul said, not knowing what a clinic was. "I will talk to Bree about it." Stan quickly turned to walk back to the snooty Parent Group with no thought of a good-bye or a see you around.

Saul's plan had been to talk to Bree about club ball in the coming week. He hadn't planned on doing it that very moment. With this clinic thing, the mind-conditioning needed to begin as soon as possible. He decided he could use his meeting with Stan as a conversation starter with Bree. He was Savannah's dad, after all.

He decided he would bring it up in the car. Suddenly, flashback images of Bree crying during the dreaded 7th grade tryout fiasco rushed through his head, but he quickly refocused his senses on the matter at hand. He only had a few minutes to gather himself and think of an enticing incentive for the bribe home.

CHAPTER EIGHT

THE BIRTHPLACE OF SPORTS PSYCHOLOGY

The bribe didn't totally work. It didn't get Bree to the clinic that night, which Saul knew was a stretch. It was too short-notice for Bree, and Veronica supported her on that.

"But Savannah will be there," Saul emphasized.

"I don't care. I don't want to go to her club. It's too good," Bree insisted. "And I don't want to go to SkyHi or MadDogs or any of those other clubs either. Those girls are too good."

But the bribe did help in one way. Saul had yet to hear the word no and Bree's eyes had yet to water up. She wasn't ruling out club ball. It just had to be the right club for her. She didn't have a huge hang-up over her whiff at the end of the game either, which was promising.

"I tried it and it didn't work out, Daddy," she said. "Savannah was glad I tried it."

"I'm glad you tried it, too," Saul reassured her. "You'll be able to spike it soon."

"Do what?" Bree asked, looking confused.

"You'll be able to spike the ball pretty soon," Saul said, trying to make himself more clear.

"Daddy, spiking went out of style like twenty years ago," Bree said.

"What are you talking about?" Saul asked. "What Pamela did was a spike."

"No, it wasn't. She killed the ball."

"I know she killed it," Saul said. "She killed it while spiking it."

Bree groaned with disbelief. "Dad, you don't understand. What Pamela did is called a kill!"

"No, it's not. It's called a spike," Saul assured her.

"Dad, I can't believe you," Bree said with disgust. She began typing on her iPhone and quickly googled the words volleyball and kill. She showed Saul the definition and he was surprised.

"Are you sure about this?" Saul asked, wondering why the word would have disappeared from volleyball nomenclature.

"Yes, Dad. Please don't use that word spike again. It makes you sound like you don't know what you're talking about."

Somewhere in that brief conversation Bree had grown up a bit. She showed some force and will in her conversation. And she started sounding a bit more mature, maybe because Saul noticed her calling him Dad instead of Daddy. It was a subtle change but it was a significant moment to Saul in a life full of subtle changes.

Club tryouts were the following Saturday and Sunday. Saul spent the better part of his Monday in the office researching club options. He was amazed to find out there were clubs all over the Dallas-Fort Worth metroplex. Obviously, he didn't want to drive to Fort Worth so he limited his options to the North Dallas area. He saw SkyHi and MadDogs and Advantage, their Websites filled with honors and awards and college recruiting information. And there was a host of other club options within a reasonable driving radius of their house. He felt like flipping a coin because they all started sounding the same. We want to make your daughter the complete athlete. We're dedicated to helping your daughter be the best player she can be. We strive for excellence both on and off the court, etc. etc.

As he continued his search, he kept coming back to one particular club. And they weren't really a club but they seemed to have a decent reputation. Plano Sports Authority, or PSA as they were known in the community, was a huge athletic facility that catered to a variety of sports. They were more known for their recreational leagues but they fielded teams to compete at the club level, too. Plus, they were five minutes from the house which was important to Veronica, since she would probably have to do much of the driving. Saul gathered all his facts from the website and was prepared to discuss it that evening at dinner. As they sat down at the table, Bree was the one who surprisingly started the conversation.

"Dad, are you going to make me play volleyball in 8th grade?"

Saul wasn't prepared for that question so it took him a few seconds to compose an appropriate response. "Well, Bree, I hope I won't have to force you to play, but . . ."

Veronica suddenly interrupted him. "Bree, we believe as your parents, that the best education a kid can receive is both a mental and physical education."

Saul looked at Very with a stunned look, while Bree did a double-take making sure it was her mother who was talking.

Veronica continued. "So we are definitely going to support and encourage your athletic education. It makes you more of a complete individual. And it's important to have extracurricular activities on your resume when you start looking at colleges."

"Colleges? Mom, I'm in the seventh grade. Can't I do choir or band if I want to?"

Saul, still speechless, waited for Very's reply.

"Of course, you could, if you wanted to," Veronica admitted. "They're less physical in nature but do require skill and talent. But I didn't see much passion from you when we paid for those piano lessons a few years ago. If you want to start playing an instrument now, that's okay with me. Is that okay with you, Saul?"

All Saul could say was, "Yes." He was still trying to convince himself that this was Veronica talking.

"But I would still have to do the physical thing, too?" Bree asked.

"Yes," Veronica replied. "We have to ensure your body is getting the physical attention it needs. Band or choir won't cut it."

"What about marching band?" Bree asked.

"Oh, Bree. Come on. All they do is walk. You know that," Veronica exclaimed. "It's just art."

"Bree, just play volleyball," Harper said. "You're good at it."

"I'm not that good, Harper."

"I think you are," Harper assured her.

"Well," Bree said, barely acknowledging her sister's compliment, "If I will be trying out for 8th grade volleyball, I better play club ball so I can get better."

"I couldn't agree more," Veronica said. "Saul, you've been researching club options, right?"

"Uh, yes, I have," Saul said, somewhat convinced now that it was his wife at the table. "I think I've found one."

"One other thing first, Dad," Bree interrupted. "If I make a team, can I get the Dr. Dre head phones instead of the Sony ones?"

Saul knew those head phones were $50 more but he wasn't about to stop the momentum following Veronica's sudden interest in physical education.

"Yes," he said. "If you make a team, you can get the Dr. Dre headphones." He didn't want to look at Very. He knew she would be giving him the death stare.

"Cool," Bree said. "Where are we trying out?"

Later that night, Saul was pacing outside on the patio, patiently waiting for Veronica to come out so their parent meeting could begin. She had been washing the dishes and helping the girls with some homework and getting them ready for bed. It was taking much too long from Saul's vantage point. Finally, she arrived with two glasses of wine in tow. Saul didn't wait to dive in with the questioning.

"What the heck got into you tonight?"

"What do you mean?"

"That whole mental and physical education thing. That was impressive stuff. Did you mean it?"

"Yes, I meant it."

"Well, why the sudden passion for sport?" He asked incredulously.

You mean her physical education?"

"Yes," Saul nodded.

"Well, I had a long conversation with Savannah's mom today," Veronica began. "She started talking to me about the problems with teenage drinking and drugs and sex and nude selfies."

"Nude selfies?" Saul exclaimed.

"Yes, nude selfies," Veronica assured him. "That stuff is not just happening in high schools. It's happening in middle school, too."

"What?" Saul said in disbelief.

"And, not only that," Veronica continued, "but after she told me the things that happen on the school buses nowadays, I might be driving our daughters to school from hereon through college."

"What happens on the school buses?" Saul asked curiously.

"You don't want to know."

"But this is Plano," Saul exclaimed. "Middle America at its finest."

"Plano, Schmano. It doesn't matter where you live or what prestigious school you go to. If it's around, kids will find it."

"So what does this have to do with playing club ball?"

"It keeps them occupied."

"Occupied?"

"Yes, Saul. Occupied. It helps keeps them away from the bad boys and the mean girls and the bad cliques and all the other bad influences that are out there."

"I see," Saul said. He understood where Veronica was coming from, but he was mainly satisfied to know that she wouldn't be fighting him on the club front. He now had a true ally in the continuous pursuit of his Master Athletic Plan.

That week, Bree stayed pretty calm leading up to tryout day. There were no meltdowns or continuous questions about why she had to play club. It wasn't until she loaded into the car with her father to head to the PSA facility that her nerves started getting the better of her and she started rifling off questions.

"How many girls do you think will be there?" She asked.

"I have no idea," Saul replied.

"Do you think they will be very good?"

"I don't know."

"Do you know how long it will take?"

"Three hours."

"What do you think they will make us do?"

"I don't know. I'm sure it will be like tryouts at school."

Then, a long pause of silence occurred until the final question. "Dad, do I have to do this?"

She had that sweet, pathetic innocent look on her face. The one that tears your heart out and makes you feel guilty about enforcing any kind of parental mandate. "Bree, we discussed this. This is about you getting better. This is about you preparing yourself for the 8th grade team."

"You're right," Bree sighed.

"Listen, if you don't make the team, you don't make the team. We will try another club."

"Another club?" Bree asked.

"I have two or three other options," Saul said. "Tryouts go on tomorrow, too, so we will have time."

"Forget that. I'm making a team here. I don't want to have to go to another place."

"Good. Keep that attitude on the court today," Saul said. "Just focus on yourself. Don't worry about the other girls out there. You will do fine."

Saul became worried when they pulled up in the parking lot and had trouble finding a place to park. The facility was huge so hopefully the owners of all the vehicles were there for something besides volleyball. He became even more concerned when they walked in the door and saw the multitude of girls on several volleyball courts warming up. God, he thought to himself. There are other sports to play. Why are they all here?

Bree wasn't saying anything. He could see the glazed look on her face and the lump in her throat. He tried to remain cool and calm. They saw the registration line and prepared to check in. Saul saw a tall, attractive looking lady at the registration desk and approached her. She must be six feet two, Saul assessed. She seemed to be the one in charge. When she saw Saul and Bree approaching, she smiled welcomingly.

"Hi, we're here to check in. We're new at this and don't know exactly what to do," Saul began.

"That's no problem. We have a few things for you to sign. What's your daughter's name?"

"Bree," Saul said.

"Cute name. I'm Autumn, by the way. I'm the 13s coach."

"Nice to meet you," Saul said. "Bree's thirteen.

"Has she played club before?" Autumn asked, sizing Bree up and down as they talked.

"No, this is her first time."

Saul then could swear he noticed Autumn looking him up and down just like she did with Bree. He was sure she was checking him out. Could she be coming on to him?

"Here is her bib to put on," Autumn said.

"Her what?" A distracted Saul uttered.

"Her bib with her number. We use that to keep track of the girls."

Bree grabbed the bib and started tying it around her waist.

"That's all I need for now. Thanks for coming and good luck. Bree, I need you to go to court two."

"Okay," Bree said and quickly scampered off with no word to her father.

"Where are you from?" Autumn asked Saul.

Uh-oh. Here we go. She is coming on to him. "Here," Saul answered. "But we spent the last ten years in Seattle." Saul then thought he better add, "With my wife."

"Good for you," Autumn said, thinking his answer strange. "I've been here five years. With my husband."

"Congratulations," Saul said, feeling a bit like a schmuck.

"Has Bree played any volleyball?" Autumn asked.

"Yes, she has played in some recreational leagues."

"Good. Well, I'm eager to see how she does. I've got to get ready so I will see you later."

She walked over to a group of other coaches. Saul figured the wife comment did what it was intended to do and scared her off, husband or no husband. He moved over to the bleachers, which were packed with parents prepared to watch the proceedings. There were fathers and mothers motivating, stretching, coaching, pacifying, criticizing, photographing, bib-retying, and hydrating their daughters. Incredible tension filled the air. Every parent was there for one thing. To see their daughter make a team. Saul nodded to a few parents, but didn't get much of a response. It was hard to be nice to people whose daughters you were competing against.

The tryouts began and the players were divided into five courts with each court hosting a specific drill. There was a serving drill, a passing drill, a hitting drill, and drills Saul had never seen before. Coaches were on each court with clipboards scoring girls as they served or passed or hit. Parents would gasp when their daughter made a mistake or pump their fists when their daughter did something good.

Autumn, the head coach would walk from court to court, taking in all the action. When she approached the court Bree was on, Saul crossed his fingers hoping Bree did something good when Autumn's eyes were on her. You didn't want Autumn to be watching when your daughter did something stupid like shank a pass.

This was pretty severe pressure for a 13 year old, Saul had to admit. He was proud with the way Bree was handling it all. He could always make her out when he saw her long, skinny arm go up in the air and try to hit the ball. She seemed to be having more good moments than bad, but then again, he was the biased father.

After about an hour, the drills ended and the girls were allowed a water break. A rush of girls approached the bleachers to find their water bottles and talk to their parents. They desperately needed their parents' approval on how they were doing. They needed reassurance that everything was or would be okay. Some came to the bench in tears and ready to leave because they were playing poorly. The parents had to decide if they pushed their daughter back on the court or modestly left the facility, pulling their daughter with them in surrender. Major parental psychology was in play here. Saul now understood why sports psychology was such a thriving business. How your daughter felt when she went back on the court for round two was crucial. Bree's face was red with sweat when she approached Saul.

"How am I doing?" She asked, as she was somewhat out of breath.

"You're doing great," Saul said. "Your good plays are a lot better than your bad ones."

"I shanked a couple of passes," Bree said concerned.

"I know you did but so did everyone else. Keep playing big," Coach Saul said. "Use your size to your advantage when you're blocking and spiking."

"Dad, don't say spiking!" Bree exclaimed.

"Just kidding," Saul said. He wanted to lighten the moment a bit. "Now get back out there and show them what you've got."

"Okay. Thanks for the water."

Bree ran back to the court and round two began. Now the coaches had the girls scrimmaging, or simulating game situations, with some courts playing six-on-six or three-on-three.

Coach Autumn, walking like the one with supreme power, surveyed the courts discerningly. She then started telling coaches to move certain girls to different courts. Saul wondered why this was happening. It took him a while but he slowly started to catch on. Autumn appeared to be dividing the courts up by talent. The girls on court one now seemed to be filled with the better girls. These were girls that had stood out in Saul's mind. If his thesis was correct, court five should have all the bad players. He quickly looked over at court five and saw three missed serves, four shanked passes and all the slow girls that couldn't jump. He was right.

He then quickly searched for Bree. He had lost track of her. He finally found her on court two. Damn. Not what he wanted but not the end of the world, either. The whistle blew and round two had come to an end. Bree hustled over for another water break.

"Dad, did you see that hit I had?" She said excitedly.

"Yes, of course, I did. It was great." Actually, he had not seen the hit. He was too busy assessing the competition and proving his thesis on the court system. But all Bree needed was encouragement right now so a little white lie was in order.

"Keep swinging like that and you'll make it."

"You think so?" She asked, hoping he wasn't just saying that to make her feel better.

But he would say anything right now to make her feel better. "Of course," he said. "You're doing great."

"I don't want to go to another tryout," Bree, short of breath, insisted.

"I know you don't," Saul said.

"I think I have a chance," Bree said, wanting reassurance, while having no knowledge of the importance of what court she was on. "These girls are not that great."

"Bree, you're the one that's great, okay?" Saul said. She actually smiled with a little confidence. "Now swing it like you mean it," Coach Bryson commanded as she ran back to the court.

Saul noticed more and more girls with their heads down, some crying as they exited the facility in failure. He saw some girls begging their parents to stay, while the parents were ready to go to another club to tryout. Those parents probably figured out the meaning of court five. Then there were the parents like him, urging their girls on, not giving up hope, convincing them they were destined for success, ready to ride it out for the full three hours. The only problem being there was still probably fifty girls left in the facility fighting it out for twelve spots. Not the best of odds.

The third and final round began and this is where they just let the girls play. Bree, who was still on court two, continued to play hard and fight through the uncertainty. She continued to stay focused and give it everything she had. She went up to hit one ball pretty aggressively but it went way out of bounds, but at least she went for it, Saul was pleased to see.

At that point, he noticed Autumn moving a couple of players off court one and on to court two. Autumn then walked over to Bree and directed her to court one. Saul's blood began to pump faster in his veins. This is when she needed to shine.

"Is that your daughter?" a voice next to him said.

"Yes, how did you know?"

"I saw you get a little excited when she was moved to court one."

"It's that noticeable?"

"Hell, I've got my hands in my pockets so no one will see them shaking," Saul's new acquaintance said. "The name's Fred."

"Hi, I'm Saul. Who's your daughter?" He pointed to a tall, brown haired girl who was playing on court one. "She's good," Saul said. "I guess it's good to be on court one."

"I think so," Fred said. "Has your daughter been to any clinics or had any lessons?"

"No. We didn't know about them. We're new to this club world."

"We've had a few lessons with Autumn. It's definitely helped our chances of getting a spot."

"A spot?" Saul asked.

"A spot on the team," Fred said. "A lot of these teams are already planned out before tryouts."

"Really?" Saul asked, totally surprised. "I had no idea."

"They don't make any official offers. Against the rules," Fred winked. "But they'll let you know where you stand."

"So your daughter's in a good place?" Saul asked.

"Yeah, I think so. As long as your daughter doesn't push her out."

Saul didn't know how to respond to that. After an awkward pause, Fred started laughing heavily. "I'm just joshing with you. Don't worry. This is America. The land of capitalism and competition."

Saul then noticed Autumn walk on the court and pull two girls from court one and on to court two. Uh-oh, another court shake-up. Saul got worried when he saw Autumn walking towards Bree. She's going back to court two, he told himself. Get ready for disappointment.

Autumn grabbed Bree by the hand and walked her off the court, but she didn't take her to court two. They started having a conversation and Saul was going crazy that he, the parent, otherwise known as the private coach and personal sports psychologist, was not included. What could they be talking about? A few seconds later, their conversation ended and Bree ran towards Saul. Saul couldn't tell if she looked happy or scared.

"Oh, my gosh, Dad. She made me an offer." Bree said, shaking nervously.

"Really?" Saul asked. "What does that mean?"

"We have to decide if I want to be on her team. It's a national team, too, that gets to go and play in Denver this year. Oh, my gosh, what do we do?"

"Well, do you like Autumn?"

"Yeah, I think so. She seems nice."

Saul liked her to, not because she was coming on to him, but because he was able to read her resume during the tryouts. She had been a club coach for over five years. She had played college ball at Stanford, where she was an All-American for two years. She played professionally in Europe for three years. He also, in the span of only a couple of hours, liked how she handled herself on the court and talked to the girls. She appeared to have a good disposition that would fit well with Bree.

"You don't want to try some place else?" Saul asked, just being sure. He still felt a little uneasy about just looking at one club and not exploring others.

"Heck, no, Dad. You think I want to go through this for another three hours? We need to hurry up though, because she has a lot of girls to talk to and if we say no, she will give my spot to someone else."

Saul didn't like being rushed into the decision but his gut felt good about this. "Okay, then go tell her yes."

"Great, Dad. Thanks."

As Bree ran off to go tell Autumn, she was still shaking with excitement. Saul figured she was either in shock for getting an offer or just relieved that the process was over. He had underestimated how stressful and emotional the day would be.

He also underestimated the cost as well. The club required half the amount up front so he handed them his credit card for a nice $1,500 charge. The next installment was due in mid-season. This didn't include hotel and airfare and gas and food and snacks and tournament tickets and practice shirts and bribes to his daughter and all the other ancillary costs associated with club membership. Oh, well, he told himself, he never said his MAP would be cheap. This was now what it cost to keep your daughter competitive in school sports, he deduced, and to keep her occupied enough to meet Veronica's wishes.

When they were done, Bree asked if she could stop and get her $200 headphones.

"You bet we can, Bree. You deserve it." Saul said.

When they were leaving the facility, Autumn stopped them in the doorway. "Mr. Bryson," she shouted.

Saul turned and saw her approaching. There was that sly, curious smile she was giving him when they first met.

"Thank you for joining our team. I'm really excited to have Bree."

"Thank you. We are excited to be a part of it."

"I really feel with my training I can make Bree a great player. I was a middle blocker in college and I love training middles. While I wish she would have played club last year, she's got a lot of good basic skills and isn't too far behind the other girls. Her body is still growing but she has decent coordination for her age. And she's got a dad that's what, six foot six?"

"Around that," Saul said smugly.

"Well, we hope she keeps on growing. We'll see you at practice, okay?"

"Okay," Saul said.

"Bye, Coach Autumn," Bree said.

As Saul drove to get Bree her headphones, it finally dawned on him that he had been a complete and utter idiot. Autumn wasn't fawning over him. Autumn was fawning over his height. She saw in Bree what she saw in him. The potential of a really tall middle blocker that could lead her PSA club team to success. She knew Bree had a growth spurt in her and she was willing to wait it out. Saul wouldn't tell Bree about this. He didn't want her to know that her dad's height might have helped her get an offer. As her personal coach and psychologist, this wouldn't be a good thing. Bree's the one that put it all out there on the court for three hours. She earned it. He may have just helped her gain a little more notice, that's all.

Later that night, Saul exhausted but relieved to be a part of a club team, would share with Veronica all of the highs and lows of the day, including the sweat and tears and the unbearable atmosphere of pressure those 13 year old girls had to endure. He would also celebrate the roll he was on with his Master Athletic Plan. In the span of just a few months, his daughter had made the 7th grade A Team, finished second at the district championship, and now was a member of Club PSA 13s. Things were coming together. He and Veronica would also laugh at his story about Autumn and how he thought she was coming on to him before he realized she was only interested in his height, and the benefit that Bree might have received from it.

"Hey, every little edge counts," Veronica said.

He would soon learn that those words were never more evident than in the world of club volleyball.

BREE'S DIARY
November 1
I told Callie I made a club team today. She was happy for me. She's been on a club team for three years now and has to be really good. She couldn't talk long. She mentioned another friend she likes. I hope she's not her best friend. Savannah and I are having a sleepover at her house this weekend. That should be fun. Bobby sat by me at lunch today. I was totally shocked. He is too cute.

CHAPTER NINE

CROSSROADS

PSA's practice schedule would begin the week after Thanksgiving. The team had the month of December to prepare for their first tournament, something called the New Year's Eve Classic.

Saul had his own practice schedule in mind before the club practices began. He wanted to practice Wednesday evening, i.e. Thanksgiving Eve, and also practice the Friday, Saturday and Sunday following Thanksgiving. He was thrilled to have a five-day weekend to work with Bree.

As Saul drove home from work on Thanksgiving Eve, he was eager to roll out the net and set up Bryson Court. It had been a while. They hadn't had as much practice time on Bryson Court during the school season with two hour after-school practices and homework and all. When he turned on to his street, he applied the brake immediately. He was shocked to see that Bryson Court was already set up. How could this happen without his vital expertise?

His girls were playing without him. That would have been okay if not for one problem. The girls were playing a game of two-on-two with two other people. And to make matters worse, the two other people were boys. And to make matters horrible, he recognized the two boys. They were part of that obnoxious trio that insisted Saul move his net out of the cul-de-sac so they could play basketball.

What the F, Saul thought to himself as he slowly released the brake. While he didn't have thoughts of running the boys over, he did have thoughts about how to run an orderly practice without teen-age boy distractions. As he pulled into the driveway, he saw Harp and Bree waving at him with their smiling faces. He waved back but his smiley face was missing.

"What's going on?" He asked Veronica, not bothering to kiss her hello.

"You remember that discussion we had the other day about outside influences? Well, they knocked on our door today."

"I see that," Saul said.

"Some boys were playing basketball and I guess they got bored with it. A few of them left but those two outside came looking for Bree."

"Does she even know them?" Saul asked perplexed.

"Yes, she knows them. They are both in her English class."

"Who set up the court?"

"They all did. They figured it out."

"Doesn't Bree remember that these are the same boys that rudely asked us to leave the court?"

"She didn't seem too concerned with that."

Saul moved over to the front window to watch them play. "I had a practice scheduled for tonight," he said with disappointment.

"Well, you can try to stop them out there, but I doubt you will be very popular. They seem to be having a good time."

Saul was not prepared for this type of interference. Bree had just turned 13 but in his mind, she was not a teenager yet. The evil boy scum that now lurked just outside their door shouldn't be calling on his daughter this early in her life. He needed her to focus on club ball and the tireless quest for a college scholarship. After several minutes of deliberation, he reluctantly decided not to interfere with their fun. He could tell they were enjoying themselves. It was a five-day weekend, after all. They had plenty of time to get some work in.

"Thank God, club practice starts next week," Veronica said before walking back to the kitchen. "How many practices are there?"

"Three a week," Saul answered.

"Wish it was seven."

At dinner that night, Saul found out that the evil boy scum his girls had been playing with had names. They were called Bobby and Robby. The rhyming scheme was too cute for his taste.

"Which one do you like the best?" Saul asked.

"Oh, my gosh, Dad. I like them both the same. They're just friends."

"I like them both the same, too, Daddy," Harper said, feeling the impulse to get her view across.

"How come you haven't told us about them before?" Saul asked.

"I don't know. We just started talking to each other in class."

On the plus side, he reasoned, at least Bree was starting to gain more friends. She had gone quite a length of time without claiming any kind of serious acquaintance at school. Then Savannah from school ball came along and now it was Robby and Bobby. Bree was still texting and face-timing Callie, which amazed Saul. When he was young and had to move away, he never stayed in touch with his old friends. It was too hard and too time-consuming for a young boy to call or write letters on any kind of consistent basis. But with a smart phone, that had all changed. Bree and Callie still communicated all the time and remained good friends. Saul and Veronica questioned whether it was healthy or not, and if her relationship with Callie prevented her from making new friends at home. So, they were a little relieved to see her interacting with others her age at school, even if they were of the male gender.

Saul still managed to get his practices in on Friday, Saturday and Sunday. The girls didn't even complain about spending a large part of their holiday on Bryson Court. Harper, all of ten years now, loved the game and loved playing with her sister. Saul couldn't wait until she turned 12 so she could play at the club level. She was a lot more aggressive than her big sister and she had to be if she wanted to impress Bree and convince her she belonged on the court with her. Bree had a great three days of practice, too. After a satisfying weekend at Bryson Court, Saul was certain of one thing. No other volleyball dad in the area was holding three practices during the Thanksgiving holiday weekend.

Advantage Daddy Bryson.

BREE'S DIARY
November 26
I played volleyball with Bobby this week. He is so cool and funny. He cracks me up. My dad saw us playing and I thought he was going to go crazy but he didn't. He asked me if I liked Bobby and I told him we were just friends, which was kind of true. I tried calling Callie but she didn't answer. I talked to Savannah tho and told her all about playing volleyball with Bobby. She had asked Bobby today if he liked me and he said yes. I've got to find out what he means by like!!!

The night of Bree's first club practice, Saul made sure he got home in plenty of time to take her. Bree was fairly calm and seemed interested to see what this club thing was all about. After walking into the huge PSA facility, it took a few minutes to figure out where their court was. There must have been at least twenty basketball courts with various games and practices going on. Saul finally found the lone volleyball court back in a corner off by itself.

Autumn was greeting her players as they arrived and told them to get loose. Saul found a row of bleachers to sit on and secured his spot. He didn't see many other parents around. Could he be the only father that was interested in watching? Advantage Daddy Bryson again.

The practice was very structured and organized and required a lot of effort from the girls. Saul was immediately impressed with how Autumn ran her practice. Except for a few water breaks, there was little down time. The entire two hour practice was focused almost entirely on passing and defense. Autumn had the girls getting down real low in a very tight defensive posture. If there was a ball that would come anywhere near them, they were expected to touch it even if it meant diving spread-eagled on the floor. The girls wore knee pads to help protect their knees, but that didn't seem to offer much protection.

In the car ride home, Bree had scrapes and dark bruises on both knees. Veronica would need to administer Neosporin immediately when they entered the house. Bree was exhausted and claimed that it was the toughest practice she had ever been a part of. The practices at school were a joke compared to this, according to Bree. She had learned more about passing technique in one practice than she learned the entire season in school ball.

The next couple of practices continued to focus on passing and defense. Autumn would yell at them, "If you can't pass, you can't win." She would place a large hula hoop in the center of the court next to the net. This was the prime target area where the girls were expected to pass the ball to. Autumn had her clipboard out and was tracking every pass by every player to see where it landed. The girls had to run a lap around the gym for

178

every pass that didn't land inside the hula hoop. Needless to say, there was a lot of running going on.

After practice, an exhausted Bree would take her knee pads off to see that more bruises surrounded her knees, along with new bloody scrapes that complimented the old bloody scrapes that had lost their scabs after the first dive of the night. Saul couldn't help but cringe when he saw Bree's bony knees and the pain she must be feeling, but it didn't seem to phase her too much. She looked at her knees with a sense of pride, like they were a badge of honor.

During the second week of practice, Autumn backed off from the defensive side and began focusing on offense. She worked with the girls' arm swings and tried to correct flaws in their hitting motion. This interested Saul because he didn't have a clue about what made up a good arm swing. By watching Autumn's animated motions, he could determine one thing. The wrist snap when contacting the ball was extremely important. Autumn would constantly extend her arm high in the air and cock her wrist down. She sort of looked like a Pez dispenser when doing this, Saul mused. Evidently, the wrist cock was needed to create top spin, causing the ball to move in a downward direction.

Autumn also spent a lot of time working with the middles. She had Bree and two other middles working on a number of footwork drills. Saul had recognized Fred's daughter as one of the middles from tryouts but he didn't recognize the third middle, who seemed a bit clumsy. That was okay with Saul. The clumsier the better, if she was competing with his daughter for playing time.

The holidays arrived and this created a little tension in the Bryson home. Bree was on Christmas break but this didn't mean club practices were cancelled. Autumn was preparing the team to play in the New Year's Eve Classic and she expected the girls to attend regularly scheduled practices. Some players came. Some players didn't. Some were out of town. The Brysons had Veronica's parents in for the holidays and Veronica didn't think it appropriate that Bree attend practice and miss out on quality family time.

Saul disagreed. It was just two hours out of her day, he reasoned.

Veronica countered that it was really three hours when you included travel time to and from practice. Okay, Saul agreed, it was three hours, but just three hours and no more. They could still schedule their shopping and family time around it. Veronica relented, but Bree didn't.

She didn't want to leave her beloved Grandma and Grandpa. She didn't like the fact that Harper got more quality time with the grandparents. She wanted to stay with them and enjoy the holidays. So Bree threw a little temper tantrum that gained the sympathy of Veronica and the grandparents, but annoyed Saul to no end.

"Other girls are missing practice," Bree exclaimed.

"I understand that but you are not those girls," Saul reasoned.

"I don't want to go!" Bree demanded. "It's not fair Harper gets to stay and I don't."

"Harp is not old enough to play club yet," Saul said. "So you can't make that comparison."

"What if Stacy and Clair are at practice?" Saul asked. Stacy and Clair, Saul had learned, were the names of the two other middles, i.e. the competition. Stacy was Fred's daughter.

"I don't care if they are," Bree said matter-of-factly.

"Well, I do," Saul said. "Do you want them getting quality time with the coach while you're not there? Do you want them setting an example with the coach about how dedicated and committed they are and you're not?"

Bree thought for a moment. "No," she had to admit.

"Bree," Saul implored, "Ninety percent of life is just showing up."

Bree looked confused. "What does that mean?" She asked.

"It means if you are where you're supposed to be, odds are that good things will happen and success will follow."

"But I'm supposed to be with my family, too," Bree countered.

She was getting better at these arguments, Saul admitted to himself. He then grabbed her hand to add more meaning to his next few words. "You're with your family right now. Make the most of this time now instead of worrying about a two-hour practice tomorrow."

Bree didn't have an answer for this. "Okay," she sadly conceded, and quietly disappeared from view.

Saul was relieved. He had won the debate and without even the need for a bribe. It was the Season of Giving and with twelve gifts under the Christmas tree bearing her name, he was dead-set against offering her an incentive at this particular time of year.

She went to the practices during the holidays and, as it turned out, she was glad she did. Both Stacy and Clair were there. They all three got a lot of quality time with Autumn as practices were adjusted to accommodate the players that showed up.

Before they knew it, Christmas had passed and it was time for Bree's first club tournament, the New Year's Eve Classic.

Game time was 8 a.m. Saturday. Autumn wanted the girls on the court by 7 a.m. The tournament was in Garland, Texas, a thirty minute drive but Saul wanted to allow a little extra time since they had never been to the location. Departure time was set for 6:15 a.m. Bree's wake up time was set for 5:45 a.m. She scoffed at the thought of setting her alarm clock that early.

"I've never woken up before 6 a.m. in my life," she moaned.

Saul had no trouble waking up. He was up and about preparing for his debut club tournament experience. Bree was a different story. She was not a morning person. You were lucky to get two words out of her before she left for school each day.

When Bree came down to eat that morning, she wore a harsh frown on her face for everyone to see. The frown didn't leave her face during breakfast or during the whole car ride to the tournament. If you tried asking her a question, you either got a grunt for an answer that you could not understand, or a deep stare that said go to hell for asking such a meaningless question.

When they arrived at the volleyball facility, however, she saw her teammates and she immediately evacuated the car to go be with them. Her frown was gone, as if it was only meant for parents who make their kids get up at 5:45 in the morning.

Saul was somewhat surprised at the location in Garland. They were in an old urban warehouse setting. He couldn't tell if most of the warehouse buildings were still in use. The morning sun had yet to appear so it was still very dark and eerie. It didn't seem to be the safest location in the world, but there was nothing really threatening about it, either. As he would go from tournament to tournament that season, he would realize that most of the locations were in urban settings such as this one. Apparently, these urban warehouses were the best places to house numerous volleyball courts because they had high ceilings and lots of square footage. The rental fees or ownership costs were probably very attractive, too, if the vacancy rates were low.

Saul and Veronica pulled Harper out of the back seat. She was still snoozing, cuddled up with little red Elmo, and was irritable when they made her get out of the car. Walking into the facility, Saul was immediately taken in by the experience. There before him were at least ten volleyball courts with teams warming up left and right. The place was extremely noisy with the pounding of volleyballs, the shouting of coaches, and the chattering of kids echoing off the walls. There was definitely no money spent on acoustics for these warehouse locations. You could tell the owner's primary mission was to fit as many volleyball courts into the space as possible. There wasn't much room for the parents and family members to sit, either. Saul and Veronica managed to find a bench to sit on and placed Harper there, who was now wide awake and admiring the cool, claustrophobic atmosphere.

Fred was waving to Saul from a distance and Saul spotted him. Saul went over to say hello to him. Fred was a pleasant man and Saul enjoyed his talks with him. Similar in age to Saul, Fred was also a former basketball player so they had many stories to share. Fred was a devout Southern Baptist, though, and by Southern, we're talking Deep South Southern, so Saul had to be careful at times when Fred wanted to discuss religion or politics. Saul was a non-practicing Methodist, which made him ripe for Fred's personal testimony. Fortunately though, Fred loved to discuss volleyball more than anything else.

"Great to get the season underway. Are you excited?" Fred asked.

"Sure, I'm looking forward to it," Saul said.

"Looks like we've got a MadDog team today."

"How do you know?"

"Looked at the pool sheet," Fred said, pointing to a bunch of schedules that had been posted on a nearby wall.

Saul walked over to study the pool sheets, but Fred was more than willing to impart his knowledge and give Saul a quick education on how these tournaments were conducted, whether Saul wanted the information or not.

"We are playing at the 13 Open level," Fred began. "There's also a 13 Club level but that's for the crummy teams. Pool play is always on Saturday and bracket play is always on Sunday. Pool play means that teams are lumped into pools of usually four teams. You have to finish first or second in your pool to advance to the Gold Bracket on Sunday. If you finish third or fourth in your pool, then you're banished to the Silver or Bronze brackets. Those brackets are very bad," Fred stressed. "Like you've been thrown into hellfire and damnation. You spend Sunday playing meaningless games atoning for your sinful play from the previous day. Probably means your team sucks and you should be playing at the 13 Club level."

"There are also waves," Fred continued. "There are morning waves and afternoon waves. Since there are so many teams in the tournament, half of the pools are played in the morning wave, which starts at 8 a.m. and half of the pools are played in the afternoon wave, which begins at 3 p.m."

While Fred was rambling, Saul was examining the pool sheets and counting the number of pools. He was conducting his own statistical analysis. There were 16 pools with four teams each. That meant there were 64 teams. Multiply that by ten girls a team on average and that meant 640 girls. Holy cow, Saul thought. 640 13 year-olds. And this was just at the Open level. Saul had no idea volleyball was this big. He was a bit in awe of his surroundings.

"This is volleyball, North Texas style," Fred told him.

"What does that mean?" Saul wondered.

"It means North Texas is one of the largest volleyball regions in the country. It means this is one of the most competitive volleyball regions in the country. Our churches are big and so is our volleyball. It's darn fun to be a part of."

Saul walked back over to court seven, the court Bree was on. As he walked past court two and court four and court five he couldn't help but just stare at the sheer number of girls, i.e. Bree's global competition. How many of them had fathers like him who had Master Athletic Plans of their own?

Bree's team was seeded third in their pool. Fred made sure Saul knew the schedule. They played the top seed, MadDogs, at 8 a.m., were off at 9 a.m., reffed at 10 a.m., played the second seed, a club called Ace, at 11 a.m., played the fourth seed, a club called Assault at noon, reffed at 1 p.m. and then they were done for the day. Saul was surprised to see that the girls had to ref games in their pool but it made sense. The cost of hiring scorekeepers and line judges for all the games was probably very high.

Fred assured Saul that they would probably lose the Mad-Dogs game since they were the top seed in their pool. The key for them would be to beat Ace and Assault. That would ensure them of finishing second and advancing to the Gold Bracket, while maintaining their sense of dignity.

The match with MadDogs was set to begin. Saul's nerves began to fill his body as he wanted an answer to one question. Who would be PSAs starting middle? That was the big question for at least three of the dads, although Saul had yet to meet father number three, Clair's dad.

Saul did notice that a lot of parents were there for the game, many more than attended practice. He didn't understand why more parents didn't come to practice. To some, maybe it was just a form of babysitting. To Saul, it was a form of gathering vital data. He wanted to know what his $3,000 in club dues was buying him. He wanted to know if his daughter was getting better. He wanted to know what his daughter's weaknesses were so he could get a sense of what to work on at Bryson Court. He wanted to know who his competition was and whether Bree, in his mind, was the first middle, second middle or third middle. And, last but not least, he wanted to know whether or not his ranking of the middles meshed with the coach's own ranking. He didn't want the coach playing favorites unless it was his daughter that was the favorite.

Because the retrieval of accurate information was so crucial to his Master Athletic Plan, he would make it his duty to attend every practice he could, even if it meant leaving the office a little early. He had now secured a solid confidence with his boss, Mr. Anderson. Anderson knew Saul got things done on time and wouldn't take issue if Saul was on the freeway at 4:30 p.m. fighting rush hour traffic to make a 5:30 p.m. business meeting up north, which in truth was a 5:30 p.m. practice.

Darn. Saul noticed Stacy was the starting middle on the floor. Advantage Fred the Baptist. While not a surprise, it was still a disappointment. He had guessed that would be the case. Stacy had more experience and knew the position better than Bree. She had spent time working with Autumn in the summer, too. Saul tried to catch a glimpse of Fred and there he was, wearing that smug look of pride on his face that all parents of starting players have. Then Saul noticed Fred lock his hands and bring them to his chin. He was saying a prayer before the match. Saul wanted to ask God what he was praying for. Hopefully, it was for all the girls and not just Stacy.

There was good news, though. Bree was the second middle that rotated in after Stacy and Saul could accept that for now. Even though they were playing against the feared MadDogs,

Saul was encouraged to see how competitive the game was. MadDogs won both games, 25 to 20 and 25 to 19, but it wasn't a slaughter.

Bree didn't have too many highlights during the match and neither did Stacy. The setters seemed scared to set the middles which was common for this age, Fred assured Saul.

"Ninety percent of the sets in a game are high, lofty sets to the left side or right side pin hitters. They are easier sets to make. Sets to the middles are quicker and lower and require a sense of timing that takes getting used to," Fred lectured Saul, whether he wanted to be tutored or not.

Both Saul and Fred hoped for more offensive production from their daughters in the next match against Ace, but that didn't happen. In fact, something worse happened. Clair, the third middle got to play the first set, while Bree sat out. Clair also got to play the second set, while Stacy sat out. This was unacceptable to Fred and Saul. Clair was not very good and was costing the team points in their estimation.

"The game wouldn't be so close if they left our daughters in," Fred whispered to Saul.

Saul agreed wholeheartedly.

It appeared Autumn was trying to give Clair some playing time since she didn't get to play the first match, but it almost cost them a game. PSA ended up prevailing, 25 to 23 and 25 to 22, but it was much too close for comfort.

The final match of the day was against Assault, the fourth seeded team. Fred figured the match would be a little easier since they were playing the weakest seed, but he was wrong. The match became even closer because of Autumn's decision to play Clair. Both Stacy and Bree had to sit out one game again. Fred was fuming and Saul let Fred know he was fuming, too. PSA still ended up winning 26 to 24 and 25 to 22 but Fred and Saul were not happy.

"She's lucky we won that one," Fred said, referring to Autumn. "Don't know what she's thinking, risking our place in the Gold Bracket like that."

"Is there some rule about playing time?" Saul asked.

"Heck no," Fred answered. "This is North Texas club volleyball. Playing time is earned, it's not guaranteed."

Saul wanted to talk to Autumn to see what she was thinking but Fred reminded him that PSA had a rule. Parents could not discuss playing time issues during a tournament. They had to wait 48 hours after the tournament was played to talk to a coach. Fred called it the cooling off period.

Saul cooled off that afternoon. He decided not to worry about it. It was early in the season. The coach had to see what these players could do.

The morning came and Gold Bracket Day was upon them. Saul and Veronica drove a grumpy Bree and a sleeping Harper back to the tournament, back to the warehouses of Garland where urban sprawl had once thrived but was now nothing more than a placeholder for the volleyball aspirations of 13 year old girls. When they arrived, Saul immediately went to search for Fred, his loyal volleyball buddy. Fred was already scoping out the day's bracket.

"Looks like we'll be done early today," Fred muttered.

"Why is that?"

"We should win our first match at 8 but if we win, we are going to have to play MadDogs at 9."

"Again? What's up with that?"

"This is a different MadDogs team. A better one."

"Well, how many teams do they have?" Saul asked.

"For this age group? A lot. Probably four or five."

"Will we play their top team at 9?"

"Nope, it's their second team."

"What team did we lose to yesterday?" Saul wondered.

"Their third team."

Damn, Saul thought. PSA got smoked by MadDogs' third team. He suddenly realized where PSA was in the pecking order of things. While he knew PSA was not one of the top clubs, he was still surprised at the depth of talent a club like MadDogs possessed. Bree had some improving to do.

PSA's opening match was against a team called Apex. According to Fred, Apex was the type of club you didn't want your daughter to play for.

"They are all about revenue and not at all about winning. Their motto is if your daughter wants to play club volleyball, she will find a home at Apex. There are no tears shed at Apex's tryouts because everyone makes a team. If forty girls show up at tryouts, they will have four teams. If sixty girls show up at tryouts, they will have six teams. If you don't have a lot of confidence in your daughter's ability, or if you don't want to endure the stress of tryouts, Apex is your place. We will smoke them."

He was right. PSA routed Apex 25 to 15 and 25 to 12. And to Saul and Fred's delight, Bree and Stacy played both games. "Praise Jesus for bracket day," Fred said. "No time for sympathy play," referring to Clair's status of riding the bench.

PSA played MadDogs' second team next and, as Fred predicted, they lost in two and didn't put up much of a fight. Both girls played the entire match but other than that, there wasn't much to cheer about. Saul assumed it was time to go but Fred told him they had to ref. As was usually the case, the losing team on bracket day had to ref the next match on the court. On the positive side, Saul reasoned, by losing early he would get home in time to watch a slew of New Year's bowl games.

"We finished tied for ninth today," Fred told Saul.

"That doesn't sound too bad," Saul surmised.

"No, it doesn't. But seven other teams tied for ninth, too. Won't help us much in the rankings."

"There are rankings?" Saul asked.

"Heck, yeah. This is North Texas Volleyball, Saul. The North Texas Region ranks its teams like every other region in the country. That's how they seed tournaments. We're currently number 14 in North Texas."

That's cool, Saul pondered. An actual ranking system. This was big-time stuff. All in all, Saul was satisfied with the weekend. Bree got to play most of the time. She was clearly the second best middle. The team had some decent talent that would only improve and he was confident Bree would improve, too. It was a good weekend for his MAP.

When the next practice came around, Saul finally met Clair's father, albeit in a slightly awkward fashion. Saul had entered the PSA facility and was headed to the concession stand for a diet soda when he noticed Autumn on a court with two girls. One of those girls was Clair. What's going on, Saul wondered. Practice didn't start for another twenty minutes. He made his way over to the court to see who the other girl was, but he didn't recognize her. She looked like she played middle though because all they were working on were middle drills.

Bree's team was warming up and stretching, while Saul took his usual seat and continued to watch Autumn provide quality teaching time to Clair, Bree's primary competitor for playing time. When the session ended, he saw a man walk over to Autumn and hand her some money. She must have been giving the two girls a lesson, Saul figured. After the cash handoff, the man walked over to the bleachers where Saul was sitting. He held out his hand and introduced himself to Saul.

"Hi, I'm William, Clair's dad."

"Saul Bryson, Bree's dad. Nice to meet you."

"Just getting a lesson with Autumn," William felt obliged to admit. "I could tell from last weekend that Clair has some catching up to do."

The duel was on, Saul's radar sensed. It was now Mano a Mano or Padre a Padre, or something Spanish like that. He could hear the over-the-top dramatic music from Clint Eastwood's spaghetti westerns playing in his head as he struggled for something polite to say. "It seems these girls are always trying to catch up. Trying to get better," he said somewhat calmly. "Who was the other girl in the lesson?"

"A friend of Clair's from school. She wanted a partner. Doing a lesson with just one girl gets pretty exhausting, especially with practice immediately after."

Saul nodded as if he understood what he was talking about, as if Bree had done the lesson and practice thing several times.

"Have you had many lessons?" Saul inquired.

"Just a few, but we will need to ramp them up now."

Saul wanted to draw his light saber after those words. He would have if he were Obi Wan, but he wasn't. All he had to draw was his iPhone out of his shirt pocket. He put the phone up to his ear. "Excuse me a minute. I've got to take a call." Saul got up and walked away. He had to get some space between him and William and the awkward conversation they were having. He hoped that William wouldn't stay for the whole practice. He hadn't been to a single one until now, but last weekend's tournament must have opened his eyes.

The next tournament was two weeks away and Saul was debating whether to schedule a lesson with Autumn. He brought it up to Bree but she resisted as usual claiming she had too much homework to do. Clair ended up having two more lessons with Autumn leading up to the tournament. Saul wanted to see if the lessons would pay off in additional playing time.

They didn't, which relieved him. The playing time at the MLK Classic, the name of their second tournament, was virtually the same as in the previous tournament. There was no Gold Bracket play for Clair. But Clair was getting better and Bree needed to see this. She needed lessons of her own if she wanted to keep getting better.

PSA finished tied for 9th again just as they did at the New Year's Classic. Saul began to notice that a wall existed between PSA and finishing in the top 8 and it was very difficult to break. That wall was talent. The stronger clubs just had more of it.

According to Fred the Baptist, the team needed to break through to the top 8, the quarterfinals, at some point if they wanted to have a shot at Nationals.

"What is Nationals?" asked Saul.

"What is Nationals?" Fred asked incredulously. "It's the Holy Grail, the Super Bowl and World Series for our sport. It features the best teams and talent in the country. There are different divisions you can qualify for like Open, USA, National and American, but Open is the highest. Open is like being saved and going to Heaven, USA is like still being in Catholic Purgatory, National is like still being here on Earth, and American is like, you know, hell. You get there by either qualifying at a National Qualifier or at Regionals." Fred got out his schedule from his pocket and showed Saul. "We are going to two National Qualifiers, Colorado Crossroads in Denver and Lone Star right here in Dallas. And one other thing, you can only play at the Open level at Nationals by qualifying at a qualifier. "

Wow. Saul thought the Denver trip was just a fun experience to travel and play different teams. He didn't know there was something at stake. Fred was causing his competitive juices to flow.

"If we don't qualify at the Qualifiers," Fred the Baptist continued, "then we have a shot at Regionals, which is our last tournament of the year. Regionals is where all the teams from North Texas play who haven't qualified yet."

"And if we don't qualify at Regionals?" Saul asked.

"Then you can enjoy a lot of free time in the summer to read your Bible. Or your girl can play in a meaningless summer league that's a total waste of time because all the superior talent is practicing and preparing for Nationals."

Saul loved Fred's passion for the sport and his drawn out Southern drawl. It was like listening to a preacher giving a fiery sermon. He couldn't wait for the qualifiers to come around. Colorado Crossroads and Lone Star, these were tournaments that really meant something. And it was for a bid to Nationals, where the best players in the country are featured. Suddenly, another important and essential goal had been added to his Master Athletic Plan. He and his girls had to qualify and go to Nationals so they could experience volleyball nirvana.

Denver was less than a month away. He hoped Autumn could get the most out of the girls and have them ready to play their best. He asked Bree again if she wanted to have a lesson and again she refused. This ticked off Saul a bit because he hoped she might want to make the extra effort to be her best. This attribute was an inherent part of his MAP. He didn't want to go through the anguish of forcing her to have a lesson, but he just might have to.

His daughter, or athlete, was expected to be all in. He didn't like the fact that she was settling for second middle. She had the ability to challenge Stacy for the top spot, but that didn't seem to motivate her. It might be because she and Stacy had become good friends, Saul contemplated. Stacy and Bree constantly chatted throughout practice and walked together everywhere. If one had to go to the bathroom, they both went. If one needed a drink of water, they both drank. They were inseparable on the volleyball court. Bree, in all her politeness and good nature, might think winning the top middle spot could harm their relationship.

Whatever the case, it was something Saul would have to work on and address at some point. Bree was growing. She probably had two inches on Stacy. Saul could see Bree's potential at the position, but the real question was when would she see it?

She hadn't seen it in time for Denver. Bree and Stacy were seated next to each other giggling innocently, like they were toddlers. They were on the same flight together. Saul was seated next to Fred. As much as Saul was amazed at the amount of jabbering two girls could do, Veronica was equally amazed at the amount of jabbering two men could do. She had dropped the whole gang off at the airport, including Fred and Stacy.

She didn't go to Denver because Harper didn't need to miss any school. And both parents agreed that Daddy Bryson should be in Denver instead of mom in case Bree needed coaching or psychological support, and to also monitor any playing time controversies that might occur.

On the plane, Saul and Fred were immersed in pool play and bracket-ology. They were studying the team's schedule for the entire weekend. Who they would play. When they would play.

Where they were seeded. What court they would be on. What would happen if they finished first or second in their pool. What were their chances of qualifying. Fred also educated Saul on who the top clubs were nationally, like Wave, Coast and Vision from the West Coast, and KC Power, Northern Lights and CYC from the Mid-West, and OVA and A5 from the South.

When Game Day came that next morning, the fully informed Saul was wide awake and ready to go. Bree was not. He thought she might be a little more excited since this was Denver and a Qualifier, but she was in standard morning grinch mode. He had room service brought up for her. She quietly picked at her food, nibbling on just a few bites, while wearing her frown of thorns. He made sure she had the necessary things in her sports bag: snacks, water, Gatorade, band-aids, etc.

Bree's frown turned to a smile when she saw Stacy and the rest of her teammates in the lobby. She quickly ran over to be with them, not bothering to acknowledge her dad or to at least say, "see ya."

The team and parents began their short walk to the tournament facility, which was housed in the downtown Denver Convention Center. As they walked into the convention center, Saul's first thought was that this was a definite upgrade from the urban warehouses they were forced to play in back home. Lots of space, lots of room to maneuver. Then, when Saul walked through the doors to the actual playing area, his mouth dropped open in awe. There before him was a vast display of volleyball court after volleyball court, more than the eye could see.

"There must be a hundred courts in here," Saul gasped.

"More than that," Fred said.

As they walked through the maze of courts, Saul continued to be engulfed by the staggering numbers. Looking down the length of the convention center, which must have been at least three football fields long, Saul saw hundreds of balls being vol-leyed back and forth. It looked like something out of a video ar-cade game. Balls arcing together in unison banking from one side of the net to the other. It was like Pong, but with a million balls.

It took them a while to find their court amongst the mayhem, but they did finally. Just as Saul took his seat, a voice on the PA system asked the audience members to stand for the National Anthem. Impressive, Saul thought. More big time stuff. A player from one of the teams in the tournament sang the Anthem and she did an outstanding job. Saul thought it was a nice touch.

Fred joined Saul and they sat court-side together and right before the match started, Saul noticed Fred saying a prayer.

When Fred finished, he looked at Saul and said, "You're in-vited to join me anytime."

"Thanks," Saul said. "I'll let you know. What are you asking for in those prayers?"

"I pray for their health, both teams' health, that is. And I pray for everyone to do their best. And I pray for safe travels."

"Is that it?" Saul curiously asked.

"Yes, but sometimes I'll add a special prayer for Stacy like any parent would."

"You ever pray for a win?"

Trying to conceal a guilty expression on his face, Fred said, "Satan tempts me sometimes, I'll admit, but my pastor has counseled me on not using the Lord's will in that way."

"Well, I can still hope for a win," Saul said. "Hope isn't the same as prayer, is it?"

"Only if there's a Dear Lord in front of it."

Saul chuckled at his friend's comment and they both turned their attention to the match at hand.

Day one of the tournament consisted of pool play with four teams in each pool. That meant there were three matches to be played, with their first opponent being a team from Iowa. PSA started the match very well taking an early five point lead they never relinquished. Stacy had a block and scored on a tip before leaving the court to let Bree rotate in. Bree got set a couple of times, too, which was surprising to Saul. They seemed to be making the middles more a part of the offense. Maybe the practice time with the setters was finally starting to pay off.

In the next game, Bree swung hard at a ball but it sailed way out of bounds. Saul could tell Bree was embarrassed by the mistake. Bree looked over at Autumn who had her arm stretched high with her wrist cocking downward. Autumn, looking like that Pez dispenser, was telling Bree to snap her wrist to hit the ball down. Autumn had told the middles this at least a hundred times. It had to be a hard thing for a 13-year old to grasp because all three middles struggled with throwing down a quick set.

When Bree rotated out, Saul could see her face was very red, which was odd for this early in the match. Bree was fanning herself with her hand to cool off. Saul got Bree's attention and mouthed the words, *What's wrong?*

I don't know, Bree mouthed back.

The girls continued to play well and won the match in two games. Clair did not get to play, but Saul wasn't concerned about that right now. He noticed that Bree continued to labor through much of the match. He motioned for her to come see him and she walked over.

"What's going on?" He asked.

"I don't know. I'm having trouble breathing," Bree said in a panicked manner.

"It's okay, calm down. It must be the altitude," Saul told her.

"The altitude?"

"Yes, it takes your body a while to adjust. Plus, the climate here is very dry. Stay hydrated and drink lots of water."

"Okay," she said and then hurried over to be with her teammates.

Great. That's all he needed, something like the altitude to potentially interfere with his daughter's playing ability. He had enough things to worry about regarding his daughter's play. He didn't need the Rocky Mountain air added to the list.

The next match they played was against a team from Arizona. They again started hot out of the gate and built a large lead. Saul noticed Bree laboring again, though. She managed to get through the first game without making any errors and she actually scored on a block, but her face was deep red again when she returned to the sideline. Their opponent showed some resolve in the first game and fought back to make it close but PSA still won 25 to 22.

During the switchover, Bree mouthed words over to Saul. He thought she said, "I can't breathe." Whatever she said, she said it with an extreme look of concern. Saul motioned for her to drink some water.

Game two of the match began and the team from Arizona took the early lead. When Bree rotated in, the team seemed out of sync. Much of that was due to the improved play of their opponent, but Saul could tell Bree was still having trouble. To make matters worse, it started affecting her play. She didn't react quickly to a ball that was near her and that cost them a point. She was also slow to react to an easy overpass from the other team that came right to Bree. It should have been an easy point for her, to just push the ball down with both hands for a kill. Instead, she pushed it right back to the hands of a defender who kept the point alive and turned it into an eventual point for their team.

Autumn had seen enough. She motioned for Clair to come in. For the first time that season, Bree was pulled for poor play. Bree looked at Saul helplessly from the sidelines.

She mouthed to him something like, "I can't help it." And Saul mouthed back, "It's okay."

"Is she okay?" Fred asked..

"I don't know," a worried Saul replied.

Bree would have to watch the rest of the match from the sidelines. PSA lost game two and proceeded to lose game three as well. Bree never went back in. Clair bumbled her way through the match making a few costly errors but it wasn't her fault they lost. It was a total team loss.

"We have to win the next match," Fred told Saul. "If we lose, we're out."

"We're out?" What do we do the next couple of days?" Saul asked.

"We spend our time playing all the other teams that sucked today," Fred said. "Is your daughter going to be able to play?"

"I have no idea," Saul said, sounding very concerned.

"Mr. Bryson," Saul heard a voice from behind him. It was Autumn. "Look, Mr. Bryson, I don't know what is wrong with Bree, whether she's asthmatic . . ."

"She's not asthmatic," Saul quickly said.

"Whatever it is," Autumn continued, "the altitude or whatever, she's saying she can't breathe and that it feels like her throat is closing up. I suggest you take her to the first aid area and see if they can do anything for her, because right now, I don't feel comfortable playing her."

"Okay," Saul said. "We'll get back as soon as we can."

Saul got Bree's attention and they started walking as quickly as they could to the first aid area. PSA's next match was immediately following the match they just loss so there wasn't a lot of time to spare. When they found the first aid area, there was a waiting line for players to get their ankles taped. Saul tried to find someone who could help him. He found a person who was a physical therapist but she wasn't qualified to diagnose Bree's condition. Saul was told to wait for the nurse.

"Where is the nurse?" Saul asked.

"She's at a court helping a girl who probably just tore her ACL," the physical therapist said.

Saul sighed as their wait began.

"I'm sorry, Dad," Bree said in a hoarse, barely-audible voice. She sounded worse than any sickness she had ever had, be it the flu or strep.

"It's okay, Bree, we'll get you taken care of," Saul assured her.

"I don't know what's wrong with me."

"That's why we're here."

Ninety minutes later, they got the diagnosis. Nothing serious. Just a slight touch of altitude sickness. Her body needed a little more time to adjust to the change in altitude and climate. That, plus she was probably allergic to something in the Colorado air. The nurse gave her Claritin and Sudafed and told them she needed to take it easy the rest of the day and could play tomorrow.

"Thank you," Saul told the nurse, as he grabbed Bree's hand and they began to rush back to the court. "Tomorrow may be meaningless," he muttered aloud to himself.

"What did you say, Dad?" Bree asked.

"Nothing important, Bree. And don't try to talk. Your voice needs a break."

As they approached the court, PSA's match had just ended. The teams were shaking hands. Saul was trying to read the body language of the players to see who won and who lost. He didn't have to. He saw Fred. Fred gave him the big thumbs-down sign as Bree ran over to be with her teammates.

"What happened?" Saul asked.

"Got beat by a better team," Fred simply said.

"How did Clair do?"

"She did okay," Fred said, thinking about it for a second.

What did that mean, Saul wondered. Did she do better than expected and Fred didn't want to tell him? He decided now was not the time to push Fred on the question. He didn't want to come across as overly concerned. Saul then walked over and gave Autumn the diagnosis, that Bree would be able to play tomorrow.

"Fine," Autumn said, not phased by the news and sounding like someone who had just lost and was knocked out of the chase for the Gold Bracket on the very first day. He could tell she wasn't in the best of moods. "We'll have ample time to try new line-ups the next couple of days," she added. She quickly removed herself from the conversation and Saul was left to wonder what that last comment meant. He told Fred about it at the bar that night over a round of beers.

"It doesn't sound good," Saul said. "Sounds like nobody is safe in their position."

"Better not be my daughter. She played her ass off today," Fred boasted.

While Saul couldn't totally agree with the comment because he didn't watch Stacy play the last match, he didn't think her play was that stellar in the first two matches. He nodded in agreement anyway to keep the peace with his buddy.

The next two days were rough for all of the parents to watch. Autumn kept to her word and changed the line-ups. She moved left side hitters to the right side. She moved right side hitters to the left side. She had middles playing right side. She had a setter playing back row defense. The girls spent the two days in total confusion, but Saul slowly figured out there was a method to her madness. She wanted all the players to understand the responsibilities of the other. They finished the weekend winning just as many matches as they had lost. They ended up in 31st place out of 64 teams.

As for the battle of the middles, there were no answers to be found. Bree felt better and played the last two days. All three girls played the same amount of time. Saul did notice some improvement with Clair and that worried him. She was much quicker in transitioning to the ball and she was timing her hits much better. He didn't know if Bree saw it, though.

As the Colorado Crossroads came to an end, Saul felt Bree was at her own crossroads in her battle with Stacy and Clair. He wanted to sit by her on the plane ride home to discuss it, but Bree wanted to sit by Stacy. He wanted to bring it up in the car ride home from the airport but Harper and Veronica were too busy getting their own updates of the trip. He wanted to talk with her before she went to bed that night, but she was already asleep when he got up to her room. She was exhausted from the weekend.

In the morning, Saul was about to leave for work and Bree came stumbling down the stairs for breakfast. Her hair was in disarray. Her frowning face still bore the sleep marks from the night before.

"Have a good day, Bree," he dared to say, knowing that an unaffectionate grunt was the best thing he could expect in reply.

"Dad?" She said, munching on a bowl of Cheerios.

"Yes," Saul answered, astonished that there was no grunt.

"I think I want a lesson."

Saul couldn't believe his ears. His day didn't normally get off to this good a start. "I think that's a wise idea, Bree," he said, controlling his composure. He didn't want to act like this was that big a deal. "I'll see about setting something up."

"Thanks," Bree said.

Her frown was still there and she was still half asleep, but she had passed a big test in Saul's mind. She had come to a fork in the road and after careful deliberation, chose the road less traveled, the road chosen by all committed and dedicated and highly-successful athletes, a road that demanded sacrifice, pain and hard work, and more importantly, a willingness to outwork the competition.

BREE'S DIARY

February 28

I had so much fun in Denver with Stacy and my teammates. I told Savannah and Pamela everything about the trip. I talked about my sickness and I sent them pics of these funny shots of my team in front of this giant blue bear statue outside the convention center. Pamela said they were cool. I'm liking Pamela more and more. She's nice. She is jealous of me and Savannah going on these club volleyball trips. She says she doesn't get to do that that much with basketball and soccer. Me and Savannah are sleeping over at Pamela's this weekend and I can't wait. Savannah is hanging out with Robby at lunch now. They sit by me and Bobby and lunch just flies by because I laugh at all the things Bobby and Robby say. I don't dare tell this to my parents tho. Savannah doesn't tell her parents, either.

CHAPTER TEN

SWEET REVENGE, SOUR AFTERTASTE

"I'm glad you decided to do this," Saul said, as they drove to Bree's first volleyball lesson. Bree was finishing up a text to someone and then focused on what her father was saying.

"Dad?" She asked, putting the phone on her lap. "Do you think Clair is better than me?"

"Of course, not," Saul said. "But, she has gotten better," he admitted. "Don't you agree?"

"I guess so."

"That's why we need to work a little harder. So we can stay ahead of her. It also doesn't hurt to have a little more face time with Autumn, either."

Bree reached over and touched Saul on the shoulder. "No matter how good this lesson is, Dad, your lessons are still the best."

Saul was heartened by the remark even if it wasn't totally sincere. "You know, Bree, I hate to admit it but you're getting to the point now where my lessons aren't that helpful."

"Yes, they are," Bree claimed.

"Bree, I appreciate the support but let's get real for a second. I never played volleyball. I don't know the mechanics of a good arm swing. This is why this lesson with Autumn is a good thing."

"You think she would consider coming to our house and giving me a lesson on Bryson Court?" Bree asked, laughing at her suggestion.

Saul laughed with her. "Never hurts to ask."

When they arrived at PSA, Saul was hugely disgruntled to see Clair, of all people, also at the lesson. So you had middle number two and middle number three battling it out for more playing time by incurring more practice time, and expense. A lesson was $75, yet another line item to be added to his volleyball budget. The lesson went well save for an initial awkward moment with William.

"How are you doing William?" Saul asked.

"Good," he said with a slight look of distrust. "What brings you here?"

"Just thought we needed to work on a few things." Saul could tell William was a little deflated. He knew he'd just lost whatever edge Clair might have gained. Score one for Team Bryson.

William was a nice man, but he was thin, pale and balding. He always had a forlorn look on his face, like the day had beaten him down before he ever got out of bed. The cost of the lessons and the volleyball fees might be what's beating him down, Saul supposed, especially if his daughter wasn't substantially improving.

For the remainder of the season, Bree had one lesson with Autumn per week and Saul could see Bree develop before his eyes. She was timing her jump well and making consistent contact with the ball. There were no more whiffs or shanks or bad touches on the ball. Bree could consistently hit the ball down, albeit with not much power, but it still was effective for that age level. She was also much better at handling bad sets and figuring out a way to get them over the net. Another benefit of the lessons was that Saul had Harper attend a few of them so Autumn could work on her game, too.

Harper was growing fast, faster than Bree's pace. Her body was broad and dense, unlike Bree's which was still thin and scrawny. Harper's increased size and strength was evident.

"I want her for my 12s team when she's ready," Autumn told Saul.

He smiled with satisfaction knowing he had a place for Harper when she was of age.

As much as Bree was improving, her team was not. It had reached its peak early in the year and there was not enough talent to push it beyond its typical ninth place finish. The quarterfinals remained out of reach. PSA wanted to be the little club that could, but unfortunately it was the little club that couldn't.

They went to their second qualifier, Lone Star in Dallas, with hopes of a magical weekend that might propel them to a bid to Nationals, but it didn't happen. Saul was impressed with the event, though. Like Colorado Crossroads, Lone Star was a huge tournament that had teams from all across the country attend. PSA ended up placing 19th out of 48 teams, but like Denver, failed to reach the illustrious Gold Bracket.

Bree's playing time became more consistent though, and Saul could tell Autumn was much more confident with her on the court. Bree was becoming more of an offensive threat than Stacy. On the last day of Lone Star, Saul was surprised to see Autumn inserting Bree into the starting line-up for the last couple of matches. This brought an awkward silence to Fred, a man that had no fear of sharing his knowledge or opinions. Saul didn't say anything as he watched Bree take the court, but he couldn't help but bare that same smug sense of satisfaction that all parents of starting players bare. He hoped Fred didn't notice.

As Regionals, the last tournament of the regular season and the last chance to earn a bid to Nationals, neared, Saul made sure Bree had one more lesson scheduled with Autumn. They arrived at PSA and there again was William, looking more forlorn than ever. Even though Bree had won the war, William was still fighting the battle, hoping against hope that Clair would somehow have a breakthrough. And then, to Saul's astonishment, he saw Fred the Baptist approaching. He was walking over to the court with Stacy.

OMG, Saul thought as he came strolling over. "What brings you here?" Saul asked.

"Cut the bull crap, Saul," Fred bluntly said. "You saw my daughter play last week. She needs to get some work in."

And so the dads of the three middles on the same team shared the same lesson with Autumn, all hoping their daughters playing-time would increase, all hoping their daughters' performance at Regionals would be amazing, all hoping their daughters would remain top-of-mind with Autumn when next year's tryout season came along.

At Regionals, PSA needed to finish fifth or better to get a bid but fell two victories shy of qualifying for Nationals. They finished ninth, their allotted spot in the annals of that club volleyball year. Bree played well and so did Stacy. Autumn ended up rotating them as starters throughout the tournament. As disappointed as Saul was in the team not making Nationals, he was pleased with Bree's development. She had at least reached Stacy's level and that was a victory in itself. Bree still had some catching up to do when it came to competing at a higher level. There were some better middles in the North Texas Region but not many. With Bree's potential, newfound passion and willingness to outwork the competition, he could see her moving up the club ranks quickly.

With PSA's season completed, Saul immediately turned his focus to school ball. 8th grade tryouts were just three months away. He would have to consider what was needed to best prepare her for those brutal three days of tryouts. Should she play in a summer league? Should she have lessons? Should she participate in camps or clinics? Or was it a combination of all three?

At the same time, there was still their summer vacation to plan, plus Callie was coming to visit for a couple of weeks. So much to do and so little time, Saul fretted, when all you really want is for your daughter to get better at volleyball while everyone else is wasting time and goofing off. He reminded himself though that the girls who qualified for Nationals were not wasting time or goofing off. Those girls were Bree's competition and Saul's MAP envisioned Bree at that level.

At the request of some of the PSA parents, Autumn was asked to coach a summer league team made up of the girls from the 13s team. They wanted this for a couple of reasons: to make Autumn happy since she was earning a little more money, and to keep their daughters on Autumn's radar screen when it came time for tryouts next club season.

The summer league was pretty much a joke for the serious player. As Fred had told him, all the good players went to Nationals and didn't take the time to dawdle in the summer league. Saul vowed there would be no more summer leagues for his daughter after this season. Achieving a bid to Nationals was now a major stepping-stone in Saul's Master Athletic Plan. Autumn's team mowed through the league without losing a game or match. The most points an opposing team scored in a game was 11. The games were yawners but the girls did get quality time with Autumn and she was able to monitor their development.

One day at practice Bree had an especially good hitting day and Autumn made a point of walking over to Saul and telling him she wanted Bree on her 14s team. This made Saul feel extremely good, not that he had been that worried about making the team. It was just nice to see the extra work that Bree had put in was paying off.

Saul had grown to respect Autumn's ability as a coach. She had the perfect demeanor for handling girls that age. She also had a deep respect and love for the game which Saul discovered during a team dinner one night in Denver. Saul ended up sitting next to Autumn at a large table set up especially for the players and parents at an Olive Garden restaurant.

Any inclination that Saul had about Autumn coming on to him was quickly dispelled when she received a call from her husband just as they were sitting down at the table. Saul overheard part of the conversation and could tell by the interaction there was the sweet spell of young love and devotion at play. This made Saul feel a little more at ease even though he never had anything to worry about.

He and Autumn ended up having a great conversation about the game of volleyball. Saul asked her what she loved about the sport and she didn't hesitate to answer. "It's the best team sport there is, bar none."

"Really?" Saul challenged. "More so than basketball?"

"Basketball? Are you kidding me? Look at the NBA. All you need is Lebron James on your team and you can win a championship. He can single-handedly win games for his team. When he wants the ball, the other players on his team just get out of the way and let him do what he wants."

"What about football and its 11 players on offense and defense?" Saul proposed.

"If the defense sucks, the offense can still outscore the other team. If the offense sucks, the defense can still win games through sheer tenacity. Trent Dilfer won Super Bowl XXXV with the Ravens, remember? But they didn't win because of Trent Dilfer. They won because of Ray Lewis and their incredible defense. All Dilfer did was hand the ball off and pray the running back didn't fumble."

"And baseball?" Saul persisted. "There are nine players on the field, after all."

"And one of them can win a game for you on any given night. Nolan Ryan had seven no-hitters in his career. He didn't need much help on those nights. Reggie Jackson hit three home runs in one World Series game. I know you have to have the catchers and fielders to help with the put outs, but when Roger Clemens strikes out 20 batters, there is not much help that is needed from your teammates."

"So what makes volleyball the best team sport?" Saul asked.

"Pass-Set-Kill," Autumn began. "People think it's all about the kills, but it's not. Yes, that's the flashy part. But you can't kill a ball unless you have a good set to hit. And you can't set the ball unless you have a good pass to set. Multiple players are required to make that happen. The art of great volleyball starts with the perfect pass. If you can pass well, chances are you are going to set and kill well, too. When you have all three elements working in tandem, it's a thing of beauty. There is a rhythm you actually start to feel on the court . . . "

Saul was enjoying the conversation immensely. He was getting somewhat aroused, not in a sexual way but in a bromance kind of way, listening to Autumn talk about the game she loved. She was talking like one of the guys and as she continued the conversation, he started to find himself more in love with the game than he realized. The cadence of her voice had him lost in the wonderful game of volleyball.

" . . . And when you have two teams, on different sides of the net," Autumn continued, "Both in the same rhythm, playing the game the way it's meant to be played, you watch in amazement as both sides become one and points turn in to long, sustained rallies. Points are harder to terminate because one side knows what the other side is doing. The rhythm of it all, it's not unlike a well-oiled . . . "

A well-oiled what? Saul wanted to know. He was so wound up he was on edge waiting for the next word when he heard out of nowhere, "May I have your order, sir?" Saul looked up and it was the waiter. The waiter noticed something hanging from Saul's lip. He reached for Saul's napkin and handed it to him. Saul didn't understand why.

"Above your lip, sir." The waiter pointed.

"Oh, thank you," Saul realized. He wiped his lip and saw that a tiny breadcrumb was the culprit.

Saul never got to finish their conversation that night. The bromance was abruptly extinguished. Autumn got pulled away by the volleyball mom sitting on the other side of her and she would never let her go. Parents were always sucking up to the coach any chance they got, thinking that might help their kids' chances.

He wanted to ask Autumn at what age does this rhythm thing start to happen. When do you really see the beauty of the game? He knew it didn't happen at 13s. Instead, he was relegated to eating his salad, pasta and two breadsticks with Fred, relying on his buddy for conversation the rest of the evening.

When Callie came to visit that summer, the girls acted as if they had never been apart, playing together with such ease. Saul and Veronica remained in awe of the strength of social media and how it connects us. Callie was still playing volleyball and was a member of one of the top club teams in Seattle. Saul managed to work a clinic in while Callie was visiting. He suggested they both go and, to Saul's amazement, they both agreed. They also spent a fare amount of time playing volleyball with Robby and Bobby. Saul, always leery of the boys, couldn't find anything troubling about them. They innocently played on Bryson Court and after an hour or two would leave for home. He never saw them looking at the girls in any kind of lewd or mysterious way like most boy scum do.

After Callie flew back home, the family managed to work a vacation in right before school and then suddenly, the whirlwind of summer was done and it was time for school, or more importantly, time for tryouts. Bree was much more calm and confident about school tryouts as they approached. She and Saul had open conversations about what to expect. There was no summer long silence or the surprise-attack conversation just days before school was to start like last year. This year, Bree felt very prepared.

Saul left work at 4 p.m. for a business meeting that was conveniently located near Plano's Wilson Middle School. It was tryout day one. He parked his car and waited impatiently for the recap like the rest of the impatient moms. But wait a second! Saul noticed there was a man waiting, too. This was a first. Could he be a volleyball dad? The mysterious man was demonstrating incredible bad form because he was snooping around the door to the gymnasium looking inside, which infuriated Saul because this was against the coach's rules.

The gym doors suddenly slammed open and a wave of girls came flushing out. Saul lost track of the Mystery Man and refocused his attention on his first concern, which was new arrivals. You never knew when you had a move-in from out of state or a transfer from another district. He didn't care if a setter or a defensive player moved into town as long as it wasn't another middle. Last season, there was Pamela and the other middle that wasn't really a middle but was playing middle because she knew the game better than either Pamela or Bree did.

He immediately began looking for new faces and if he saw one, he would quickly assess their height to see if they could play middle. He soon realized his process was a waste of time because he couldn't tell if a new face was a seventh grader or eighth grader because both grades were released at the same time. He remembered he had this same problem last year. He then saw Bree running his way and she was smiling, thank God. That was a rarity for his thirteen year old, the prolific possessor of multiple moods.

"Hi, Dad," Bree said as she plopped down in her seat.

"Hi, Sport. How was day one?"

"Pretty good. My teachers all seem nice."

Saul was not concerned about the teachers but he felt he better act like his daughter's education was important. "That's good to hear. Any homework?"

"Yes. In three classes. Can you believe it?" Bree exclaimed.

Saul shook his head in disgust. Bastards. It never ended. More homework meant more work for the parents and less work for the teachers.

"So how was tryouts?" Saul said, quickly changing to the subject that really interested him.

"It was fine. Kind of boring, though. A lot of basic drills and stuff."

"Any new faces trying out?"

"A few, but they don't appear to be any good."

Good to hear, Saul told himself. "Are all the same A Team girls back from last year?"

"Yeah, I think so, but guess what?"

"What?" Saul asked, his interest peaked.

"Remember Katie?"

"Katie, Katie, who was Katie?" Saul couldn't remember.

"Dad," Bree said annoyingly. "The other middle from our team."

"Oh, her. Yes, the middle that wasn't a middle but still played middle. Yes, I had forgotten her name."

"She's moving to setter."

"Really?" Saul said, intrigued by the new development. Could that mean there was one less middle to worry about? "Are they going to add another middle?" He asked.

"I don't know yet. There were really no good middles on the B Team last year so I don't know who they would add."

"What about Pamela. Is she still playing?"

"Yeah."

Saul winced at the answer. He was hoping this was the year she would focus on just her primary sports. Did she have to play everything?

"But she's terrible, though," Bree added.

Bree might think she's terrible but Saul knew if Pamela ever set her mind to it, she could be a force. She had the athleticism to do anything she wanted.

"I got a lot of compliments today," Bree boasted.

"From who?"

"From all the club girls. They were impressed with how much I improved."

Bree was definitely flowing with confidence, which was okay to a degree. He didn't want her getting too overconfident, though.

"They all want me to come try out at their clubs."

"That's nice of them," Saul commented.

"My coach said if you want to get better, you need to try and be on the best team you can find."

"That's a compelling thought," Saul said, his interest peaked.

"But I still like Coach Autumn and PSA. We have a good team. Don't we, Dad?"

"Sure you do," Saul answered. If you like finishing ninth. He didn't say that but that was the first thing that came into his mind.

He had never even thought about changing clubs at this point. He was happy with Autumn and the training she had provided Bree. But maybe her school coach had a point. If you want to get better, you have to challenge yourself and play against the best competition you can find. It made sense. And it fit within the framework of his Master Athletic Plan. Saul needed some time to think about this. Along with a beer or two, this would take a few nights with Veronica in the Conference Room for Private Family Discussions to talk through.

Club ball was a major topic of conversation at the Wilson Wrangler volleyball games, too. Just as impressed as Bree's teammates were with her improvement, the parents, check that, the snooty club parents that snubbed their noses at Saul all last season were now amazingly interested in Bree's club career. He was now officially part of the group. He and Veronica now got to sit with them as they oohed and aahed over Bree's transformation. In between points or games, one parent would whisper in Saul's ear that she needed to come to MadDog. Another parent would urge him to go to SkyHi. And then another parent would talk about Premier or Advantage. She needs to go to a real club, they would say.

"What do you mean, a real club?" Saul would ask.

So they would talk about the benefits their clubs had over PSA, which they insisted was not a real club. Parent A would say PSA was a little volleyball team living in a huge athletic center that made its living on other recreational sports. MadDogs has its own facility with eight courts. It's totally dedicated to volleyball. You don't have basketball courts or indoor soccer courts or anything like that. Parent B would say SkyHigh has age groups going all the way to 18 years old. They prepare you to play in college. PSA has age groups going only up to 15. What are you going to do after that? It will be awfully hard to break into a top club at that point. Parent C would say Advantage has at least three teams for every age group, which means your daughter has a good chance to find a team and position that's just right for her. PSA has just one team per age group. Parent D would say MadDogs has over ten quality coaches on its staff. You have more opportunities to get a quality lesson that fit within your schedule. You want to join a volleyball club, not a recreational center.

These words, at first, felt harsh to Saul. He was proud of his first year at PSA and he felt lucky they had found a coach like Autumn. But these club parents were more experienced at this than he was and they all seemed to have valid points. It was hard to get a lesson when Autumn was the only one available. Where would Bree go after the age of 15?

As the school season got into full swing, the club tryout season also began. Last year, Saul was unaware of the club tryout season. He just showed up at tryouts clueless, and was fortunate Bree got selected. The club tryout season consisted of one to two clinics a week. If you were considering three to four clubs, you were adding a lot to an already busy schedule, not to mention adding a lot of stress to your daughter. This didn't even count the lessons that parents would try to get with key coaches, not necessarily to get better, but to increase their daughter's visibility with the coach of the team they wanted her to play for.

During PSA's first tryout clinic of the so-called Club Tryout Season, Saul cornered Fred the Baptist to talk about what he was hearing from his new club parent buddies at school and how they were encouraging him to leave PSA.

"Don't say a word to anybody else," Fred whispered sternly to Saul. He looked to both sides to make sure no one else was listening. Fred's actions made Saul feel like he was in a spy movie, that Fred was about to pass along important military secrets. "But I've been thinking the same thing myself."

"Really?"

"Where are we going to go after 15, Saul? And there's no guarantee Autumn will even coach that team. She likes the younger ages. After her, PSA's coaching depth is horrid."

"You're right," Saul said.

"You and I would make a better coaching team," Fred added in jest.

They then looked at each other for a brief moment as if they were seriously considering the possibility.

"We would be a complete failure," Fred assured him.

"You're absolutely right. We would be way in over our heads."

"Not so much as in over our heads," Fred paused. "Yes, we would be in over our heads. Hell, I can't even hit a down-ball."

"Me, neither," Saul agreed. "I don't even know what a down-ball is."

"Getting back to reality," Fred continued. "You know what makes me even more concerned?"

"What?" Saul asked.

"Look who showed up here tonight and who didn't."

"What do you mean?"

"Just look around."

Saul began to look around and then slowly realized what Fred was getting at. "Our best hitters aren't here."

"Bingo," Fred added in agreement.

"Well, where are they?"

"Word on the street is that they have been showing up at SkyHi and Advantage."

"What?" Saul exclaimed. "Does Autumn know about this?"

"I have no idea. But if we try to go somewhere, we've got to be stealth."

"Stealth?"

"Stealth," Fred whispered emphatically.

"Why?"

"Because if Autumn found out, it could jeopardize our place on her team. She might invite a few other middles into the fray."

"I see," Saul realized.

"This discussion is TBC," Fred whispered suddenly.

"What is that?"

"To be continued."

Saul didn't know why Fred was ending the conversation until he noticed William lurking, the father of the third middle who cost everyone more money by having lessons early in the season.

"How are you guys doing?" William asked.

"Good. Good to see you," Saul said politely.

William then probingly asked, "So since you're here, I guess you're coming back to PSA?"

"That's the plan," Fred said.

William sighed. "That will make it tough for Clair. She wants to stay at PSA but I've got to make sure she plays more next season."

"Makes sense," Saul said. "She's a good player. She should be playing more."

Saul noticed Fred looking at him with a look of why are you softening up the enemy.

"Thanks. We'll see what happens, I guess." William then slowly walked his way over to talk to another parent.

"Don't trust that guy," Fred cautioned. "We don't need a mole inside our team."

"A mole?" Saul laughed.

"If he catches wind of us going somewhere, he'll be the first one to blab it to Autumn. Believe me, he wants us somewhere else. It helps his daughter."

Saul slowly understood. He guessed he would be doing the same thing. Every dad was about helping his own daughter. Every little edge counts. Saul had to ensure he was doing everything he could to help his daughter, to make sure she had the edge she needed. It was then and there that he decided they needed to take a chance, to go on a five-week mission to seek out new clubs (cue the *Star Trek* theme music), new forms of coaching and competition, and to boldly go where few fathers have gone before.

He now had to decide the best time to bring it up to Bree. She was feeling good about herself so hopefully she would take it well and not have a meltdown. On the other hand, part of the reason she was feeling good about herself was because she liked her role on PSA and she liked her teammates and coach. But Saul knew he had to do it. In the brief athletic career of a teenager, time was of the essence. They grow up too fast and so does the competition.

BREE'S DIARY
September 4
I made the 8th grade A team last week!! Not too surprised, tho. Savannah and Pamela couldn't believe how much better I've gotten. I'm still thinking about what a great summer it was. Seeing Callie made me feel really good. I was worried we were drifting apart because she has so many friends now, but we had a great time. She likes Bobby a lot, too. She has a new boyfriend, too, that looks really cute. Pamela wants to play club volleyball but her dad won't let her. I feel sorry for her.

Game Night was upon the Bryson family and Saul was more fired up than usual because the Wilson Wranglers had a home game with their arch rival, Schimelpfinig. They weren't really the Wranglers arch rival. They were Saul's. He couldn't stand the name, let alone pronounce it or spell it, and he didn't want his Wranglers to lose to a team with that name.

The Wranglers were actually really good this season. Their club players had developed nicely. Their outside hitters, Millie and Tracy, were still a little under-sized but they were effective scorers. Both Bree and Pamela could hold down the middle, Bree with skill and Pamela with old-fashioned athleticism even if she didn't know what she was doing half the time. Savannah, Bree's buddy, and Katie were a strong setting tandem, and the team's back row defense was solid.

The Wranglers were undefeated thus far and to Saul's enjoyment they stayed that way. They finished off Schimelpfinig with ease, 25 to 15 and 25 to 16. And to top it off, Bree scored the last three points in a row. Such a satisfying feeling, but Saul was already looking ahead. He couldn't wait for the matchup with Renner, last year's district champions. It was coming soon and he wanted to see if this year's Wranglers team could take them down.

After the game, and after Saul had been flooded with compliments about Bree by all his new club parent buddies, a man approached him. Saul recognized him immediately. He was the snoopy Mystery Man from tryout day.

"Are you Bree Bryson's dad?" The Man of Mystery asked.

"Yes, I am."

"I'm Brent. I'm Pamela's father," he said, extending his hand like it was some sort of peace offering.

"Oh, nice to meet you. I haven't see you around before."

"I haven't been around much. I'm still coming to grips with this volleyball stuff. I noticed you at the school tryouts, though."

"You did?"

"Yeah. You and me were the only dads there."

"Sorry, I didn't see you," Saul lied.

"I just wanted to say how impressed I am with your daughter."

"Thanks," Saul said, a little suspicious of his motives, if he had any.

"Pamela told me she's really improved a lot in the last year."

"Yes, she has."

"Did she play club last year?"

"Yes, she did. It really helped her pick the game up."

"Where did she play?"

Uh-oh, Saul feared. Do I give up my sensitive and valuable Intel? I can't lie about this, though. He would find out soon enough anyway. I just better not see Pamela show up at the next PSA tryout clinic.

"She played at PSA, a small club team at the Plano Sports Authority rec center."

"Well, it looks like it's made a difference. Pam's got to make a decision soon, you know. She can't go on playing three sports forever."

"Bree told me she plays basketball and soccer."

"Yep. She's great at both and now, for the life of me, I don't know why she wants to try this volleyball thing out. I want her to stay focused on soccer and basketball. We've invested a lot of time and effort in those sports."

"Well, at least you have options."

"Yeah, I guess so," Brent said, and then started to laugh. "But every option costs me money."

Saul laughed with him. "I hear you, Brent."

"Congratulations again, tonight."

"You, too," Saul said. They shook hands and Brent walked away. To Saul, he seemed nice enough, but he would remain the Mystery Man to him until his motives were made more clear.

During the car ride home, Bree was high-fiving Harper, Veronica and Saul. She was elated with her play and all she wanted to talk about was her last three points. She kept talking about the game when they arrived home and chattered before she showered and after she showered and when she got in bed. Saul went up to tuck her in and overheard her describing to Harper how she was able to score one of her points.

"Harper, time for you to be in your own bed," Saul said as he entered Bree's room.

"Okay, Daddy," Harper said, annoyed that she had to leave.

"And you, my girl," he said, pointing to Bree. "You need to get some rest, too."

"I'm sorry, Dad, but it's so hard to come down from such a rush. I never scored so many points in a row before."

"That's not true. You ran off quite a few points in that exciting spring league from a couple of years ago."

"Oh, please," Bree blushed. "Those girls were terrible."

Saul laughed with her and then he thought this might be as good a time as any to talk about what he now termed Operation Club Search. "You know, Bree. I've been thinking about what your coach told you. About finding the best team possible to be on. Have you thought about that at all?"

"A little."

"I think it's a good idea and, frankly, something we should do."

Bree pondered his statement for a moment. "But what about Autumn and my teammates."

Saul sighed, thinking of what to say. "I think Autumn is a great coach, but I think it's possible your other teammates are looking for better teams, too."

"You think so?" Bree asked disbelievingly.

"They haven't all been at the PSA clinics, have they?"

"No, they haven't," Bree said, now wondering where they were going.

"And I think we may be able to get Stacy to go with us if that would make you feel better."

Bree had already made up her mind. "Dad, I think we should do it."

Saul was stunned at her decisiveness. "Okay. Then I'll start looking at options."

Saul got up and turned the light off. Before he shut her door, Bree said, "Dad, I want to try out at MadDogs."

Saul was stunned again. "You do?"

"Savannah's been asking me to go and so have some of my other friends. I think I might like it there."

"MadDogs it is," Saul said. He leaned over and kissed her goodnight one more time. "You were great tonight."

As Saul walked down the stairs to meet Veronica on the patio, he was pleased with how easy the conversation went. And he was happy she brought up the club. MadDogs would have definitely been on his list.

"Are you sure we aren't moving too fast," Veronica cautiously asked. This was the first time she had been included in the conversation about Operation Club Search. "Autumn's a great coach and she still has a lot to learn."

"I know, Very, but MadDogs has great coaches, too, and we've got to be where the talent is. That's where the winning occurs and the more you win, the more you get noticed."

"By who?

"By better club teams and by colleges, eventually. Very, I want her to have the best available chance to succeed at this."

"And since when has winning become so important? What's happened to good old-fashioned fun?"

"Winning is always important," Saul stressed. "Forget the old adage, please. It's not how you play the game. It's whether you win. And speaking of fun, it's more fun to win than lose."

Veronica's face was flush with concern. "I'm worried you're getting a tad obsessive over all this, Saul. She's just in eighth grade."

"Very, you've seen the competition. All these girls are starting so early. The sheer number of them is hard to fathom. You've got to do what you can to get ahead and stay ahead. Besides, this is important to me. I want to do everything I can to give her the opportunity my dad was never able to give me."

"Which was what, to get a scholarship to a bigger college? To play professionally?"

"I don't know. I just know I could have done more as a player if he didn't . . ."

Saul stopped in mid-sentence. He didn't want to go there. He didn't want to bring up the death of his father. It was too painful a subject to him. He had told Very the story once, and only once. He could see she knew what was running through his mind right now.

"Honey, I'm sorry," Veronica pleaded.

But it was too late. There he was again, back in his freshman year of high school, ready for his first basketball game of the season. He and his dad had practiced together vigorously to get ready. Harper Sr. promised him he would leave work early to come watch him play. And he did leave early. He just never showed up at the game. Struck by a speeding driver while crossing a street, Harper Sr.'s promise to his son remained unfulfilled, and the bond they shared was suddenly forever shattered. Saul was left with his loving, but distraught mom who didn't know sports and even if she did, she wouldn't have the time given the sudden demands of going back to work and providing for her family.

Veronica immediately walked over and put her arms around Saul, kissing him on the cheek. "It's alright, Dear. I understand. I'm sorry for doubting you. I know you will do the right thing for Bree."

Saul didn't answer. He remained silent, sheltered in Very's warm embrace, trying to erase a memory that cannot be forgotten.

That weekend, Saul and Bree ventured out to the MadDogs tryout clinic for the first time. It was on Saturday night at 5 p.m., which meant they could still go to PSA's clinic from 2 to 4 p.m. Saul hoped that Bree would still be fresh for the MadDogs clinic after two hours at PSA. He was confident she would be because usually, due to the extreme number of girls, there was a lot of waiting in line until you got your turn to participate in a drill.

Walking into the door of MadDogs was a little intimidating at first. There were eight courts in their facility and all of them were full of activity. You had girls ranging from Bree's age all the way up to 18. It was organized chaos. It was especially busy at that particular hour as you had people exiting from their clinics and people arriving for their clinics. It made finding a place to park very challenging. Bree was overwhelmed at first but once she saw Savannah and Stacy and a few other familiar faces she was fine. Saul felt the same way when he saw Fred the Baptist.

"Can you believe this place?" Saul asked.

"It's all about the volleyball here, isn't it? Pure and simple."

"Sure seems to be. They even have a lounge for the parents."

"If there's a keg in there, I'm sold," Fred said jokingly. Fred was that rare southern Baptist. As devout as he was, he had no problem with drinking a beer or two. "If the disciples drank wine, he could drink beer," he would tell Saul.

"Look at all the banners hanging from the rafters," Saul pointed out. They have won a lot of tournaments."

"They won Nationals this past summer," Fred said.

"Really?"

"Yes," Fred confirmed. "Their 13s team."

"Wow. I hadn't heard that."

"Some of the girls from that team are here. Have you heard of Tina Dulles?"

Saul shook his head no. Fred described her and pointed her out to Saul and Saul realized he had seen the girl before.

"That's the Renner girl," Saul exclaimed.

"That's right," Fred said. "She goes to Plano Renner. You know how Ronaldo is to soccer?"

Saul didn't know Ronaldo or much about soccer for that matter, but he acted like he did.

"She is the Ronaldo of our age group here in North Texas," Fred stated.

Saul remembered her well from their matches last season and how hard it was to stop her. He found himself even more excited about the upcoming battle between the Wranglers and Renner.

The clinic began and both Fred and Saul refocused their attention on their girls, watching their every move to see how they were doing. Fred would wince when Stacy made a mistake, then clutch his fist with satisfaction when she did something well. Saul was more focused on their competition. What other middles were there that could challenge his daughter for a spot on one of their teams? He recognized a few faces from the two

MadDogs teams they played last year, but he thought Bree was better than any of them. Saul could always spot Bree by her long, skinny arm that raised up out of nowhere when it was time to swing at a ball. He felt Bree was having a good day and he saw the coaches talking to her from time to time. Fred had wandered off to inspect the conveniences of the lounge area when Saul was tapped on the shoulder. He turned around and there stood, what appeared to be, a MadDogs coach.

"Are you Mr. Bryson?"

"Yes I am," Saul replied, quickly standing at attention.

"I'm Frances Morgan and I am the owner of the club."

"Very nice to meet you," Saul said, as he shook her hand.

"Our coaches have been watching your daughter play and they like what they see."

Saul could tell she was not prone to chit-chat. She got right down to business. "That's good to hear."

"Where did she play last year?"

"At PSA."

"For Autumn?"

"Yes. For Autumn." Small world, Saul thought. All the coaches must know each other pretty well.

"She's a great coach. Not the best club, though," stated Frances matter-of-factly.

"She helped Bree a lot last year," Saul stated, feeling obliged to give credit where it was due.

"I'm sure she did. Well, we would like to help Bree this season," she said, putting the emphasis on "this".

"That's good," Saul noted. "Where do you see her playing?"

"She might be able to crack our top team, but our top team is really good."

"I heard that. They won Nationals, didn't they?" Saul interrupted.

"They did. It was so fun to experience," she beamed. "But getting back to Bree, I can definitely see her on our second team. There would be fewer concerns about playing time and she is still a little raw. She probably would fit in better with that group. And don't get me wrong. Our second team will be really good."

"I believe it," Saul said. "We lost to them a couple of times last season."

"Well, let me know if you have any questions and we hope to see you at the next tryout clinic."

She quickly shook his hand and then moved through the crowd of parents, probably to find the next volleyball dad to discuss the recruitment of his kid.

Fred came walking back soon after. "Nice digs in the lounge. Very comfortable."

"Good to hear," Saul said, still thinking about his meeting with the owner. He debated whether to tell Fred about his encounter. If he did, Fred might get bummed that Stacy hadn't been noticed yet. Saul decided not to talk about it. He needed more time to process the information anyway. He also needed the friendly confines of his patio to talk through the pros and cons with Very. While never the sports enthusiast, she was the best listener a husband could ask for and it was always important to avoid the death stare by keeping her in the loop.

All the hype leading up to the Renner vs. Wilson duel ended up being just that. Hype. And most of the hype was a figment of Saul's imagination, blown up in his head all out of proportion for nobody else to hear or see but him. Like many dads, he got overly amped up for the game and thought is was going to be a great match. Two undefeated teams, the top two teams from last season, playing on Wilson's home court. Renner came in and throttled them though, on the strength of Tina Dulles, the Ronaldo of North Texas volleyball.

She had a great game. No one could block her. She scored at will. It appeared that Wilson was definitely overconfident after their undefeated start. The final score was 25 to 10 and 25 to 17, but it felt like they were skunked. They wouldn't get to play them again until the championship tournament.

With the Renner game drama over, Saul continued to take Bree to MadDogs and PSA tryout clinics. The club tryout season was starting to take its toll. He kept sweating it out when he was at the PSA facility. He had this fear that Autumn would corner him and read him the riot act for treasonous behavior. Did she know what he was doing? Had a mole ratted him out?

As fewer and fewer players from Bree's PSA team were showing up, Bree was becoming more and more comfortable at MadDogs and knew that whatever team she would make there would be better than her PSA team. She had many school friends playing at MadDogs and it was truly a club atmosphere. Saul knew the decision had been made in his mind and even though Bree hadn't said it publicly yet, he knew it wouldn't take much swaying for her to make the move.

The Wilson Wranglers regular season ended with just one loss and they were seeded second in the district championship tournament behind the unbeaten Renner Middle School. To make matters more challenging, the tournament was being hosted by Renner. The best team in the district also had the home court advantage. And to add further difficulty to the day, the parents and players were ready to get the tournament done because afterwards, many girls had to go to their various tryout clinics.

This was the last weekend for clinics. Next weekend was the try-out period for Bree's age group.

As Saul expected, the first couple of rounds of the tournament were yawners. Both Renner and Wilson marched through the quarterfinals and semifinals and were set for the rematch. Saul was hopeful that the girls would give them a better contest today. As he was watching the girls warmup, he was distracted by a familiar face. Entering the gym was none other than Mad-Dogs' very own Frances Morgan, greeting parents and apparent friends.

What was she doing here? Saul wondered to himself. Was she here to scout Bree? Saul nudged his new club buddy Stan Mason, Savannah's dad. "Do you see who's here?"

"Not surprised. She always gets around to watch the kids from time to time. She's got a good eye for talent. Plus, she has to continue to coddle Tina, her superstar."

Saul thought that made more sense. Tina Dulles was worth coddling. Either way, he hoped Bree didn't see Frances. She didn't need any additional stress or distraction right before the biggest game of her young volleyball life.

Saul looked around to see if Mystery Man was in the gym. He was not a part of Saul's snooty Parent Group. You had to be a club parent to achieve that status. Finally, he noticed Brent high up in the corner of the bleachers all by himself, his face almost blocked out by the shadows of the rafters, which ironically gave him the aura befitting Saul's nickname for him.

The match started and to everyone's surprise, Renner came out flat. It was if they weren't ready to play. It was the perfect start for Wilson. They needed this kind of start to build their confidence and erase the memories of the first match. Before you could blink, the Wranglers were up 12 to 3. They could do no wrong. Their outside hitters were on fire and Bree and Pamela each scored a few points to keep the Renner defense off base. Saul, along with his club parent buddies, was getting fired up. The noise from the cheers the Wilson parents were making was echoing loudly through the gym. It seemed to add to the burden the Renner players were feeling. Wilson won the first game 25 to 15 and the Renner players were in shock. Saul could hear their coach slam down a clipboard in anger and was doing everything he could to wake them up.

Meanwhile, Saul was starting to think and hope that this could be it. This could be the one. This could be the first real championship win of Bree's career. There were to be several of these per his Master Athletic Plan. He told himself to remain calm, though. Renner had Tina "Ronaldo" Dulles, national championship team member, on their side. Saul's instincts were correct.

Ronaldo came out smoking. She began to patiently place her shots with sharp angles that made it harder for the Wrangler defense to adjust to. She stopped trying to overpower the ball and began using more finesse. It was working. She possessed a lot of different shots for being such a young player. The amount of topspin she could put on a ball was more than any player Saul had ever witnessed. And to add to her many attributes, she was jumping much higher than she did last year, which made the angle of her ball flight more difficult for the defense to handle.

Wilson would not back down, though. They were still putting up a fight, but as a very well-known sports cliché teaches, talent ultimately wins out. Like last year, Renner's depth of talent was starting to show. While Tina was the superstar, they still had eight other high quality club volleyball girls and they knew how to play. Wilson began making some unforced errors that allowed Renner to seize control of the second game.

Pamela made a few boneheaded mistakes at middle like shanking bump passes to the outside hitters. These were mistakes she normally made but the team had learned to live with them. Against Renner, you couldn't afford those kind of mistakes. Saul found himself huffing and puffing and gasping with disgust with the rest of the snooty club parents. He wanted to shout out something like, 'Get her off the court!!' But he didn't. He caught himself. He suddenly realized he was in danger of becoming one of those snobby club parents that screamed at Bree last year. He told himself he would not become that person. It wasn't Pamela's fault that she didn't play club volleyball. This was school ball. She was just trying to help her school team win as best she could. He looked over to the upper corner of the bleachers and there was Brent, his head in his hands. Reclusive Mystery Man or not, Saul knew and felt his pain.

Renner finished off the second game with relative ease winning by eight points. Now it was time for the rubber game, game three. Saul was chastising himself for getting his hopes up too early. You don't do that in sports, he reminded himself. It's never over until it's over. You've already endured two heartbreaking runner-up finishes in the Catholic league and at the district tournament last year.

Wilson was going to have to find a way to curb the Renner momentum. The Renner parents were on their feet at the start of game three. The noise was deafening. It was amazing the level of hysteria forty to fifty passionate parents can generate. As game three began, the momentum stayed with Renner. They surged to a 7 to 2 lead.

Saul, being a middle dad, was getting irritated that they weren't setting the middle at all. Bree had a high success rate at converting her sets to points. He watched as she rotated off the court, disappointed that she didn't get an attempt as they fell further and further behind. But then, a momentum change occurred. It was barely noticeable at first, but it began to gather steam. And it came from the unlikeliest player, Pamela.

She began getting her hands on every hit Renner attempted, either blocking them for a point or deflecting the ball enough to slow down its pace and make it easier for the Wilson defensive players to pass the ball. Tina Dulles went up for a hit, her arm outstretched, and slammed it as hard as she could, but Pamela was there, arms high in the air, in perfect position to block the ball for a score. Tina Dulles tried again on the next point, but the wall of Pamela was there again for another Wrangler score. It was as if Magneto from *X-Men* had christened her arms with special magnetic powers, or at least with the power to attract a leather volleyball. The Wilson parents were back in the game cheering loudly.

"That was awesome," Stan yelled to Saul. "Did you see that?"

"I sure did," Saul had to admit.

When Pamela rotated off the court, the score was tied at 12. You could sense the Renner players were frustrated and a little discombobulated. Nothing was working with their offense. Bree ran in and it was now her turn to do battle. Her teammates were intense and focused and Saul had never seen such a look of determination on Bree's face. The next play they ran was actually a set to Bree. Saul couldn't believe it. "Finally," he muttered to himself. It wasn't a great set, but Bree was able to make something out of it. She tipped it to an empty zone on the court for an easy point.

"Nothing flashy, but it worked. Smart play." Stan yelled, now providing his game commentary on every point.

Wilson continued to run their offense effectively and keep Renner off balance. Every point they scored was a point closer to

25. Saul couldn't help but tell Stan, "Eight more points! Seven more points! Six more points!" after every score.

The Wranglers had maintained a slim lead and were up 21 to 19 when Pamela rotated back in. Did she still have her special powers? Saul hopefully wondered.

Pamela immediately deflected one pass but it dropped on the Wrangler side of the net for a Renner score. On the next point, she got a perfect set to hit and rose up high ready to pound the ball. For a moment, Saul sensed this could be a carbon copy of her amazing smash in last year's championship game. But it wasn't to be. She smashed it into the net. The score was tied.

"Come on, Fitty-Fitty!" Saul passionately yelled.

Stan looked at him confused. "What did you say?"

In a mad rush of excitement, Saul had spoken his internal nickname for Pamela out loud. Fortunately, he didn't have to answer Stan because the next point was ready to be played. Tina Dulles next connected on a sneaky roll-shot over the out-stretched hands of Pamela and the Wranglers had lost their lead. And Pamela had lost her mojo. Tina Dulles then moved to the service line, which was a good thing. At least she was off the front row, Stan assured Saul. It turned out to be an even greater thing when Tina Dulles served her ball into the net.

Point Wilson. It was tied again at 23 and a team had to win by two. The two teams traded points and it was now 25 all when Bree was rotated back in. Saul heard a familiar voice in the distance.

"Oh, my God," Veronica exclaimed. Veronica and Harper were sitting with the club volleyball moms. This was the first time this season Very had exclaimed to the Almighty.

Savannah was serving and Stan grabbed Saul's arm. Saul looked at him. "For luck," Stan told him.

"I understand," Saul said, assuring him he knew there were no sexual undertones in the arm grab. This was just an innocent bromance moment. Nothing more, nothing less.

Savannah served a long floater of a serve that immediately appeared to be sailing well out of bounds. But six feet from the end line the ball started diving so fast the defense didn't have a chance to respond. The ball landed in the back corner for an ace. Wilson had moved ahead 26 to 25. Savannah jumped up and hugged Bree like they had just won the match.

"One more point," Stan yelled.

Everyone in the gym was now on their feet as Savannah readied to serve again. She hit another floater serve but it didn't have the distance of the previous one. It was a safe serve that was easy for Renner to handle. They set the ball to Tina Dulles, of course, who went up for the kill. She hit the ball with tremendous force and Saul thought for sure it was a point but the ball went right into the arms of a Wilson defender who passed it perfectly to Savannah.

"What a dig!" Stan screamed.

The ball was passed high in the air and Savannah was patiently waiting for it. Bree was transitioning and readying herself for a set if it came her way. The ball finally landed in Savannah's hands and she set a quick set to the middle. Saul, while excited at first, quickly realized the set was too high. Bree had left her feet and was jumping as high as she could but the ball was too far away. As Bree started her descent, she swung that long, skinny arm of hers as hard as she could, lunging for the ball just enough to get a piece of it. It might have just been a fingernail that brushed the ball, but it was enough to propel the ball barely over the outstretched fingernails of the defense. It seemed like an eternity, like the ball was in slow motion, but it finally fell to the ground before a diving Renner defender could reach it. Wilson had won.

Saul couldn't believe it. He jumped so high he stumbled on the bleachers when he landed. After gathering himself, he hugged Stan and the rest of the parents. Veronica hugged her fellow club volleyball moms. Harper ran over to give her dad a high five. Bree and her teammates were in a pile on the court, ecstatic at what they had just pulled off. Saul looked up at the corner of the bleachers to find Brent, but was surprised to see he had already vanished. He looked back down at the girls celebrating and enjoyed the moment of Bree's first championship, the memories of past failures suddenly vanquished.

He then noticed Pamela pulling herself up from the pile of girls and running to the other side of the court. There was Brent. Pamela had ran up to give him a huge hug. And then suddenly, Saul felt a punch to the solar plexus. There next to Brent was none other than MadDogs owner, Frances Morgan. And next to her was his club buddy Stan Mason. Saul had wondered where Stan had run off to so fast. They appeared to be making introductions, the three of them chatting it up. Frances then started talking to Pamela. What could they be talking about? He then let out a long, loud heavy sigh. No one could hear it though, because of the raucous celebration. Don't kid yourself, Saul. You know what they're talking about. Bree's going to have another middle to contend with at MadDogs.

Most of the Wranglers were still on the court celebrating their upset win, a sweet win that avenged their loss in last year's championship game. But for Saul, he couldn't help but feel a bitter aftertaste in his mouth. Watching Frances Morgan give her recruiting sales pitch to Pamela and Brent, he stood there just dazed with a terrible feeling in his stomach, wondering to himself, did I just get out-fathered?

By the notorious Mystery Man, no less.

BREE'S DIARY
October 26
My team won district and I got the winning point. So excited. And MadDogs was there to watch. I hope it helps me get on one of their teams. Pamela is wanting to play club volleyball but her dad doesn't want her to. He told her she would have to give up basketball and soccer because volleyball would cost too much. I hope she plays club because that would make our school team better. I asked Bobby to come to the game today but he didn't show up. A little bummed about that. Hoping Savannah and me can make the same MadDogs team. Haven't heard from Callie since summer. Need to call her.

PART FOUR

THE FRUITS OF OUR LABOR

CHAPTER ELEVEN

THE BUSINESS GAME

The district championship celebration lasted all of fifteen minutes. The girls took photos with the trophy and quickly went their separate ways. Many were trying to get to a club tryout clinic on time. Some were just ready to get home. Saul spent the entire ride home wondering about the outcome of Brent's conversation with Frances. He figured he would find out in a couple of hours. That's when Bree's next MadDogs clinic started.

He arrived at the clinic the same time as Fred. Fred was getting nervous because he didn't know where he stood with Mad-Dogs. And he continued to worry about what Autumn might do if she found out he had been disloyal. He had yet to talk to any MadDogs coach and no coach had approached him, like Frances had with Saul. Fred decided he was going to talk to a coach that day and get a sense of where Stacy stood.

Saul was focused only on who would be walking in the door that day. Would Pamela make an appearance or not? To his relief, she did not. Must have been a false alarm. Maybe Brent and Pamela talked it over and decided to stick with basketball and soccer. Or maybe Brent was taken aback at the annual cost of club volleyball dues. As Saul had soberingly found out, Mad-Dogs' fees were a thousand dollars more than PSA's. Oh, the joys that come with membership, Saul sarcastically chuckled inside.

Fred had found a MadDogs coach to talk to and he approached Saul to relay his intel.

"How did it go?" Saul asked.

"Not good, not bad. She's on the bubble for the second team."

"So what are you going to do?"

"I don't know yet. What are you going to do?" Fred shot back.

"I still have to talk with Bree but I'm going to encourage her to come here."

"I think that's the right thing to do," Fred agreed.

After the clinic, Saul and Bree stopped to get ice cream. Ice cream had helped him before when there was a serious topic to discuss. But today there wasn't much to discuss.

"Dad," Bree began, while rapidly licking her cone. "I want to try out at MadDogs."

Saul didn't hesitate to agree with her and just like that, the discussion was over. They then moved on to different lighter topics like what team she would make, who would make her team, would Savannah and Stacy be on it, etc.

That evening, Saul and Veronica enjoyed a relaxing stress-free evening. They celebrated their 8th grade championship in fine fashion with a bottle of wine. They applauded their daughter's maturity in making the right club decision, not knowing for sure how it would all turn out, but at least she took a leap forward from the safety net that was PSA. And with relief, they toasted Pamela and her spectacular future on the soccer field or basketball court.

Tryouts were scheduled for 4 p.m. on Saturday. This was a little bit awkward because PSA's tryouts were scheduled at the same time. Autumn would know something was up once Bree didn't show. Saul felt bad about not telling her but his gut told him he had to keep all options open until the last possible moment. You never knew when some six-foot five-inch girl would walk in the door and take your daughter's spot.

Stacy had wimped out. She decided to go to PSA, which was the sure thing. Fred wasn't happy about it but as he told Saul, he knew there were risks involved if they went to MadDogs and he didn't have enough convincing rationale to sway his daughter in that direction.

Meanwhile, Saul was amazed at the number of girls trying out at MadDogs. There had to be over 200 players there. A knot started building in his stomach just out of habit. This was crazy, he assured himself. He knew his daughter was 99 percent likely to make the second team, which would be a great team, yet he was still on edge. He was thinking about going to the lounge and not even watching, but he knew he couldn't do it. He had to give Bree his positive mental vibrations. Those vibrations became tremors when he saw Mystery Man walk in the door with Pamela.

What the F, he thought.

Brent saw him and waved and then came over after Pamela was registered. "How ya doing?" Brent asked.

"Good. How are you?" Saul asked, trying to look happy to see him.

"Just fine," he smiled. "Glad I got Pamela to finally make a decision."

"And what decision was that?" Saul asked curiously.

"It kills me but she really wants to play volleyball."

Saul's heart sank, killing him, while he tried to look upbeat. "That's great," Saul said. "Good for her."

"The MadDogs owner watched her play last weekend and really saw a lot of potential. Said she would make a team for sure."

"That's fantastic," Saul lied. "Did she say which team she would be on?"

"No. I told her Pamela was just learning and we'd be happy with any team."

"I see."

"What team is Bree going to make?"

"Don't know yet. I'm hoping she'll make the second team at least."

"You kidding me? You're daughter's so good I'm sure she'll make the top team."

"Thanks, but that top team is pretty good. They won Nationals last year."

"They did? I didn't know that. Guess we've come to the right club, huh?"

"I hope so," Saul said.

The tryouts began and Saul had to watch alongside Mystery Man, his new club buddy, and Stan Mason as their daughters battled it out against the other girls in the building. Saul was still upset with Stan for introducing Brent to Frances. How would Stan like it if he invited a new setter into the fold to compete with his daughter, Saul fumed internally. But Saul couldn't dwell on it. He had to focus on Bree right now.

Bree looked strong throughout the tryout. Pamela looked confused and lost, which wasn't unexpected given her rookie status. Saul was still concerned because he couldn't gauge what the club would do with a girl like Pamela, someone with such athleticism and potential, but no skill or clue about how the game was played. She was able to wing it and get away with it on the Wilson Middle School team, but that didn't seem possible here. There was too much competition.

Thirty minutes into the tryout, Saul got an unexpected call on his cell phone. It was Fred the Baptist. "What's it like over there?" Fred asked, whispering again as if he was in spy mode.

"Very crowded. At least 200 girls."

"I just got a call from the MadDogs coach asking me where Stacy is."

"Really? What did you tell her?"

"I told her the truth. We're at PSA. The coach then said Stacy had a spot at MadDogs if we wanted it."

"That's great, Fred. So what are you going to do?"

"The talent sucks here. Hardly anyone from last year's team is here, except Clair of course. William is licking his chops. You can tell Autumn is upset, though. I'm going to try and pull Stacy out and get the heck over there, but I feel like such a Judas."

"Good luck," Saul said.

"This isn't a sin, is it, Saul?"

"Not if you're a Methodist."

"Thanks. You're a big help."

"Get your butt over here," Saul implored.

Sure enough, fifteen minutes later, Fred was in the MadDogs facility with Stacy. He quickly registered her in and Stacy took to the court. Fred walked over to Saul and breathed a big sigh of relief.

"Is there a keg in that lounge or not?"

"I'm afraid not," Saul said. "But I'm glad you made it."

Saul introduced Fred to Brent and, after a brief stare-down, the three middle dads watched intently as the drama continued to unfold. After almost three hours of grueling drills and play, the tryout finally ended and Frances gathered all the girls to the center court. She asked five coaches to go to various spots in the facility. They were the coaches of the five teams to be named.

"Five teams in our age group?" Saul whispered to Fred.

"Ka-ching." Fred said. "They've got the talent and the demand. Enough for two national teams, two regional teams, and one local team."

Frances first called out the top team and to no one's surprise, the team remained virtually unchanged. They were National Champions, after all. While Saul had held out a one percent chance of making the team, he wasn't too discouraged for Bree's sake. And Bree didn't have her sights set on that team. She wanted the second team.

Frances then introduced Coach Nixon, the coach of the second national team. Coach Nixon looked tough and carried a stern look on her face. Saul did not want to get into a rumble with her. As she began to announce the girls' names, Fred the Baptist was deep in prayer.

Saul began to feel a little queasy after the third name was called and Bree had yet to be named. The silence in the building was deafening. Finally, Saul heard the name Bree Bryson and he breathed a sigh of relief. She made it.

Fred, Brent and Stan gave Saul a quick thumbs-up sign, but their ears were still focused on Coach Nixon's voice. And then, after ten names had been called, Fred heard Stacy's name announced and he bent over with relief.

"Praise Jesus," Fred uttered

"Congratulations, Buddy," Saul said.

"Thanks for the intel," Fred joked. "That was a close one."

They then realized that Pam and Savannah's names had yet to be called so they decided to hide their joy, while Brent and Stan were still in their midst. Brent was getting impatient and concerned. Pamela had not made the second team and as the third team coach called names one by one, he still had not heard his daughter's name. Stan was relieved to hear Savannah's name called. She had made the third team again.

As it turned out, Brent wouldn't hear his daughter's name until the fourth team coach announced it. While not too pleased, he shook it off and told Saul, "You gotta start somewhere."

Once all five teams were announced, the other 100 or so girls that were left were invited to a second day of tryouts tomorrow. That tryout was for spots that might open up if any of the girls selected today turned down their offer. Most of the 100 girls quickly scrambled out the door to head to another club's tryout or to talk with their parents about Plan B, Plan C and, God forbid, a Plan D. Many tears were being shed by the unwanted girls and much dread was being shared by parents at the thought of having to go to another tryout.

Bree seemed happy as she met her new 14s teammates. Most of them she knew from the previous clinics. From what Saul could tell, they had some pretty solid talent and had the potential to be a very good team. Then, as Bree's age group was clearing out, Saul noticed a lot of younger girls filing in. They looked so tiny compared to Bree and the other girls.

"Look at those little tykes. Are those twelve-year-olds?" He asked Fred.

"Don't know. Let me check." Fred quickly searched Mad-Dogs' website on his phone. "Believe it or not, those are 11s and younger," Fred said. "It's time for their tryout."

"What?" Saul exclaimed. "I thought 12s was the youngest club age."

"Are you kidding? This is how MadDogs built their empire. On starting them young. That's how they won nationals at 13s this year."

"I didn't realize it or I wasn't paying attention," Saul told him. His thoughts were now on Harper. This was the perfect opportunity for her. If he could get in touch with Veronica, they still had time to make some of the 11s tryout. Panicking, he searched all his pants' pockets to try and find his phone before he realized it was in his coat pocket. He had to call Very before it was too late. She was taking Harper to the movie during Bree's tryout. He called her but she didn't answer. She was a stickler for silencing her phone while in the theater. Darn her good manners, he cursed to himself.

He didn't know which movie they were seeing or which theater they went to. It was a hopeless situation unless she returned his call. Harper didn't have a phone yet, either. She was too young according to the Bryson by-laws of parenting. She hadn't reached the age where volleyball bribes for iPhones were necessary. But Harper was a different animal altogether. She was all in, gung-ho, and ready to play every time a volleyball activity came around.

Saul continued to kick himself for not being aware of the 11s team. Evidently, according to Fred the Baptist, every young girl in North Texas that wants to play volleyball wants to come to MadDogs. Over a span of just a few years, they had built a reputation for being the best at the younger ages. While the other top clubs specialized in the the older ages, MadDogs secured every talented girl that walked in the door before the age of 12.

"It's quite a farm system," Fred told him. "And you know what they call their pre-12 program?"

Saul shrugged. He didn't know.

"The PoutyPups."

Saul laughed. "That's genius."

"Heck, yeah, it's genius. Every little girls wants to be a PoutyPup and their logo and merchandise is so cute it melts girls' hearts, and the hearts of the moms, too."

"What a business!" Saul proclaimed.

At home that evening, Saul was having to hide his disappointment with himself and with Fred for not conveying the 11s information sooner, because Bree was still chatting it up about making her new team and how good it would be. She expressed her disappointment about Savannah not making the team. Savannah made the third team again and wasn't too happy about it, according to Bree. Bree was thrilled to have Stacy on the team and she wasn't surprised at all that Pamela made the fourth team, given her inexperience. Bree still claimed she was terrible. Saul wanted to reprimand her for not being nice, but decided to let Bree gloat in her success for the time being.

Veronica and Harper had yet to come home. He looked at his watch and knew it was too late for any PoutyPup tryout tonight. Bree finally got tired of talking and went up to shower and do some studying. When Veronica did get home, Saul was finally able to vent to someone.

"You forgot to turn your phone back on after the movie," he said annoyingly.

"Oh, you're right. Sorry about that." She looked at her phone. "Whoa, I've got a few messages," she was surprised to see.

"Don't worry about them. I'm sure they're all from me."

"What happened?"

"I'm just upset with myself. I dropped the ball on Harper."

"In what way?"

"MadDogs has a team for 11 year olds and I didn't even know it. Harper could have tried out tonight. I've been so absorbed with Bree I just didn't even think to look for it."

"I thought you told me 12s was the age when clubs started."

246

"I thought it was. I didn't know MadDogs was such a trend-setter with the tykes."

"Isn't there a second tryout tomorrow?"

"Yes, but all the spots will have been taken," Saul said deject-edly.

"You know that for sure?"

"No, but I'm 99 percent sure."

"Take her tomorrow. What do you have to lose?"

"Nothing, I guess. Other than Harper feeling rejected."

The next morning at the breakfast table, Saul told Harper about the second tryout and she was totally on board. Saul cautioned her about his mistake and that she might not make a team but she didn't care. Harper had been laboring in recreational league hell for the last two years, the kind of league where everybody gets a trophy because participation is such a noble effort. It didn't matter whether you were good or not. Even Harper couldn't understand why last place teams got medals.

The rec teams she played on had been terrible, yet still finished first. Harper's skill set was way above the competition. At her age, the service line was moved up to where it was only twelve feet from the net. Most of the girls still couldn't get their serves over. The game was totally decided on who served the best because you could be sure of one thing, the ball wasn't coming back. If a player served a ball that actually cleared the net, the defenders remained frozen and watched the ball slowly drop between them. Then, they would stare at each other with a look of Why Didn't You Get the Ball? If a serve was coming right at a defender, her instinct was to move out of the way and let some-one else take it.

Sometimes there would be a serve that was actually returned, like when one of Harper's hard serves caromed off a girls head and back over to Harper's side for a point. That was rare, but when it did happen, parents cheered wildly because they knew that would be the longest rally of the match.

The games were extremely tedious and unexciting. Harper's ability was kept in check because, to make it fair, a server was only allowed three serves in a row. So Harper, who was the best server on the team, wasn't able to serve out the game with 25 straight serves. This irked Saul and Harper to no end.

When they arrived at MadDogs that day, one thing was certain. The amount of cars in the parking lot on day two of tryouts was significantly less than the day before. Saul walked in and got Harper registered and she hustled over to where she needed to be. The facility was eerily quiet and gave off a most certain vibe that all teams were filled. This didn't stop Harper. The tryouts began and she gave it her all, hustling every chance she got. She was one of only ten girls there but she was clearly the stand out player. The coaches were good with her. They talked to her a lot and bragged on her when she did something great. Harper beamed when she received a compliment and looked over at Saul with a look of Did You See That? Before the tryout ended, Saul was greeted by a familiar face. It was none other than Frances Morgan.

"We didn't know you had a second one waiting in the wings," she began.

"Yes, I do," Saul said proudly.

"She's a little fireball. We really like her."

"That's great to hear," Saul said, feeling a bit encouraged.

"Unfortunately, though, we don't have a spot on the 11s team for her."

"I see," Saul said, trying to mask his disappointment.

"We already have twelve girls on that team and they've been playing here together the last couple of years and we decided to start our 11s program this year with them."

"That's too bad. Harper will be disappointed."

"But," Frances continued, "we do have a program for our younger girls and hope Harper will join in. What we will do is put Harper on a team with girls her age and they will practice and scrimmage each week. They won't be playing any tournaments, but it's a great way to keep them active and let them learn the game."

Saul didn't want to say yes because he was still upset with his stupid mistake, but he knew he couldn't let his emotions get the best of him. The only answer he could possible say was, "Yes." This was MadDogs, for crying out loud. If this was the only way he could get her through the door, it seemed like the right thing to do. So Harper would be a PoutyPup for a year whether she liked it or not. Frances was pleased with his answer and walked over to get him the paperwork.

When the tryout ended, Harper pestered Saul, wanting to know why Frances was talking to him. Saul could sense Harper felt good about her tryout and was dying to hear if she made a Mad-Dogs' squad.

"What happened, Daddy. Did I make a team?"

"Yes," Saul said. He wanted to tell her yes so bad because the look of hope on her face was too much to bare.

"Really?" Harper asked excitedly.

"Well, no, not exactly," Saul had to say.

"What do you mean?" Her sense of excitement had transitioned to worry.

"Well, they really liked you. They think you are a great player and they want to put you on a team with a group of girls your age and you will get to play each other every Friday night."

"So I'm not on the 11s national team?" Harper asked, with a sad look of beleaguered innocence.

"No. I'm sorry, Harper. They filled that team yesterday."

Harper wanted to cry but she didn't. She was pretty good at holding back tears, unlike her big sister who could cry a bucketload with the most minor of meltdowns.

"I knew it. Bree's better than me," she pouted.

"No, she's not, Harper. You guys are in two separate situations. Besides, this is not a competition between the two of you."

"But she got on a national team and I didn't!" Harper frowned.

"Bree made their 14s second team. They don't have a second team for 11s. If they did, I'm sure you would have made it. This new program you're in is sort of like making a second team," Saul said, doing his best to allay her disappointment.

"You think so?"

"I know so," Saul said. "They aren't making offers for this program to everybody."

Saul didn't know that. In fact, he was quite sure MadDogs was offering it to anybody that was willing to pay the $700 fee. But his daughter's confidence was wavering. If it took a lie to perk it back up, he could live with that.

Harper felt better after the conversation and she felt even happier when he stopped on the way home to get ice cream. She would position her status to her sister as like being on a second team even though it was not a second team. Saul begged Bree ahead of time not to challenge Harper on this. He wanted to maintain sanity in the household.

The Bryson home now consisted of two MadDoggers, which meant the merchandise budget would be increased. Veronica didn't hesitate to pick out a few things the first time she was in the MadDogs' gym. She fawned over the adorable items as much as the girls did.

The season with MadDogs ended up being a huge success for both girls. By being in the PoutyPup program, Harper got noticed. The MadDogs coaches could see her talent on display and Harper liked the attention. Saul felt this would bode well for her next year in making the top team. With Bree, she earned the starting middle spot early on in the season over Stacy. This took some getting used to for Fred. He and Saul never really talked about the competition between the two daughters, but Saul could tell it bothered Fred a bit. On the other hand, Fred was very glad to be on the team.

Ultimately, both dads were very happy because there was no third middle on the team. That meant their daughters played almost every game of every match. Occasionally the coach would put in a right side hitter to play middle just so she had some experience in case Bree or Stacy got injured, but that was the only time.

During the first few practices of the season, Saul and Fred watched in enjoyment at the talent level of the team. They had outside hitters that could actually put the ball away, i.e. terminate points with force. Their defensive players were strong. The only question mark was the setter. She was a tall setter who had good hands, which was probably her best feature and what drew her to the club. But she was in the middle of transitioning from a different position. The club wanted to use her to run a 5-1 offense, which meant she would be the only setter on the court. She would not be rotated out for another setter, which is what happens in a more traditional offense called a 6-2.

During the first tournament of the season, the fathers got to finally watch the team on display. The girls were a little rusty at first and made a lot of mistakes, but managed to make it out of pool play unscathed. This was the first tournament Saul experienced where Bree's team actually won the pool on day one. Last year, PSA was always fighting for second place. This year, it was always an easy trip to the gold bracket on Sunday. Such are the pleasures of being on a better team.

In fact, such pleasures also included making it to a quarterfinal match, finally. For the first time, a club team Bree was on would finish in the top 8. The monotonous tied for ninth finish was now in their rearview mirror. Where Bree's team would meet their match though, was in the quarterfinals. It was very tough to make it to the semi-finals because that's where the top teams of MadDogs, SkyHigh and Advantage resided. So Bree's team would have to battle it out with them or another top team from a highly-regarded club in the quarterfinals.

For Saul, this meant witnessing first hand the best the North Texas Region had to offer. This also meant Bree got to play against the best as well. Their first tournament ended with a loss to Advantage in the quarterfinals. Bree's team put up a fight in the first game but lost the second game by a large margin. It was obvious that the new setter was in over her head during these bigger matches and the opponent took advantage of her rookie mistakes. MadDogs 14 Red, the official name of Bree's team, finished tied for fifth.

As the season progressed, it was beginning to feel a bit like déjà vu. MadDogs Red kept on finishing tied for 5th, just like PSA the year before kept finishing tied for 9th. You were ultimately defined by the talent you had, Saul conceded. There was no question that Bree was on a better team now. But their limit seemed to be capped at fifth place. They didn't quite have the oomph to make it to the final four of a tournament. Some of that was due, in Saul's mind, to the inexperienced setter. At times, she looked great and at times she looked goofy, tripping over her feet or letting a set drop between her two hands, which was the ultimate humiliation for a setter. As a parent and as a fan, you held your breath on every set because you didn't know what to expect. Saul could only imagine how the hitters felt. His nickname for her was Double Trouble, because she had a knack for getting doubles called against her by the referees. A double is when you contact the ball twice when trying to set it.

He often wondered why they didn't put Savannah on the team. Yes, she was smaller, but she was experienced and could run a good offense. The club obviously made a business decision that it was worth investing the time and effort in grooming Double Trouble for future greatness.

Bree and Double Trouble did start to generate some chemistry as she gained more confidence setting the middle. Saul would still get annoyed with Bree because she didn't kill the ball. She would score and get kills on the stat sheet, but they weren't KILLS, meaning terminating the ball with force in Saul's vocabulary. Bree was an expert at the tip to the open zone and she was effective at hitting the ball down to an open zone, but she would hit the ball timidly, safely, and definitely not up to the standards of Saul's Master Athletic Plan.

Saul knew she could do it, though. He had seen her unlock her killer instinct before. On Bryson Court, she did it all the time. Saul would put the ball in front of her face and say, "Pretend this is Harper's head, the little sister that gets on your nerves so many times during the course of a day. This is your chance to wham that head into submission."

Bree would laugh and so would Harper, but it did get his point across. She would proceed to hit the ball as hard as she could and it was awesome to watch. But for some reason during actual games and even during practice, she would hold back. Her coaches noticed it, too, and would push her to snap her wrist and swing her arm with authority.

Saul told her that all she had to do was survey the other side of the net to see what the defense was doing. If they were double-blocking you, a tip might be the right play. But if they were merely single-blocking you, you had to pick an angle to go for and just swing away.

Now at the age of 14, most of what Saul would tell her would go in one ear and out the other. Some of that was due to the fact she was a teenager and teenagers are genetically engineered to tune out their parents. The other fact was that she was now a two-year club veteran and, in her mind, she knew more about the game than her father did. This new know-it-all attitude was annoying to Saul. He admitted that she probably knew more about the game. Saul still didn't understand the rotation sequence and when players subbed in and subbed out, for example. He only knew when his daughter subbed in and subbed out. Bree would get frustrated with him at times when she tried to explain some of the rules.

But what Saul did know was sports. This is what she didn't understand. He could tell when Bree made poor decisions in the flow of the game or when she hit safely when she should have hit aggressively. When they would have their game recaps in the car, he would carefully try to critique her performance but she became increasingly defensive. He was always wrong. She knew what she was doing and he didn't.

As the season played on, he continued to try and find ways to motivate her to hit hard. He prepared a mix tape to play in the car on the way to tournaments to get her pumped up. He was so tired of her morning grumpiness, he was willing to try anything.

He thought playing some of his and her favorite tunes would get her going, and would at least make her stop yawning during the first points of the first match of the day. Didn't work. Nothing worked until the final couple of tournaments of the season. And it wasn't even Saul's doing.

While the season had been a success for Bree because she held down the starting middle spot, received tons of playing time and was considered one of the better players, the team couldn't be considered a success because it never seemed to reach its potential. To Saul and Fred, it was clearly due to the setter's inability to run the offense on a consistent basis. A lot of talent was going unused because Double Trouble couldn't get the hitters involved. Her sets were never where they were supposed to be. The team played in three qualifiers that year and hopes were high that they were good enough to get a bid to Nationals, but it didn't happen. Too many errors at the wrong time. They had two tournaments left in their regular season, one was a meaningless local tournament and the other was Regionals, their last chance to qualify for Nationals.

Saul and Fred would be in their huddle commiserating during practice about their team's problems. Sometimes they would be joined by Brent, who was bored to tears by Pamela's team. At times, they enjoyed having Brent join the group because he would tell hilarious tales about how bad Pamela's team was. Brent would talk about how his daughter never got set and how the passing was so bad a shank was considered a moral victory. Saul and Fred enjoyed the comic relief.

Brent would continue to complain about how they could never run their offense and Pamela wasn't getting a chance to get better because she never got any opportunities. He thought he wasn't getting what he paid for. Saul and Fred had less sympathy for him because they had both been there. It was about paying your dues, both monetarily and mentally, in the business of club volleyball.

Brent didn't have to pay his dues for long. Soon after that discussion, Saul and Fred strutted into the MadDogs gym one day and were shocked to see Pamela getting private lessons, and not with just anyone. She was having lessons with none other than Frances Morgan. This was unheard of.

The MadDogs owner did not give lessons to just anyone. Her time was too valuable. She gave lessons to only those she deemed worthy, like Tina Dulles, her college-bound all-star. Saul and Fred became a little jealous of Pamela's new tutoring. Brent's complaining must have gotten some real results. Saul tried to contact Frances for some lessons for Bree and she never returned his phone calls. Fred did the same but also didn't get a response. They then knew their daughters were not Frances-worthy. While that didn't sit well with them, a few weeks later something occurred that would rattle their cages for the rest of the season. Pamela showed up at one of their practices.

"What the heck is going on?" Fred asked Saul.

"I haven't a clue," Saul responded.

He looked around for Brent, but he was missing in action. Comic relief or not, the Mystery Man label still applied.

At the end of practice, the coaches told the players they had a new player. The team didn't have a third middle and it was beneficial to have one in case somebody got hurt. They talked to them about Pamela being new to volleyball and that the experience of practicing and playing with this team would help her and would also help the team.

"How can they do that?" Bree asked Saul in the car ride home.

"It's their business, Bree. They can do whatever they want. They have an unhappy client and they are trying to make him happy."

"But I'm not happy. Are you?"

"No, I'm not happy with it, but it's their club. They can do what they want."

"But isn't it against the rules?" Bree asked.

"No. It's not against the rules. You can change teams within your own club."

"But she's not that good," Bree exclaimed.

Saul wanted to say "Yes, she was and she was going to be better than you if you don't start hitting the ball harder," but he didn't. Instead, he said, "Evidently, the club sees some potential in her and they want to give her a chance to play with better players."

Saul was at least happy about the passion Bree was showing. It was good to see her blood boiling. He wished he could see this much passion in the mornings on tournament days. As much as Bree's blood was boiling, it couldn't match the venom that was running through Fred's veins. Fred had to call Saul every night to vent for at least an hour. This interrupted Saul's own venting time with Veronica on the patio. So after an hour on the phone listening to Fred, Saul would have to spend the next hour venting with Veronica about what Fred had said and then add what he had to say. They vented every night up until the next tournament, which was a meaningless local tournament. Since it was meaningless, Saul and Fred figured Pamela would get plenty of playing time.

On the morning of the tournament, Bree was actually a little perkier in the car ride to the tournament. "Dad, would you put on the mix tape?" She eagerly asked.

"I sure will," Saul said, thinking her request a bit strange.

Thrilled with his daughter's positive morning demeanor, Saul happily inserted the CD. Songs that ran the gamut from The Black Eyed Peas (Bree's choice) to Bruce Springsteen (Saul's choice) to Taylor Swift (Bree's choice) to Pat Benatar (Saul's choice) to Miley Cyrus (Bree's choice) to Cheap Trick (Saul's choice) played in the car. Saul began dancing in his seat as best he could but the seat belt restricted some of his better moves. He wanted the girls to feel the pounding 80s power pop urgency and thrill of Benatar's "All Fired Up" or Cheap Trick's "Tonight It's You" or INXS' "New Sensation". These were the songs he had turned to in his youth to get him seriously ready for action. Bree and Harper had a hard time making the connection. They were more charged up by the Peas' "I Got a Feeling" or Cyrus' "Party in the USA." Saul didn't really care who the artist was as long as Bree was awake and ready to play.

Saul later realized that Bree's newfound morning spunk had nothing to do with the music they were playing. She was fired up because there was a new middle in town. Bree seemed to be dead set on proving herself capable of holding down the top middle spot. She played with a sense of urgency that weekend. She actually had a couple of good power kills that impressed Saul.

As expected, the coach worked Pamela in a lot during the first day. It was pool play and there wasn't any concern about losing to the opponents that were in their pool. The three middles shared the time equally even though two of the middle dads were still displeased. Fred was especially. He would tell Saul maybe the reason they brought Pamela up was because they were not happy with Stacy's play. Saul tried to ease those fears but he didn't seem to calm Fred's concerns. Brent again didn't show his face that day, which Saul thought was strange. Maybe he was too uncomfortable to face the rest of the parents. Pamela did fine when she was in. She was still like a fish out of water at times but she could rely on her athletic ability to make up for most of her lack of experience.

Sunday, Gold Bracket Day, came around and MadDogs Red were in their usual position. They had made it to the quarterfinals, but this time they had a more favorable draw. They didn't have to play one of the Big Three, Advantage, SkyHi or MadDogs' top team, to advance to the semi-final. Bree's team played a club called Tejas that was one of the newer clubs on the rise in the area.

Double Trouble stepped up in the Tejas match and probably played her best two games of the season. Bree stepped up as well and contributed six kills in game one and four kills in game two, which were pretty solid stats for a middle blocker. MadDogs Red won the game 25 to 22 and 25 to 21. Saul was encourage by the win, not just because they made the semi-finals for the first time that season, but because hopefully they were gelling at the right time. Regionals was next weekend, their last chance to make Nationals, the Holy Grail of Junior Volleyball.

The reward for beating Tejas was a match with SkyHi. SkyHi was one of the top two teams in the area. They vied with Advantage for the top ranking in their age group for most of the season. Saul was excited to see what Bree's team could do against them. The match started well. MadDogs Red continued their momentum from the previous match and jumped out to a 9 to 3 lead. Bree sparked them with a couple of kills and a couple of blocks. SkyHi never panicked, though. They methodically worked their way back into it and soon tied the game at 15. To Fred's disappointment, Stacy was not having a good game. She missed a couple of easy kill opportunities and seemed to be out of sorts. When she rotated off the court, Saul could see the coach telling Pamela to get ready.

"Crap," Fred said under his breath.

Saul didn't say anything. Anything he said might just make it worse. Plus, he was too wrapped up in his own daughter who was actually having a great game. Bree was on fire and she continued to pound the ball consistently. This was the first time she showed this much aggressiveness with her hitting. Saul watched as Bree's coach smiled with excitement over Bree's play. SkyHi didn't have a middle blocker that could stop her.

Equal credit also had to go to Double Trouble who was running the offense with great efficiency while at the same time, not getting called for any doubles. When Bree rotated out, they were still tied at 21 all. Saul painfully watched as Stacy was then subbed out for Pamela. He could only imagine what fury was running through Fred's body. With Bree out of the game now, the team lost their momentum. A couple of loose passes by their back row cost them two points and SkyHi took advantage of it. SkyHi ended up winning the game 25 to 22.

Game two started and SkyHi took an early lead. Bree continued to connect for scores that were beautiful kills. Her killer instinct had finally come out of its shell. Saul could feel the testosterone surge in his body every time she slammed one down. It was a great feeling. He could only imagine what it felt like for a player. When Bree subbed out, they were only down by two points. It seemed like they were down more if you looked at Fred's face. Saul tried not look at him, but couldn't help it when he saw again that Pamela was coming in for Stacy. They could be down 20 or up 20 but it wouldn't matter to Fred right now. His face clearly showed the anger and disappointment of the coach's decision.

When Pamela was in, she had a couple of good blocks to help the team stay close, but that's all MadDogs could do was stay close. SkyHi was now playing great, mistake free volleyball. Saul was impressed with how they maintained their composure and adjusted to the game as it went on. Bree subbed back into the game with MadDogs trailing 17 to 13. Since she was hot, the team was gearing their offense around her. She quickly got a set and went up for another smash when suddenly, the ball came right back at her. The SkyHi middle blocked her for the first time. A couple of points later, Bree got another set to hit but again she was blocked and the ball fell back on her side of the net for a SkyHi point.

"They're triple blocking her," Fred said.

Saul was surprised Fred was saying anything. "What are they doing?" Saul asked.

"They are pulling the outside pin hitters in to help the middle blocker block Bree."

Saul finally understood what he was saying as he watched how SkyHi maneuvered the block at the net. They had basically shut down Bree with the adjustment. That took the wind out of the sails of Bree's team. SkyHi ran off the last few points of the game to win game two easily 25 to 15.

Saul didn't let the loss bother him, though. He felt like they had won the tournament. MadDogs Red finished tied for third. They broke the fifth place barrier. And Bree had her best day ever as a player.

"Your daughter played great," said a familiar voice from behind him. It was Brent, who had magically reappeared.

"Thanks, Brent. She did have a good day. And welcome to the team, by the way," Saul said awkwardly.

"Thanks. Pamela is excited to be on it. She's glad to be around girls that actually know how to play the game. I was totally surprised when Frances suggested the move. I hope the parents aren't too upset, though."

Saul didn't know exactly what to say so he decided the truth was best. "I don't think there is much concern amongst the parents right now, except for maybe one."

"I understand," Brent said. "I'm feeling pretty awkward myself."

After their brief conversation, Saul looked around for Fred but couldn't see him. He must have exited very quickly. Saul would have to call him at some point, but he figured he better let the venom wear off.

The car ride home for the Bryson's was like a house party. Saul had the music back on, the windows down, and the beat blasting through the air. Saul was already thinking about Regionals next week, which meant another play of Benatar's "All Fired Up" was in order. He even got the girls to sing along. After the song was over, he turned down the volume to make an important statement.

"Girls."

"Yes, Dad." They giggled

"Are you listening to me?"

"Yes, Dad." They giggled again.

"There are good days and bad days in volleyball. Did you know that?"

They looked at each other and shrugged. "I guess so." Bree said.

"And today was a very good day," Saul proclaimed. "Bree, today you went from being a good volleyball player to a great volleyball player."

"Thanks, Dad," Bree beamed.

Harper was looking at her enviously and patted her on the head. "You did great, Sis," she said.

"Thanks, Harp." The two hugged each other as only sisters can.

That evening, Saul and Veronica shared a bottle of wine and toasted the day's success. Bree played her best tournament ever and her team finished in third place, allowing Bree to receive her first ever club volleyball medal. But more importantly, the winning was happening. Their labor was starting to bear fruit. It was becoming more of a regular occurrence.

After one glass, their celebration was suddenly interrupted by a phone call. It was Fred the Baptist. Saul decided to put Fred on speaker because he was too tired to hold the phone to his ear. Veronica sat quietly and listened to Fred's fire and brimstone rant. Like the most long-winded of pastors, Fred's rant lasted an incredibly long time. He railed on the coach. He railed on Pamela. He railed on Brent. He railed on Frances Morgan. He railed on wanting his money back. He didn't pay for the team in its current configuration. He paid for his daughter to be the second middle, not the third middle. He talked about pulling Stacy from the team.

Saul and Veronica listened and didn't say much. They didn't have to. Saul would sit there and agree with him to make him feel better. He did say pulling Stacy from the team was an irrational move right now with only one tournament left. When Fred was done and had cooled down, Saul told him he would call him tomorrow.

"I do feel sorry for him and Stacy," Saul told Veronica. "They're getting screwed."

"I do, too. But what can you do?" Veronica asked.

"Nothing. The club is doing what it thinks is best for the club. It's about making sure your clients are happy but it's also about winning. Winning is key to their business success. They obviously see Pamela as someone that can help them in the future."

"But they sacrificed one client's happiness for another's," Veronica said, trying to make sense of it all.

"I guess they thought it was a risk worth taking."

Saul then poured another glass for him and Veronica and started thinking about what he just said and how business, even in the world of club volleyball, could be cutthroat at times. He wondered what he would do if his daughter's happiness was ever sacrificed at the expense of another's. That kind of incident had never been factored into his MAP. His daughter would always be too good to have that happen to her.

Trying to pull him out of his deep thought, Veronica raised her glass and said, "Here's to our great day."

"Very, you have such perfect timing." He raised his glass to hers and quickly derided himself for having such bad thoughts on such a good day. A very good day, in fact. He proceeded to take another sip of wine and opted to put the business of club volleyball out of his mind, instead focusing on the wonderful game itself. And how good Bree had become at it.

BREE'S DIARY
April 14
So fun to show off my new medal to my friends. Shared a pic wth Callie but she hasn't responded. I wish we chatted more. Feel so bad for Stacy. I like Pamela and all but I like Stacy, too. Pamela's starting to bug me, tho. She's been acting strange ever since she joined the team. Maybe it's awk for her. Sometimes she says crazy things like she wants to make MadDogs top team next year. Good luck with that. Bobby's not sitting by me at lunch anymore. He is spending time with a cheerleader who is a total slut. I am so done with him.

CHAPTER TWELVE

NICKED

Saul had hoped that MadDogs Red were gelling at the right time for Regionals. Double Trouble had just had her best tournament of the year and so did Bree. Unlike last year with PSA, this MadDogs team seemed to have the talent to get it done. The task was made even easier because Advantage, SkyHi and MadDogs' top teams had all received Open bids at the qualifiers they attended. That meant they wouldn't be at Regionals where there were four bids at stake, two National and two American. The National bids were considered more prestigious but Saul didn't care. He just wanted a bid, any bid that would take him to Nationals so he could experience it just once.

Bree's team didn't come through for him. They laid an egg on Gold Bracket Day. All they had to do was win two matches to make it to the final four and ensure a bid. They won the first match but lost the second in agonizing fashion. Everything was going the way it was supposed to in the second match. They won the first game 25 to 20. They were playing a team they had beaten twice already that year. But in the second game, Double Trouble started playing like she did earlier in the season. The set would be too high or too low or she would double the ball with her hands (i.e. the reason for her nickname), which was illegal and would cost the team a point. No one had a clue where her sets were going. Her nerves had obviously gotten the best of her. They lost game two 25 to 15.

Pamela played in that game instead of Stacy. The coach switched them in and out of every game that weekend. Saul guessed an attempt was being made to keep both dads happy. Thankfully, Bree started all the games and was never taken out.

MadDogs still had a chance to pull it out in game three but the setting woes continued. It was sad to see, especially when there was a bid on the line. They lost game three in embarrassing fashion by only scoring six points. Nationals was not meant to be. Their season was over.

After the match, one of the parents from the team, a mother of one of the outside hitters, came up to talk with Saul. He thought it strange at first because he had barely talked to her all season.

"Bree played great this year," she said.

Saul was flattered. "Thank you," he said proudly.

"And she's gotten so tall," she exclaimed.

"Yeah, she's still growing. Hopefully, she won't stop for a while."

"Is she cycling?"

Saul thought the question kind of strange but answered it anyway. "Uh, yes. She's been riding a bike since she was four."

"No, no, no, silly. I mean has her period started?"

Saul was speechless. He couldn't believe a woman he barely knew was asking such a delicate question. "I d-don't know," he stammered. "I don't think so, but I haven't been copied off on that one."

"Well, hopefully she hasn't started for your sake. You know what they say, after you start, you only have two years of growing left."

"I didn't know that," Saul said. "But thank you. That's good to know." The mom wished him a happy summer and walked away.

What was she saying? Saul wondered. He had never heard of this before. He immediately began searching for Veronica. If true, he needed to know if Bree was menstruating and, if so, when it started so he could calculate when her height would stall out. He couldn't find Veronica but found a nervous Fred instead..

"What did you think of the weekend?" he asked. "Who played better? Pam or Stacy?"

"Stacy," he confirmed. Although truthfully, he thought they played about the same.

"Good," Fred said. "I thought so too, but I'm the dad, you know."

"I know," Saul said, still searching for Veronica. He didn't have time for Fred right now.

He also needed to confirm if Harper had started cycling. She was only eleven, but he had no idea what the normal age was. Harper was growing faster than Bree so did that mean her period started earlier? He finally found Veronica but she was with a group of other volleyball moms. His questions would have to wait.

In the car ride home following the disappointing loss at Regionals, the music wasn't playing and everyone was a bit down after the unsettling defeat. Harper felt the need to interject something up-lifting.

"Dad," she began.

"Yes, Harp."

"There are good days and bad days in club volleyball. And today was a bad day."

"Thank you for clarifying, Harp," Saul said.

"I'm so mad at my team," Bree cried out, after holding it all in for a while.

"Don't be mad," Veronica said. "You guys just had an off day."

And what an off day it was, Saul thought. Maybe they were all menstruating simultaneously and that's what contributed to their poor play. He had never looked at these 14 year olds as women before, but that's what they were becoming. All Saul could think of right now was that he needed some alone time with Veronica STAT.

"I have never heard of that before," Veronica stated firmly, while sitting in the peaceful confines of the Conference Room for Private Family Discussions.

Saul had forced Veronica into the backyard as soon as they got home. "Are you sure?" Saul asked.

"Yes. It's got to be an old wives' tale."

"Well, just in case it is true, has Bree started her cycle?"

"Yes," Veronica answered.

"And you never thought to tell me this?"

"You never asked. I figured you didn't want to know about such private female matters. It's her body anyway. She probably would be upset with me for talking to you about it."

"So when did she start?" Saul asked.

"Six months ago."

Saul did the quick math. Maybe a year-and-a-half left if the wives' tale was true.

"Has Harper started?"

"No. She's barely 11 for goodness sake."

"Well, I don't know these things," Saul said defensively.

"May I go tend to the dinner now?" An annoyed Veronica asked.

"Yes. Please do. Thanks for the information," Saul said. He didn't know why she was being so short with him. He was just trying to get the data necessary to make an easy, but important calculation. Height was an important factor for volleyball, especially for college coaches.

The end of club season meant the end of school was near. Bree would soon complete the 8th grade, which meant she would be a freshman in high school next year. Saul couldn't believe how fast she was growing up. That meant she would be trying out for one of three teams: Freshman, Junior Varsity or, if he wanted to really dream big, Varsity. He had to get Bree in the gym a lot this summer to maintain her focus and her game.

Saul had planned a two-week vacation to the Grand Canyon so that would take away some of the available practice time. To his surprise, Bree didn't want to visit Callie this year. Maybe the distance was finally catching up with them. Or maybe Bree felt like spending more of her time with her school friends. Bree didn't talk about it much. As long as she wasn't spending time with Robby or Bobby, he was okay with things. Bree not going to Seattle meant a couple of extra weeks of workout time, which was good because the summer workout window was already cut short because high school volleyball started the first week of August, a few weeks before school even began.

Bree's MadDogs coach had suggested she play beach volleyball over the summer. Bree was told beach would increase her mobility and force her body into working muscles she didn't normally work. She was up for it once she got Stacy to agree to join her. There was only one problem with playing beach volleyball in Plano, Texas. There was no beach. There was also no cool breeze coming off the ocean to soothe you from the heat. There was no body of water to quickly soak in and clean the sand from your body. The correct name of the sport, if you played it in Texas, was called Sand Volleyball. And Sand Volleyball was not fun. At least it wasn't fun to Bree, Stacy, Saul and Fred.

The girls had to play in heat exceeding the century mark most days. There was no shade. And every thirty minutes, they had to delay play so they could spray water on the sand because it got so hot it burnt the girls' feet. Saul and Fred got dry-mouth while watching their games. The sweat was unstoppable. The girls complained about getting sand in their private parts when they would have to dive for a ball and with no pool around to rinse off, that pretty much put an end to the sand volleyball experiment.

As the summer neared its end, Saul began trying to research Bree's competition for the upcoming school tryouts. There was much more competition in high school ball than in middle school ball. There were several middle schools feeding into Bree's high school so Saul had to try and remember who the players were on those teams and if they posed a threat to Bree. He also went on the Plano High School volleyball website to look at the rosters of the Varsity and Junior Varsity. He noted that the Varsity team did not have many seniors last year. That meant a lot of returning players, which hurt Bree's odds of making Varsity as a Freshman. The Junior Varsity had six juniors on its team from last year. That meant six spots that needed to be filled either by members of the Freshman team last year or by incoming Freshman like Bree. Making the Junior Varsity squad seemed like a reasonable goal to set for Bree. It also seemed to fit well within the code of his Master Athletic Plan, the one where his daughter was expected to overachieve at all times.

Leading up to tryouts, Saul took Bree to MadDogs for a few lessons. He was sometimes discouraged to see Pamela there getting lessons with Frances. He could tell Pamela was getting better. He just couldn't tell by how much because she wasn't playing in a game. She was doing a lot of hitting drills and he could tell Frances was unlocking her power and quickness. Pamela was also getting more consistent in making solid contact with the ball.

Saul wanted desperately to meet the high school coach and make sure she knew about Bree's resume. It compared more favorably to the other middles she would be competing against. He wanted to tell her about how Bree was on the MadDog second team and Pamela was on the fourth team. He would, of course, omit any mention of Pamela being elevated to the second team during the season. He wanted to expound upon Bree's excellent hitting percentage, her smart play and her ability to keep errors to a minimum. In the end though, he chickened out. He didn't think it would be appropriate to stick his nose in the coach's business.

But how would the coach really see Bree's potential in just a three-day tryout? The coach never came around to club games to see how good or bad these girls really were. And she never came to watch any of the middle school games, either. Saul finally decided to send a corny email that introduced the coach to Bree and mentioned how successful she had been on her club team and middle school team and how excited she was to be trying out. Saul never told Bree he did this.

After he punched SEND, Saul then started to worry that since tryouts occurred three weeks before school even started that the coach might not even be checking her email. What was he to do? He could only cross his fingers and hope that she got the email in time.

Tryout day one came. Bree's goal of making the JV had been established between her and Saul the night before. As she ate her cereal that morning, there was tension between each loud munch she made. Saul drove her to the tryout before he went to work. For three days, the kids had to endure two three-hour practices a day with an hour break for lunch.

Saul didn't get much work done at the office. He would check with Veronica to see if she heard anything and she would say no. Saul left work early that day to pick Bree up. He told his secretary he had a dental appointment. When he arrived at the high school, the parking lot was flooded with moms waiting for their volleyball girls. Saul again seemed to be the only dad in the lot until he noticed Mystery Man from far away exiting the gym door.

Was he in the gym watching? Saul wondered. If he was, he wanted to call foul on him and tell the coach this was a violation of volleyball interscholastic rules and that Pam should be disqualified from competing for a spot on the team. He would console Brent and tell him it's okay, not to worry. Pamela could always go back to soccer or basketball. Saul then noticed Brent was waving hello to him from afar and Saul was forced to somewhat awkwardly wave back.

The gym doors opened and the girls came pouring out. Saul was amazed at the size of some of the girls. They must have been the varsity athletes, he told himself. He had a hard time imagining that Bree might be that big in a few years. Bree came walking out with Savannah by her side and the two exchanged their good-byes before getting into their cars.

"How did it go, Champ?" Saul asked.

Bree let out a heavy moan as she loaded her backpack into the car. "I'm exhausted."

"Was it that hard?"

"Yes. We did a ton of conditioning and drills."

"Well, how did you do?"

"Good. But we didn't do much hitting or anything today."

"How did the other middles do?"

"Fine. I guess. Pamela has gotten better."

Uh-oh, Saul thought. She noticed. "In what way?" Saul asked.

"I don't know. I can just tell. She knows the game more. But we didn't play any games today so I can't really tell."

"Any other middles that are good?"

"I don't think so."

Saul was at least encouraged to hear that. "Did you hit the ball hard today?" The last words Saul had told her before dropping her off were "Be aggressive."

"I didn't really get a chance to. Like I said, we didn't do much hitting today."

"Okay," Saul said. "Just be sure and stay aggressive."

"I think I'm on the JV court though."

"That's good. How do you know?"

"I can just tell. Most of the freshman players are on another court."

Maybe the coach read his email, after all, Saul hoped. "Are there any other freshman on the JV court?"

"Savannah and Pamela."

This was not what Saul wanted to hear, at least the Pamela part. "How many middles are left from the JV team last year?"

"Two."

Drats, That meant only one freshman middle will probably make it.

Day two of tryouts came and Saul got to the parking lot a little bit earlier. No dentist appointment today. He had a client meeting instead which just happened to be in the Plano vicinity. Bree was one of the first girls out the door and she seemed perky. She didn't seem exhausted like the day before.

"Guess what, Dad," she said excitedly.

"What?"

"I'm still on the JV court!"

"That's great," Saul said.

"They moved me back to the freshman court earlier in the day, but then moved me back to the JV court an hour later. They let a lot of freshman go back to the freshman gym today, too."

"So they are out of the picture for JV?"

"Yes. And one of the varsity girls told me it's always a good sign to be on the JV court at the end of day two. That usually means you've made it," Bree said with nervous excitement.

Saul was excited, too. "That's great, Bree. Just keep working hard and don't assume anything, okay?"

She nodded in agreement.

"So how many freshman are left on the JV court?" Saul asked.

"I think four. There's me, Pamela, Savannah and a defensive player who played on MadDogs championship team last year."

All Saul heard was Pamela. The battle was going to go the distance, all the way to tryout day three. Would they take two freshman middles? He didn't want to ask Bree because he didn't want her to worry. She seemed pretty fired up right now and confident that things were going her way.

Tryout day three arrived and Saul decided not to push the outside office appointments to a third straight day. He planned to take a half-day of vacation and leave the office at noon so he could celebrate what he hoped would be good news. At 11:45 a.m., his boss, Anderson, the Chief Financial Officer, walked into his office and proceeded to ruin his day. He asked him what he was doing for lunch. This was the first time the CFO had ever asked him to lunch so Saul couldn't tell him no. Apparently, there was urgent business to discuss. The CFO had made reservations at The Capital Grille, a high-end steak restaurant in downtown Dallas.

Steak restaurants at lunch time can take forever. Bree's try-outs ended at 3 p.m. and he was desperate to know if she made the JV. He had to text Veronica to be on-call to pick Bree up since he had been detained at work.

The lunch took about as long as it could take. Anderson had to talk business for the first thirty minutes before they even looked at a menu. Anderson then ordered an appetizer course, along with a salad course, along with a steak entrée course. Internally, Saul was hot under the collar because the big business that needed to be discussed was not that important. He deduced the CFO just wanted a fancy free meal that day and was using him for the expense account. On any other day, Saul would have been fine with enjoying a deliciously expensive meal, but not today.

They left the restaurant at 2:30 p.m. and Saul sent the SOS text to Veronica, that she would need to pick up Bree. When they got back to the office, Anderson informed him he needed to come up to the C-Suite so he could hand off a few files. Finally, at 3:15 p.m. Saul got back to his office. He was extremely worried because he had not received a call or a text from Bree or Veronica with any news.

Not a good sign. Maybe the practice was running long. He debated getting in his car or just staying the rest of the day since his half-day of vacation had already been wasted. He decided to sit it out and wait. He closed his office door so he could nervously pace while looking out at the Dallas skyline. The call finally came. The caller ID said Veronica. Knowing it was Veronica and not Bree meant it had to be bad news. Saul answered hello.

"She didn't make it," Veronica said.

Saul could feel the invisible blow to his gut.

"She's crying her eyes out and worried that she's disappointed you. I can't get her to the phone."

"I'm coming home," Saul said. He departed his office without any hint to his secretary of what he was doing. He was more or less in a trance the whole drive home. This was not a chapter he had foreseen in his MAP.

He kicked himself for not visiting the coach in person before tryouts. She apparently didn't read his email or if she did, she didn't give it much consideration. Saul was trying to figure out what he could do or say to make Bree feel better. He wanted to keep things positive and get her back on track. He wanted to make sure she knew that wasting away on the meaningless freshman team for one season was not a career de-railer. He wanted her to know she was still a special player, although there was nothing really special about a freshman making the fresh-man team. Stop it, Saul, he told himself. Think positive thoughts.

The first thing Saul did when he got home was give her a hug. He held her for a few minutes because he couldn't say any-thing until her sobbing stopped. Her tear ducts were set for flash flooding. When her sobs turned to mere droplets, he finally as-sured her that everything was okay.

"I'm terrible," she cried.

"No, you're not," he assured her.

"I'm so embarrassed," she cried some more.

"There's nothing to be embarrassed about."

"I'm sorry I didn't make it, Dad," she sniffed pathetically.

"There is nothing to apologize about."

Finally, the tears and the sniffles subsided and all that was left was a puffy, bloated face with bloodshot eyes and red cheeks. "So tell me what happened," Saul began. "Who made the team?"

"Savannah and Pamela. And I'm better than both of them," she moaned.

"The star defensive player from MadDogs didn't make it?"

"No. And she was really mad, too. I think her parents are going to complain to the principal or sue the school or something."

Saul had to chuckle a bit. "Well, if she didn't make it, Bree, you shouldn't feel that bad, either. They just didn't need a defensive player. They must already have enough."

"But what about Savannah? She was on that crummy third team and still made it."

"It sounds like they needed a setter. Do you set?"

"No."

"So you can't be too alarmed by that, can you?"

"I guess not."

"So Pamela beat you out. They only needed one freshman middle, correct?

Bree nodded. "But I'm better than this other sophomore middle that made it."

"Maybe you are, Bree, but she's a sophomore. Maybe the coach is favoring seniority a bit. Let's talk about the girl that's your age. Why do you think Pamela beat you out?"

"I don't know. She's gotten better."

"How so?"

"She hits the ball really hard."

"Were you hitting the ball hard?"

Bree hesitated to answer.

"Were you being aggressive?" Saul asked again.

"I guess I could have been more aggressive at times, but I wasn't put with the best setter."

"Let's not worry about the setter. Let's focus on you."

"Alright, I could have been more aggressive," Bree confessed. "I still scored a lot, though."

"I'm sure you did."

"And I'm a better all-around player," she emphasized again.

"I think you are, too, but let's not dwell on what we can't change. Let's use this as a teachable moment."

"What does that mean?" Bree asked confused.

"Let's focus on what you can change, okay?"

Bree nodded yes but still didn't know what he was talking about.

"As you're getting older, the game is getting faster and more powerful. The ability to terminate points quickly will become even more imperative. Let's use this freshman season to focus on terminating points with authority. You know you can do it. I've seen you do it. Remember your game against SkyHi?"

Bree nodded and actually smiled a bit.

"You've just got to do it consistently. That is what will make you stand out to coaches in the future. Make sense?"

"I guess so."

"Good. Now, I want you to go upstairs and wash your face. You're as red as Elmo."

Bree laughed and started up the staircase.

"And be sure and text congratulations to Savannah and Pamela for making the JV."

"Ah, Dad. Do I have to?"

"It's the right thing to do," Saul assured her. "They've been your teammates and they will be your teammates in the future."

Saul had to do the same thing at the first game of the school season. Bree was playing with her freshman team on a court that was buried way back in the anal recesses of the high school, while the JV were playing on the main varsity court. He found Brent and Stan and congratulated them on their daughters' success. They both told him that Bree should have made the team, too, and Saul lied by saying "It was for the best and it will all work out."

BREE'S DIARY
August 24

Still devastated I didn't make JV. I congratulated Savannah and Pamela. Savannah was very sweet but Pamela barely acknowledged me. Something's going on with her. She's not the same person anymore. Tried to vent to Callie but can't get her attention. So sad she's not there for me anymore. I guess Savannah is my official best friend now.

There was a certain luxury with being on the freshman team. Bree didn't have to worry about playing time. In fact, she played all the way around, which meant she also got to show off her defensive chops. In addition to focusing on her aggressive hitting that season, she also developed a nice jump serve that was very effective. Bree ended up enjoying her stint on the team. She was clearly the best player and all the players seemed to rally around her. The team itself was actually good, too. They won most of their games and finished second in the district. Sadly though, the freshman team did not get to play in a year-end championship. It was a subtle reminder by the Plano Independent School District that freshman squads were second class citizens and not tournament-worthy.

During the season, Saul was able to catch glimpses of the JV games. He watched Pamela play and saw her improve game after game. Her power was undeniable and her ability to jump up and block high was continuing to improve. There was little doubt in Saul's mind that she had surpassed Bree. As good as Bree was, she didn't have the muscular strength that Pamela possessed. Bree was still thin and Saul didn't know if she would ever add any beef to her bones. While both her and Pamela had grown to the same height, about 5 feet, 11 inches, Pam had the natural athleticism to hit the ball a little harder and jump a little higher.

As club tryout season drew near, Saul began formulating an idea in his head. He recalled what Bree's school coach said last year. You need to try and be on the best team you can be on to improve. Saul concluded that it was time for Bree to make a top club team. While being on MadDog's second team helped Bree to develop into a great player, it was now time to take the next step. The big question was what top team?

Saul started at the top of the list He began recalling the middles from Advantage and SkyHi and MadDogs' top teams. He remembered that Advantage had two middles that were over six feet tall. While they weren't that coordinated, he thought Bree's chances there would be slim. MadDogs' top team had two really good middles that would be tough to beat out. They were holdovers from their championship team of a couple of years ago. Plus, Bree would also still be competing with Pamela who was learning under the watchful eye of Frances Morgan, the owner of the club.

SkyHi, while a great team, didn't have impressive middles. Saul remembered the great game Bree had against them and how they had to put up a triple block to stop her. Maybe SkyHi was a viable option. It would only be viable if he could get Bree to one of their tryout clinics. So, just prior to the first MadDogs tryout clinic of the new club year, he cautiously broached the subject with Bree, catching her totally off guard.

"They are too good, Dad," Bree said emphatically. I don't want to go there."

"Bree, don't you remember how well you played against them? Yes, they are good, but their middles aren't that strong."

"But I have a lot of friends at MadDogs. I like my team."

"But doesn't your school coach want you to be on the best team you can be on?"

"Yes. But why can't I just try to make MadDog's top team?"

"You can," Saul reasoned. "But what if you don't make it?"

"Then I play on the second team again."

Saul was a little flustered with her response. He didn't want his daughter settling for second team status anymore. "Bree, this is your time to make a significant move. You're a great player that needs to be on a top team now."

"But what if I don't make the SkyHi team? What will I do then?"

"We will try a few other clubs. You can always end up back on MadDogs' second team if it doesn't work out." Saul realized that was somewhat of a bold statement given clubs' resentment at times for trying out at other places. But Saul was confident in Bree's ability and the value she could bring to a team. He knew MadDogs Red would take her back.

"Bree, don't you wonder if you're good enough to make a top team? Don't you at least want to know?"

"I don't know," Bree sighed.

"Just remember my magic statement. Don't say no to something you don't know anything about.'

Saul watched as she rolled her eyes at hearing the statement she had no answer for.

"I'll think about it, okay?"

Saul was okay with that answer for now. As it turned out, the tryout clinic at MadDogs that night was his best ally in convincing Bree. Several new middles in the gym were there from other clubs. They were all testing the water to see if they could make the move to MadDogs. This made Saul and Fred and Brent all uneasy. Saul was sure it made Bree uneasy, too.

Midway through the clinic, Pamela was moved to the top team court which offered Brent some relief. She played on that court the rest of the night, a clear sign that she was being strongly considered for the top team. Bree and Stacy didn't step foot on that court. While Saul was irked that Bree didn't get an opportunity, the slight to his daughter sparked her resolve.

"Dad," she said, jumping in to the car after the clinic ended, "When's the next SkyHi clinic?"

"Tomorrow night," Saul answered.

"Let's go try it."

Those words were music to Saul's ears. He couldn't wait to get to SkyHi and assess what they had to offer. Seeing all those new middles in the MadDogs gym made him feel a bit queasy, though. What if SkyHi didn't work out? Maybe she wouldn't have her spot on MadDog Red, after all. He felt it was still a risk worth taking though, even if the nausea boiling in his stomach didn't agree.

The next evening Bree got a chance to show her stuff at SkyHi. She had a great workout and it didn't go unnoticed by the SkyHi coaches. One of the coaches talked to Bree for a long period of time after the clinic. Saul wanted to walk over and join in on the conversation but thought better of it. Bree didn't waste anytime debriefing Saul in the car.

"They really like me," Bree shouted. "They think I have potential to play on their top team and they want me to come back next week."

"That's great," Saul said.

"They said I was clearly one of the best middles for my age group, too!"

"Outstanding," Saul began to gloat. He was as excited as she was.

"And I really liked the coaches. I learned a lot from them."

Saul continued to soak it all in. Bree had a legitimate shot at SkyHi. And so would begin the brutal process of attending both MadDogs and SkyHi clinics, while at the same time playing Freshman school ball and, almost forgotten in the process, making sure she stayed on top of her homework. They would have to show up at MadDogs to keep her spot secure on the second team, while secretly striving for top team gratification at SkyHi. After a couple of weeks, Saul was exhausted. More importantly, so was Bree. Saul was concerned she might be getting too tired and would not be able to play her best when she was auditioning at SkyHi.

"Are you sure you're doing the right thing?" Veronica would caution. "It seems like you're pushing her too hard."

"This is the time we have to push," he assured her. "It's now or never."

Bree then got a call from SkyHi to attend a VIP clinic, otherwise known as a Special Super Secret Invite clinic. The Super Secret Invite was an additional tryout clinic clubs would arrange that featured just the girls they were really serious about. SkyHi's Secret Invite was Wednesday night at 7 p.m. Saul was happy as this was further proof that Bree was high on their list. A couple of days later Bree got a similar Secret Invite from MadDogs. Saul read the email. It was scheduled for Wednesday night at 7 p.m., the same time as SkyHi's.

Are you kidding me? Do they do this on purpose? He then thought to himself that they probably did. This was a club's way of knowing for sure how serious a girl was about them. Both Bree and Saul felt they had to go SkyHi since that was her best chance at a top team offer. Saul was at a point where he felt they probably should stop going to MadDogs' clinics anyway so Bree could rest a little bit. The process of the last few weeks was taking its toll. He could see it in Bree's dark eyes that she was not getting enough sleep.

Saul decided the best thing to do would be to talk to Frances about Bree's status. Frances would know something was up after Bree didn't come to their Secret Invite. He thought it best to address the situation head on. He arranged to meet Frances at her office. He figured he could kill two birds with one stone. He would also talk about Harper's status for next season, too. Harper had been turning heads as a PoutyPup all season. She continued to improve and develop and was one of the tallest girls in her age group at the club. Saul was certain she would make the top 12s team but felt he better at least talk to Frances about it to be sure.

The 11s team that Harper had failed to make the previous year had a strong season. They finished near the top of every tournament they played, which was remarkable because they were playing against girls a year older. But they needed height and Harper was the obvious remedy for that need.

Harper wasn't too keen on playing with the girls. Saul assumed she might have been a little intimidated by them. Her PoutyPup team would scrimmage them from time to time and she told Saul they were too cocky. Most of the girls on that team had been in the MadDogs program since they were nine and seemed to have a sense of entitlement. Saul also sensed some cockiness in them but he felt that was normal to see in great athletes. Granted, he wasn't used to seeing it in 11 year olds.

The conversation with Frances began pleasantly enough. She was happy with Bree and Harper's development and looked forward to having them back next season. Saul congratulated Frances on her club being recognized as one of the top five clubs in Texas. He was unaware of this until walking into the club that evening and seeing a new brochure they had recently produced. He then proceeded to dive into the meat of the conversation.

"About Bree," he began. "Can you see her making the top team this season?"

"Possibly, but unlikely," Frances answered. We have two good middles on the team as you know. We might move one to right side but I haven't decided yet. We have several middles that we are looking at and I haven't seen enough from Bree yet to convince me she is ready to play at the level we need on the top team."

Saul wanted to say that if you gave her lessons like you were giving Pamela you would have plenty of opportunity to see what she could do, but he didn't. This needed to be a civil conversation and he had another daughter's future to worry about, too. He did appreciate her candor even if she wasn't saying what he wanted to hear.

"Will you carry three middles on the team?" Saul asked.

"Definitely. But I don't think placing Bree in a third middle spot would be best for her. She needs to play more and continue to improve. I'm just concerned there would be few opportunities for her to get on the court."

"But you definitely see her on the second team?"

"Yes," she said with certainty.

Saul was at least relieved to hear that, in case the SkyHi opportunity fell through.

"But let me clarify one thing," she cautioned. "Today, I see her on the second team, but we still have a few more weeks of tryouts left. Things could always change."

"I understand," Saul replied. He also understood that she was covering her ass if they did something to piss her off like go to another club's clinic, or if a 6' 3" girl-wonder came walking into her club one day and booted Bree out.

He then figured it was time to change the subject and talk about daughter number two. "How do you feel about Harper?"

"We love Harper. I hear nothing but great things about her."

This wasn't a surprise to Saul but it was always good to hear positive feedback. It was time to ask her the no-brainer question. "And do you think she can make the top team this season?"

"No," Frances said without any hesitation.

What did she just say? No? And she said it so matter-of-factly, without any thought whatsoever. Saul had to recompose himself mentally and get back to his line of questioning. "You don't see her for the top team?"

"No. She's very good but she still needs to improve her all-around game. We have two very good middles on that team and we don't want to mess with the chemistry they have developed."

"But Harper is five inches taller than one of your middles." Saul exclaimed.

"She is taller, but she is also slower, and her arm swing still needs work. We feel the middles we have now give us the best chance to win this year."

Saul was beside himself. He couldn't believe they would keep Midget Middle over his daughter. Couldn't they see Harper's potential?

"Listen, Mr. Bryson," Frances assured him, "We believe in Harper and want to see her develop. I just think the top team this year is a stretch. She'll be better off on our second team, which will also be very good by the way."

Bull poopy, Saul fumed to himself. His emotions were controlling him now. He courteously excused himself from her office and began the drive home. Believe in Harper, my Uranus. They didn't believe in her. If they did, she would be on the top team. Midget Middle gives them a better shot of winning? Not a chance.

In reality, at the age of 12, height is not that important in volleyball. The game is more about serving and ball control but Saul didn't know this at the time. He was all about his daughters making a top team. His daughters had languished in PoutyPup Land and Second Team Land long enough. When Saul got home, he immediately went to the computer and searched for SkyHi's web site. He found the tryout clinic schedule for the 12s age group. He told Harper that night that they were going to SkyHi.

"Okay," she said without any hesitation. She was on board. She was always on board, There was no pushing her like you had to push Bree at times.

The family decision had been made, although it was pretty much Saul's decision. The Bryson's were going all in with SkyHi. They were risking their second team status at MadDogs for a top team offer at SkyHi. The only thing left to do now was sweat out the actual tryouts.

It wasn't easy telling Fred the Baptist about his decision. They had been together for two years and he had enjoyed their camaraderie. He tried to compel Fred to send Stacy to SkyHi, too, but she didn't want to go. She didn't feel like she was good enough. She was content with staying on MadDogs Red.

Brent gave Saul a call a week later after he noticed Bree and Harper were not coming to the clinics. Saul updated him as to why they were moving and Brent wished him well.

"Thanks," Saul said. "And good luck. I'm sure Pamela is a lock for Frances' top team."

"We feel good about it," Brent said. "We'll let you know what happens."

The tryout weekend for 12s came first. It was a non-event. Saul had taken Harper to a couple of SkyHi clinics beforehand and their coaches immediately assured him she would make the top team. There was nothing really to worry about. Except, you still worried. You worry anytime you see a couple hundred kids competing for the same spot your daughter is competing for.

Saul was thankful he got Harper involved so early. He now regretted not making Bree play club the first year they had moved from Seattle. She was still playing catchup from that lost year. But her catching-up period might be over if she managed to make the SkyHi team.

Even though it was a fait accompli, it was still a joy to watch Harper get selected to SkyHi Blue, the top team. She was beaming with pride and started making friends with her new teammates immediately. From what Saul could tell, they had the makings of a very good team, though probably not good enough to challenge MadDogs.

Bree's day at tryouts came next. She was extremely nervous. Her outcome was still in doubt. Saul had one brief conversation with the 15s coach a week earlier who told him she would probably be the second or third middle. But he also gave out a warning similar to the one Frances gave. "You never know who's going to come walking in the door on tryout day."

One such girl that day just happened to walk in. Saul had never seen her before. She was at least six feet tall, taller than Bree for sure. And when she started doing the drills, she actually looked pretty good. He started to sweat and began worrying about their decision. This could turn into a disaster, he worried. He could be walking back to MadDogs with mud on both his face and hind legs.

He started polling some of the parents to ask if they knew who she was and where she was from. He finally got word that she was injured last year and didn't play. She had some kind of ankle injury. Saul now watched Bree's every swing intently. Her swings had to be perfect since she was being challenged by a girl that was clearly taller than her and more physically imposing.

The girls took a timeout for a water break and Bree came over to ask Saul how she was doing.

"You're doing great, Bree. You're clearly standing out. Keep hitting it aggressively."

"Okay. Thanks." Bree gulped her water and quickly ran back to the court.

Saul didn't know if she was clearly standing out or not. The talent level in the gym was the highest he had ever seen. SkyHi had enough talent to fill three top teams if they wanted to. As the next drill began, Saul saw another talented hitter go up to kill a ball and the hitter's swing bore a striking resemblance to another hitter he had seen before. He could have sworn she looked like Pamela. After two double-takes and a triple-take, Saul was sure it was her. What the F, he moaned. It can't be. He looked around to see if Brent was in the gym. He couldn't see him anywhere, but his ears had the privilege of hearing him first.

"How's it going, Buddy?"

Saul turned around and there was Brent. "What are you doing here?" Saul asked, looking aghast.

"Frances wouldn't commit to us."

"What do you mean she wouldn't commit to you?" Saul asked.

"She wouldn't guarantee us one of the top two middle spots. She promised third middle only and we thought heck, let's go see what SkyHi can offer. You said they needed middles, right?"

Saul didn't know what to say. He was speechless. He looked down and saw Bree looking up at him with the same *What the F* expression he was now wearing. He now had Pamela and the

Unknown Girl that Walks Into a Gym on Tryout Day to deal with.

For the remainder of the tryout, Saul tried desperately to send every ounce of mojo he could Bree's way, while at the same time trying to carry on a polite conversation with his buddy, Brent, who at this particular moment was the enemy. With the tryouts nearing the end, Brent got pulled away by Pamela who had been signaled to go talk to the coach.

Saul knew this wasn't a good sign. He watched as the coach talked to Brent and Pam. He saw a lot of nodding heads which also wasn't a good sign. His arm was then suddenly yanked by Bree who had come out of nowhere.

"Dad, the coach wants to talk to us," Bree loudly whispered.

She pulled him through the crowd of parents and over to where the coaches were standing. Coach Carpenter was the name of the 15s coach and he was wrapping up his conversation with Brent and Pamela. As they left, Brent gave Saul the thumbs-up sign, whatever that meant. Was that a thumbs-up for Pamela and a thumbs-down for Bree? Or a thumbs-up for both of them?

"Mr. Bryson?" Coach Carpenter began, grabbing Saul's attention. "We've had an interesting day here today. We've had two girls walk in that we weren't really planning for. I know Bree wants to play middle and we have a spot for her if she wants it."

"What's the spot?" Saul asked.

"Third middle."

It wasn't what Saul wanted to hear but it wasn't a disaster, either.

"Who are the first two?" Saul asked curiously.

"Cathy, who was on our team last year and is really solid, and Pamela. She's one of the new girls that came today. She is just too dynamic for us to pass up."

"Yeah, we know who she is," Saul admitted. He was actually a little relieved that Bree was ahead of Unknown Girl that Walks Into a Gym on Tryout Day.

"But listen, we really want Bree as a third middle. She will get great training. You just need to decide what you want to do. She could also be the starting middle on our second team, which will also be a very good team."

Saul didn't want to hear about the second team. "If she takes the top team, will she have every opportunity to compete for playing time?" Saul asked.

"Yes, definitely," the coach said.

"Can you give us a couple of minutes then?"

"Sure, but we need to know soon because if she doesn't want it, we will probably give it to the other new middle that walked in today."

"Yeah, I know who she is, too," Saul uttered under his breath. He pulled Bree aside who had been hyperventilating through the entire conversation.

"What do we do, Dad? What do we do?"

"What do you want to do, Bree?"

"I want the top team. That would be so cool to make their top team," she said, having a hard time controlling her emotions.

"I understand that, but you are the third middle. That means you will have to beat one of them out for playing time."

"I know, but I think I can do it. Don't you?"

Saul didn't know what to think. And he didn't know what was going through Bree's head. Did she really think she could do it or was she so in love with making the top team it was clouding her thinking. But then Saul started to do his own thinking. He knew she probably couldn't beat out Pamela. Pamela's upside was too high. But the other middle, Cathy, didn't stand out much to him. She didn't hit the ball hard and she didn't really move that well, either. Plus, she was the middle Bree played against last year and dominated. He was feeling better about Bree's chances. Plus, it was the damned top team!! This is what they had been working for since the dawn of the Master Athletic Plan's creation. Of course, she could do this.

"Yes, Bree, I think you can do it, too," he said excitedly.

Bree jumped up and down with delight.

"But you're going to have to work your butt off," Saul warned.

"I know, I know. Let's hurry up and go tell the coach." Bree didn't appear to be registering anything he was now telling her.

When it was all said and done, Saul had endured another successful tryout day. This one had been the most stressful yet. He couldn't wait to go home to Veronica and celebrate the day and relay to her all the events that occurred. He still couldn't believe Bree beat out the Unknown Girl that Walks Into a Gym on Tryout Day. She would be someone Bree would probably have to contend with next season. But for now, Bree had made the top team. She was a member of SkyHigh Blue, one of the best teams in North Texas and Bree's best shot yet to qualify for Nationals. Saul felt that same proud feeling watching her being selected just as he felt for Harper.

Bree and Pamela, destined to always be rivals it now appeared, still managed to hug each other with excitement when their names were called. Saul shook Brent's hand as well, but there would be no hugging between the two of them. Saul couldn't help but feel some resentment at the Mystery Man's ability to always show up at the most inopportune of times. It wasn't that Brent had done anything wrong. He was watching after his daughter's interests just like Saul was watching after his. They were both looking for any edge they could find. But this was the first time Saul had felt the nick of another volleyball dad's blade.

The Mystery Man had out-fathered him again.

BREE'S DIARY
November 2
Can't believe I made SkyHi's top team. All my friends are jealous. Feels so good. I'm okay with Pamela making the team. She's gotten better, but she still doesn't talk to me much. I don't know what I did to upset her. She kept cutting in line hitting before me at tryouts which was really annoying. She needs to chill.

CHAPTER THIRTEEN

SKY LOW

Being on a top team for a top club carried with it a lot of expectations and Coach Carpenter, Bree's new coach, made that abundantly clear soon after tryouts. He held a meeting with the parents and told them their goal was to win Nationals. It was not just to qualify for Nationals, which was all Saul was hoping for, but it was to win the whole darn thing.

Carpenter talked about how deep the team was in talent and that they had the ability to compete with anybody. He said that they would have one extra practice a week because you couldn't win championships unless you outworked the competition. He talked about how he kept meticulous statistics and would use those to educate the girls on how it influenced their playing time. Carpenter emphasized that the key to winning volleyball games was to make the fewest mistakes, and keeping good stats would show the girls how minimizing errors leads to wins. He also talked about the value of nutrition and that the girls would have to keep a food log so that they could better understand what they were eating. He wanted them to learn about good food and bad food and what type of food their bodies needed to perform at a high level. He talked about how the girls should conduct themselves on and off the court and what they should be wearing when they traveled and how they would be responsible for setting alarm clocks and going to bed at the specified curfew time. He talked about how teamwork breeds discipline which breeds confidence which breeds champions.

Carpenter was preaching to Saul's internal choir. Saul was impressed and totally on board with the coach's philosophy. He never realized all the responsibilities that came with being on a team like SkyHi Blue versus a team like MadDogs Red or PSA.

He was even more impressed with the training. The practices were extremely well organized. There was no downtime for the players. They were lucky if they got one water break a practice. All the drills were set up to where there was always a competition at play. You either won or lost the drill and if you lost, you had to deal with the consequences. That normally meant some kind of conditioning exercise like sprinting, lunges, burpees or abdominal crunches. Saul got exhausted just watching them. Over the course of just a few weeks, he could see his daughter getting better and stronger. At the same time, he could see Pamela getting better and stronger, too.

Saul continued to believe Bree had a better chance of beating Cathy out for a middle spot than Pamela. Cathy, while very good, didn't have Bree's arm-swing and she moved a little slower. She was more deliberate in her movements. She almost looked lazy. Saul could tell that Coach Carpenter would get annoyed sometimes with Cathy's lack of hustle to the ball. Regardless of Cathy's shortcomings, she was still an effective scorer and Bree had her work cut out for her.

The talent on the team was impressive. Even Saul could tell that. The back row players were all excellent passers with great technique and great instincts. The outside hitters had a lot of power and could display a variety of shots. He was extremely impressed with one of the hitters who was already being recruited by some major colleges. She had a confident air about her and nothing seemed to rattle her. Saul thought she could tone down her cockiness just a tad. She liked to stick out her chest and strut after every kill she made. She did have one distracting feature that rattled Saul and all the other parents.

Her shorts, or spandex sliders as they were called, were always skin tight and hiked up too high. She was always having to pull them down after every hit to cover the bottom of her bottom, but it didn't seem to bother her. She didn't have a problem showing off her rear assets, and neither did her parents who seemed to be oblivious to it. Because of this, Saul couldn't help but call her Butt Cheeks, which embarrassed Bree every time he referred to her in conversation.

The setter on the team was one of the best in the area. The team's quarterback and captain, Lauren Kennedy, already had a scholarship locked up at the University of Texas. She had been setting for SkyHigh since she was 12 and she was the only setter on the team. They ran a 5-1 offense like MadDogs Red did with Double Trouble, but Lauren Kennedy did not make double contact errors like Double Trouble.

Carpenter had told Saul that Bree would improve a great deal just by hitting off of good setting. Saul was impressed with Lauren's setting motion and her ability to make great sets even with the poorest of passes. He couldn't wait to see Bree play with her during real matches.

When the team scrimmaged six-on-six during practice, it was fun to watch. The quality of volleyball on display was the best Saul had ever witnessed. Everyone hustled all the time and very few balls hit the ground. The players would dive for balls they had no chance of saving, but they dived for them anyway. That was the mentality that had been drilled into the girls.

Long rallies were normal during the course of their scrimmages. Excellent defense on both sides of the net made it harder to score points. Saul, for the first time, began to witness the true rhythm of the game just as Autumn had described to him. The passing, the setting, the hitting, all being conducted in such harmonic fashion. Volleyball was not just the ultimate team sport, as Autumn had so strongly debated. It was also a game of great, physical beauty. Finally, at 15s, Saul was able to see the game as it was truly meant to be played. The girls had matured enough, both mentally and physically, to play the game at a level that resembled something like the games' forefathers probably had in mind when they created it.

The great game of beauty would soon turn ugly again when Saul had to attend one of Harper's practices. Watching 12 year olds try to play the game was far different than watching 15s. The slowness of the game became more apparent. Their underdeveloped muscles were always on display. The silly errors the girls would make made the parents pull their hair out. And these were supposed to be the good 12 year-olds.

Aside from MadDogs, Harper's team was considered the next best team in North Texas. Saul had a hard time believing that when he watched them practice but the coaches seemed confident they had the talent to compete well. Saul assumed they knew their business better than he did. It definitely took a different kind of coach to coach 12s. In college, they must have pulled a double major in patience and anger management.

You can't scream at 12 year olds. If you do, they mentally check out and forget how to play the game. You have to provide encouragement constantly and if you want something to sink into their little brains, like how to properly pass a ball, you have to tell them several hundred times before the instruction starts to take hold.

While Saul was ecstatic to have two daughters in club volleyball, he soon realized a couple of minor things. First of all, it meant he was now paying twice the money, and the cost per daughter had increased because SkyHi's dues were $1,000 more than MadDogs. It seemed the better the team you were on, the more you paid. Second, with two girls playing now, it meant two separate schedules with a lot of tournament overlap. So, he and Veronica would have to manage the schedule and decide which parent would go to see which daughter and make sure neither daughter got their feelings hurt. This also meant a new video recording device would need to be added to the budget so both parents could film their daughter play so the other parent who was not in attendance could watch the game at home. Oh, the joys of having two girls playing sports simultaneously.

The first tournament up was Harper's. SkyHigh Blue 12s made their debut and a promising debut it was. They won the tournament rather easily. Not all the top teams were in attendance though. MadDogs Black, the infamous top team, opted to play up in age at a 13s tournament that weekend. Saul joked with Harper that they were avoiding the real competition.

It was still a promising weekend with Harper starting at middle blocker the entire tournament. She had several kills and was the primary force at the net. Saul was especially pleased that the team won all their matches very easily. While a few notable teams did not attend, it did establish Harper's team as a force to be reckoned with in the region.

The next tournament up was Bree's. Saul didn't know what to expect with his daughter residing at third middle status. He was hoping that she had beat out one of the middles by the time of the first tournament, but he couldn't really tell by the coach's substitution patterns during practice.

Saturday's pool play was not a deciding factor, either. He started Cathy and Pamela in the very first game of the day, but Bree ended up playing the same number of games as the other middles. She played well but so did the other two middles. All of the matches in Pool Play were against inferior teams. He wouldn't really know Bree's status for sure until Gold Bracket Day, when the real competition heated up.

The competition heated up quickly the next day along with Saul's body temperature. Bree didn't play in a single game. There were opportunities to insert her, but the coach refused. Pamela made several mistakes over the course of several games but the coach let her play through them. Saul was extremely discouraged.

He was even more discouraged by the play of Cathy. Not that she played poorly, she played great and that was the problem. He never realized how good she was until they played the better teams. Cathy, as slow and methodical as she was, could score at will. She didn't do it with power. She did it with patience, finesse and smarts. After three years of playing with Lauren, the best setter in the region, Cathy had developed a rapport with Lauren that was incredible. Their timing was impeccable. Each one knew where the other would be at any given time. Cathy would jump up and float in the air waiting for Lauren's set to be where it needed to be and then she would proceed to eye the other side of the net, see the open spot and direct the ball to that exact spot.

She didn't have to hit the ball hard. She could tip it, tap it, push it, but she could hit it hard if she needed to. The number of points she racked up that day were too many for Saul to keep track of. Saul's underestimation of Cathy startled him. He thought because she didn't demonstrate a lot of power that Bree could overtake her. He was so wrong. He knew that Bree wouldn't be beating out Cathy for a spot. How was he to know that Lauren and Cathy were the Lennon and McCartney of club volleyball?

He already knew that Pamela and all her athletic ability was going to be nearly impossible to beat out. Pamela was Carpenter's project player. His focus was to develop her into the best player she could be by Nationals. In order to do that, he would have to play her as much as he could.

Thus, after just the first tournament of the year, Saul had a terrible feeling in his gut that they had made a huge mistake. What were the middle school coach's words? Play on the best team you can make? Bree did just that. But what happens when you don't get to play? The coach should have warned him by adding an addendum: Just be sure and don't sit on the bench of the best team you can make.

Saul soon discovered there was nothing fun about paying $5,000 to see your daughter twiddle her thumbs on the bench, while simultaneously losing all confidence in herself. Saul had to come up with some line of BS that would keep Bree feeling good about herself. After the nightmare of not making the junior varsity, he had meticulously coaxed her through the freshman volleyball season and managed to keep her attitude positive. Being a benchwarmer for SkyHi could send her over the edge.

The car ride home after the first tournament was pretty quiet. Bree was wearing a first place medal around her neck. Her team had won the tournament without her setting foot on the court on Gold Bracket Day. Harper was admiring her medal and comparing it to the one she won the prior weekend. It was late in the day and everyone was tired. This was the latest the Bryson's ever had to stay for a tournament. When you're on a winning team, you suddenly realize the days are longer because you have to play more games. Gone were the days of PSA when they would lose at ten in the morning and Saul could make it home in time for a noon kickoff.

Saul could see Bree's eyes welling up with tears through the rear-view mirror. He could tell she wanted to say something but she probably didn't want Harper to hear. When they got home, the girls went upstairs to shower and change and the parents went outside to the patio to vent and moan.

"What have we gotten ourselves into?" Veronica started.

"It's just one tournament," Saul said. "Let's see how the rest of the season will play out first. Things could change."

"You really think that?" Veronica fired back.

"No," Saul said. "I'm working on a line of BS for Bree. I just hope she buys it."

"She's not stupid, Saul."

"I know she's not."

"It's just so painful to see her standing there. She's such a good player but she's just standing there," Veronica pleaded.

The sound of the door opened and Bree walked outside interrupting their conversation. She still had wells of water in her eyelids.

"What's up, Champ?" Saul asked, trying to break the ice but not the dam.

"I'm not a champ." Bree said with disdain.

"That medal you won says otherwise," Saul countered.

"I didn't do anything to win that medal. I'm terrible."

"Bree, you're not terrible. You're on the best team in the region."

"But Coach Carpenter wouldn't play me. Pamela makes all those mistakes and he still wouldn't play me."

"We know, Bree. We're disappointed, too," Veronica empathized. "But it's still early in the season. It's just one tournament. Let's see how the rest of the season plays out."

Saul looked over at Veronica with a quizzical look on his face. He was surprised to hear her saying his line of BS. "Mom's right, Bree. A lot can happen in a season. You just have to keep working hard and proving yourself."

"Did you see how good Cathy was?" Bree asked. "She's unbelievable. I will never be that good."

"Don't say that," Saul cautioned. "You don't know how good you can be right now. All you can do is keep working hard and getting better."

"And Bree, learn from Cathy," Veronica added. "You are on a team filled with great players. Take advantage of that and let them make you a better player."

"Your Mom's right again, Bree." Do you see how Cathy studies the other side of the net before she hits the ball? That's something you can work on and get better at."

Bree nodded and it was obvious to Saul she was getting tired of the pep talk.

"I guess you're right. I'll keep trying."

"That's my girl," Saul said. "Now give me a hug."

Bree got up and hugged her parents and went back inside. The two parents looked at each other with some satisfaction. They had successfully kept the dam from breaking at least for one night. "She is getting better," Saul said.

"You really think so?" Veronica wondered.

"Definitely. You should see her in practice and all the work she puts in. That's the real frustration. She's getting better but she's not able to show it on the court.

"And she doesn't know she's getting better," Veronica reasoned.

"Would you if you were 15 and sitting the bench?"

The next tournament weekend was going to be chaotic. Both girls were playing simultaneously at different sites. Without hesitation, Saul told Veronica he needed to go with Bree. She was the one having playing time issues. Saul needed to monitor the games and the coach to see if Bree was being fairly treated. Harper was clearly the lead middle on her team and playing time was not an issue.

For Bree, the tournament began like the last one. She played the same amount of time as Cathy and Pam during Saturday's pool play. On Gold Bracket Day, it was more of the same. Bree was not going in. It was even more humiliating for Bree because the first opponent that day was her former team, MadDogs Red. Bree had to watch from the sidelines as her former teammates put up a valiant effort but still lost in two games to SkyHi.

She was able to catch up with Stacy after the game and also with Savannah, who had been elevated from MadDogs third team to the Red second team. Saul caught up with Fred, too, who cautiously asked him how the SkyHi experience was going. Saul commented how great the practices were and that she was learning a lot, but that the coach still didn't have the confidence to play her in critical games. He was hoping that things would get better from a playing time standpoint. Fred wished him well.

In the semi-finals that day, there was a minor breakthrough. Pamela was having a horrible game. Carpenter kept her in for the longest time until it got to the point of embarrassment. He motioned for Bree to enter the game, which caught Bree totally off guard. This was her chance, Saul hoped. His nerves quickly shifted into high gear and he felt a rush of adrenaline surge through his body, the kind you normally feel when your kid is actually playing. Saul didn't like Bree being in the position of only going in when a player did poorly. He didn't like being swayed to pull against a teammate for his own daughter's gain, but that's what being a third middle dad can do to you. He thought of poor old William, the third middle dad from the PSA team and how pathetic he looked at times. Saul actually had empathy for him now.

303

Speaking of pathetic, Saul could see Brent was covering his face with disappointment after Pamela was removed. Brent was known to moan and groan when Pamela made a mistake and he had been groaning non-stop since the start of the match. The two dads had remained amicable during the course of the season, but there wasn't a lot of idle chitchat. They were interested in one thing and one thing only, their daughters' playing time, and it was too awkward a subject for them to talk about amongst themselves.

Bree made the most of her time in the game. She scored a few points and had a couple of key blocks and did not make an error. He was ecstatic to see her playing well against such tough competition and under difficult circumstances. It wasn't easy coming in cold off the bench and contributing but Bree was doing just that. For the first time that season, Bree felt like part of the team and Saul felt like one of the team parents. He was on his feet cheering like many of the dads did. Lauren's dad, in particular, was always extremely vocal. He would stand at the side of the net and cheer the girls on, and also let the referee know when he or she made a bad call.

The intensity level was high during these final matches of the day. They had more meaning to both the players and the parents. The core of the team had been together for several years now and rivalries and pride had developed into something of enormous importance. In the past, Bree and her former teammates would shake off a loss with little concern. If SkyHi Blue 15s lost, however, it would be a devastating experience. The goal to be the best team in North Texas drove this core of girls. It had been their mission, along with the club's expectation, since they started playing together as 12 year olds.

To Saul's satisfaction, Carpenter left Bree in for the remainder of game one and all of game two as SkyHi won and headed to the finals. After the match, Saul could tell Bree was excited with her opportunity. He was hopeful the coach would leave her in for the final. But it didn't happen. Cathy and Pamela played the entire match. SkyHi ended up losing to Advantage in a close three setter. Pamela made a couple of critical errors but Carpenter didn't budge. He left her in for the duration. Lauren's dad was despondent with the loss, although he did come over to Saul and compliment Bree's play in the previous match.

In the car ride home, Bree let Saul have an earful. "I go in the game and I play well and I don't even get a chance after that," she fumed. "And do you know what it's like to have to sit there and watch your old teammates play a game and have them looking at you the whole time while you're doing nothing on the bench? It's humiliating. Oh, I'm so frustrated."

"I know you're frustrated, Bree. But let's look at the positives here."

"What positives?" She shouted back.

"He put you into an important match for the first time. He had the confidence to do that and you performed well. This may be the beginning of more playing time for you in key games."

"He didn't put me in the final," she argued.

"That's true," Saul had to admit. "But we did take a step in the right direction today. And I loved some of your kills. I saw you scoping out the defense on the other side of the net before you swung. You're getting much better at that."

"Thanks," Bree said, in a defeated manner. "How did Harper do today?"

"They won again. But MadDogs wasn't in the tournament."

"I'm sure Harper got to play all the time, didn't she?"

Saul grimaced at the question but had to answer, "From what I heard from your Mom, yes."

"Dad, why did we move to SkyHi again? I could be playing and having fun with my friends on my old team. Savannah's on that team now."

Saul sighed. "Because we wanted to be on the best team you could be on. And we did that. Bree, I know you find this hard to believe right now, but you are getting better."

"Yeah, right," she jeered in disbelief. "I think I might have wanted it for the wrong reasons."

"What do you mean by that?" Saul asked.

"I thought it would be cool to tell my friends I was on SkyHi's top team," Bree said, staring out the window and not focusing on anything in particular. "It would show everyone how good I had gotten. Today though, I didn't feel so cool when talking with Savannah and Stacy after the match and trying to provide answers about why I'm not playing."

"Just stay positive," Saul compelled her. "You might be surprised how things turn out."

BREE'S DIARY
February 13
So mad at Coach Carpenter. Don't understand him. I don't know why he doesn't play me. Pamela ignores me more and more. She's becoming good friends with Lauren and doesn't give me the time of day. So embarrassed talking to Stacy and Savannah today and acting like it was no big deal I was not playing. The worst feeling in the world is after you have won a game and all the parents come over to congratulate the team, but they don't know what to say to me, the one who doesn't get to play.

Things had been turning out well for Harper. Two tournaments and two wins made Harper feel pretty good about herself. Her next event was an important ranking tournament, which helped decide how the teams were ranked in their age group. Saul discovered that MadDogs would be playing in the tournament, too. At last, he would get to see how Harper's team would match up against them.

MadDogs was seeded first in the tournament and SkyHi was seeded second, which meant they would meet in the finals if both teams won all their matches, which they did. Both teams were barely tested in the matches leading up to the final. When it came time for them to play each other, the intensity level in the gym started amping up. Saul had heard that the MadDogs parents were extremely vocal.

The two club organizations had been battling each other for several years now. They were based only a couple of miles apart from each other, which made it natural for heated rivalries to develop. Before the two 12s teams had even played each other, the atmosphere felt like a rivalry.

It didn't feel like a rivalry after the match, though. SkyHi was clearly intimidated and nervous. MadDogs came out and served them off the court. The SkyHi defenders had trouble passing the ball throughout the match, which meant the setters didn't have good balls to set and the hitters didn't have good sets to hit. Harper did not get any opportunities to kill a ball. To make matters even worse, Midget Middle, the girl Saul had argued to Frances that Harper was better than, scored a ton of points. She had a great arm swing that generated a huge amount of topspin. It was a potent weapon for someone who could barely reach the top of the net.

Saul also had to watch as one of their outside hitters did a cocky pull-out-your-pistol-from-your-holster strut after every kill she made. Saul didn't think it appropriate for a 12 year old to simulate mowing down your opponent with a .38 special, but he guessed he was in the minority. This was Texas, after all. Six-

Shooter, as he would now call her, had a dad that would howl obnoxiously after every point was scored, which eventually forced Saul and Veronica to move to the other side of the court.

Regardless of the annoyances, MadDogs was clearly the better team and SkyHi would have to settle for its second place standing. Harper, who since exiting Veronica's womb never liked to lose, was furious after the match.

"I'm so upset with my teammates, Daddy. We shouldn't have lost. And I don't like those MadDogs girls, especially the one that acts like she's shooting a gun."

Based on Harper's rants, Saul could tell that from this point on, the rivalry with MadDogs would forever be branded in her soul.

With Bree, the only thing branded in her soul was her contempt for Coach Carpenter. Her playing status remained unchanged. She would go in when Pamela was having a bad game and would play well, but even though she played well, Carpenter would always reinsert Pamela back into the lineup for the next game. As the season progressed, Bree was getting fewer chances because Pamela was getting better. So, the fewer mistakes Pamela made, the fewer opportunities Bree had.

Frustrations came to a head at the Colorado Crossroads Qualifier in Denver. Bree was back in the city of high altitude and Saul made sure they got there a day earlier than the rest of the team so she could adjust better to the climate. To Bree, it didn't matter since she wasn't playing anyway. Saul didn't expect much from the weekend since they would be playing top competition from the start. He was sure Carpenter would play his regular line-up throughout the tournament. Pamela had been playing well and her timing with Lauren was improving.

Pamela and Lauren had also become good friends off the court, which seemed to be helping with their chemistry on the court.

Bree, on the other hand, was getting used to life on the sidelines. She had become friends with two of her fellow benchwarmers, Morgan and Bailey. Morgan was the third outside hitter and Bailey was a third right side/defender/utility player. Both would be inserted from time to time but, like Bree, they spent a lot of time on the bench and found it hard to break into the regular lineup.

While the matches were being played, the trio would find themselves in deep discussion about a variety of topics. They would cheer when they needed to cheer so they looked like they were supporting the team, but their minds were really elsewhere. It was disruptive when Coach Carpenter would motion one of them to enter the game because it interrupted their conversation flow.

Saul ended up getting to know Morgan and Bailey's dads pretty well, too, especially Scott, who was Morgan's dad. Together they would commiserate about their daughters' lack of playing time. While Scott was no Fred the Baptist, he did do a first class interpretation of Coach Carpenter that would make Saul crack up.

On day one of the qualifier, Bree's team played three matches and won all three. Bree didn't get to play. On day two of the qualifier, Bree's team played three matches and won all three. Bree was inserted into one match because the team they were playing was surprisingly bad. Carpenter decided to rest Cathy and give Bree some mercy play. On day three, the team made it to the semi-finals. If they won that game, they would get a bid to Nationals. Even though his daughter was not playing, Saul still thought it would be cool to go to and experience the biggest tournament of the year.

SkyHi was playing a team from Atlanta called A5, who came in as the number one seed. A5 lived up to their billing in the first game. They started the match with a fury of impressive points. They had two great outside hitters that were both as good as Butt Cheeks, but they didn't have to adjust their spandex sliders after every kill.

Pamela was out of her element from the start. For whatever reason, she appeared lost and wasn't adapting to the speed of the opponent. To Saul's surprise, Carpenter quickly inserted Bree into the match and she seemed to settle things down at the net. She blocked their outside hitters a couple of times and helped stem their momentum. The Atlanta team still won the first game 25 to 17 as their early lead was too big to overcome.

Game two began and Saul was thrilled to see that Carpenter left Bree in the match. SkyHi started better this game and adjusted to some of the plays their opponent had success with in the first game. Bree remained strong at the net and her block was giving the Atlanta team problems. The one thing that Saul kept waiting for was a kill attempt by Bree. That was her strength and Saul felt Bree could take advantage of the other team's middle. For whatever reason, Lauren would never set her and there appeared to be several opportunities for a middle set, but Bree never got a chance to kill one. Saul was getting annoyed and didn't understand why Lauren wouldn't set her at least once, if for no other reason than the element of surprise. He could tell Bree was getting a little flustered, too, as she was working hard to transition and try to create an opportunity.

Saul couldn't be too alarmed though because the team was winning. Lauren kept pushing the ball to the outside pins and the hitters were having success. Butt Cheeks was heating up from the left side and the Atlanta team couldn't stop her. SkyHi won game two 25-21 and prepared for the rubber game.

Game three started and the teams traded points out of the gate. Cathy was the starting middle, which was expected but who would be the next middle in? Saul waited with anxiety. To his delight, Bree came bouncing onto the court when Cathy rotated off. He looked over at Brent for a split second and could see the helpless displeasure on his face.

Bree continued to block well at the net and SkyHi built a three-point lead, 7 to 4. In club ball, the third game of a match went to 15 points instead of 25. Every point was crucial in the third game because if you got behind by even a slim margin, you had fewer opportunities to make up the deficit. The SkyHi parents were getting rowdy as they closed in on the victory. Lauren's dad was spurring the girls on one point at a time with loud, sonic cheers of encouragement.

Still, with all this excitement, Saul was waiting for one offensive chance for Bree. Give them the element of surprise and set a quick set to my daughter please, he begged internally. But it never happened. She was playing the defensive game of her life, but her offensive game was invisible. When Cathy came back into the game for Bree, they were still up by three points. The teams traded a flurry of points and the lead was still three when it was time for Bree to rotate back in. The score was 13 to 10. Two more points and they had the bid! Perhaps she could score the winning point, Saul dreamed. But the dream quickly turned into a nightmare when Carpenter motioned for Pamela to sub in for Bree.

"What the F," Saul said aloud. Luckily, no one heard him because the crowd noise was so high.

Bree walked back to the bench with a look of confusion, but she quickly turned her attention to the final few points. A missed serve by the Atlanta team gave SkyHi a game point. The next point seemed to take forever. It was a long pressure-packed rally with neither team willing to cede ground. Finally, SkyHi got a free-ball to convert, a free-ball being a high, lazy pass by the opposing team that is easy to take advantage of.

Lauren got the perfect pass to set and what did she do? For the first time in the match, she set the middle. Pamela rose up and killed the ball with authority and the game was over. The girls swarmed around Pamela and fell onto the ground in a frantic huddle. Morgan, Bailey and Bree, the three benchwarmers, were the last to join the pile, but the pile was too high to jump on so they feebly made an attempt to join in. Saul was high-fiving the parents with muted joy. He was happy to finally be going to Nationals but it was bittersweet to see Bree being taken out of the game at such a crucial point, especially when she had played her ass off. Lauren's dad came over and congratulated Saul on Bree's play in the previous match, but it was all Saul could do not to go off on him and ask him why his superstar setter didn't set his daughter. Saul's cooler head prevailed. He tried his best not to be one of those crazy sports dads that like to create a scene in the arena.

As hot as Saul was, Mystery Man was even hotter. Saul was surprised to see Brent pulling Pamela aside and reading her the riot act. He was in her face letting her have it. He wasn't screaming so Saul couldn't hear what was being said, but his face was turning red with fury. Pamela was near tears when Brent walked away from her. Saul had never seen Brent so intense. He felt sorry for Pamela that she had to endure the public flogging. He never thought of Brent as a crazy sports dad, but maybe his true colors were starting to show.

In the championship match that followed, SkyHi didn't show up to play. It was as if they were so relieved to get a bid, they were still drunk from the celebration. They got smoked by a team from California, while Saul had smoke coming out of his ears. Bree didn't get to play at all in the championship game. It was as if her effort in the previous match was forgotten. He was so upset he decided to do something he had never done before. He was going to talk to the coach about his daughter's playing time. He had seen other parents do it and have success. For Bree's sake, it was time for him to try.

He knew Bree's patience was reaching the breaking point not only with Carpenter, but with him and his monotonous displays of encouragement, You're Getting Better, Keep Working Hard, You've Got to Stay Positive, Good Things Will Come From This. With her silver medal draped around her neck and a National bid secured, what should have been a moment of extreme happiness was instead a moment of extreme depression. For the first time, he could see in Bree's eyes that terrible deflated look of defeat. The only thing keeping her from saying "I want to quit" was probably the public setting they were in. He would call Carpenter when he got home and schedule a meeting. He would keep it a secret from Bree.

BREE'S DIARY
March 1
I'm done with Coach Carpenter. He has no confidence in me and I have no confidence in him. And Lauren doesn't have any confidence in me, either. If my dad tells me I'm getting better or that everything is going to be okay, I will barf. Please let this season end!!! Pamela continues to upset me. She told me today that I shouldn't play for SkyHi next year. That was not a nice thing to say. Altho it's probably true.

The meeting seemed to go very well. Carpenter said all the right things. He said he would look for more opportunities to get Bree in games. He said she was working hard and was not far away from Cathy and Pamela, but he did caution, she was still the third middle. Saul asked him why they didn't take advantage of Bree's offense in the match versus the Atlanta team. Carpenter said they should have but Lauren said she didn't trust Bree would be there in time for the set. She said she was a step slower than Pamela in transition.

This was the first time Saul had heard this about Bree. He didn't believe it and even if it were true, he challenged Carpenter that it still made sense to set her once or twice just to see what would happen. Carpenter agreed. Saul reminded him about Bree's high kill percentage and asked him why this new reference of being too slow had never surfaced before. Carpenter didn't have an answer.

Saul had an answer but he would never be able to prove it. His theory was Lauren wasn't setting Bree because she had become friends with Pamela. She didn't want to give Bree a chance to take Pamela's spot. Saul didn't bring this up to Carpenter because he had no proof other than a biased father's hunch. Regardless, the meeting ended well and Carpenter said he would work with Bree and Lauren more and try to get them in better sync. He didn't want Bree to lose confidence in herself. He even suggested getting a lesson with Lauren outside of practice when they had time. Saul thought this was a great idea.

He asked Bree to ask Lauren if they could have a lesson together and Lauren said yes. Saul was encouraged by this; maybe his hunch was wrong. The lesson never happened though, because Lauren never had the time to fit it into her calendar.

As the remainder of the season played out, Saul remained discouraged because nothing changed in terms of Bree's playing time. If anything, her playing time lessened. Pamela continued to improve and she kept her errors to a minimum, which decreased Bree's chances. All the positive things that Carpenter said were just words, Saul reckoned. He just said what any dad would want to hear. Say all the right things and get the meeting over and hope the parent wouldn't ask for another meeting.

Saul didn't ask for another meeting. He knew it was pointless. He decided to let the season play out. In the process, he watched his daughter's attitude decline severely. The few times she did get in games she was tentative and not aggressive. She knew she wasn't going to get set so why bother. Her confidence level was dropping. He kept reminding her she was on a team and she had to be a team player and support her teammates, even if her role was a benchwarmer. Bree listened but she didn't hear what he was saying. She was tuning him out.

To make matters worse, Bree had to watch her little sister get to play all the time and talk about how great her team was. Harper wasn't trying to rub it in Bree's face, she was just truly happy about her status on SkyHi 12s. Bree tried to act happy for Harper but Saul and Veronica could tell she was envious of Harper's position, which was now the exact opposite of Bree's.

Harper's team had continued to prove to the North Texas Region that they were the second best team in the area. The only local team they had lost to was MadDogs. They played MadDogs a second time and played them tougher but it was still a decisive victory for Midget Middle and her teammates. Harper played better in the loss but MadDogs just had more quickness and experience. Harper fumed afterwards like she did with any loss and insisted they wouldn't lose to them a third time.

SkyHi Blue 12s went to Baltimore to try and qualify for Nationals but fell one spot short. They lost to a Puerto Rican team who was incredibly good. For some reason, Puerto Rico had great teams in the younger age group. Saul swore they were over age. He wanted their birth certificates checked because they all looked and played like they were 15 years old.

Because they didn't qualify in Baltimore, they had to play at Regionals and try to get a bid there. Saul was a little nervous because SkyHi was the number one seed. MadDogs had qualified at the Spokane qualifier so they wouldn't be at Regionals. SkyHi had soundly beaten all the other teams in the field and they were the clear favorites. The only problem, as Saul knew, was that they were 12-years old and with 12-year-olds, anything can happen.

Harper and her teammates breezed through the first day's pool play but in the last match, Saul and Veronica had a scare. Harper dove for a ball and got herself in an awkward position. She heard something pop in her right leg and when she got up she had trouble walking. The coach quickly removed her from the game, which was meaningless since they were ahead 21 to 6.

Saul watched Harper on the sidelines. She didn't seem to have a noticeable limp, which was encouraging. After the match, he asked her where the pain or pop was felt and she pointed to the back of her leg just under her buttocks. Her coach diagnosed it as a hamstring injury. Saul questioned her at first because he had no idea the hamstring extended so high up in the leg. A few minutes later, the trainer on duty confirmed that she strained her hamstring. The trainer said to ice it and rest it the remainder of the day and see how she felt in the morning.

Great, Saul thought. They were just a few wins away from a bid and now this had to happen. Harper stayed off her legs the rest of the day and woke up the next morning feeling a little better. She said the leg was sore but that she could still play. Saul told her that she shouldn't push it. A hamstring injury was dangerous, especially if you damaged it further. It could take a long time to heal. On the other hand, they were playing for a bid and if they didn't get one, she would have the whole summer for the injury to heal.

On Gold Bracket Day, Harper's team managed to march through to the semi-finals with little problem. A win in the semi's would guarantee them a trip to Columbus, Ohio where Nationals was being held. The match was a little scary because they were pushed to a third game by Tejas, a club that was based near Fort Worth. They had played them three times already that year and had won every time. SkyHi didn't panic though. They jumped out to an early lead in the third game and never looked back.

Harper provided some key points even though she was moving gingerly. She had done a masterful job of managing her injury the whole day. She wasn't putting much pressure on her injured leg, which meant she was barely jumping at all but she was still able to be effective. On game point, the setter set the ball to Harper for the win and Harper went up as strongly as she could and finished the game off with a kill. The girls swarmed around her and celebrated their bid. Saul jumped up with excitement, too. His daughters had double-qualified. They were both going to Nationals.

As the girls went to the net to shake the hands of the opposing team, Veronica said, "I think she hurt herself again."

"What do you mean?" Saul asked.

"She's limping very badly."

Saul located Harper at the net and Very was right. She wasn't moving well at all. Harper then made eye contact with Saul and he could tell by her face she was in pain. He moved over to the sideline to talk to her.

"What's wrong, Harp?"

"I think I hurt my other leg."

"How did you do that?"

"I don't know. On that last point, I may have pushed it a little too much."

He asked her to point to where it hurt and oddly enough it was in the same location as the other leg. "Did you hurt your other hamstring?" he asked.

"I think I did," she said, trying to hide her pain.

The coach came by to check on her and agreed that she must have hurt the other leg while she was favoring the injured leg.

"Damn," Saul said. "Can you do anything, Harper?"

Harper tried to walk around and simulate a jump but could barely move. The coach told her not to play in the finals, that everything was okay. They got their bid. She now needed to rest up and heal.

"How long does something like this take to heal?" he asked the coach.

"It depends on the girl. Everyone heals differently. It could be anywhere between four to twelve weeks."

Nationals was in six weeks. He needed Harper to be a fast healer. He and Veronica decided to get an expert opinion so they visited an orthopedic doctor who took some X-rays. The good news was there were no major tears. The bad news was there were minor tears in both legs. He told them this was common for a tall girl her age. It was part of the growing pains that a kid had to endure. He also suggested for her not to play at Nationals. It would be too risky and she could easily re-damage the muscles and make the healing process even lengthier with the scar tissue that could build up.

Saul didn't like this suggestion and decided to get a second opinion from another doctor, who ordered an MRI to be done. The second opinion agreed with the first opinion.

"I'll get a third opinion, just to be sure," he told Veronica who looked at him disbelievingly.

"I'm your third opinion," she responded back sharply. "She's not playing at Nationals."

Saul let out a long sigh and knew she was right. He just couldn't admit it. Here he was, finally going to Nationals, The Big Dance, the tournament he had been waiting for, but he had two daughters that couldn't dance at the ball. One was out because she needed a third leg to stand on, the other was out because she would always be a third stringer in her coach's eye.

Saul was demoralized. There was no mention of third stringer status or injury in his Master Athletic Plan. Nationals was six long weeks away and he would have to put up with the moaning from both girls, both of them angry because they wouldn't be playing.

The trip to Nationals couldn't come soon enough. Harper was tired of her physical therapy treatments and Bree was tired of her team. To make the experience even more unpleasant, the schedules of the two teams did not overlap. Harper's team played the first four days of Nationals and Bree's team played the last four days. Thus, the Brysons had to reserve eight nights in exciting Columbus, Ohio.

Even though his daughters weren't playing, Saul decided he would still try to enjoy the experience of Nationals as best he could. This was what everyone played for. He wanted to see what kind of environment was on display. When he arrived at the Columbus Convention Center, he was a little disappointed. On the surface, the tournament had the look and feel of any other national qualifier. Colorado Crossroads and Lone Star were actually larger tournaments when it came to the number of courts.

He didn't really get it until he saw the large colorful stadium court. Built to hold a few thousand people, the stadium court hosted all the championship finals. At the start of every final, the National Anthem was played and then all the players were announced over the PA system. All the finals were streamed live over the Internet with broadcasters commenting on the match. They had official referees at every position on the court. They also had ball boys and ball girls that shagged loose balls for the players so they didn't have to chase after them. It was all done in a first class fashion.

Over the course of his eight day stay, Saul got to watch a few of the finals at the stadium court and he got wrapped up in the drama of it all. A season's worth of action coming down to just one match, one game, maybe even one point. The excitement of the girls and parents when they won was a blast to watch. To top it off, they then climbed the medal stand to receive their medals and other individual honors.

Saul dreamed about seeing his daughters up there one day. The stadium court was a natural milestone to achieve in his MAP. He hoped his daughters might make it to the medal stand this year. Even though it would be less rewarding since they weren't playing, it would still be a unique experience.

Harper's team didn't cooperate with his dream. They fought gallantly at times but weren't quite ready for the big stage. They missed Harper a great deal, too, but Saul's modesty kept him from relaying that to the other parents. The third middle they used in place of Harper was very weak. SkyHi Blue 12s finished 17th, which wasn't a bad showing. It was a far cry from the stadium court, though. Their arch rival, MadDogs Black, had an outstanding tournament. They finished third and Saul and Harper watched enviously as they approached the medal stand to receive their bronze prize.

"I want to do that," Harper told Saul.

"I do, too," Saul said.

Harper looked at him with a funny face. "I mean I want you to do that, too," Saul corrected himself. "Obviously, I can't do it."

"That's right, Dad. You're too old."

"Thanks, Harp."

"Plus you're a boy," Harper added.

With MadDogs finishing third, it did speak to the strength of the North Texas Region. SkyHi now knew that if they could hang with MadDogs, they could hang with anyone in the country. The question was how long would it take for them to reach MadDogs' talent level.

Speaking of talent, talent was widely on display in the 15s Open Division. Saul couldn't believe how good all the teams were. Bree's team got off to a great start and won a grueling eight team pool that spanned the first few days of the tournament. By winning their pool, they received a bye that advanced them to the final eight teams. One more win and they would at least assure themselves of a medal.

Everyone on the team was playing well except for the bench players, of course. Bree had yet to see the court and her benchwarmer buddies, Morgan and Bailey, were providing much needed comic relief on the sidelines by creating improbable scenarios of how each of them would make the all-tournament team.

Their next opponent was a team called SVC. They were a surprise team that didn't have a high seed coming into the tournament. Because of this, Saul felt good about the team's chances and also about seeing his non-playing daughter on the medal stand. And, they were only two wins away from playing on the stadium court, which would be great to witness even if his daughter was on the bench.

Coach Carpenter ended up being right about his team. He said at the start of the season they could compete for a national championship and here they were on the verge of fulfilling that quest. Saul wished that Bree would gain some satisfaction from being on such an elite team that finished high at Nationals. Just to make the team showed she was a quality player, but when you're 15 years old, playing means you're good and not-playing means you're a failure.

During warm-ups for the SVC match, Bree was going through her routine when she began hearing her name called from somewhere on the court. The voice sounded somewhat familiar but she couldn't quite place it. Then, her eye caught a figure waving to her from the other side of the net.

"Oh, my God," Bree blurted out.

Saul, looking on, noticed it was Callie, her old friend from Seattle who she hadn't talked to for the longest time. They ran to meet each other and gave each other a hug, once they awkwardly figured out who was going to walk under the net to get to the other side.

"What are you doing here?" Bree asked, flushed with emotion.

"I play for SVC. We're playing you guys."

"Oh, my God. This is crazy," Bree exclaimed. "I didn't realize SVC stood for Seattle Volleyball Club. This is bizarre."

"I know. This is crazy," Callie echoed. "but I've got to go now. The coach wants us. Good luck."

"You, too," Bree said as she watched Callie stamper off.

Watching the exchange between the two girls, Saul was amazed. What a small world, but a great one. Where else can you have a sport that connects players and families like this. In Columbus, Ohio, of all places.

The game started and Saul could tell Bree seemed more nervous than usual. She probably wanted to win the game more than usual so Callie could see how good her team was. She also probably wanted to play so Callie wouldn't know she was a benchwarmer. She didn't have much control over either scenario, though.

The longer the game played out, the more unsettled Bree looked. Saul could only imagine what was going through her mind. Did Callie think she was a loser for not getting into the game? She would have to answer all the awkward questions of why she wasn't playing, just like she had to answer them for her old teammates from MadDogs Red.

Callie was still a great player, Saul quickly deduced. That was easy to see as he watched her make a tremendous athletic play that led to a point for SVC. She still had a great serve, too, but her outside hitting wasn't as strong. She had stopped growing over a year ago and her size of five feet nine inches was starting to catch up with her. She got blocked quite a bit because she couldn't hit over the outstretched hands of the defenders. Her team was very good though. They gave SkyHi all they could handle in the first game. SkyHi played an almost perfect game with only two errors and managed to squeak out a 25 to 23 win. In game two, however, Callie's strength came into play.

With the game tied, she approached the service line and started to reel off a string of jump serves that were impossible for SkyHi's back row to handle. Her serves came over the net with such topspin and dived to the ground so quickly it left Bree's teammates in a state of confusion. Saul could tell by Bree's facial expression that she wanted a try at passing one to show her teammates how it was done, but that wasn't going to happen.

After five service winners in a row, Carpenter had to call a timeout to try and stem Callie's momentum. The timeout worked. They won the next point and got Callie off of the service line. The five point lead she had built was too large to overcome, however. SVC continued to play well and kept SkyHi from putting together a rally. They won game two 25 to 22.

Tensions were high as game three began. Lauren's dad was up leading cheers for the parents hoping it would get the girls fired up. Girls from a couple of other SkyHi teams that were done playing gathered around the court to cheer on their fellow club mates. Saul noticed a wall of people surrounding the court, maybe five or six people deep. Everyone was watching to see which team would make it to the medal round.

Game three began and the gravity of the moment was taking its toll on the girls. What had been a perfectly played match for the first two games suddenly turned into a game of errors. Players were missing serves and hitting shots way out of bounds. Even Callie missed a couple of serves at crucial times. Surprisingly, the girl that was making the most mistakes was Cathy, normally reliable Cathy. Her offensive game had disappeared and she wasn't closing the block on defense at all. Her last serve was hit so poorly it actually went under the net. Saul knew that she wasn't coming out, though. She had not come out of a game all year.

Pamela, on the other hand, was having a great match and was helping to keep SkyHi in the game. The score was going back and forth. One team would take a one point lead and then the other team would bounce back and retake the lead. Pamela rocketed a kill through the defense and tied the score up at 13 when it was time for Cathy to rotate in for her.

Cathy came in and Lauren quickly set her the ball. Cathy went for one of her patented tips to an open zone, but almost whiffed the tip. The ball fell short of the net and SVC took a 14 to 13 lead and had match point. Then Saul's heart stopped beating for a moment. He noticed Carpenter motioning for Bree to go in.

"Oh, my God," Veronica shouted.

What the F. You're going to put her in now? Saul didn't want her in. She was as cold as ice. She had barely played the whole tournament. What was Carpenter thinking? Yes, Cathy had been having her worst game of the season, but don't you stick with the horse who brung ya?

Bree walked somewhat reluctantly onto the court. Saul could tell she was nervous. She was being thrown into a fire, a situation she didn't deserve to be in. One mistake and the game was over. One mistake and her best friend, or former best friend, would win the match.

Saul was concerned that Callie might be a distraction for Bree, but he also figured Bree could be a distraction for Callie as well. The next point was ready to be played and it was almost unbearable to watch. Lauren set the ball to Butt Cheeks a couple of times during the rally but SVC somehow dug her shots and kept the rally going. Lauren then set Bree, which caught Saul totally by surprise. As Bree went up, Saul was praying for a forceful kill but it didn't happen. Bree hit the ball safely over the net to an SVC defender.

"Hit the ball," Saul heard Butt Cheeks screaming at Bree.

If Bree heard her, she pretended not to notice. She concentrated on getting to her block. Callie was going up for the kill and Bree launched herself in the air high enough to touch the ball and slow it's pace down.

Lauren immediately screamed at Bree, "Zone Five! Zone Five!", which meant she was about to set Bree again and she needed to hit to the zone five area. The set came again to Bree and again she hit it safely, but it was to zone one instead of zone five.

"Hit the ball!" Saul shouted with disappointment.

Bree wasn't playing aggressive. She had wasted two opportunities in a row from Lauren, the setter who Saul had once questioned but not now. Saul was glad he didn't make a scene with her dad back in Denver. Lauren was trying to get Bree involved but Bree was playing not to lose instead of playing to win. She didn't want to make a mistake. It also didn't help that her confidence had been totally shot the last couple of months.

"I told you zone five," Lauren screamed at her.

Again, Bree didn't act like she heard her teammate's criticism. She also didn't act like she heard Saul's loud outburst. She kept her focus on what to do next, which was preparing for another block.

SVC was running another play to Callie. She was coming hard to the net and Bree was there in plenty of time to set up the block. Her arms went up high and Callie swung with all her might. The ball went right into Bree's hands and caromed back to the SVC side of the court. Saul jumped high with excitement They had tied it at 14 and Bree's teammates were starting to celebrate the point when everyone heard the loud whistle of the head referee.

"What's going on?" Saul asked, turning to Veronica. He then saw the head referee signaling that the game was over.

"Game over?" Veronica asked perplexed. "We won the point."

"No, we didn't," Saul said dejectedly. "The down ref said she was in the net."

"In the net? Who? Bree? She's never in the net?" Veronica said.

"I know," Saul agreed. "She never makes that mistake."

But she did today. At match point of the third game of the quarterfinal match with a national medal on the line. The call was a common one. It happened a lot. A player can't touch the top of the net with her arms or hands when attempting to block the ball. Saul heard the grumbling of the SkyHi parents talking under their breath. They were either criticizing Bree or Cathy or Coach Carpenter for making the substitution, or all three.

He watched as the players gathered at the net to shake hands. He could tell Bree was distraught. She quickly went through the line and shook the players hands. When Callie reached out for Bree's hand, she tried to maintain the grip and pull Bree closer to her, almost like she wanted to give her a hug, but Bree pulled away forcibly. The SkyHi girls walked back to their bench, many of them with tears in their eyes. Carpenter said a few words and then released them to go be with their parents. The season was over.

Saul and Veronica waited with Harper for Bree to come over, but she didn't come over. She immediately walked away in the opposite direction.

"Where is she going?" Harper asked.

"I don't know. Maybe she doesn't see us." Veronica suggested.

"I'll go get her," Saul said.

"No, I better get her," Veronica insisted. Saul thought that a mother's touch might be the right move. He nodded for her to go ahead. As she walked through the flow of people, she spotted Bree and saw that she was heading for the bathroom. She caught up to her and grabbed her arm. "Hey, Bree,"

Bree turned around and Veronica saw her sad, depressed face. Saul was watching from a distance. He watched as Bree faced Veronica. He saw Bree say a few brief words to her and then head into the ladies restroom. While hanging onto Harper's hand, Saul walked over to Veronica.

"What did she say?" Saul asked.

Veronica looked at him and then looked at Harper. "I'll tell you later," she said.

Saul got the hint. Whatever it was Bree said, Very didn't want Harper to hear. Saul reached in his pocket. "Hey Harp, would you do me a favor and go get you and your sister some Dippin' Dots."

That was music to her ears. "Will do," she said, grabbing the money and heading for the line.

"So tell me what she said," an extremely concerned Saul asked again.

Veronica thought a few seconds about how she should phrase it, but she thought it best to just say the words as Bree said them. She said, "I'm done with this game."

Saul bowed his head and sighed. He now wished he would have been the one to chase after Bree. Maybe she would have said something different. Or maybe not. If this was how she felt, this was how she felt. She needed to get the misery of the past few minutes, heck the past few months, off her chest.

And so did Saul. His Master Athletic Plan was beginning to fail him. Ironically, there had been lots of winning this season, more than Bree had ever experienced. But it didn't feel like a winning season for Saul or Bree. For the first time, he felt a little helpless. He had a daughter who wanted to quit. There was no chapter in the MAP for dealing with quitters. Quitting was not a part of his DNA. All he could do now was hope it was not a part of Bree's, either.

CHAPTER FOURTEEN

THE OTHER SIDE OF THE NET

While Harper was getting her Dippin' Dots and Saul and Veronica were waiting for their daughter to exit the restroom, Callie came walking over looking for Bree and asked them where she was.

"She's very upset right now, Callie," Veronica said. "I'll have her call you, okay?"

Callie looked disappointed. "Okay. Would you tell her I'm sorry I haven't called for a while? I really miss her."

"You bet," Veronica said. "I know she misses you, too."

Saul had barely heard the conversation. He was too wrapped up in what Bree had said. This wasn't the time for Bree to quit. He knew the season was tough and had a lot more downs than ups but Bree was still a great player. There were a ton of clubs she could play for and there was always school ball.

Bree finally exited the restroom and the family walked out together. Harper shared her Dippin' Dots with Bree, which broke the awkward silence a bit. They reached their hotel room and began packing for the flight home. Saul was getting tired of avoiding the elephant in the room. "Do you want to talk about the game, Bree?" he asked.

"No," she said decisively.

"You know, it wasn't your fault."

"I don't want to talk about it," she said as she forcefully shoved some items in her suitcase. "And it was my fault, by the way. I cost the team the game by hitting the net."

"The coach never should have put you in that position."

"Darn right," she huffed. "Because I'm not good enough."

"That's not true. I didn't mean it that way."

"Oh, really? I had Lauren yelling at me and Butt Cheeks yelling at me. Then I had my own father yelling at me. All during one point! I hadn't played all weekend and I was supposed to be a hero then?"

"I'm sorry I screamed at you. I was caught up in the moment. You did have a chance to kill the ball, though. You've got to take advantage of those opportunities next time."

"That's what you want to talk about right now? Thanks for the advice, Dad, but there isn't going to be a next time."

Saul knew he had said the wrong thing at the wrong time. "Listen, Bree, I'm sorry . . ."

She wasn't listening to him. "I'm done with your advice and I'm done with this game. Didn't Mom tell you?"

Saul didn't respond. He looked at Veronica. He didn't know if he would be betraying Veronica's confidence or not.

"Harper," Veronica said. "Let's go get some ice cream."

"Really? But I just had Dippin' Dots," Harper exclaimed.

"I know but I didn't have any. You can share with me, okay?" Veronica grabbed her purse and the two exited the room.

Saul broke the silence. "Bree, I know you're upset but . . ."

"I never had the killer instinct anyway," Bree interrupted him. "That's always bugged you about me, right Dad?"

"That's not true, Bree. I . . . "

"I'm tired of having to be aggressive," Bree continued. "I'm tired of having to be the boy you always wanted. I'm tired of being something I'm not. And I'm tired of listening to you talking about what's happening on the other side of the net. You know why?"

Saul shrugged. He didn't know how to respond.

"Because I feel like you're always on the other side of the net. I feel like you're always against me. Like I can never do anything right. You're never on my side of the net."

"Bree, I'm always on your side."

"I can never make you happy. I'm always doing something wrong and you know what? I've finally realized that all I have been trying to do is make you happy. I've been playing this silly game for you and not for me."

Saul was speechless. He couldn't comprehend the words that were coming out of her mouth. They cut hard and deep. He knew the season was difficult but the vitriol she was now spewing had to have been stored inside for quite some time.

"Bree, I'm sorry you feel this way," Saul began as he was trying to search for the proper words. "But don't be reckless, you have college to consider and . . ."

"College?" She asked incredulously. "Dad, I don't want to play in college. That may be what you want but it's not what I want. And how would you even know? We've never even discussed it."

"But how do you know if . . .?"

"If what? I don't want to play in college? Because I just do, not to mention the fact that I'm just not good enough."

"But you don't know unless you . . ."

Bree cut him off again. "And don't tell me not to say no to something I know nothing about. Dad, I've played this game for almost five years now. I know plenty. I've talked to girls at the club who've played in college and I don't want to do it."

Saul decided it was best if he didn't say anything. She wasn't letting him talk anyway. He could only hope her outburst would help her heal whatever scars she was bearing, some that might even be his doing.

"Bree, I'm going downstairs to check out. Please finish up your packing." He walked to the door and opened it, but stopped before heading out. He didn't want to leave her this way. He felt he had to say something. "For what it's worth, you always make me happy. Please don't forget that. And I love the fact that I have two beautiful daughters. You give me such joy."

A tear dropped from Bree's eye but Saul couldn't see it because she had turned away from him.

"If I wanted a boy so badly, believe me, your Mother and I would have kept trying. But this is about me and you. And if you don't have a true love for the game by now, that's fine. You don't have to play anymore. I won't make you. Heck, you're about to be 16. It's time for you to start making decisions about your life and I'm sorry I've put you in this situation. I was only trying to make you a better player."

Bree was breathing heavily, like she was letting out a huge weight inside her soul. Tears were running down her cheeks.

"But Bree, regardless of what decisions you make going forward, you do have a special talent for this game. If you don't realize that by now, it's a shame. I know you're tired of my speeches and my coaching and my advice, but this is your dad talking now, not your volleyball dad. You have many other talents as well. Please don't ignore them. They are gifts and to waste them will keep you from being the best person you can be." Saul was satisfied. He said what was on his mind and she didn't interrupt him. He shut the door and left Bree in the room to finish her packing, while Saul was left to figure out how to restore whatever bond, if any, he and Bree had forged together prior to this point.

Not one word about volleyball was spoken on the trip home or when they got back. The summer was shortened because of Nationals. June was already past. They decided not to have a vacation that year and just enjoy the house and pool. Veronica let the kids unwind when they got home. She kept wanting to talk to Saul about his conversation with Bree but thought it best to wait for him to bring it up. For some reason, he never did. He went off to work and every evening she thought this might be the night they would talk about it, but it didn't happen.

There was no talk of volleyball. And there was no talk of school volleyball, which was soon coming up. There was no talk of volleyball practices on Bryson Court. There was no talk of even setting up Bryson Court, if only to play a pick-up game.

Veronica told Bree about seeing Callie after their match and Bree called her up. She apologized for not visiting with her in Columbus and they both apologized for not talking to each other and promised not to let that happen again. Their friendship rekindled, Bree asked if she could go visit Callie in Seattle and Saul and Veronica said okay.

With Bree away in Seattle and Harper at a friends house one evening, Veronica decided to have a quiet, romantic dinner poolside on the patio with Saul. While the setting was romantic, her intentions were anything but. She thought the ambiance might relax Saul a bit and they could finally have their conversation about what happened with Bree.

Saul sat down at the table. He was tired from work. He told Veronica he spent most of the day in the CFO's office listening to him practice a speech he was giving to the Dallas Chapter of the American Institute of Certified Public Accountants. After four run-throughs, it was all he could do to keep his eyes open while showering his boss with praise.

"Where is Harp?" he asked as he sat down.

"At a friend's house. Want some wine?"

Saul held up his glass for her to pour. "Heard anything from Bree today?" he asked.

"I talked with her for a few minutes. They were going hiking at Mt. Rainier today."

"Good for her. That's something we never did when we lived there."

"No. We let the rain keep us from doing a lot of things."

"That's true," Saul laughed.

"It was nice of you to let her go there on such short notice."

"She needed it. We both needed some away time, I think. Besides, it's not like there's any need to practice."

"What does that mean?" Veronica wondered.

"It means she's done. She told you that, remember?"

"Of course, I remember," Veronica replied. "But I never heard what happened after you two talked."

"She basically told me that I was impossible to make happy, that I was never satisfied with her, that I wasn't on her side, that I had been making her play this silly game all along, that she was playing it for me and not for herself, basically she said everything a proud father loves to hear about his parenting skills."

"You know she didn't mean all of that. She was just upset about things."

"I don't know what she meant and didn't mean. I let her get her feelings out. It was tough to hear but maybe there was some truth in it. Maybe I did push her too hard. I told her she didn't have to play anymore."

"But how is she going to spend her time? Volleyball was also our plan to keep the bad outside influences at bay. Remember?"

"Sure, I remember. But she's almost 16. We can't keep the bad influences away forever."

"I guess you're right," Veronica hated to admit. She took a sip of wine and started to reflect. "When Bree was younger, I used to think you were pushing her too hard. Making her play sports she didn't want to play. Dragging her out to the ballparks. Sending her to clinics and tryouts she screamed bloody-murder about. In the end, though, I think you were doing the right thing. She never would have done anything without a little nudge."

"There's a nuance to finding the right balance, though," Saul thought aloud.

Veronica agreed. "It's hard to find that balance. I guess a lot depends on the kid. We've got to figure out how much to push them and how much we let them pull us."

Saul put down his glass. "I still can't believe she ever thought I was against her. I promise you I never said or did anything to make her feel that way."

"I know you didn't. Like most kids, Bree has a problem handling criticism, especially when it comes from her father. I do believe she was playing for you, though."

"You do?

"Not in a bad way. I think she was playing for both you and herself. But every daughter wants to make her dad happy."

"Maybe you're right," Saul pondered. Whatever she ends up doing, I will always believe, deep down, she found some joy in that game. As much as she resisted it at times and as much as she reluctantly went to tryouts, when she made the PSA team, I heard the excitement in her voice. When she beat Renner in that district championship game, I saw the passion on her face. When she went up for a set and killed it with authority, I saw her smile wide with satisfaction."

"Well, you have another daughter that wants to make her dad happy, too. When are you going to start practicing with her?"

"With Harp? Heck, she doesn't need the practice. She'll have no problem making the 7th grade team. She's turned her competitive desire of being better than her sister into a desire to beat every girl on the planet."

"So let her pull you," Veronica said.

Saul looked at Veronica, not understanding what she meant at first. Then he smiled.

"She still needs her Dad's attention and guidance, even if she is a natural born killer . . . of the volleyball, that is."

"You know, Very, you may be right. I've been so worried about Bree's volleyball career, I've probably took Harper's abilities a little too much for granted. Maybe it is time to focus more on her."

"And remember to do what?" Veronica cautioned.

"Let her pull me."

"Good," said Veronica as she rose from the table. "Time to bring out the dinner."

At Harper's urgent request, she and Saul began working together the next evening. Harper had been cleared by her physical therapist to start working out a week earlier. Saul was careful not to push it the first night. He wanted to slowly work her back into playing shape. As it turned out, that didn't take very long.

Harper enjoyed having the sole attention of her dad while Bree was visiting Callie. They worked on a lot of different types of hits, not just middle hits. Saul was amazed at Harper's power for her age and the heaviness of her arm swing. The sound she made when she contacted the ball echoed from the cul-de-sac down to the end of the street. He told her not to jump high and to go at half-speed, but there was no half-speed setting for her arm swing. She loved to hammer the ball every time she could.

She continued to do her leg exercises daily to strengthen her hamstrings and as the school season was approaching, Saul could tell she was jumping higher than she had ever been jumping before. The strength training the physical therapist assigned was starting to pay dividends.

Bree returned home from her visit to Seattle and seemed very happy and at ease. She talked with Saul about all the things she and Callie did. She talked about how their friendship was as good as it had ever been and that Callie was going to come visit them next summer. They didn't talk about volleyball at all and Saul was not going to be the one to bring it up.

Time was ticking, though. Tryouts started the first week of August for high schoolers, which was less than a week away. If she were still playing, this next week would have been a big deal; maybe a chance for her to make the varsity team. But with each passing day, Saul told himself it wasn't to be.

He continued to work with Harper, though. Harper would ask Bree to come play with them, but she refused. Harper would get dismayed and ask Saul what was wrong and he would just say she's decided to move on from volleyball.

"Move on? What does that mean?" Harper asked. "She's too good to quit."

"It just means she's ready to do something else."

"You mean, like date Bobby?" Harper asked innocently.

"What? No. Of course not. Why would you say that?"

Harper had that look on her face like she said something wrong.

"Harper," Saul said sternly. "Do you know something we don't?"

"I thought you knew."

"Knew what?"

"Dad, please don't say anything because Bree will kill me."

"Is she dating Robby?" Saul asked.

"Bobby," Harper corrected him.

"Robby, Bobby, whatever, is she dating one of them?"

"I don't know for sure. I think they've been hanging out some."

"Where?"

"When Bree goes over to Savannah's house, Robby and Bobby go there sometimes."

Saul ended practice immediately and went to find Veronica. He called for an emergency conference meeting on the patio ASAP. He confronted her to see if she knew what was going on.

"Of course not. This is the first I've heard of it."

"So Bree's never mentioned anything to you about the boys?"

"No. Oh, why this now," she moaned flailing her arms in the air. "She's got all this extra time on her hands and now she's going to use it to hookup with a boy."

"Don't say that word."

"What word?" Veronica asked.

"Hookup."

"But that's the word they use."

"I know it is but I get a very horrible vision of my daughter when I hear that word."

"You need to make her go to tryouts," Veronica insisted.

"I'm not going to make her go to tryouts. I've told her she didn't have to play anymore."

"Well, I never agreed to it. I can make her."

"Okay, Very, calm down for a minute. Would you listen to yourself? We don't really know anything right now. For all we know, they are just friends. We've got to trust Bree to do the right thing here."

"Thanks, Dad."

Saul turned and there was Bree approaching them. "Bree, hi," Saul said somewhat startled. What's going on?"

"Harper told me what she said to you so I thought I better come down and explain things."

"Okay. Thank you," Saul politely said.

"Robby and Bobby have been hanging out over at Savannah's. Nothing naughty has happened, but I do like Bobby."

"Bree," Veronica began, "when you're over at Savannah's with Robby and Bobby hooking . . . I mean hanging around," she quickly corrected herself, "is her Mom there?"

"Yes, Mom, of course."

"Okay, good. Just checking."

"But I want you guys to know Bobby is nice and a lot of fun. He's asked me out this weekend and I want to go. Is that okay?"

Saul and Veronica looked at each other. They were not ready for this type of question. Their Master Parenting Plan never assumed their daughter would be asked out on a date before the age of 18.

"Who's going to drive?" Veronica asked.

"His dad."

"And where would you go?" Saul inquired.

"To see a movie."

Saul looked at Very and then said, "I think that's fine then. You guys go and have fun."

Very nodded in agreement and Saul was relieved she wasn't upset with him for his answer.

"Thanks, Mom and Dad. I'm going back inside now."

When Bree shut the door behind her, Veronica wailed, "Oh, my God."

"Oh, my God is right," Saul said. "It's happening and she's taking it out on me. She's so pissed off she's decided to date the boy that kicked me off the volleyball court that day."

"You think she's rebelling?" Veronica asked worriedly. "It's my fault, too. I didn't let her pull enough."

"Let's get a grip for a moment, Veronica, we've got to keep some faith in our parenting skills. We're not that bad. We took them to the Grand Canyon, for God's sake."

Veronica sighed and tried to calm down. "You're right. She's just going to the movies. Everything will be okay."

After they both settled down, Saul knew the boy crush was not a good thing. Tryouts were the furthest thing from her mind. Any ounce of hope he claimed just disappeared thanks to the boy scum that now was called Bobby.

BREE'S DIARY
July 21
Thanks to my little sister, it happened. My parents found out about Bobby. It's not that big a deal, tho. It's not like we've been dating. We just sort of reconnected over the summer. Just like Callie and I reconnected. It's nice to have my friend back. My parents have been pretty cool, tho. For me spazzing out like I did at Nationals, I'm surprised they haven't locked me up at a crazy house. Playing volleyball with Callie in Seattle reminded me of our younger years. It reminded me that I still love the game. I've got to figure out what I want to do. I have an idea but my parents will think it's stupid.

Saul continued to work with Harper to keep his mind off things. Harper was always gung-ho when he asked her to help him set up Bryson Court. She and Saul had it down to a science. It took them just a few minutes to set up the net and take it down. They were outside playing when Bobby came to pick Bree up that Saturday night.

He didn't go to the door. Bree came out to him. The manners of kids these days, Saul thought. Somewhere along the line, this generation had lost proper dating protocol. Bree saw Saul and Harper and waved to them. Saul waved back. Bobby waved, too, but Saul gave him a half-wave out of spite. Saul checked to see if there was a responsible driver in the front and there was. He didn't bother circling through the cul-de-sac like other drivers did. Bobby probably told his dad to turn around in the driveway.

Coward, Saul deduced.

When Bree arrived home at 10:30 p.m., she scampered upstairs with no conversation whatsoever. Saul and Veronica were in bed watching the news when they heard her arrive.

"Should you go up for a debrief?" Saul asked.

"I'll just wait until morning."

The morning debrief was quick. How was your evening? Fine. How was the movie? Good. How was Bobby? Fine. What was Bobby's dad like? Fine. They were the usual in-depth answers from their reigning member of the National Honor Society. She didn't see any need to elaborate any further. She spent the rest of the day by the pool with her headphones on listening to her iPod.

That evening, Saul was out playing with Harper before dinner. Veronica sent Bree outside to tell them dinner would be ready in thirty minutes. Bree walked outside and yelled the information to them instead of walking a bit closer and relaying the information in a more respectful manner.

Harper yelled back, "Come out and play with us."

Bree seemed to act like she didn't hear. She went back inside and Harper frowned. "She's still mad at me for telling you about Bobby."

"She'll get over it," Saul assured her. "Let's work on your serving."

341

Harper went back to serve the ball but before she did, she saw Bree walking toward them. Bree had changed out of her swimsuit and into some shorts and a shirt.

"Alright if I play?" she asked.

"Sure." Harper said.

It seemed like a lifetime to Saul but for the first time in five weeks he saw Bree touch a volleyball.

"You serve and I'll pass, okay?" Bree suggested.

"Okay."

Harper's face lit up with happiness. She had her big sister back on the court again. Saul didn't say a word. He stood back and shagged a loose ball when he needed to. He was enjoying just watching the interaction between the two girls. Bree bragged on how good Harper's serve had gotten and that just made Harper want to serve better. Bree was rusty, which wasn't a surprise but it didn't matter. Whatever compelled her to come back outside wasn't important. He was just glad to see her playing with her sister. They were having a good time.

At dinner that night, Bree asked if they could move the table settings outside to the patio. She wanted to be out where the conference meetings took place. She told Veronica she had a conference of her own to conduct, which spiked everyone's curiosity.

They were finishing up a nice family meal when Bree said she had an announcement to make. Please don't tell me you're engaged, Saul thought. Or please don't say you want to move away and disown us.

It was neither of those.

"First, I want to thank you for allowing me to have some space this summer," she began. "It allowed me to do a lot of thinking and spend some time with some important friends."

Saul thought that was a nice touch to begin with.

"And Dad, I want to thank you for letting me get some things off my chest and not throwing me out of the house afterwards."

"You're welcome," he said. He didn't know what else to stay.

"As I'm sure you know, tryouts start tomorrow morning. I've decided to go to them."

"That's great to hear, Bree," Saul and Veronica said in unison.

"Mom, Dad, please stop. I'm not finished yet."

The two apologized in unison as well and urged her to continue.

"Dad, you were right. I do love the game. I've missed it. But from now on, I want to do this my way."

"That's okay," Saul assured her.

"You're not going to like this, but I don't want you taking me to the tryouts and I don't want you picking me up after they're over."

Saul took the news as best he could. Was he torn up inside? Yes. Did he feel the agony again of a thousand failed sports dads in his gut? Yes. But he did his best not to show it.

"I don't want any expectations, Dad. I don't want any advice. I don't need any motivational techniques. I'm going there to have fun. I'm going to play volleyball with my friends. I'm going to enjoy the game. I know I haven't played in over a month. I know I'm not in shape. If I make the junior varsity, that's great. If I get cut, that's okay, too. But I hope you both will support me on this."

Saul and Veronica looked at each other to see who would talk first. "Of course, we will, Bree. We're just happy with your decision," Saul said.

"So you're playing volleyball again?" Harper asked.

"If I make the team, yes," Bree answered.

Harper got up and gave her sister a big hug. "I'm so happy you're playing. You're my hero, Sis."

Bree laughed as Harper showered her with affection. "You want to go out and play some after dinner?"

"Let's go now," Harper said.

"Can we be excused?" Bree asked.

"Go right ahead," Veronica said. "It's your Dad's turn to clean up."

The two rushed away and left the parents there to make sense of things.

"Well?" Veronica said, waiting for a reaction from Saul.

"I think I'm on volleyball dad probation," Saul said. "One more violation and I am without visitation rights."

"At least she's trying out," Veronica responded.

"Oh, I'm happy with her decision. I'm not complaining. I'm glad to let her do things her way." She wasn't following the steps of his Master Athletic Plan, but that was okay. He still had Harper who was rapidly exceeding his Plan's expectations.

Veronica took Bree to tryouts in the morning and Saul went to the office. He did his best to stay focused on his work. He didn't call Veronica to see if she heard anything. He didn't lie to his secretary and leave the office early to go spy on the tryouts. He stayed in his office until the day was over and he drove home. He had dinner that night with his family and he did not make mention of the tryouts at all. Neither did Bree. When he asked Veronica in private if she had heard anything, she said no. The next day was more of the same. He went to work. He stayed at work. He went home, had dinner, and no mention was made of the tryouts.

The third day came and he knew he would have to hear something. This was the last day of tryouts, after all. It was the day they selected the teams. He went to work. He stayed at work. He didn't call Veronica. He waited for a call but a call never came. He figured it had to be bad news. He left his office at the regular time and drove home in typical rush hour traffic.

After pulling into the garage, he walked inside. There was nobody around.

"Hello? Anybody here?"

"Dad, you've got to close your eyes," Harper shouted from upstairs. "We've got a surprise."

"I like surprises," Saul said. "My eyes are closed."

"Okay, you can open them now," Harper ordered.

Saul opened his eyes and there was Bree standing before him in a gray Varsity letter jacket.

"How do I look?" Bree asked.

"You look great," Saul said. "Does this mean what I think it means?"

"I made Varsity," Bree screamed. "Can you believe it?"

"That's fantastic, Bree. Of course, I believe it." He went over to give her a hug.

"How did you get the jacket? I thought you had to wait a year or something."

"It's not mine. I borrowed it from Bobby."

"Oh," Saul said. He looked at Veronica with a worried look. She motioned for him to check his phone. He pulled it out and checked his messages. There was one from Veronica that said 'She's just borrowing it. They aren't going steady.' Saul looked at her with relief.

The family dinner was very lively that night, almost like the terrible falling-out Bree had with Saul was way in the past. Saul didn't have to ask a question. He listened to Bree talk about the last three days. She bragged about how she was the only person from the Freshman team that made Varsity. She said that both

Savannah and Pamela made Varsity, too. She talked about how all her friends supported her. Callie told her she had to keep playing so that they could see each other again at Nationals next year. Bobby told her she had to keep playing so she could have her own letter jacket to wear. Savannah begged her to play because if she didn't, she would want to quit herself. And Pamela, of all people surprised her the most. She told her she couldn't quit because if she did, their team would be terrible. The Varsity needed two middles and she was the best middle out there.

"That was very nice of her," Saul had to admit.

"And Dad, I know this sounds crazy but being on SkyHi last season made me a better player. The coaches were all impressed that I was on a team that finished fifth in the country."

Saul acted like he was hearing this for the first time. He had tried to tell her several times last season she was getting better, but she would never believe it. She only saw the embarrassment of sitting on the bench. Saul listened intently as Bree rambled on about her new teammates and how she managed to play well for those three days even though she hadn't touched a ball for weeks.

"Every day I got better and better," she told him. "It was sort of like riding a bike. It didn't take long before my game came back."

And to Saul's relief, his daughter was back playing her sport. Maybe not at the MAP level he wanted, but she was back nonetheless. She was growing up right before his very eyes, making mature decisions and finding her own independent streak. More importantly, his daughter was no quitter. The Bryson DNA strand remained intact.

Even with Bree's good news that evening, there still something that bothered Saul, something that had yet to be fully repaired. And it had nothing to do with volleyball. Yes, he and

346

Bree were talking again but their conversations didn't feel the same. They lacked substance and feeling and depth. He didn't feel like she shared with him anymore and that was devastating to him. Quite simply, there was no bond living or breathing or growing between them now and he didn't know what to do. He knew maybe all they needed was time. Time heals everything so they say. But he didn't want to wait for time. She would be in college in two years, for crying out loud.

He wanted to reconnect now but how do you reconnect with a 16 year old? He knew it would require more than just taking her out for a scoop of ice cream.

BREE'S DIARY
Wednesday, August 13
I had a hard conversation with my dad this week. I think he took it well. I think he knows I still need him. I had a conversation with my mom, too. She wanted to talk volleyball since me and dad aren't talking volleyball. She tried giving me advice about volleyball and competition. She mentioned her experience as being a flute player and how she had to compete for first chair in the orchestra just like I had to compete with Pamela and others. Every day, a new flutist would challenge her for her chair. It made her a better flutist. At first I thought she was crazy. Music is just art, after all. But the more I thought about it, the more I admired the pressure she was under. I think she has a sense of what I go through. Parents are still out of control, tho. Pamela made peace with me after making peace with her dad. I understand now why she was so mean to me. Her dad was putting tons of stress on her to get a scholarship, making her feel guilty about quitting basketball and soccer. It made her feel she couldn't be nice to me because she had to compete against me. I guess my dad is not so bad after all. Anyway, she apologized to

me in the nicest way. She voted for me to be captain of the school team.

CHAPTER FIFTEEN

DREAM TEAM

The trio of Bree, Pamela and Savannah was the future of Plano's Varsity volleyball team. All three played prominent roles that season, which was rare for a bunch of sophomores since they lived in one of the largest school districts in the state that was home to a plethora of experienced club volleyball girls. Part of their good fortune was at the expense of a few veteran seniors who succumbed to outside influences, the kind that Veronica always worried about.

While no one ever knew the true facts, the string of rumors posted on Facebook, Twitter and every other form of social media suggested the veteran seniors got caught indulging in several forms of controlled substances. They were immediately kicked off the team and their absence allowed for the younger girls to move in.

Pamela had secured her spot as the starting middle and Bree won the second middle spot, beating out a couple of juniors in the process. Savannah was the second setter, which meant she was paired with Bree. The two had a blast playing together having been friends and playing partners since the 7th grade. Even Pamela became good friends with Bree who, after years of competing with her, had come to the realization that Pam was just plain better. They enjoyed each other's company considerably more now, knowing what their respective roles were and that they weren't having to fight each other for playing time.

Saul enjoyed the school season and it had nothing to do with winning. They won a lot of games but they lost a lot, too. They ended up being basically a .500 team and just missed out on making the playoffs. The loss of the seniors had obviously hurt their chances, but that didn't matter to Saul. He enjoyed watching Bree play again and he enjoyed watching her love for the game reappear. She was truly having a good time. It was hard to believe only a few months had passed since the pain and agony of the SkyHi season. Thankfully, that was in the rearview mirror now.

Something else that was in the rearview mirror was the Mystery Man. A few games into the school season, Brent approached Saul and said he had something important to tell him.

"I want to apologize to you, Saul."

"Apologize? What for?"

"I haven't behaved in a way I'm proud of. I've put too much pressure on my daughter and, in turn, I think Bree's been the whipping post for some of Pamela's behavior. I didn't know it was happening and it's all my fault."

"I'm a little confused. Bree never mentioned anything to me."

"Well, Pamela mentioned it to me. We had a little falling out and everything hit the fan. Let's just say us volleyball dads, sometimes we'd be better off taking a little Valium to take the edge off."

Saul laughed. "You might be right about that."

"Anyway, I'm glad our daughters are getting along again. Hopefully, we can continue to get along, too."

"Brent, I think we are fine."

And with that understanding, the Mystery Man nickname was laid to rest. Saul was sad to hear that Bree experienced more than just playing time issues with Pamela. He wished she would have said something about it. Maybe that said something about the current lack of connection between them. He didn't know for sure.

While Bree's high school coach encouraged her players to get on the best club team they could, Saul would not make the same mistake again. In theory, it's good advice, but in reality, you want your daughter to play. It's a great game and if you're watching it from the sidelines, you're not playing the great game. Yes, you get to play in practice and get better and all of that, but so what. The game is at its most meaningful when you're in uniform, playing against a true opponent and showcasing your talent, good or bad. Not to mention the fact that $5,000 is a lot of money to shell out just to watch your daughter be humiliated sitting on the bench.

His daughter was playing again and that's all that mattered. And she made Varsity as a sophomore, which was a great accomplishment regardless of the fact certain seniors squandered their opportunity. She was now on track to be a three-year Varsity letterman, which was in perfect alignment with the goals he envisioned in his MAP. But Bree was following her own map now and he had to support it. He still had never brought up volleyball issues with her since their falling out. He would only discuss them when she initiated the conversation. He was still searching for a way to reconnect with her, but the moment, whatever that would be, had not presented itself yet. At least, that's how he justified it in his mind. But he also secretly worried he was just choking away any bond he might ever reclaim with Bree due to his own inept reluctance.

Harper, who was still under the tutelage of Saul's MAP, also had a great school season. She made the seventh grade A Team, which wasn't a surprise. There was little doubt when after the first day of tryouts Saul picked her up and asked her what the competition was like at the middle position and she answered, "Dad, there is no competition."

Even with no drama, Saul still dropped her off and left work early to pick her up every tryout day. He celebrated with her by stopping to get ice cream when she told him the obvious, that she had made the A Team. He didn't want to make light of what was still a great accomplishment, so he felt a scoop of Rocky Road was in order.

Watching Harper play that season, Saul was constantly filled with great pride. And it wasn't just because he was watching his daughter play. Every time he walked into the Wilson Wrangler gym, he got to look up and admire the banner that was hanging down from the rafters. The banner was there to honor Bree's 8th Grade team and their District championship. All the players names were listed, including Bree Bryson. It wasn't the Boston Garden, Saul admitted, but it was still a nice touch. To know your daughter's name would live for eternity in the Wilson Wrangler gymnasium was enough to make any parent proud.

Harper's team won 25 matches that year against only two losses. One of those losses was to dreaded Renner, the team that gave Bree's squad so much trouble. But this Renner team didn't have the great Tina Dulles. Wilson, on the other hand, had three very strong club players, including Harper. Maybe the socioeconomic tide was turning a corner in the Wilson Middle School zone, or maybe it was just lucky timing.

Wilson won the regular season district title and was seeded first for the district championship. They rolled through the tournament all the way to the finals. Renner was the team that stood between them and a district trophy.

"And a banner," Saul told Harper before the match. "You win this game and you get a banner hanging in the gym just like your big sister."

Harper's eyes lit up at the very thought. "Oh, yeah," she said with envy.

That was all the motivation she needed. Harper ran off to remind her teammates of the banner opportunity and the trophy was theirs. They won the match with relative ease, 25 to 16 and 25 to 18. Harper played lights out but so did the rest of the team. Saul couldn't wait to walk into the Wilson gym next season and see both of his daughters' names hanging from the rafters for all to see.

After the championship match, most of the girls had to run to club tryouts, which had started that day. Saul had a brief discussion with Harper about considering other clubs, maybe even trying out for MadDogs again, but she shut that down quickly. She wanted to stay at SkyHi, especially when she found out who her coach was. Bree's PSA coach, Autumn, was hired by SkyHi to coach 13s. Saul was pleased. He thought she would be a great fit for Harper.

Autumn assured Saul she wanted Harper on the team. Saul was worried she might hold a grudge against him for moving Bree to MadDogs a few years back but she didn't bring it up. It was a blessing going to tryouts knowing your daughter would most likely have a spot. Most parents in the club volleyball world aren't afforded that luxury. There was a lot of talent in the gym that day. Saul saw several familiar faces from last year, girls who played at different clubs and were coming to SkyHi to see if they could make it. He didn't see any players that might threaten Harper for her spot, but he did see several good outside hitters that could help their team improve.

Harper's team had 10 girls on it last year. She had become friendly with most of her teammates. They were all in the gym that day hoping to secure their spot. Saul wondered what the SkyHi coaches would do. They had a good team last season that qualified for Nationals so he assumed most of the team would stay intact.

The end of tryouts is one of the most stressful and nervous times in a young volleyball girl's life. She sits there waiting for her name to be called and if it isn't, it's on to the next tryout. As the names were called for SkyHi 13s Blue, Saul slowly realized his assumption about keeping the team intact was wrong. Harper's name was called early but as he listened, new name after new name was announced. The club had switched out half of the team. Five new girls were added and five veteran girls were demoted to the second team, SkyHi 13s Black.

Parents that he had come to know last season were aghast. They couldn't believe their daughter didn't make the top team. Saul tried to console them and tell them what they didn't want to hear, that the second team would still be a strong team and that they might make the top team again next year. He heard fathers cussing under their breath and desperate discussions between spouses murmuring about what to do. Do we take the second team offer? Do we go to Advantage or MadDogs or some other club to see if we can make it there? It was a point where a parent has to remain calm and objectively assess the situation. Instead, most parents' anger and pride take over and they leave the facility in a huff.

"My daughter is not playing for no second team," he heard one father say.

"Screw them, we'll go play on a second team somewhere else," he heard one mother say. "I'm not going to give them the satisfaction."

He even heard one dad berating his daughter's performance in the tryout. "If you would have played better today, you would have made the team so quit your darn crying," he shouted at her.

Lost in all this was rational thought and discussion. Many times the discussion didn't even include the daughter and what her pride and ego were feeling at that moment. Most girls are happy with a second or third team. Most just want to have a good time and make new friends. But most parents have an un-realistic view about their daughter's talent and potential and they let that cloud their judgment at times. Saul felt lucky to be in the position he was in with Harper. However, he knew that every year would be a battle to protect her spot, but for this year at least, she was safe.

SkyHi was a club but it was a club with a mission to win, not just to create a place for friends to congregate. They had third teams and fourth teams for the girls that valued socializing over winning.

When Saul got to know the new girls that were added to the roster, he could see why the changes were made. They were cho-sen to shore up some of the weaknesses from last year's team. While it was tough for Harper to watch some of her friends move to the second team or walk out the door, she understood it when Saul explained the reasoning.

"Plus," he told her, "SkyHi Blue would have a better shot at beating MadDogs now." Once she heard that, she seemed to be more at peace with it all.

What Saul wasn't at peace with was Bree's plan for club ball, or if she even had one. He was worried sick about it but he couldn't say anything because he was honoring Bree's wishes for more space. He didn't even know for sure if she was going to play club ball. He assumed it was a given since she had a successful school season and would need to keep her game up if she wanted to make the Varsity team next year. For all he knew though, she might just want to play in a ghastly rec league.

Tryout clinics were currently being conducted and if she was going to try out she better start showing up at them. He asked Veronica if Bree had talked with her about club ball and Veronica said no. He asked Harper and all she would say is "I think she's still thinking about it."

Saul had a brief discussion with Coach Carpenter about Bree during Harper's tryout and he told him that Bree would be on the bubble for the top team. Saul told him he did not want another experience like last year, that Bree needed to play. Carpenter understood and recommended the second team. The SkyHi second team finished among the top ten in the region last season, which was respectable. Saul didn't know how that would play with Bree because she wouldn't have a conversation with him about it. She might prefer to go back to MadDogs' second team instead. Who knew?

As tryouts for the 16s age group approached, Saul was about to breech etiquette and confront Bree about her plans. He just had to know. He was worried she was going to make the wrong decision and take the club season off. If she did, it would most likely mean an end to her high school career, too, in addition to any pipe dream Saul had about her playing in college. 16s was the year when colleges started making scholarship offers to club players.

He was sitting in his office pondering how he would start the conversation with her at dinner when his phone rang. He was happy to see it was his old pal, Fred the Baptist.

"Hey, stranger," Saul answered.

"Just calling to see if you needed any volleyball advice. Haven't heard from you in a while."

"I always need volleyball advice," Saul said, glad to hear his old friend's voice. "Although I'm probably more in need of parenting advice at the moment."

"I hear that. When they reach 16, they take a turn for the worse, don't they? They think we're the dumbest people on the planet."

"You got that right," Saul concurred.

"So tell me what's going on with Bree and SkyHi?"

"To be honest, Fred, I don't know yet. "We don't discuss volleyball much anymore. She's doing her own thing, now, whatever that is."

"Well, she's doing something," Fred cautioned, "Because she's trying to recruit my daughter to come play there."

"What? Say that again?" Saul asked, not sure he heard Fred correctly.

"She wants Stacy to play with her at SkyHi."

"On what team?" Saul asked.

"Any team they can be on together, I guess. I'm sure they are thinking it will be the second team."

Even though the news caught him by surprise, Saul was relieved to hear Bree had her sights set on playing club ball. Playing on the second team was a much better option than taking the season off.

"Are you okay with that?" Fred asked. "Do you like the club okay?"

"The club is great. We had our issues last season as you know but that was our own doing. We took a chance and it didn't work out. But the training was great and she did improve. It helped her make the Varsity team this year."

"I saw that. Good for her. Stacy had to settle for the JV team this year at her school."

"How are things at MadDogs?" Saul asked.

"Things are fine but Stacy may need a change of scenery. She's played on the second team now for two years. They keep bringing in new talent and I'm worried that she may not make the team again. She's a small middle now. Remember when our girls used to be tall?"

"I know what you mean. I was hoping to get a couple of more inches out of Bree but it didn't happen."

"I hear Bree is trying to recruit Savannah, too."

"Really?"

"Savannah's looking for a new team. MadDogs told her she was too short to set for them now."

"Unbelievable," Saul said. "That's a shame. She's really good, too."

"These clubs get more serious the older these girls get. And the girls more serious, too. They can be real mean at times."

"Tell me about it," Saul laughed. "Bree's vocabulary expanded this season on the Varsity team. She heard words being said on the court she had never heard before. A lot of smack talk is going on now."

"A far cry from when they used to smile and giggle and wear little pink ribbons in their hair," Fred laughed.

Saul laughed along but then quickly looked at the clock on his desk. He was late for a meeting. "Listen, Fred, I've got to run, but keep me posted on things. I hope this can work out for Stacy and Bree."

"Hell, I hope it can work out for you and me. It'd be nice to have my old partner-in-crime with me again."

"I'll keep my fingers crossed," Saul said. He hung up and sat back in his chair with relief. Bree had a plan after all. She was trying to put together a team with all her friends. He had to admire her cunning, although he didn't know if it would work. SkyHi's priority isn't about putting the best friends together. It's about putting the best teams together.

After Fred's call, he didn't feel the need to press the club issue at dinner that night. As it turned out, he didn't have to. Bree brought up the issue on her own.

"By the way," she started matter-of-factly like what she was about to say wasn't a big deal, "I just want you guys to know I've decided to tryout at SkyHi again."

"That's great," Saul and Veronica said in unison.

"Are you trying out for the top team again?" Veronica asked.

"No. I'm not doing that again, Mom. Do you think I'm crazy?" Bree fired back in that sassy sweet 16 kind of way.

"Of course not, Bree," Veronica answered. "It was just a question."

"I'm hoping for the second team but I'm okay if it's the third team, too. But the second team would be nice. They have some pretty good players and if you add me and Bailey and Morgan, it could really be a good team."

"Do they both want to move down to the second team?" Saul asked.

"I don't know for sure, but I know they don't want to sit on the bench again. And did you hear the other big news?"

Saul and Veronica looked at each other and shrugged.

"Autumn is going to coach the 16s second team."

"Oh, my God," Veronica said. "We could have both of you playing for the same coach."

"That's so cool," Harper said.

"Yeah, it would be fun to play for her again," Bree said. Her phone then buzzed signaling she had received a text. "Oh, I've got to run."

"Where are you going?" Saul asked.

"Tryout clinic. Savannah is picking me up."

"She's driving now?" Veronica asked.

"Yep. Just got her license."

"Well, please be careful. Saul, are you okay with this?"

"It's okay, Very. It's just a five mile drive."

"I thought Savannah played at MadDogs," Harper asked.

"Not anymore. See you guys," Bree said as she shut the door behind her.

"Do we have to deal with driving now, too?" Veronica asked. "I'm already worried about her grades, her volleyball, her boyfriend, her posture. Does she have to get behind the wheel of a car?"

"I'm more concerned if Savannah is tall enough to see out the window," Saul replied.

Harper cracked up laughing. "That's funny, Daddy."

"Thank you, Harp."

Saul got a kick out of making Harper laugh. And he also liked it that she still called him daddy. Based on his experience with Bree, he knew that wouldn't last much longer.

Tryout day for 16s came and Saul was actually allowed to go with Bree to the club. Saul was fully prepared to sit it out, but he quickly said yes to her invitation. Bree, who had just gotten her driver's license drove them to the SkyHi facility. There was not much chitchat in the car because Bree liked to remain deadly focused while behind the wheel. The calming silence allowed Saul to think about what he wanted to tell Bree right then and there. How could he go about reconnecting with her? He had been thinking about what he should say for a long time and he felt this might be as good a time as any to work at piecing things back together.

When Bree pulled into park, she reached back to grab her volleyball bag.

"Wait," Saul said, grabbing her arm in the process.

"What's up?" Bree asked.

"There's something I've been meaning to talk to you about."

"But Dad, I've got to get in there. Tryouts are about to start."

"I know, but tryouts can wait for a few minutes, okay?" Saul insisted. "This is something that's important to me."

"Tryouts can wait? I can't believe you just said that."

"I know that doesn't sound like me but I need to tell you why I sound like I do. I mean, like I normally do. I need to apologize to you for being the way I am."

"Dad, you're sounding weird."

"Just hear me out, Bree," Saul said, cutting her off quickly. " There's a reason I am the way I am. I know I'm obsessive. I know I live and breathe the sport you play. I know you think I'm crazy at times. But it's only because I want you to have what I didn't."

Saul paused a moment and saw that Bree's face showed puzzlement and concern.

"Dad, I still don't know what you're talking about. And I don't think you're crazy."

"Bree, please. Let me finish. You know about my dad, right?"

Bree nodded with a look of cautious surprise. "Mom's told me the story."

"Well, I don't like to talk about it, but as you know, he wasn't always there for me. And I've placed a lot of blame on him for not being there for me. And ever since he's been gone, I swore to myself that I would always be there for my kids. And while it's no excuse for the way I've acted, I have to be honest with myself. I want you to know his loss is a big part of why I always feel I have to be there for you."

"Dad, I'm glad you're there for me. And I think I understand what you're telling me."

"You do?"

"I think so. And I hate what happened to your dad. I would be crushed if I lost you or mom. But you don't have to engineer and organize everything about my life anymore."

"I know I don't. You're doing quite well on your own."

"On my own? Dad, I don't want to be on my own. I'm sixteen. I just want your help when I need your help. I want you to be there for me. But you know what?"

"What?"

"You don't have to be there, to be there."

Saul wore a look of confusion on his face. "What do you mean?"

"I mean you don't have to be at every tryout I ever sign up for or every practice that I attend. If you're not there, I still have you and all your many volumes of advice, good or bad, with me. But ultimately, it's up to me if I make a team. It's not up to you."

Saul chuckled to himself. He had just gotten the best advice of his life from a teenager who couldn't drink, vote or fight for her country.

"And Dad, don't blame your father. He's still with you. He always has been and always will be."

Saul didn't know how to respond. Bree leaned over and kissed him on the cheek.

"I've got to run now. Love you."

Like a flash, she exited the car with her volleyball bag in tow. Saul held his tears in check long enough for her to get out of the car. And then he let out a cry that rivaled one of Bree's dampest. He didn't know for sure what had come over him, he just knew he had to let it out.

His dad was with him. Deep down, he always knew that and maybe that made it easier to blame Harper Sr. for his son's shortcomings. But it wasn't his dad's fault that he didn't make varsity until his senior year. It wasn't his dad's fault that caused him to miss a game-winning shot that kept his team out of the high school playoffs. And it wasn't his dad's fault that he didn't get the scholarship to UCLA or Texas. The truth was, he just wasn't good enough. But it wasn't for lack of trying. He tried his heart out, with all the love of sport he could muster from his dad's memory. That heart and fight is what ultimately got him to where he was today. But in the end, talent ultimately wins out. And then your next generation comes along and you hope against hope that they are more talented than you.

Saul's sobbing finally came to an end and when he felt he was emotionally stable enough to endure tryouts, he entered the SkyHi facility. There was less pressure today. There were no plans to try out at another other club. Whatever team Bree made, even if it was SkyHi's local non-traveling team, she would take it. He was still keenly interested in the make-up of the team, however. He wanted it to be a solid team. He knew Bree was just in it for fun, but it was still more fun to win than to lose.

Saul pitied the poor parents who forked over thousands of dollars so their daughter could play on a team that was ranked at the bottom of the region. You spend your tournament weekends getting the crap beat out of you, while your daughter is pursuing her dream and hopefully having fun and enjoying the benefits of a team environment where they all learn how to lose well together. Maybe it builds character, Saul thought. Or maybe it builds stupidity. It probably depended on the daughter and the parent.

Saul was excited when he saw Fred in the gym. He saw Stacy racing over to give Bree a hug. He also saw Savannah's dad, Stan, and Morgan's dad, Scott. Being new to the club, Fred and Stan and were both a little nervous. It had taken a while but Saul had finally forgiven Stan for recruiting Pamela to MadDogs. Saul tried to keep both Fred and Stan calm. They didn't know what to expect but they seemed to be content with whatever happened. If their daughter made the top team, great. If they made the second team, that would be okay, too, because they knew it had the potential to be a good team. Scott, on the other hand, was still desperately hoping Morgan could make the top team again.

The tryouts started and the pressure slowly built with each passing hour. There were fewer girls trying out than the year before but that was common in the older ages. As girls grew up, their interests changed or they would succumb to the realization that they weren't good enough and would hang up the shoes and spandex sliders. Even with fewer girls in attendance, there were still enough girls with good talent to keep all the dads concerned.

Saul watched as Bree moved back and forth between courts two and three, which he assumed were for the girls they were considering for the second and third team. He didn't want Bree on the third team, although he had no say in the decision. Bree's friends were being moved between courts as well.

Saul also noticed Unknown Girl that Walks Into a Gym on Tryout Day from last year's tryouts. It appeared that Coach Carpenter, who was coaching the same team again this year, was considering her for his top team. Pamela and Cathy wouldn't like it, Saul guessed. He was glad he wouldn't have to navigate through that three-middle drama.

The whistle blew, signaling the end of tryouts, and the players were asked to huddle in the middle of the court. Saul was starting to get nervous even though he kept telling himself there was no need to be. Coach Carpenter began the process of calling out his team's players. The usual suspects were named for SkyHi Blue: Lauren, Cathy, Pamela, Butt Cheeks, etc. They were the core that could not be broken. A few names were called that Saul was not familiar with. He guessed they were probably the new set of benchwarmers, the girls who were thrilled to be making one of the best teams in the country but who soon would be drowning in their own humiliation.

Scott looked extremely disappointed. There would be no hilarious mimicking of Coach Carpenter today. He was holding out hope that maybe his daughter could have broken through to the Blue core, but it wasn't meant to be. Saul was surprised to see that Unknown Girl was not among the names. She would be a lock for the second team and could jeopardize both Bree and Stacy's chances.

Coach Autumn was the next coach to announce her team and Saul moved closer to Fred. "Good luck," he said.

"Got my fingers crossed."

"So do I," Saul said. Then he heard Fred the Baptist begin to mumble an indecipherable prayer. Whatever he was praying for, it wasn't for the girls' health. The playing was over for the day.

The first names called were five girls that were on the team last year. All were quality players but they were not middles. The next name called was Bree's and finally Saul could relax. Any fears of a grudge held by Autumn for leaving her PSA team were put to rest.

Fred patted Saul on the back and said, "Congratulations."

The next name was that of Unknown Girl, which wasn't a surprise given her exclusion from the top team.

"Two middle spots gone," Fred whispered to Saul.

Bailey's name was then called and Bree cheered happily as Bailey walked towards her. A fellow benchwarmer alum had joined her but this time, hopefully, they would spend time on the court together. Savannah's name was called next and a loud "Yes" was heard through the facility. It was Stan jumping up and down with relief. Savannah ran up to be with Bree who was beaming. They hugged each other and celebrated the fact they could now be club mates in addition to being school mates.

Two other names were called who were players Saul did not recognize. That brought the count to 11 players. There was only one name left to call. He was worried sick for Fred's sake, but he didn't have to be. Autumn called Stacy's name and she jumped up uncontrollably and hopped over to her new teammates like a bunny rabbit. Fred breathed a sigh of relief. "Dear Lord, why does she always have to be the last name called?" He asked incredulously.

Saul gave him a man-hug and welcomed him to the club. He couldn't believe it. Bree had gotten her way. She was selected for Autumn's team and all her friends were selected as well. It would be a fun group of players to watch regardless of how they finished. Then Saul suddenly realized one girl had been left out, Morgan, Bree's other bench-mate. Her name wasn't called. Oh crap, he thought. He looked around to try and find her father, Scott, but couldn't see him. He caught a glimpse of Morgan walking through a crowd of girls. She was in tears. He followed Morgan as she walked into her father's arms in shame. Saul walked over to Scott and asked him what he was going to do.

"I don't have a clue, but we're not going to be on a third team. We're headed to MadDogs. It's the closest place."

"I don't want to go there," Morgan objected.

"We've got to go somewhere, Morgan. We don't have a back-up plan." He then looked at Saul. "I'm so pissed. Carpenter told me she was on the bubble but I thought that meant on the first team. I just assumed she would be a lock for the second team. We've got to go."

"Good luck," Saul said.

They didn't hear his good wishes. They were out the door in a flash. Saul felt horrible for them. He couldn't believe Morgan was out. She was a solid hitter and defensive player and she got more playing time than both Bree and Bailey combined last year. But Scott made a tactical error.

He assumed.

He should have picked up the phone and contacted Autumn to get a sense for where Morgan stood, just to be sure. But he didn't. Many volleyball dads, Saul would find, were afraid to talk to coaches. He didn't know if they were just afraid of hearing something about their daughter they didn't want to hear, or if they just felt it was all in their daughters' hands. Saul had learned that most coaches were happy to give you a sense of where your daughter stood. It helps guide your decision process on where to try out or where to focus your efforts.

Scott knew this better than anyone else. He was a veteran of the club game. He just got a little too careless, thinking that the second team was an automatic since his daughter was on the top team last year. Coach Carpenter or Autumn could have provided him some warning, Saul figured, but sometimes club coaches don't volunteer the information. It's their job to keep every girl they can in the gym, to keep them from going to a competitor.

After Saul and Bree signed up for the team, Bree went to the dressing room to try on uniform sizes. Saul made his initial deposit for the coming club season and as he was placing his credit card back in his pocket, Bree came running back towards him.

"Dad, do you know where Morgan is?"

"I think they went to MadDogs. Why?"

"One of our players declined the offer. Autumn is trying to find Morgan to offer her a spot on the team."

Saul quickly got on his cell phone and called Scott. He didn't answer. Bree tried texting Morgan but didn't get a response.

"Can you drive us over to MadDogs?"

"Sure," Saul said. "Who is us?" Before he knew it, he was in the car driving Bree, Stacy, Savannah and Bailey to MadDogs. They felt they needed their collective girl power to bring her back. Saul pulled the car up to the front door and the girls rushed inside. They all had SkyHi T-shirts and Saul noticed a few of the MadDogs girls eyeing them suspiciously. What were their arch enemies doing on their turf?

Bree spotted Morgan and Scott. They were at a table talking to a couple of MadDogs coaches and it appeared they were about to sign with a team. The girls rushed over and swarmed Morgan, pulling her away from the table. Scott spotted Saul and asked him what was going on.

"One of the girls turned down the SkyHi offer. Autumn is wanting Morgan now."

"Over my dead body," Scott said. "I'm not going back there after being treated like that."

"Come on," Saul pleaded. "We're going to have a great team."

The two dads looked over at their girls who were laughing and giggling. The SkyHi teammates were still circling around Morgan and were forcing her to leave with them. Morgan was enjoying the attention. They started moving their circle towards the door, not allowing Morgan to escape.

"Dad," Morgan screamed. "I can't help it." Once they got outside, they pushed Morgan into the car. Bree ran back in to get Saul.

"Dad, we got her. Let's go."

Saul looked at Scott helplessly. "I hate to kidnap your daughter, but it's in the best interest of the team. You've got to come back over."

He looked at Saul as if he was crazy. "Come on," Saul begged. "It's club volleyball. No club is perfect."

Scott couldn't help but laugh. "Saul, that's the truest thing you've said yet." He sighed and considered what to do next. "If Morgan's okay with it, I guess I can swallow my pride."

"Along with that twenty percent deposit," Saul joked. "Glad to have you back on board."

The two exited the MadDogs facility and Saul noticed Scott pulling things out of the trashcan located just outside the door. He was pulling a few SkyHi shirts and some other merchandise out of the waste. Saul then noticed that the SkyHi decal sticker on the rear window of Scott's car had been scraped off in an apparent fit of rage.

"Sorry," an embarrassed Scott said. "I was angry."

"I understand," Saul said, sounding now like he was a true veteran of the game.

Through the years, he had seen what the world of youth sports can do to a multitude of families, including his own. It could be joyous at times. It could be cutthroat at times. You take it day by day. On this particular day, he managed to convince Scott to drive back to SkyHi. Much to Bree's joy and satisfaction, Morgan signed with SkyHi Black.

Saul had to give his daughter all the credit. Her Dream Team was complete.

CHAPTER SIXTEEN

GAG REFLEX REDUX

"**S**kyHi 16 Black is going to rule, Dad. We're going to be a great team," she said as Saul was driving her home from the tryout.

"You think so?"

"I know so. And we're going to be better than Blue. You just watch."

Spoken like a jilted first teamer. Everyone always wants to get back at the club or team that told them no. And every girl on a second team always wants to beat the club's top team. They have an unending desire to show the club how wrong they were. The problem was it rarely, if ever, happened. The Coach Carpenters of the world know this more than anyone. Saul let Bree dream though. He didn't want to steal her thunder or put a damper on what was, for her, a very good day.

As it turned out, it was also a very good season for Bree. She was in good hands with Coach Autumn, who did a great job with the girls. Saul could tell that Autumn was a little bit nervous coaching a 16s team, having never coached girls that old before. It was a lot for her to take on, especially with the added pressure of changing clubs and also coaching a highly regarded 13s team. But the positive attitudes of Bree's teammates were intoxicating. They all wanted to be on that team playing together, which was rare for a second team. Many second team players spent their days bemoaning the fact they were relegated to second team status. They would watch the top team with envy and wonder why they had to be on an inferior team with unhappy players like themselves.

SkyHi 16s Black was filled with players that wanted to be there. They knew they had a good team and they also knew they would enjoy each other's company. The challenge would be making sure the fun they were having was translating to wins.

Thankfully, the winning happened quite regularly. At local tournaments, they had no problem finishing first in their pool on Saturdays. On Gold Bracket Day, they consistently finished tied for 5th, which was what you would expect of a good second team at a major club. Advantage, SkyHi Blue, MadDogs Black and Tejas usually finished in the top 4.

During the third tournament of the season, Bree's team got their chance to play Blue in the quarterfinals. This was their chance to make a statement. All the girls were fired up. The last thing you want to happen if you're a member of a top team is lose to your club's second team. That's too much crow to have to digest, especially if you've been a part of the core group of that team for years.

All the pressure was on Blue, while Black looked loose and confident. They were the underdogs and didn't have anything to lose. If they lost, they would finish tied for fifth again. They had no worries. The core of the Blue team, Lauren, Butt Cheeks, Cathy and Pamela played like they had no worries, either. They came out with a force Saul hadn't seen before. Their play was close to perfect as they forced Black into mistake after mistake. Autumn called a timeout to stop the bleeding. They were losing 12 to 4. For the first time that season, Autumn was raising her voice at them. She was talking so loud all the parents could hear.

"You're not playing your game," she yelled. "They are controlling all the points. Let's start passing like we're capable of and get back in this thing. And let's start moving on defense. You guys look like my 13 year olds out there."

They broke the huddle but the fiery speech didn't seem to help. Blue controlled the rest of the game and won easily 25 to 16. Autumn changed her line-up in game two moving Stacy to right side. Butt Cheeks had been killing them with her outside hitting and Autumn was probably hoping Stacy could block her more effectively. Stacy hadn't played right side before, but she looked up to the challenge. She had been sitting the bench most of the season as the third middle behind Unknown Girl and Bree, so she was just happy to get a chance to play in a big match for a change.

Stacy's blocking did have an impact. She slowed Butt Cheeks down a bit but Blue's overall quickness and experience continued to dominate the match. Stacy also miss-hit a lot of sets, which wasn't unexpected given the fact she hadn't played the position before.

Blue won game two 25-18 and Bree's Dream Team left the court with their hopes and heads down. This was their chance to play like top team players and they failed. Autumn didn't waste any time railing on the girls after the match, again her voice a few octaves higher for all the parents to hear.

"You are a great group of girls," Autumn assured them. "You love and support each other and that's great. But if tied for fifth is all you want to be, then let's decide that today because I'll just have fun and laugh and joke around with all of you the rest of the year. We'll coast to the end of the season and wish each other well and have no worries. But if you want to get better, if you want to go to Nationals, if you want to compete with the likes of MadDogs Black and Advantage and Blue, then you've got to start pushing each other to be better NOW."

The girls were all nodding their heads while listening to her, but Saul couldn't tell if Autumn was getting through to them or not.

"I don't want any benchwarmers on this team," she continued. "You've all had your share of that, haven't you? You're better than that. I want every one to have a role and I promise you I will sub you in when that role is required in every match we play. But if we're all here just to have fun. Then I guess playing time is not that important. You can have fun on the bench just as easily as you can have fun on the court."

She looked at them all to try and gauge what they were thinking. "Any questions?"

There was no response. "Then I'll see you at practice."

Autumn left the girls alone to ponder her words. Not much was said between them. They picked up their gear and headed over to their parents to leave.

Bree was in a very low-key mood in the car ride home until she finally asked Saul a question.

"Dad, we didn't do that bad, did we?"

"No. You finished tied for fifth. There's nothing wrong with that. You're clearly the fifth best team in the area which is great for a second team. Why do you ask?"

"I don't know. Autumn gave us a big speech afterwards. She sounded a lot like . . ." Bree hesitated.

"Like what?" Saul asked.

"Like you."

"I guess you don't mean that as a compliment," Saul interjected.

"I don't know. I was just surprised at how she reacted to us losing to Blue."

"Do you still think you can beat them?"

"Yes. I think we can beat them. I want to beat Butt Cheeks so bad I can taste it. I'm getting tired of her smack talk. And watching her pull her stupid sliders down every time after she hits a ball."

Saul chuckled a bit, then asked, "What kind of smack talk does she say on the court?"

"Just the usual stuff. Take that, bitch, and stuff like that."

"Really? The referee lets her get away with that?"

"They don't hear it. She says it under her breath."

"I'm shocked," Saul said.

"It's not like I've never heard the word, Dad. I guess if we want to shut her up, we just have to play better."

"And how are you guys going to play better?" Saul asked.

Bree thought about it for a second. "I guess we just need to practice harder."

"Sounds like you've got it figured out."

BREE'S DIARY
February 23
Bobby is thinking of coming to one of my club tournaments. He has never been to a club game before, only school games. Maybe that's a sign he wants to get more serious. I don't know. I don't know if I want to get more serious. Some things are starting to bug me a little bit. Like why has he started to chew tobacco all the time. I can't stand that. It doesn't make kissing very fun. I told Callie about this and she told me to ditch the guy. I don't think I'm ready to do that. Callie has already planned her trip to come see me this summer. I can't wait to hang out with her. Lost to Blue today and that sucked. We can beat them, tho if we get our crap together. I hate playing against Pamela, tho, because she is so good. She told me today she wished she was on our team. I wish she was, too.

The next few weeks Bree's team seemed to rally around Autumn's speech. Bree came to the next practice with a renewed sense of purpose and gathered the girls around to talk about how they would conduct themselves in practice going forward. They would keep their fun and silly antics to a minimum on the court. They had plenty of time for that stuff before and after practice and during water-breaks.

Autumn started working them harder in practice and began developing more individualized roles for each girl as well as areas each girl needed to improve on. Stacy, for example, was moving to right-side because her blocking was better than Morgan's, the now former right side. Bailey would be the new third middle but would remain the team's go-to server because she had a killer jump serve that you couldn't keep on the bench. Unknown Girl would continue to work on her quickness and become a bigger blocker at the net. Morgan had to work on being a better hitter down the line because she was too predictable with her cross-court hitting. Savannah had to become a better back-setter, which meant she had to gain more confidence in setting the ball to the right side and setting slides for the middle blockers. Too often, she would set the safer, easier set to the left side. And Bree needed to get better at hitting slides, which required her to jump off her left foot and hit a backset while moving to her right. It was basically a lay-up move like in basketball, but she was never able to perfect it due to her supposed left-footedness. Autumn challenged her to get better at it. "Every 16 year-old middle should be able to hit a slide," she said.

The team started seeing their improvement take hold when they flew to Kansas City for the Show Me National Qualifier. They decided to play at the USA level, which was a lower level than Open. They had little competition the first two days and made it easily into the Gold Bracket on Sunday. Saul had expected some tougher matches on the final day but SkyHi 16 Black made it to the finals without dropping a set. In the process, they secured a bid to Nationals, which was to be held that year in, of all places, Dallas, Texas.

In the Show Me championship game, they lost a close three setter to a team from St. Louis, but they still had their bid. Autumn told them she was proud of them but that they still had more work to do. They were winners and needed to believe they were winners. She told them that the championship match was theirs for the taking, but they didn't take it. They played too cautiously.

The next tournament on their schedule was the Lone Star Qualifier in Dallas. Because they had their USA bid and a trip to Nationals secured, Autumn decided to move them to the Open Division level. The girls were excited about the challenge and felt inspired that Autumn had the confidence in them to compete at the highest level, a level usually just reserved for top teams.

All of Texas' best teams were at Lone Star along with a few out-of-state teams, too. Three National bids were at stake and four teams in the field had already received bids at other qualifiers: Advantage, MadDogs Black, SkyHi Blue and a team from Orlando called OVA. Because of the tournament's trickle down rules, if three of those qualified teams finished in the final six, the other three teams in the top six would get the three Lone Star Open bids. The big question was could SkyHi Black finish in the top six?

Thirty-two teams were in the Open field and the first day was broken down into eight pools of four teams. Bree's team received a pretty favorable draw. They were seeded second in their pool and two of the teams in their pool they had beaten before.

It was always good to know you could beat a team, even if there was a revenge factor at play from the other side.

SkyHi 16 Black took care of business though. They played confidently from the start and beat their first two opponents without dropping a game. Their last match was against the top seed in their pool, OVA, a team that had already qualified for Open. OVA had one of the top players in the country. She had already verbally committed to the University of Florida. Bree and her teammates spent most of the match watching in awe at her ability. They couldn't stop her and they couldn't stop OVA. They lost in two games and finished second in their pool, which was still good enough to advance.

The field had been whittled down to 16 teams for day two with there being four pools of four teams. You had to finish in the top two to advance to day three. Looking at the pool, Saul knew they had their work cut out for them. Two North Texas nemeses, Advantage and Tejas, were in their pool along with a team from Houston, called Woodlands Wave. Saul figured they needed to win two matches to have a chance, which meant they had to knock off one of North Texas' Big Four, Advantage or Tejas, something they had yet to do. Tejas was their first opponent.

Autumn got the girls fired up with a passionate pre-game speech, basically telling them that this was their chance to prove they belonged with the top teams. The girls came out and played what was probably their best match of the season. They won the first game 25 to 23 with truly inspired play by everyone. Stacy was firing hits from the right side, Bree had a couple of key blocks and Bailey was killing it with authority on the left side.

Tejas responded in game two with some great play of their own. They began matching SkyHi's intensity and their defensive play rose to a higher level. They were digging balls Saul couldn't believe. He thought for sure they were kills but the Tejas defenders somehow managed to keep the balls in play. SkyHi kept it close but lost game two 25 to 23.

During game three, the excellent play from both teams continued. The largest lead was two points the entire game. Both teams traded points and were knotted up at 13. It was time to sub in Bailey for her big serve, which seemed like perfect timing to have your best server in the game. Unfortunately, Bailey served her worst serve of the weekend. It hit the tape on the top of the net and didn't bounce over. Tejas had a one point advantage.

"It's okay, we're still in this," Fred shouted in support.

The Tejas server stepped up next and drilled a ball deep in the left corner that fooled Morgan. She decided to let the ball go hoping it would sail out, but it didn't. It hit the line. Tejas won 15 to 13 and just like that, the game was over. Their most well-played match of the season came down to a game of inches. A missed serve that clipped too much of the net and a made serve that caught the line.

Saul shook his head in disappointment. So close, he moaned to himself. He had remained skeptical about the team's upside potential all season, but he still pulled like crazy for them. Against Tejas they had actually shown some real backbone, but they still came up short. It was so hard to break through the top team talent barrier.

The girls were dejected but Saul watched as Autumn compelled them to fight on. They had two more matches to play. "You are not out of this," she said. "You were right there. You were in the match all the way. You can play with these teams. Just remember, every point matters."

The girls took the message to heart in their next match against Woodlands Wave. They didn't let the heartbreak of the previous game linger. Wave was one of the best teams from the Houston area, but historically, the Houston area teams were not as strong as the teams from North Texas. Saul figured they had a decent shot against them.

To his delight, he was right. SkyHi played at a level consistent with that of the Tejas match and it proved too much for the Wave team to handle. SkyHi won a hard fought three-setter.

Now, they had to play Advantage, the top seed in the entire tournament. Saul knew they didn't have a prayer as he watched Autumn doing her best Vince Lombardi impression to try and fire them up. They blew their chance to advance by losing to Tejas, he figured. If they would have won that match, they would still be in it tomorrow.

The match against Advantage didn't take long. Bree and her team were spent. They had given it their all the first two matches. Advantage's talent and depth were just too strong. Advantage won 25 to 14 and 25 to 16. The outcome was never in doubt. With only one win in pool play, they figured their chance for a bid was gone. It was now out of their control.

"We still have one dash of hope left," Fred said to Saul.

"What's that?"

"We need Wave to beat Tejas. If that occurs, there would be three teams tied with one win and two losses."

"That means a playoff," Saul said excitedly. "Where are they playing?"

"Two courts down," Fred said.

"Let's go," Saul said.

He and Fred the Baptist led the other parents along with the rest of the team to the court where Tejas and Wave were playing. The match was in the third game and Wave was ahead 10 to 7. Saul sensed new life. He and the SkyHi contingent immediately became Wave fans and even began joining in on the cheers with the Wave parents, who welcomed the support enthusiastically. Feeding off their new fan base, Wave went on to win the third match and just like that, SkyHi was back in business.

Another stroke of good fortune then occurred. The seeding of the three team playoff was determined by set differential first, and point differential second. The set differential of the three teams ended up being equal so point differential was the deciding factor.

"We have the best point differential," Fred screamed at Saul. "That means we get a bye and the other two teams have to play first."

Tejas and Wave, being the other two teams, would have to play a one-game playoff to 25. The winner of that game would then play SkyHi in a one-game playoff to 25. And the winner of that game would advance to play another day.

Having the bye was a huge advantage. The girls had already played three grueling matches with most of them going three sets. It was getting late in the day and it was natural for the girls to start to fatigue. The Tejas-Wave match began and Fred and Saul watched intently to see who their opponent would be.

"I hope they have to play to 45 points," Saul told Fred. "The more tired they are the better." Deep down, Saul was hoping they would play Wave. He knew they could beat them. They had yet to beat Tejas. Plus, the Tejas team and parents were pissed at them for cheering for Wave. It was considered bad form to cheer against your fellow region, but an Open bid was at stake for crying out loud. He didn't want to have to face their vengeful wrath.

Luckily though, ever since the Advantage loss, things continued to go SkyHi Black's way. In what was an edge-of-your-seat nail-biter, Wave somehow pulled out a 28 to 26 thriller. They didn't play to 45 as Saul had hoped, but it was still enough to drain them of some valuable energy.

SkyHi took the court next and had to beat Wave one more time. This was their chance to make one of tomorrow's Gold Pools. If they won this game, they would be in Lone Star's version of the Elite Eight. Two Gold Pools consisting of four teams would remain. Saul tried not to think about tomorrow. He tried to focus on the game at hand. Coming into the tournament, he felt SkyHi Black had an outside shot at getting a bid and this was the kind of game you had to win to keep your outside shot alive. Tomorrow, they would have to beat a really good team like a SkyHi Blue or MadDogs Black, but today all they had to do was beat Wave in one game to 25.

SkyHi's good fortune continued. They opened the game with a spurt of six consecutive points, which basically knocked out their tired opponent. Wave had nothing left in the tank. Bree and her teammates cruised to a 25 to 12 win and they were still in contention for one of the three Open bids. Even after enduring two losses in pool play, they managed to win the three-team playoff and officially take second in their pool.

An exhausted Bree bragged on her team to Saul during the ride home. "I told you we would be good, Dad. We made the final eight in Open."

"That's a great accomplishment. I'm proud of you guys. But you've got a tough road tomorrow," Saul said, doubts still lingering in his mind. They still hadn't beat an elite team, but they would get another chance tomorrow.

"We can do it," Bree said. "I know we can."

SkyHi Black's Gold Pool the next day consisted of MadDogs Black, which starred the great Tina Dulles (the Ronaldo of North Texas), OVA, which starred the great recruit from the University of Florida who had already killed them once that weekend, and Houston Juniors, the top club in the Houston area who had beaten Woodlands Wave three times that season. Looking at the schedule, Saul figured their only hope was against Houston Juniors. They had never come close to beating MadDogs and he witnessed firsthand what OVA could dish out. Their first match of the day was against Houston Juniors.

SkyHi Black picked that morning to play like a team they were trying not to be, a second team that was just happy to be there. Saul did not think Houston Juniors was all that good, but SkyHi could not get anything going offensively or defensively. They laid an egg and lost in two poorly-played games. Their next opponent was OVA, which ironically in lower-case, spells ova, another word for egg. Unfortunately, SkyHi Black laid another ova against OVA. They looked outclassed and outmanned from the get-go. OVA stomped them into submission. It was embarrassing. The girls were looking confused on the court and lacking confidence in themselves. OVA was just too good.

So it came down to their final pool match against MadDogs. Ironically, after two losses, just like yesterday, SkyHi was still alive. If they beat MadDogs, they would finish in third place with a 1 and 2 record. The win would guarantee them a spot in the top six and, more importantly, an Open bid. Here was their chance, one more time, to knock off an elite team. MadDogs was the only thing that stood between them and a bid that normally was reserved for top club teams. As much as Saul wanted to hold out hope, he knew it was impossible. He would be happy with finishing seventh. It was a very respectable finish for a second team.

As the game began, however, Saul saw a glimmer of hope. Two MadDogs starters were missing from the team. He had heard a rumor they didn't play the last match, which was the primary reason they had lost it. Apparently, the two girls had gotten ill from something they had eaten. Saul wished the entire team had eaten the same thing. Tina Dulles was still playing and that was really all that mattered.

She was having her typical dominating performance and the girls were unable to contain her. MadDogs won the first game 25 to 19 and Saul could sense their outside chance slipping away. Just one time, for Bree's sake, he was hoping the team could deliver a marquee win. MadDogs took an early lead in game two and were in control mid-way through the second game leading 17 to 13 when something odd happened, something Saul had never seen happen on a volleyball court before.

The MadDogs setter was hustling after a pass to set for Tina Dulles when she doubled over in pain. She let the ball drop to the ground and SkyHi won the point. The setter remained bent over and clutching her stomach when all of a sudden she spewed out a spray of vomit on the floor. All the girls on both sides of the net had to look away from the gross display of chunky liquid. Saul's first thought was that she evidently ate what the other two girls ate. Then, his weak gag reflex kicked in and he had to restrain himself from upchucking, so he quickly got up and looked away.

The referee called time-out to clean the court and they brought in a trainer to tend to the sick setter. Fred turned to Saul who was still trying to keep his gag-reflex under control. "I hate to be unsportsmanlike, but if the setter can't set, who's going to set for them?"

"I don't know," Saul muttered in between gags.

"We still might have a chance," Fred said eagerly. Then Fred spotted something else to his amazement. "Oh, my God."

"What happened?" Saul asked, while turning to look around.

"Another one just threw up."

"What? Who?" Saul saw another stream of liquid chunks spewing onto the court and he quickly had to turn around again. "Oh, my God, I'm going to be sick."

"That was Tina Dulles just tossing her cookies on the floor," Fred informed Saul. "We're back in business, Bud."

Saul needed a glass of water. He looked for Veronica, but Veronica was busy pulling out her Purell like all the other mothers and administering it to their daughters on the sideline. Bree and her teammates were in a state of shock as was everyone else.

"Hey, Saul, all we need is one more vomit and they may have to forfeit. You've got to have six girls on the court," Fred explained.

"That's great, Fred," Saul said, still looking away from the court. "Oh, my God, I'm starting to smell it. I've got to go the restroom. Text me if something happens."

As Saul was about to leave the circus scene, the HAZMAT crew arrived and feverishly began to clean up the court. With HAZMAT there, Saul thought he could delay his trip to the restroom, when all of a sudden, a third MadDogs girl then threw up on the sidelines. The girls scattered away from the mess but one of the HAZMAT ladies hadn't seen the puddle of fresh gruel behind her and slipped and fell to the ground. The MadDogs coach went to help her up and then walked over to the referee.

Saul swore he heard the MadDogs coach say, "We can't play. We have to forfeit." His hearing was correct. The referee suddenly motioned that the game was over. SkyHi Black had won.

Autumn turned to the girls and screamed, "We've got an Open bid!" The girls looked at each other in disbelief and huddled together on the floor like they had just won Nationals. Fred quickly rushed over to Saul to embrace in an emotional man-hug.

"We're in Open, Bud!" Fred the Baptist shouted with hallelujah joy.

Saul couldn't believe their good fortune. They finally had a marquee win, or to be more realistic, a marquee forfeit. It didn't matter. They had played their way into the Open Division, which in reality could be both a blessing and a curse, Saul figured. Yes, it was great to be in the field of the best 32 teams in the country. But he also knew the team had no shot at winning it. In the Open division, you're playing teams like Advantage, OVA and SkyHi Blue every match. Bree's team couldn't sustain that kind of quality play during an entire tournament. Heck, they couldn't do it at Lone Star. And if you're not playing well, the Open Division can be a humiliating beatdown. Four days of getting your butt kicked by really good teams.

Saul received his own beatdown after Fred released him from the man-hug. There was Bobby cheering on Bree and her teammates, and there was Bree running up to Bobby to give him a celebratory kiss and hug. Where did he come from? Saul wondered. He hadn't seen him the entire weekend and there he is showing up at victory time.

Bree and Bobby had been getting more serious, it seemed, although no one really knew. They saw each other almost every day and Saul and Veronica were doing their best to come to terms with it. Saul walked by them and told Bobby hello and gave Bree the thumbs up sign for qualifying for Open. Saul's walk-by prompted Bobby to take his hands off of her and Saul took some satisfaction in that.

He walked back over to Fred and Veronica and got his mind back on more positive things. What a treat, he thought, to have both daughters going to Nationals, and more importantly, playing at Nationals, with no injuries or bench-warming issues to worry about.

Harper's team had qualified for Open in much less dramatic fashion. They earned their bid earlier in the year at their first qualifier they played in at St. Louis. Harper had stayed healthy the entire time and was integral in leading her teammates to a successful season. The new additions to the team had made SkyHi 13 Blue a complete team and a force to be reckoned with. The only problem was there was still another force they couldn't reckon with, those dreaded MadDogs.

The MadDogs were back with their formidable line-up that included Six-Shooter and Midget Middle. They kept the core of their team intact with no new additions to speak of. The question on everyone's mind was how good was SkyHi with their new additions.

They were good enough to maintain their number two ranking in North Texas. They beat the teams they were supposed to beat, even the teams that included some of Harper's former teammates from last season, the ones who wanted to beat their former club so bad but couldn't manage to do it, their bitterness ever remaining.

Beating MadDogs was a different story. The two teams had played each other twice during the season and MadDogs walked away with two victories. Saul and the SkyHi parents were deflated. They had higher expectations for the team. In the first match, SkyHi put up a gallant effort in game one losing by only two points. They could have won it but had a few unfortunate errors by one of the new players that cost them. In game two, Mad Dogs cruised to an easy win with Six-Shooter firing her make-believe bullets after every point. It was clear to all in attendance that MadDogs was in the SkyHi girls' heads.

That was never more apparent than in the second encounter when SkyHi, after playing flawlessly throughout the weekend, reached the final against MadDogs. The mental mistakes mysteriously reappeared and Harper and her teammates played like a vastly different team. They let balls drop, they shanked passes, they missed serves. It was a wipeout. MadDogs won the match 25 to 10 and 25 to 16.

Autumn got in the girls faces after the match and let them have it, just like she let her 16s have it earlier in the season. The young tweeners were shocked that this nice angelic lady with such a playful smile, this coach of such a cute and innocent bunch of 13 year olds, that had been so pleasant and encouraging to them for the entire season, had suddenly turned into Cruella de Vil. It scarred them and they never quite looked at Autumn the same way after that.

When Saul asked Harper what she said to them, Harper just shook her head in disbelief. "I can't even remember, Daddy. Something about how we weren't worthy of wearing a SkyHi uniform or something like that. I just know I don't want to make her mad again. And I want to keep my jersey."

Whatever Autumn told them, it seemed to have an effect. The girls were all business after that, in practice and in games. They took care of their individual responsibilities and assignments. When it was time to play in the Lone Star qualifier, Autumn told them they better come prepared to win the whole darn thing. The Lone Star qualifier for Harper's team and the rest of the younger ages occurred the weekend before the older age groups played, when Bree's team so memorably secured their Open bid by watching the vomit flow.

Harper and her teammates were on a mission. At least that's what Coach Autumn had told them. They marched into the Dallas Convention Center and began mowing down teams with conviction. The scores were not close the first day. The scores were not really close on the second day either. They had reached the

Gold Bracket without losing a set. More importantly to the 13 year-old girls, their coach was smiling and there was no sign of Cruella appearing.

Sixteen teams made the Gold Bracket, which meant SkyHi needed four wins to take home the much-coveted Golden Volleyball Trophy, which wasn't made of gold mind you. It was just a volleyball covered in gold paint, but it was enough to get young girls excited.

MadDogs was on the other side of the bracket along with that pesky Puerto Rican team, the one that Saul wanted to have players carded to ensure they were of proper age. Saul was at least glad they wouldn't have to contend with either of them until the finals.

SkyHi started the day by beating MadDogs' second team, MadDogs Red. Saul thought the win was significant because they finally managed to beat a team with a MadDogs uniform on. No, it wasn't the top team but maybe it helped trigger a positive mental event in some small recess of the girls' minds.

They followed that win with a victory over a team from Oklahoma and in the semi-finals, they took on a very good team from Kansas City, but managed to eke out a 25 to 22, 25 to 23 win. They had made the finals and still hadn't lost a set, which was a very impressive run. They now had to sit back and wait to see who they would play in the championship game. MadDogs Black was playing Puerto Rico. Saul thought it was a toss-up as to who would win. As far as he was concerned, he didn't want to play either one of them. They were both so good.

In the end, MadDogs won a close three-setter so SkyHi was destined for round three with their arch rival. Both teams had already qualified at earlier qualifiers so a bid was not at stake. The only thing at stake was their pride and North Texas bragging rights.

From the start of the match, it was clear that MadDogs was a little tired from their previous battle with the Puerto Ricans. They also appeared to be taking SkyHi a little for granted after beating them twice that year. Harper's team got off to an early lead and stayed laser-focused during the whole game. They took advantage of some uncharacteristic MadDogs errors and won the game rather decisively 25 to 19. After winning game point, the girls celebrated crazily like the match was over. Saul was worried the excess celebrating might fuel MadDogs' fire.

Autumn huddled the girls together and settled them down. "Have we won this tournament yet?" she shouted at them sternly.

Saul could see the girls suddenly calm down, as if fearing that Cruella might be resurfacing.

"Then stop acting like you've won something. We came here to win this thing and we haven't done it yet. Stay focused on what your responsibilities are and go out and play our game. Okay?" The girls all nodded with a sense of relief, as if they were happy Coach Autumn was still with them. They hadn't triggered her multiple personality disorder.

Game two began and MadDogs delivered a heavy dosage of Six-Shooter and Midget Middle at the start and raced to a quick four-point lead. Their two stars had been pretty quiet in game one and the coach was obviously trying to get them more involved. Midget Middle scored a couple of points in a row and Saul could tell Harper was starting to get mad.

Harper walked over to her setter and Saul could read her lips. "Set me the ball."

The setter complied and Harper killed the ball with so much force many of the parents oohed and aahed at the sight. Her kill slowed the MadDogs momentum and SkyHi stayed close throughout the game. The longer the game stayed close, the more confident SkyHi was becoming and the more worried MadDogs was getting.

Saul was proud of the way the girls were fighting. They had taken a flurry of punches in the start of game two but they hadn't backed down. They were proving they could hang with MadDogs for an entire match. MadDogs was clinging to a 23 to 22 lead when Six-Shooter rifled an outside hit out of bounds. She flung her arms up in the air with disgust and pouted as she walked to the back row to get ready for serve-receive.

The game now tied, Autumn ordered her server to serve it right at Six-Shooter. The serve barely cleared the net but its direction was true, sailing straight into Six Shooter's arms. Six-Shooter misplayed the serve and shanked it way out of bounds. Saul could tell she was rattled. It was now game point and the SkyHi parents rose to their feet in anticipation. Autumn directed the server to do the same thing again. The ball came at Six-Shooter, this time at a higher angle and all she could do was pass the ball straight up in the air forcing the setter to run way out of system. The setter still managed to set Six-Shooter the ball, but it was a tough ball to handle and Six-Shooter swung and dumped it feebly into the net.

SkyHi had won.

After nearly two years of frustration, they had finally beaten the mighty MadDogs Black. The girls swarmed the court and mobbed each other. The joy on Harper's face was priceless. She had finally gotten some revenge from the team that was too good to have her. Saul high-fived the other dads and gave Veronica a big kiss. He felt more relief than anything else. It was nice to get the monkey off their back. Harper's team needed the boost, too. It couldn't have come at a better time with Nationals just around the corner.

They proved they could play with MadDogs, but more importantly, they proved they could play with anybody. The trip to Nationals couldn't come soon enough for Saul. All he could think of was that big, beautiful stadium court and the thought of watching his two daughters play on it. According to his Master Athletic Plan, it was meant to happen.

What wasn't meant to happen is what transpired in the parking lot following the victory over MadDogs. Saul, Veronica, Bree and Harper were walking to their car when they noticed Midget Middle and her family parked right along side of them. It was an awkward moment but both sets of parents managed to congratulate each other on a great tournament. On the other hand, Midget Middle wouldn't say a word to Harper and Harper wouldn't say a word to her. They were warriors, after all, who only faced each other in the arena.

Harper climbed in the back seat and picked up her old Elmo, which had been lying their peacefully. Yes, that same old Elmo that helped her through the yellow jaundice, the Swollen Colon Syndrome and so many sleepless nights. Elmo had been a hard habit for Harper to break and she still nestled next to him during those morning rides to volleyball tournaments.

As the Bryson's made their way home, Bree suddenly let out a shrill scream. She quickly covered her mouth with her hand.

"Oh, my God!" She mumbled.

"What's wrong, Bree?" Veronica asked.

"Look at this Instagram."

Bree showed Veronica her phone. Veronica suddenly put her hand to her mouth in a state of shock.

"What is it?" Saul asked.

Veronica showed it to Saul.

"Oh, my God." Saul exclaimed.

"What is it?" Harper asked curiously.

"It's nothing, Harp." Veronica quickly responded, with what could have been the biggest lie she ever told.

There, presiding on Bree's phone for all the world to see, or at least the world as it pertained to 13-year old volleyball players in North Texas, was a picture of Harper holding her beloved Elmo. Harper's medal was draped around Elmo's neck. Midget Middle had apparently taken the photo of Harper in the car. The postings were too numerous to mention. There were a few cute and precious ones but they mainly ran the gamut from vicious to harsh. They referred to Harper as a wimp, a six-foot tall volley baby, a Sesame Street Super Fan. There were questions like, Hey, Harper, where's your rattle and crib? Are you ready for your bottle? Is Elmo your pacifier? There was one post from Midget Middle herself asking, How could we lose to this? Not going to happen again.

Harper was getting agitated in the back seat. "If it's nothing, then I want to see it," she implored.

Veronica looked at Saul and Saul looked at Veronica. It was if they were trying to consult their parenting handbook about social media but couldn't find the right chapter. What do you do? What do you say to your daughter that doesn't even have a phone or a Facebook page yet?

Veronica finally had to give in and let Harper see the photo and related comments. Harper didn't yell or scream or curse the girls' posts. She sat their taking it all in, scrolling and scrolling, her own tears scrolling down her cheeks in unison, her face now matching the color of her old buddy, who was no longer in Harper's arms, but sitting alone against the door, as if he had been placed in timeout.

CHAPTER SEVENTEEN

ONE FLEW OVER THE VOLLEYBALL NET

The days dragged for Saul. He counted them one by one like a little kid waiting for Christmas. Christmas for him, however, was June 25th, the day Nationals would begin.

The tournament schedule would be a little crazy. Each age group played over a span of four days. Harper's age group would lead off on the 25th and finish on the 28th. Bree's age group would start on the 26th and end on the 29th. There would be three days of overlap which meant, with Autumn coaching both teams, a conflict could occur.

If a conflict did occur, Autumn's primary responsibility would be to coach 13 Blue. The club would have a roamer coach ready to sub in for Autumn for 16 Black, if needed. While the plan made perfect sense, Saul felt it was still just another slap in the face to all former, current and future members of second teams playing any youth sport in any part of the world.

After Bree qualified for Open, she texted Callie and told her. Callie congratulated her and looked forward to seeing her in Dallas. Callie's team had qualified for Open, too. Callie and Bree worked it out so that Callie would stay with Bree for a couple of weeks after Nationals. There was no sense paying for two trips to Dallas that summer, the parents reasoned.

A week before the tournament started, the pools came out. Saul had been accessing the tournament website in his office for the last few days waiting for the information. He quickly punched up the two age groups to see what was in store. Harper's team was seeded 8th overall in the tournament out of 32 teams. Not bad, Saul reasoned. The only negative was that they were in the same pool with the tournament's number one seed, OVA. Saul hoped they weren't as good as their 16s team, but they must be since they were the favorite to win it all.

The 32 teams were divided into four pools of 8 teams. Saul located MadDogs and noticed they were seeded fourth, higher than Harper's team. He was a little ticked that they were ahead of SkyHi following their great win at Lone Star, but MadDogs had beaten them twice that season and had finished high at Nationals the year before.

Saul pulled up the 16s schedule when he noticed his cell phone ringing. It was Fred the Baptist. If it was anyone else he would have pushed ignore, but Fred always had the facts for those that wanted to be informed. Saul answered hello.

"We're screwed," Fred began.

"Why do you say that?"

"Have you seen the schedule?"

"I was just pulling it up."

"Guess who's in our pool?" Fred asked in a state of depression.

Saul had little time for a guessing game. "Fred, I don't have a clue. SkyHi Blue?"

"No. Worse than that."

"Who then?" Saul said impatiently.

"OVA and Advantage."

Saul had just pulled the screen up and saw what Fred was seeing. "Ugh," was all Saul could utter.

"Every one else in the pool will be playing for third place," Fred said.

"But third is good enough to advance to the next round, right?"

"Yeah, it's good enough. The top three teams advance, but if you look at the rest of the pool, it's not easy. We've got a team from Northern California and a team from Southern California. They are always tough. We're seeded 28th out of 32 teams. The darn seeding committee sure doesn't like our chances."

"Fred, you and I both know we aren't going to win the darn thing. We just need to go there and play our best."

"I know but I don't want it to be four days of being processed through a meat grinder and then left to flounder in the entrails of hot dog mash."

Saul grimaced at Fred's description. "Fred, stop. You're making me nauseous."

"I just want us to win a few games and make it respectable."

"Like *Rocky*?" Saul asked.

"No. Not like *Rocky*. He at least went the distance. I know we aren't going the distance. I'm thinking more like *Rudy*."

"*Rudy*?" Saul contested. "He didn't play at all until the last game of the season. He only got on the field for a few seconds."

"But it was still inspiring," Fred said. "That's what I want. I want a *Rudy* level of inspiration. *Rocky* is a little too much to ask for."

The two volleyball dads ended their conversation but they both spent several hours studying the pools and all the different permutations and computations that could occur if their team finished first, second, third, fourth, fifth, sixth, seventh or eighth in their pool. Saul had to work double-time since he had two teams to analyze.

The Bryson's packed the car and left for Nationals on June 24th. They would be staying at the Omni Hotel downtown. Even though they were playing close to home, Saul wanted to stay downtown to give the tournament an out-of-town feel. Plus, he just didn't like driving in Dallas traffic. He did that enough everyday of his life. The drive down from Plano was all of 27 miles, far shorter than last year's trip to Columbus, Ohio. Saul hoped playing at home might provide the local teams some advantage, but when you're dealing with teenagers, they tend to be ambivalent to location.

Sadly, Elmo did not make the trip.

Harper left him on a shelf in her bedroom. It took Harper a few days to get over the embarrassment of such a harsh social media experience, but in a way it also helped. It forced her to distance herself from Elmo a bit, something that Veronica and Saul felt should have happened a couple of years earlier, but neither dared risk bringing it up because they felt the separation anxiety for Harper might be too severe. During the weeks leading up to Nationals, however, they saw their little Harper take the final steps from childhood to teenager-hood. Their little girl had grown up. Saul knew the transition was complete when Harper called him at work one day to ask him if she could invite a friend over. She started the conversation with Dad.

Daddy was now a name in the past.

Harper's team started bright and early at 8 a.m. on June 25th, Saul's Christmas day. Their first match was against a team from Idaho. Autumn made the girls arrive at 6:30 a.m., a half hour earlier than normal because she wanted to make doubly sure they were awake. You couldn't take anything for granted at Nationals, especially with 13-year-olds. You never knew for sure when a team would come out of nowhere and surprise you. While Idaho was not known as a volleyball hotspot, if they had a really good server who got on a roll or a really good hitter that got hot, that could make a difference in the outcome of the match.

The girls were definitely ready to play. It had been a long eight weeks since their last tournament action and they were tired of practicing and scrimmaging. They came out of the gates focused and on fire. Everyone was in sync and hitting on all cylinders. It was easy to see that the Idahoans were not used to playing at such a high level. SkyHi went on to win easily, 25 to 13 and 25 to 16.

While it was always good to get that first match under your belt, they had two more matches to play that day. Like Idaho, however, neither of their next two opponents had enough talent to hang with SkyHi 13s Blue. Harper's team won both matches easily and ended the day 3 and 0. Saul was also keeping eyes on OVA, the top team in their pool. They had an easy day of it as well and finished 3 and 0. From what he could tell, they looked really tough. They were riding a wave of momentum coming off a recent national championship win at AAU, which was held in Orlando, OVA's backyard.

Day two arrived and Saul and Veronica had a full day ahead of them, as did Autumn. Harper's team was scheduled to play in the morning and Bree's team was scheduled to play in the afternoon. SkyHi 13s did their best to make Autumn's day more manageable.

They continued their excellent play from the day before by knocking off teams from North Carolina and Virginia. Saul was feeling more confident about Harper's team. They could go deep in the tournament if they continued playing at such a high level.

Their last match of the day was a team called Imi Ike from Hawaii. Saul didn't like playing Hawaiian teams. They were always very good and well-coached. Volleyball was popular in Hawaii and it showed by the quality of their club teams. For the first time in the tournament, SkyHi 13s was tested.

Imi Ike's defensive play was outstanding and began flustering the SkyHi players, causing them to over-swing and make several hitting errors. SkyHi couldn't control the tempo of the game and lost 25 to 19. Saul was worried and felt beads of sweat suddenly start to cover his forehead. If they lost this match, it would make it really difficult for them to win the pool. They would still be in good shape to finish in the top three, but even that could be in jeopardy if they lost to OVA, too. Autumn gathered the girls around and kept them calm.

"We're okay girls. We just have to play our game and limit our mistakes. They're defense is outstanding but so is ours. It's time to show them how we play defense in Texas. Okay?"

The girls all nodded in agreement.

"And let's cut down our hitting errors. Our offense is way better than theirs. Let's just be patient and find the openings. We don't need to over-swing."

Saul loved to listen to Autumn coach. He had made a point to sit as close to the bench as possible so he could enjoy her instruction. It also helped him coach his own daughter better when they practiced on Bryson Court because he knew what Autumn was focusing on.

The girls were ready for game two and stayed remarkably composed. Their defense began matching Imi Ike's intensity and they stayed very patient on offense. The points became longer rallies because they weren't swinging for the big kill anymore. They let the points play out until they had an opportunity for an easy kill, then they took advantage of it. Imi Ike showed great resolve and wasn't going down easily. SkyHi managed to win the second game 25 to 22 but it was hard fought and well-played by both teams. Saul felt the third game was a toss-up.

Harper helped the team to an early lead by converting a couple of quick sets for easy points. She then took advantage of one of Imi Ike's few mistakes by smashing an overpass straight down to the floor. The ball must have sailed 30 feet high in the air after hitting the ground. The Imi Ike girls looked up in awe as the ball sailed above their heads. Saul hoped that this was the point that would sway the momentum in their favor. The Hawaiian girls actually looked a little intimidated now.

While Imi Ike continued to play well, SkyHi 13s played a little bit better and was able to maintain their small lead throughout the game. They won 15 to 12 and were now 6 and 0 in pool play. With the victory, they were guaranteed at least a second place finish so they knew they would advance to the next round, regardless of what happened in their next match against OVA. Saul went to check on what was happening with OVA and to his chagrin, there was no drama. They won their third and final match of the day with ease. They were also 6 and 0, which set up a battle of the two top seeds in their pool.

Even though both teams were guaranteed advancement into the next round, the game still had significant meaning. Whoever won the pool would get a bye in the next round. That meant one less match you had to win and one less quality team you had to face.

Veronica took Harper back up to the room so she could rest and have some lunch. Saul headed over to meet Fred at Bree's court. SkyHi 16 Black was scheduled to start in about an hour. "What's the word, Fred?" Saul asked as they shook hands.

"The word is one," Fred said.

"One what?" Saul asked.

"One win. We need one win today, that's all."

"You're not sounding very optimistic," Saul told him.

"We have Advantage and OVA today. Are you optimistic?"

"Guess not," Saul admitted.

"Think *Rudy*," Fred said. "Remember?"

"I remember," Saul said.

"Our only shot is to finish third," Fred explained. "To do that, we will need to go 5 and 2 or 4 and 3, at worst. We've got to win one match today to stay in this thing."

That one match would have to be against a team from Vermont.

"It's Vermont, for crying out loud," Fred exclaimed. "Do they even play volleyball there? We can't lose to them."

The two matches versus OVA and Advantage went about as planned. SkyHi 16 Black lost both and quickly fell to 0 and 2. Autumn tried to keep the girls mentally in the matches but they were too outmanned. She used what energy she had left from the long day and implored them that the season was not over. They needed to win the last match that day to help turn things around. The girls responded and played a quality match against Vermont Juniors. Saul and Fred didn't get too amped up after the win. It was Vermont, after all.

The next day would be challenging. Bree's team would have their hands full with three quality teams. Both Saul and Fred believed they were teams they could beat, or get beaten by.

"3 and 0 would be great," Fred said, "But 2 and 1 would still keep us alive."

Fred wanted to go to the bar for a drink but Saul was too exhausted. He had to get mentally recharged for Harper's match in the morning. He and Veronica told Fred good night and went up to their hotel room to check on Harper. She was tucked in bed watching an episode of *Friends*. Whatever episode it was, you could bet it was at least the tenth time she had seen it. *Friends* was the *The Brady Bunch* of her generation.

The next thing Saul heard was the alarm clock buzzing. It was already 6 a.m. and time to get up. He could have sworn his head just hit the pillow. The OVA match started bright and early at 8 a.m. When Saul got to the court, he could sense the intensity level was a little higher than normal. Parents had made it to the court earlier to ensure they got a seat. OVA had a pretty good-sized contingent of parents and family members that travelled with them. The seats were filling up fast and Saul already knew this was going to be a standing room only event.

The pre-game warmups were more flashy than usual as both teams wanted to give the other team a preview of what they were about to get. Harper was hitting the ball so hard Saul was worried she might throw her shoulder out of its socket. The SkyHi girls were wearing blue ribbons in their hair to match their blue jerseys. The OVA ribbons were white. The moms took such joy in preparing them each tournament. They would always try to top the previous mom by coming up with a new color combination or style. Easter weekend tournaments had to feature something in pastel colors. New Year's Eve tournaments had to feature something sparkly.

At 13 years of age, the ribbons were an essential part of the uniform for the girls. They wore them with pride and also because they made them look adorably cute. In no more than two years' time, the ribbons would be tossed aside and considered extremely immature and offensive to their competitive nature.

The referee signaled for the match to begin and their youthful competitive nature was ready to be put to the test. OVA came out swinging and was looking to deliver an early knockout. They showed some dazzling displays of ball control early on and they had two hitters that could jump high and pound the ball into submission.

The OVA parents were involved early and started yelling loudly. Saul could hear a couple of dads delivering some smack talk and he didn't like it. This immediately got his juices flowing and made him want to beat OVA even more. Unfortunately, he wasn't playing. He would have to rely on the girls to do that. He hoped they were just as pissed as he was.

OVA jumped to an early lead but Harper and her teammates did not panic. They had seen this kind of talent before, right in their own back yard with MadDogs. They took OVA's best shot and started showing a little razzle-dazzle of their own. They countered with some powerful outside hits and Harper contributed a couple of stuff blocks that began intimidating the OVA hitters. SkyHi took the lead 16 to 15 and the SkyHi parents began ratcheting up their own cheers. Saul wanted to taunt the smack-talking dads with a cheer of his own, but Veronica shut him up before he could begin.

This match was epic, Saul felt, or as epic as it could be when you're on court 46 and there are dozens of other matches going on around you. Parents and fans and passers-by had built a wall around the court about six people deep. Loud cheers were raised after every point. The two teams were in a slugfest and SkyHi was winning. OVA seemed to be getting a little rattled. SkyHi had stood up to them and was now taking control. They scored the final three points of the first game and won 25 to 20. The SkyHi parents were delirious.

The crowd kept getting bigger as more people stopped to watch the match as it progressed, many were curious to see what the fuss was about. Game two began and SkyHi kept the momentum they had from the first game. They built a small lead and OVA knew they were running out of time. With SkyHi up 17 to 16, the OVA coach called a timeout. Saul figured he was trying to do anything to change the momentum of the match.

Whatever he told his girls, it seemed to work. OVA came out and scored on the next two possessions and SkyHi started to press. They made a couple of costly passing errors that gave OVA two more points and before you knew it, OVA was in control of the game. OVA won game two 25 to 19.

Saul was impressed with the Florida team. They were on the ropes and, like champions, they found a way to win the second game. All the momentum had swung back in their favor. Saul wasn't impressed with their parents, though. The Smack-Daddys, as he now termed them, were chanting again in full force and their behavior was becoming more and more obnoxious.

Saul screamed out, "Let's go SkyHi" at the top of his lungs and all the SkyHi parents followed suit, echoing the phrase repeatedly while clapping their hands. They made enough noise to drown out the obsessive Smack-Daddys and Saul received much satisfaction for leading the cheer.

"Good job," Veronica told him. "And you didn't even have to taunt them."

Game three began and tensions were high. Autumn was compelling the girls to keep fighting. She reminded them how important it was to get off to a good start in the third game. For some reason, they didn't heed her direction.

OVA came out with a flourish of big kills and suddenly led 4 to 0. Saul figured the nail in the coffin was ready to be driven in. Autumn called a quick timeout and started talking at the top of her lungs. Saul couldn't tell if it was Cruella reappearing or not.

"You guys, nothing hits the ground from here on out," Autumn demanded. "You understand me? We are digging every ball they fire at us. Every point matters. Remember?"

The girls all nodded their heads in agreement, or in fear. Saul couldn't tell. They ran back on the court with a look of determination and grit, or as much grit as you could muster with blue ribbons in your hair.

OVA was ready to serve the ball and the SkyHi players prepared to dig in. That's exactly what they did. They got their hands on every serve and every attempted kill OVA threw at them. They were on a mission again like they were at the Lone Star qualifier. SkyHi's defensive play began frustrating the big hitters from OVA who couldn't believe their kills were not hitting the ground.

Harper benefited from her team's improved defensive play by getting great sets to hit and she converted on every opportunity. Even the points that OVA scored on were almost dug by SkyHi's back row. Nothing was hitting the floor as Autumn ordered.

SkyHi had built an 11 to 7 lead and the rest of the match was all Harper Bryson. She dug a couple of balls herself and converted two more huge kills. Her team won the third game going away, 15 to 7. The girls rushed the court and the parents celebrated like they had just won Nationals, but they hadn't won Nationals. They had beaten the top seed, however, and they got a bye in the next round which was very important. And just like the MadDog win, they proved that they could play with anybody. More importantly, if they won the next match, they would be in the semi-finals which assured them of getting a medal.

Several parents came up to congratulate Saul on Harper's play and he soaked it all in. She was a beast that third game and it was a thrill to watch. He and the rest of the parents had plenty of time to settle down. Their next match wasn't until 2 p.m., which worked out perfectly because Bree's first match didn't start until 3 p.m.

Harper's team had to watch the match that would determine who they would play next. Saul was concerned when he saw who the two teams were. One was Northern Lights, a top club out of Minneapolis, and the other was that darn pesky team from Puerto Rico. Harper's team had yet to beat a Puerto Rican team, for whatever reason. Saul decided he better cheer for Northern Lights, but it didn't help. The Puerto Ricans won in two games, and much too easily for Saul's liking, which added to his concern. If SkyHi 13s wanted any chance of winning Nationals, they would have to end the hex that the Puerto Ricans had placed on them.

After lunch, Bree, who had been cheering Harper's team on all morning, left to go be with her teammates and Saul told her he would be over as soon as Harper's game ended.

"Don't worry, Dad. We've got this," she said, showing more confidence than she had a right to.

Like Harper, she was carrying herself in a much more mature fashion these days. She had become one of the leaders on her team and she was starting to show a take-charge mentality, which Saul admired. She was still a little delusional at times when she talked about how great her team was, but that was okay. It was her team with her friends and she had a right to feel proud about it.

Not that Harper needed any motivation, Saul decided to give her an earful anyway. "One more win and you get a National medal, Harp," he told her. He hoped those words would carry the same inspiration for her that the banner did in middle school ball. He then pointed to the majestic stadium court in the distance. "And you see that, Harp?" She looked and nodded. "Two more wins and you'll be playing there. Wouldn't that be fun?"

Her mouth was agape and her eyes were glowing. She ran back to her teammates as they prepared to warm-up against the pesky Puerto Ricans. As it turned out, Autumn had her own pre-game speech planned that trumped Saul's.

"Girls," she began. "There are eight teams left and you are one of them. From here on out, it's win or go home. Do you want to go home?"

"No," the girls answered back.

"These girls don't know how tough we can play and they need to find that out right now." Autumn reached in her bag and pulled out a bunch of blue elastic headbands. They each had the girls' number stitched on the front.

"Cool," one girl said.

"LeBron wears one of these," another girl said.

"That's right," Autumn shot back. "Do all of you know who LeBron James is?"

Saul chuckled as a couple of girls raised their hands but the majority had confused looks on their faces.

"He's only the best athlete and basketball player on the planet," Autumn continued. "And LeBron looks tough when he's on the court. You know why?"

The girls looked somewhat afraid to answer.

"Because he wears a headband. So I want you to take those ribbons out of your hair and I want you to put these on," Autumn ordered. "And when you're out there on the court, I want you to feel tough, be tough and play tough. Okay?"

The girls told her they would as they giggled and looked at one another while trying on their headbands. Some girls looked pretty good, others not so much. Harper did, Saul surmised. She looked tough and the rest of her teammates looked like they meant business. Saul hoped Autumn's ploy would work. They needed something to combat the Puerto Ricans' mojo.

When the game began, the girls walked on the court with a little swag. The Puerto Rican team looked at them with a bit of curiosity. They didn't recognize the team they had beaten earlier in the season. This SkyHi team looked more mature, older and more confident. Saul just hoped they would play as tough as they looked.

From the first point of the game, SkyHi played with a toughness and physicality that was unusual for girls their age. They were improving right before everyone's eyes. Saul had no doubt that both teams could take on most 14-year-old teams and probably beat them. Simply put, Harper and her teammates were playing a fantastic match.

In between points, the players helped adjust each other's headbands because sometimes they had a tendency to shift or fall down over their eyes. They wanted to make sure their tough look didn't change. That mutual support spurred their play on the court as well. They made sure they had each other's back. They communicated in perfect tandem on the court so everyone knew where everyone was at any given time. They picked each other up if an error was made and they calmed each other down after celebrating a great play.

The Puerto Ricans played a great match, too, but they weren't the better team on this day. Was it the blue headbands that broke the curse? Or was it a great SkyHi team that, on this particular day, just happened to play over their heads? No one would ever know for sure, but what people would know was the score. SkyHi beat them in two, 25 to 22 and 25 to 23. The score was close but the game never seemed that much in doubt because of the poise and control the girls demonstrated. There was also little doubt about one other thing. The headbands would stay on for the rest of the tournament.

After the match, Harper was so excited she ran up to Saul and asked him, "When do we get our medal?"

"You've got to finish the tournament first silly. We don't know what place you'll finish in yet."

Harper covered her face with her hands in embarrassment. "Oh, I forgot. How stupid of me." She then ran back to be with her teammates.

Saul and Veronica looked at their watches and realized they needed to move fast. Bree's game had just started. As they headed towards her court, Saul heard a loud cheer that erupted from a few courts down. He looked over and saw that it was the 13s

MadDog Black parents. They had just won their match, too. They had made the semi-finals just like SkyHi did. If they both won, they would be in the finals. What are the odds of two North Texas teams playing in the finals of 13 Open in Dallas? Saul wondered. He tried not to even think about it. He needed to focus on Bree and her team now. They needed all of his positive mental telepathy to help them try and survive the day.

When Saul and Veronica arrived on the court, Bree's match was already under way. Veronica left Saul to be with the other moms while he found Fred the Baptist, who was saving him a seat.

"Congratulations," Fred said.

"Thanks. It was a great game."

"Nice to have one daughter leaving with some hardware."

"It sure is. So what's happening here?"

"We're struggling. I'll feel better when Autumn makes her way over here."

"Who's coaching?"

"Our assistant coach."

"Great," Saul frowned. That was not what he wanted to hear. The assistant coach was a nice girl but she was 22 years old and fresh out of college. She talked to the girls like they were her teammates. She didn't have their attention or respect.

Bree's team was trailing 16 to 12 when Autumn finally arrived. After watching a few points, she quickly called a timeout and tried to regroup them. The timeout helped. The girls began targeting zone five, the left back part of the court, with their kills. Autumn must have noticed a weakness in the defense. They kept on hitting to that zone every chance they could and they managed to come back and win the game 25 to 22. Game two was a lot easier. They won 25 to 15 as the opposing team never did anything to try and remedy their defensive problems in left back.

"We're 2 and 2," Fred reminded Saul. "We're still in it."

Bree's team had two teams from California left to play that afternoon. One was from Northern California and the other from Southern California. Like North Texas, both were major regions in the club volleyball universe. With California teams, you also had the beach volleyball factor, which these girls played year round. That meant every girl was used to diving and digging in sand, which translated into sharper instincts and quicker defensive play indoors. They had no problem sacrificing their bodies on a hard court.

The first match was against the team from Northern California. It proved to be a very frustrating game if you were a part of the SkyHi posse of parents and players. Morgan and the other girls on the back row had a hard time matching the defensive quickness of their opponent. Savannah could never get the offense in any kind of rhythm and the hitters ended up having to hit several harmless free-balls over the net during most of the match.

What was agonizing to Saul was that the team was beatable. They were not that good. Yes, they were athletic and blonde and they had good tans like all California teams do, but other than their defensive play, they were not that good. Bree's team, for whatever reason, didn't answer the bell. They lost in three agonizing games and had several opportunities to win the match but they could never seem to convert the big points at the right time.

Autumn got in their faces after the match and told them they had to adjust to California volleyball. They could never assume a point was over. You play the point until you hear the referee blow his whistle. Their opponent was too good at diving for balls and pancaking balls that SkyHi normally thought were kills. Pancaking was a term used when a player dives and extends her arm out on the floor and the ball hits the back of her hand popping it back up for another defender to retrieve. It was a cool technique when executed properly and also a great hustle play that could change the momentum of a point. Saul hoped Autumn's speech delivered the right effect. They had one more California team to play and they had to play better.

"This is it," Fred said in his constant melodramatic Southern tone. "We lose this and we're done."

The Southern California team looked even more athletic and blonde and more tan than the team from Northern California. Saul figured the darker tan was a function of sunnier days in L.A. as opposed to San Francisco. The SoCal girls also had their sliders hiked up about as far as you could pull them.

"They've got an entire team of Butt Cheeks," Saul exclaimed.

"Why do I feel like a sexual predator if I watch them?" Fred asked. "I'm not a sexual predator. I'm just a nice, Southern Baptist, Bible-totin' dude that has a 16-year old daughter that plays volleyball."

"Relax," Saul interrupted him. "Just keep your eyes on our girls and the volleyball. We're not doing anything wrong."

The match began and the SkyHi girls didn't let the SoCal girls throw them off their game. The previous match with the NoCal team had helped them adapt and adjust to the California style of volleyball. Morgan and her defensive teammates raised their level of play and even performed a few pancakes of their own.

Bree's team was able to stay in a good rhythm throughout the match and control most of the action. They were even able to cope with SoCal's penchant for sassy smack talk. Whenever they had a kill, they would utter something that sounded like, "Right back at you, Bitch."

Saul could tell this was starting to annoy Bree and the other front row players since they were the ones in earshot of the nasty comments. They didn't let it distract them, though. If anything, it caused them to elevate their desire to beat them. During a point late in the match, Stacy went up for a block against one of the SoCal outside hitters and stuffed the ball back right in her face.

"Pull your sliders down, Beeotch!" Stacy blurted out as loud as she could.

Bree and her other teammates looked at Stacy in amazement. They had never heard her utter smack before.

"Lucky block," the SoCal girl shot back.

"Your butt was roofed, girl," Stacy shouted in reply.

Bree suddenly put her arm around Stacy and pulled her away from the net to calm her down.

"Stacy's getting feisty," Saul remarked to Fred.

"It only took five years," Fred countered. He then quickly locked his hands in prayer. "Good Lord, please forgive Stacy for her language. It was not done out of spite or in any kind of vindictive way. She is just riding the excitement of your great spirit, Lord. Amen."

Fred looked at Saul. "You think He bought it?"

"Totally."

Never backing down to the SoCal girls, the girls from Plano, Texas stood up to the challenge and won a three-set thriller. Fred looked at a relieved Saul and said, "Now that was a *Rudy* win."

Saul smiled in agreement. "What does that do for our chances?"

Fred pulled out his phone and accessed the tournament scoring app. "Heck, it's hard to say," he said after studying it for some time. "OVA and Advantage are clearly one and two. Right now we have three teams that are 3 and 3 and one team that is 4 and 2. We play the 4 and 2 team tomorrow morning. We've got to win that match to tie them. Then it will come down to what the other two teams do. We could have a two-way tie, three-way tie, or four-way tie."

"Or no tie if we lose," Saul interjected.

"You're right. You're getting better at this, Saul."

"Thanks for noticing," Saul replied. "So we could be in a huge play-off situation, right?"

"Nope. They don't do playoffs at Nationals for some reason. If it's a three-way tie or greater, it will come down to set and point differential to see who advances. A two-way tie is still based on head-to-head."

"So every point matters," Saul said, mimicking Autumn.

"Yep. With four teams still in it, it's impossible to do all the what-if scenarios. It's making my head hurt. We just got to go out and do our part and win."

To win, SkyHi 16 Black would need to beat a team out of Wisconsin. They looked pretty strong based on the few times Saul had a chance to glance at them. As Fred had said, they were 4 and 2 and currently in sole possession of third place. SkyHi would have to win and hope the tie-breaking system worked out in their favor. At least at Lone Star you had a one-game playoff to decide a three-way tie. It seemed odd that, at the National Championship of all places, a team's fate could be decided by a simple statistic.

Harper's team didn't have to worry about a tie or a statistic. All they had to worry about was winning. Their semi-final opponent was a team from St.Louis called Rockwood Thunder. They were a surprise team that wasn't highly seeded, but they managed to play their way through a tough draw. MadDogs had to play OVA in the other semi-final. Saul didn't want to have to play MadDogs again, but for that matter, he didn't want to play OVA again either. SkyHi had won the previous match against both teams and Saul was always leery of the revenge factor.

He made sure both girls were in bed and the lights were out by 10 o'clock. They were exhausted and both needed to get a lot of rest. Their first matches in the morning were both survival matches. If either team lost, they were out of the tournament.

The girls slept well and so did Saul. Thoughts of playing in the stadium court filled his sleep with pleasant dreams, blocking out any nightmares that might cause a restless slumber. Strangely, he awoke that morning very much at peace. He wasn't overly nervous at all. Overnight, he seemed to have developed a more carefree sense of being. In the shower, he kept humming that song that Doris Day sang in that Hitchcock movie, 'Que Sera Sera, whatever will be, will be.' Something inside had told him there was nothing else for him to do. He had done what he could. He helped get his girls to this point. In a lot of ways, they had helped themselves. The season would soon be over. Win or lose, whatever would be, would be. Maybe his eased state of mind stemmed from the fact that his girls were playing well and that their teams were playing well, too. They were doing the best they could and that's all you could ask. He didn't know for sure. He was just relaxed and content.

His contentment continued as he and Veronica walked to the court and prepared for Harper's semi-final match.

"Why are you so serene?" Veronica asked, noticing his antsy and obsessive demeanor was missing.

"I don't know. I'm just very proud of our two girls. They handle themselves so well, on and off the volleyball court."

"Maybe our parenting isn't too bad, you think?"

"I think you may be right. It's just interesting how things work out. I've been so focused on mapping out their athletic careers, but in hindsight, I didn't need a map at all. They figured it out on their own. They chose the sport. They chose to have lessons. They chose the teams they would play on. Heck, they even taught me to forgive my dad."

Veronica grasped his hand and whispered, "Thanks for being such a caring father. I love you."

Saul stopped walking and looked straight into his wife's eyes. "Very, I may not have been the greatest basketball player. But my dad gave me the heart and desire to make something of my life. And that something is you."

He leaned over to kiss her and they shared a warm embrace.

"Now let's go watch some volleyball," he said calmly.

The girls' schedule was a tight one again. Harper played at 8 a.m. and Bree played at 9 a.m. That meant Autumn might be delayed in getting over to Bree's match.

Oh, well, Saul thought, as he kept hearing Doris Day's voice in his mind.

Harper's match started and it started well, just as Saul thought it might. SkyHi 13 Blue was playing so good no one could beat them. That sounded cocky but that's what Saul was feeling. The girls from St. Louis appeared a little shell-shocked at first, like the moment was too big for them.

With their tough-guy blue headbands, Harper and her teammates not only played like they belonged, they played like they were the better team. More importantly, they were playing to win while their opponent was trying not to lose. SkyHi prevailed in two drama-free games.

Saul stood up to celebrate with the rest of the parents, all the while remaining relaxed and content. Out of the corner of his eye, he saw the stadium court in the distance. For the first time, he was able to stare at it without envy. His younger daughter would be playing there. He would finally get to experience it. It was all meant to be.

He and Veronica then calmly walked over to Bree's court. Harper's match was done so quickly there was no real rush. Autumn would get there in plenty of time, too. He saw that Fred was walking over to him in his usual quick pace. Fred always walked like he had someplace to get to in a hurry. Today, he was just excited about the game.

Bree's team seemed ready for battle. They were relieved to see Autumn there in plenty of time. Autumn had scouted the team the night before and she told the girls the game plan. It was all about quickness and speed. The Wisconsin team consisted of stout, well-fed, beefy girls with a couple of them standing six-foot-three or taller. During warm-ups, they looked quite impressive slamming the ball down to the ground with such strong force. Their block would be formidable, but Autumn assured her girls that they could out-hustle and out-play them.

Just as the match began, Saul got a text from Harper. 'We play MadDogs in the final, ugh!!!' it read. Saul could only smile at the irony. He texted back, 'Don't worry. You can beat them. You've done it before.' Harper texted back a row of smiley faces, which was a good sign, Saul figured. He then focused his attention back to the game at hand.

From the get go, Bree and her teammates were not intimidated by the opponent's size. They came out swinging and weren't afraid to tool the block or hit into it, if necessary. Morgan's back row passing was perfect and enabled the setters to run the quick offense that Autumn was counting on. The Wisconsin girls were tall but very slow and SkyHi was able to beat them to the ball and dig more balls. Bree and her teammates had an athletic advantage that proved too difficult for the Wisconsin team to match. They could not cover the court like Morgan and the other SkyHi back row defenders could.

The result was a convincing win in two games and a 4 and 3 record in pool play. Saul and Fred gave each other the obligatory man-hug and then Fred went to check on the other two matches that would help decide the outcome of the pool. SkyHi needed the two 3 and 3 teams to lose. That would guarantee a two-way tie between SkyHi and Wisconsin and SkyHi would advance based on the head-to-head win.

Saul remained on Bree's court and took in the atmosphere and the glory of the win. A 4 and 3 record was darn good for a second team in Open. Bree and SkyHi 16 Black had exceeded his expectations, regardless of the outcome of the tie-breaker.

"Hey," a voice startled him from behind. It was Bree.

"Hey, girl. Great game."

"Thanks. Have you heard the big news?"

"What news?"

"SkyHi Blue lost this morning. That means they got second in their pool."

"That's too bad," Saul said. "They're still alive, though."

"Yeah, but guess who they play next?"

Saul couldn't recall how all the permutations and calculations played out. He had done the bracket analysis a while back but his expectation for Bree's team was never to make it out of pool play so he didn't focus on it too much.

Tired of waiting for a response, Bree told him, "They play us or whoever finishes third in our pool."

"Are you serious?" Saul asked.

"Yep, Autumn just told us. Wouldn't that be great?"

If you wanted to lose, Saul wanted to say but he didn't. "That's great," Saul said instead. "You'd get another shot at them."

"The girls are stoked. We want to beat them so bad."

Saul's phone then buzzed. He had a text from Fred. It said 'One down, one to go'. "It appears one of the 3 and 3 teams just lost," Saul told Bree.

"Really, that's so awesome. I'm going to go tell the girls."

Bree left Saul alone to ponder the drama of a SkyHi Blue, SkyHi Black match-up. He didn't want to think about it too much. He was enjoying his calm, nerve-free morning and wanted it to continue.

The other 3 and 3 team left was the team from SoCal. They were playing NoCal and had to beat them. SkyHi needed the lighter tanned girls to win. A few minutes passed by and Fred appeared and plopped down on the seat next to Saul. "SoCal won, darn it. We have a three-way."

"You mean tie, correct?" Saul asked.

Fred nodded.

"Because if you just say three-way it sort of implies something else."

"I'm in no mood for sexual innuendo after watching the SoCal girls, okay?"

Saul laughed at Fred, but quickly steered the subject back to the tie-breaker. "So who's in?"

"I don't know. I think the set differential is even between the three teams so it's coming down to points. I tried running the numbers but it's so close I don't trust my math. It's either going to be us or SoCal."

Saul had an urge to turn his phone calculator on and start doing the math himself, but he resisted. He would take whatever Doris Day would give him today. Suddenly, a burst of excitement rose from Bree's teammates, who had been sitting on the sidelines waiting for news. They got to their feet and saw Autumn approaching.

"We're in," Autumn yelled.

The girls jumped into each other's arms and screamed with joy. Fred and Saul watched them in their frenzy and could only smile.

"They're really excited," Fred said. "They should be, making the final twelve teams and all."

"It's not just that. They're excited about their next opponent."

"Who's that?" Fred asked.

"You mean you don't know?" He couldn't believe he was about to scoop Fred, the fact finder.

"No. I've been too busy watching the other two matches."

"We play Blue."

"What the . . . ?" Fred did a double take. "SkyHi Blue? Did they lose and finish second in their pool?"

"That's what Bree told me."

"Well, I'll be," Fred remarked.

"When do we play?" Saul asked.

"Just a sec, let me check." Fred searched through the tournament app and found the game. "They play on court 16 at 1 p.m."

"Uh-oh."

"What's wrong?"

"That's the same time as Harper's championship match."

"Well that sucks," Fred exclaimed.

Saul had to find Veronica and formulate a plan. Which parent was to watch which game? As much as Saul had dreamed of being on the stadium court, he felt so guilty about leaving Bree on her own without him. He had been there for her from the start, through all the tears and cheers and practices and dreaded tryouts and school seasons and club seasons good or bad.

For Harper, it had come so easily. She had the big sister that she wanted to emulate and she had such an early start that gave her a greater advantage. Regardless of Bree's new found independence and wanting to do things her way, Saul had stood by her and he didn't feel right abandoning her now. He told Veronica to go watch Harper's game and record it. He would stay and watch Bree play.

"Are you sure?" She asked. "I know how much the stadium court aura means to you."

"Now, how would you know that?" Saul asked.

"Because you talk in your sleep. Sometimes I think you're making love to that court."

"Oh, for crying out loud, Very. Quit your joking. Harper's playing there and that's the important thing. Just be sure and take some good video. No camera jiggling or indistinguishable shots of the floor or people's feet."

"I'll do my best."

Saul then saw Brent and some other Blue parents approaching the court. Brent, no longer Mystery Man, was a good buddy of Saul's after the two of them bonded while cheering for their Varsity middle blockers last season. He went over to talk with the Blue parents and wished them luck. They did the same, although it all felt a bit awkward and disingenuous. A win meant a trip to the quarterfinals. They both wanted to beat each other's brains out.

Saul's calm demeanor continued as the game drew near. They were the underdogs. There was no real pressure. A loss was expected. Fred was getting amped up and Saul tried to settle him down. "Think *Rudy*," Saul said. "Not *Rocky*. We've had our moment."

Saul then noticed a couple of familiar faces sitting down across the court from him. They weren't his favorite faces but he was learning to coexist with them. Bobby and Robby had come to watch Bree play. These guys were like magnets now. You couldn't get rid of them. The more he had gotten to know Bobby, the more he liked him but that didn't really matter. Saul knew from his own experience that you could never really trust a 16-year old boy.

Before the girls were set to warm up, Bree saw Saul sitting in the stands and came over.

"What are you doing here?" She asked.

"I'm here to watch the game."

"Dad, Harper is playing in the final. You need to go watch her."

"It's okay. Mom's taping it."

"Dad, don't worry about me. We'll be okay. You need to go watch Harper. I want you to."

"But one of us needs to be here."

Bree continued to urge him to leave. "Dad, it's okay. I'm fine with it. Go enjoy the stadium court. She's playing for a national championship, of all things. I promise I won't mind."

"But I've . . . " Saul's voice started to crack a bit.

"But what? Bree asked, looking concerned.

"I've never missed one of your games," Saul pleaded, his emotions swelling inside of him.

Bree smiled at him lovingly. "Dad, don't you remember our conversation? You don't have to be here." Then she pointed to her heart. "To be here. I can handle things," she assured him.

Saul wanted to tell her to stop all the mature talk. He was getting tired of it. He still wanted his little girl around. The more he thought about it though, the more he knew she was right. He could let her go. She would be fine on her own. Everything would be okay.

"We're gonna beat them, Dad," she told him as he began to gather his things along with his composure. Saul nodded as to act like he agreed with her, but he knew what the result would be. He told Fred to pull them through, that he was going to watch Harper play in the finals. Fred told him he would keep his seat for him.

Saul made it over to the stadium court in time for the National Anthem. He found Veronica and went to sit by her. She was surprised to see him and asked him if she should go watch Bree. He told her no. Bree wanted them here. After the Anthem, each player was announced individually. Harper Bryson's name echoed through the stadium amplifiers and it sent a bolt of chills through Saul's body. He knew they were so fortunate to experience this. Not many club volleyball players ever get this opportunity.

For the next hour or so, he would soak it all in. Yes, he hoped for a win but he didn't want to be too greedy. They had already been blessed with a medal. Seeing Six-Shooter and Midget Middle on the court again did get his juices flowing. MadDogs looked very determined in warm-ups, like they were ready to feast on revenge. SkyHi's warm-up was okay but didn't have the same intensity level as MadDogs. He hoped they were ready. He hoped the blue headbands were ready, too. He also hoped Harper didn't have any lingering issues from Elmo-Gate and would stay focused on the game at hand.

Saul again felt an unusual wave of peace move through his body assuring him everything would be okay. SkyHi was playing great volleyball. If they played their best, they would win. If they didn't, they would lose. It was as simple as that. There was nothing else he could do.

With an audience of about two thousand people filling the stands, the game started and a new chapter in the rivalry between MadDogs and SkyHi was about to be written. MadDogs came out with the same heightened intensity level they demonstrated during warm-ups. They wanted to exact their revenge quickly and prove to SkyHi the last match was a fluke.

They won the first few points and took a quick 8 to 2 lead. Autumn had to call a timeout and stop the juggernaut. The girls returned to the court and SkyHi managed to slow down the MadDogs momentum, but they couldn't cut into their lead. The two sides traded points, which was fine with the MadDogs players as they protected a five-point advantage.

Midget Middle scored a couple of points in a row and Saul got a little irritated that Harper didn't block her. He could tell Harper was getting irritated, too. And then Six-Shooter got on a roll. She hammered a point down the line with such authority, it left the SkyHi defenders in awe. She did her little pistol-waving dance and the MadDogs fans were on their feet with applause.

"Looks like Elmo just took two in the chest," Six-Shooter shouted, staring directly at Harper.

"Did she say what I thought she just said?" Veronica asked Saul.

"You heard correctly," Saul confirmed, fuming inside. His newfound serenity was being tested.

Autumn had to call her second and final timeout of the game. The girls walked over to the bench, but Harper was still in a stare-down with Six-Shooter.

"Harper," Autumn yelled. "Get over here."

Harper's teammates pulled her into the huddle. Saul could tell most of the girls were worried, fearing the worst, that Cruella would reappear one last time. Instead, to their surprise, Autumn was just smiling. She looked like she had no intention of yelling. "Look, you girls. It's very simple. My coaching is done. I've taught you everything I know. You just have to execute what you've learned. If we don't execute, we're not going to win. So what are we going to do from here on out?"

The girls looked at each other waiting for the first one to speak. After a few moments of hesitation, Harper spoke up, "We've got to play together."

"That's good," Autumn said. "What else?"

"Communicate," one girl said.

"Good. What else?"

"Play like every point matters," another girl said.

"Nothing hits the ground," a fourth girl joined in.

Then Harper added one more comment, "We're on a mission to win."

The girls all cheered Harper's last comment. They had built themselves back up and were ready to fight. As they headed back to the court, Autumn pulled Harper aside.

"That middle doesn't score again. You hear me?"

"I hear you," Harper said, taking on the challenge.

Saul saw the girls walking back to the court with a new look of determination. He could tell Harper was ready by the steam coming out of her ears. SkyHi was down 20 to 15. Even if they ended up losing the opening game, they at least needed to change the flow of the game and have some positive mojo heading into game two.

MadDogs served the ball in play and the SkyHi defender made a perfect pass to the setter who made a perfect set to Harper who made the perfect kill. She leaped over Midget Middle and stuffed the ball down so hard, the crowd erupted after witnessing such a spectacular effort. On the next play, MadDogs set a ball to Midget Middle but Harper's long arms were there in time to block the ball right back into her for a point.

Autumn gave Harper a fist pump and told her to keep it going, which gave Harper even more adrenaline The next point featured an outside set to Six-Shooter who was preparing for the kill when a teammate of Harper's came out of nowhere to block the ball for another SkyHi point.

"You need to reload!!" Harper's teammate shouted to Six-Shooter, the comment obviously rattling her. It even surprised Harper who later would tell Saul that smack talk had now officially reached the 13-year-old age group. Harper soon got another opportunity with a quick middle set and blasted it through Midget Middle's hands. SkyHi was on a roll and MadDogs had to call timeout.

Saul was feeling much better about things. He could see Harper's green eyes boiling. Autumn may have kept her Cruella De Vil inside, but Harper was unleashing her Exorcist Baby for all to see. She was playing with a fury and intensity level Saul had never witnessed before. On the sidelines, Autumn told the setter to keep feeding Harper. "When the beast is hungry, you've got to feed her, okay?" The setter understood the message.

During the next point, MadDogs again tried to get Six-Shooter the ball but she hit it way out of bounds. Saul could tell the opponent was starting to tighten up. SkyHi's confidence was growing. They were playing their best now and when they played their best, they couldn't lose. They continued to feed the ball to Harper who was having Midget Middle for dinner. In the span of just a few points, Midget Middle, who stopped growing when she was eleven, started to see her career as a front row hitter begin to fade. SkyHi had reeled off the last ten points in a row and won the game 25 to 20. Saul knew the match was over. MadDogs could not recover from such a blow.

His phone suddenly buzzed and he guessed it was a message from Fred. His text said that SkyHi Blue won the first game easily. He typed in capital letters IT WAS A BLOODBATH. Saul wasn't surprised. He turned his focus back to the game in front of him.

Game two of the championship match began with a steady dose of Exorcist Baby. Harper was playing like she was truly possessed. MadDogs couldn't stop her. They tried double-blocking her but even that wouldn't work. As MadDogs continued their focus on trying to stop Harper, it opened up space for SkyHi's outside hitters to deliver kill after kill. Game two was never in doubt. It was like the team was taking a victory lap, showing off to everyone and telling the world that yes, they were the best team in the nation.

SkyHi won the second game 25 to 16 with Harper scoring the last point in typical grand fashion, an Exorcist Baby overpass kill. The girls mugged Harper in the middle of the court and the parents ran down from the stands to be with the team. Somewhere at the bottom of the pile was Harper.

Veronica and Saul hugged every parent they could find while trying to video as much of the euphoria as possible. After catching their breaths, the girls were told to head to the medal stand for the medal ceremony. SkyHi stood high at the top of the platform with MadDogs and the other two semi-finalists on both sides.

Several of the MadDogs girls were still in tears but they and the other two teams had no reason to hold their heads down. They all had fabulous seasons and a fabulous tournament. In the end, Nationals was like any other tournament. The team that plays the best is going to win. Saul was overcome with pride and satisfaction, and the good fortune of having a daughter on a team that played well at the right time.

Amid all the revelry, he was distracted by his phone again. It must have been Fred texting him that Bree's game was over. The text read, "Playing lights out, 23 all." Saul couldn't believe the score. He was suddenly cursing himself for not getting to Bree's court sooner. All the championship haze had engulfed him. He found Veronica and they started running over to Bree's court. He looked for Autumn but couldn't see her. Maybe she had already headed over. They made it to the court just as Pamela was smashing a kill for Blue. The Blue fans were celebrating with wild abandon and Saul feared the game had just ended. He looked at the score and it was still tied, now at 26 all.

Veronica found a seat with the moms and Saul quickly took the seat Fred was saving for him. "What's happened?" Saul asked.

"We're playing out of our mind," Fred said. "And your daughter is playing great. She's probably had six kills this game."

"Who's coaching?"

"Barry, the club director stepped in."

"Is he helping?"

"I can't tell. I think the girls are coaching themselves."

Saul looked at the girls on the floor and there was Bree talking to Savannah and Morgan, and directing other girls where to go. It looked like she had taken command. He had never seen her this involved and intense. Bailey, the designated server, was scheduled to sub in when the fill-in coach held her back. If she came in, they would be out of subs.

Bree and Savannah walked over to the fill-in coach and argued for Bailey to come in. She was a role player and this was the role Autumn had committed to her. He then relented and their best server took the court. The only problem was she couldn't be subbed out after serving, which meant they would have a defensive liability on the back row. Bailey was never known for her passing skills.

Bailey took a deep breath and readied herself for her patented jump serve. She tossed the ball high into the air, timing her leap perfectly, and contacted the ball with all the topspin she could muster. The ball's arc, as it cleared the net, bore down at such a steep angle, the Blue defenders didn't even have time to react. The ball dropped for an ace and Black was up 27 to 26.

"One more time," Bree shouted at her.

Bailey went back to serve again and it was almost a carbon copy of the previous serve. Saul instantly thought it was an ace but Butt Cheeks must have adjusted her defensive position because she was able to make contact with the ball, just barely. Lauren, the setter, was able to get to the pass, setting it to Butt Cheeks who lined herself up for the kill.

Everyone knew the ball was coming Bailey's way. Butt Cheeks swung as hard as she could and Bailey positioned herself, closing her eyes in the process. The ball came at her like a bullet and caromed off Bailey's arms as perfectly as it possibly could. Bailey opened her eyes to see where the ball was heading. It was going right to Savannah who had an easy set to make. Bree was calling for a slide. Of all plays to run, why was she calling for that, Saul wondered. She was moving to her right and Savannah back-set her the ball. Saul prayed that Bree would jump off the correct foot, while simultaneously trying to keep visions of failed lay-up attempts out of his mind. Bree did jump off the correct foot. She flew as high off the correct foot as she could and slammed the ball down through Pamela's outstretched arms for a kill.

Black had won game two and the girls were going crazy. Fred and Saul gave each other a fist bump but tried to remain calm. They didn't want to appear too excited with the Blue parents just across the way. Saul turned around looking for Autumn and noticed she was standing behind him among a group of fans with a big smile on her face. She had not joined the girls. It was as if she didn't want to change the mojo. They were doing fine on their own.

Bree and the girls walked back onto the court as pumped up as they could be. She noticed Saul sitting court-side and gave him a sly wink, as if to say everything was under control. Who is this girl? Saul thought.

He just hoped Bree and her teammates were prepared to match Blue's intensity because he knew Coach Carpenter would have a new plan of attack. Saul continued to harbor doubts about Black's ability to finish the job. They had yet to finish against a marquee team the whole year.

Fred quickly turned to Saul. "Would you join me in prayer?"

"Uh, sure," Saul said. "Make it quick."

"Dear Heavenly Father, we think you for this great game of volleyball and these great young athletes. We ask that you protect both teams from injury and that they play to the best of their abilities in this final game of the match. We also ask, that if it's in Your heart Lord, for a win. For that would surely be a boost to our daughters' spirituality and overall mental health. We ask these things in your name, Lord. Amen."

"Amen," Saul echoed.

"There's a first time for everything," Fred said, giving Saul a sly wink.

Blue was the first team to serve to start game three. Saul heard Morgan shout out Autumn's rallying cry, "Nothing hits the ground." And that's basically how the whole game was played. Both teams played at a very high level with rallies that were long and fierce and reminiscent of the rhythmic beauty of the game that Autumn had described. Bree and her teammates knew their roles and responsibilities and were dead set against making a costly error.

Blue managed to stay a point or two ahead during most of the game. They had success double-blocking Bree which forced Savannah to set the pin hitters more often. Stacy, who had developed into a solid right side hitter, had several key kills to keep the game close. They were down 11 to 10 and Saul knew they had to do something to break the flow of the game or the teams would just trade points until Blue won.

Bailey was up to serve next and Saul thought the timing couldn't be more perfect. She rifled her first serve between two Blue defenders, who both let the ball drop out of indecisiveness. She drilled a second serve that was directed right at Butt Cheeks who couldn't react quickly enough and shanked the ball badly out of bounds. Those were the only two errors of the game and Blue had made both of them.

For the first time in game three, Black had the lead and Saul was actually starting to think they could do this. He didn't want to get too excited but with Fred sitting next to him, that was hard not to do. He reminded himself what the record was of second teams versus top teams. It wasn't good. 16 Blue had never lost to a second team since their core group of players first got together as twelve-year-olds. Saul just wanted to remain in his peaceful Doris Day state of mind. It had carried him through the day up to this point.

As Bailey prepared to serve again, Carpenter called a timeout to try and ice her. Saul looked around for Autumn to see if she would join the huddle. She didn't. She stayed in her same spot. She was letting the girls play this one on their own, win or lose. Black took the court and Bailey was ready to serve. She tossed the ball high like she always did. This time, however, the toss was a little off. She hit it anyway but unfortunately, the ball bounded into the net.

It was 12-all.

"We need a side-out," Fred shouted. "Right here. Right now."

Saul could hear Lauren's dad shouting with all his might from the other side. Lauren was set to serve and she served a tough floater right to Morgan who handled it with surprising ease. Savannah set the ball back to Morgan who fired it down the line for a kill. Saul looked back at Autumn and saw her grinning with total satisfaction. She had been working on that shot all season with Morgan.

With Black up 13 to 12, Bree rotated back in. Saul felt sweat on his palms for the first time all day. It was Morgan's turn to serve and, unfortunately, she served a lame duck. It was one of those I'm not going to miss serves. It sailed harmlessly to the other side and Blue was able to load up for a great hitting opportunity. Lauren set the ball to Butt Cheeks and her hit looked like a sure kill until Morgan dove from out of nowhere and dug it up. The play got a rise of oohs and aahs not just from the Black parents, but the Blue parents as well. The ball sailed high into Savannah's hands who then back-set it to Stacy who crushed the ball harder than she had all season. The ball was sailing with such velocity it was going way out of bounds until it smashed right into Butt Cheeks' face.

The crowd moaned as Butt Cheeks took the blow. She looked as if she was going to fall over but she maintained her balance. The SkyHi Black girls went over to congratulate Morgan on an outstanding dig. She was playing the game of her life against the team she wanted most to beat, the team that told her at tryouts she wasn't good enough.

Trailing 14 to 12, Carpenter had to call his final timeout to draw up a play. He also needed time for Butt Cheeks to recover from the heavy blow. The side of her face had turned beet red.

In the Black huddle, the girls were doing their best to contain their excitement. They were one point away. The club director was talking but they were barely listening to him. They were coaching each other. Bree congratulated Stacy on the facial she planted on Butt Cheeks. Savannah told Bree to prepare to block middle because she thought they would be going to Pamela. Bailey told Morgan to serve more aggressively. Morgan said she heard Coach Carpenter tell the outsides to not hit line, to go crosscourt because our block was too slow. Bree knew that was a slight at her but she took it in and used it as additional motivation, although no one needed additional motivation right now.

The girls took the court and the Black parents rose to their feet with applause. Fred looked at Saul and said, "Arm lock?"

"What?" Saul asked.

"For luck," Fred insisted.

Fred held out his arm and Saul followed suit and the two locked arms for good luck. Saul hoped they didn't look too silly but he went along with the bromance move to make Fred happy.

Morgan was ready to serve and she did serve more aggressively, but it still wasn't enough to fool the Blue defense. A solid pass was made to Lauren who back-set Pamela who was rolling to the right on a slide. The play caught the Black girls off guard and Pamela terminated the ball easily. Cathy then rotated in while Pamela went back to serve.

Still game point and Black holding on to a 14 to 13 lead, Bree screamed at the back row, "Dig deep, right here!"

Pamela then hit a low-lining serve that appeared to be heading into the center of the net. It clipped the top of the tape instead and managed to tumble over. Bree saw the ball dropping and instinctively dove for it and was able to pancake the ball back up before it hit the ground. Savannah was able to push a set over to Morgan but the ball was way off the net and all Morgan could do was keep the ball in play. Blue now had an easy free-ball to convert and Butt Cheeks bumped a pass to Lauren who quickset Cathy. Cathy swung hard but Bree managed to get her long, skinny arms up just in time. The ball deflected toward the floor back in Cathy's direction. Saul thought the point was over and was ready to celebrate, but Pamela came out of nowhere and saved the ball before it hit the ground. Lauren's only option was to go to Butt Cheeks for an outside hit. Bree knew where the ball was going. She had started shifting her block to the right side before Lauren had even set the ball. Bree knew Butt Cheeks was hitting crosscourt. Bree timed her block beautifully just as Butt Cheeks was swinging through the ball. There was nowhere for the ball to go but straight down off of Bree's hands. The ball fell to the floor on Blue's side of the net.

Bree had just executed the best block of her life. She knew as soon as the ball hit her hands that the game was won and she fell to her knees in triumph. Her teammates swarmed around her in a raucous celebration. Fred and Saul couldn't get their arms unlocked and had trouble executing their traditional man-hug. Autumn came running out and pounced on the mound of girls, hugging them one by one and then reminding the girls to go to the net and shake the opponent's hands.

As soon as Bree was done with the obligatory handshakes, she darted over in Saul's direction with the biggest smile on her face. He thought he was running towards her, but then he realized that Bobby was standing ten feet in front of him and was extending his arms out to her. She ran towards her boyfriend in full sprint, but then Saul could tell she wasn't really looking at Bobby. She was looking at him. She slapped Bobby's hand as she raced by and Bobby turned to look where she was running to. She was running straight into the arms of her dad.

She jumped up into Saul's arms and gave him the biggest embrace he had felt in years. For a brief moment, Saul knew that all was right with the world. She was as light as a feather, like a three-year-old again, that innocent age when every daughter thinks her father is a super-hero, free from imperfections. And just like that, he knew everything was okay between them. Their bond was strong again. Somehow, someway, through his patient actions or inactions, or just his willingness to let her go, he had managed to transport himself back over to her side of the net. She knew he was on her side again, even though he knew he'd never really left.

"We did it, Dad," she said, her head resting on his shoulder. "I told you we could beat them."

"You can do anything you want, Bree," Saul said, giving Bobby a sly wink as he was watching them embrace. It's not your turn yet, Saul wanted to say to him. She still belongs to me.

And then, like a flash, Bree pulled away and said, "I've got to go."

She gave Bobby a quick hug and then was surprised to see Callie who had come over to congratulate her. Saul hadn't seen Callie the whole tournament. Her team was knocked out early and was forced to play in the loser's bracket the last couple of days. He was glad she saw Bree play and witness firsthand the caliber of player she had become.

"Oh, and Dad," Bree shouted back to him. "Talent doesn't always win out." She then ran over to be with her teammates.

She was right, Saul had to admit. Sometimes talent doesn't win out. Sometimes heart, grit and determination win out. That combination provides the occasional upset or Cinderella story, or even a beautiful family like his own.

In all of the delirium, Saul had forgotten they had another match to play. They had to play some team from Kansas City. The winner would be assured of a medal and get to play in the semi-finals tomorrow morning. But in reality, Saul knew SkyHi Black had just earned their medal. They proved they were a top team. They were the first SkyHi second team to ever beat a top team in the club's history. They finished the highest that any second team had ever finished in the Open Division.

Ironically, they finished tied for fifth, the same finish they had in most of their local tournaments. The Kansas City team they played in the semi-finals beat them and beat them good. It was obvious the girls were drained after their victory over Blue. That was their championship match. Court 16, the court where they triumphed over SkyHi Blue, was their stadium court that day.

The Blue parents were good sports afterwards. Brent came over to congratulate Saul and bragged on how great his daughter had played. Pamela, while upset with the loss, was happy for her high school teammates, Bree and Savannah.

"School ball will be ramping back up in a month," Brent reminded him.

"Hard to believe," Saul replied. "The sport never ends."

"It will end someday," Brent said. "Then we'll be reliving days like these."

"I'll see you at school ball," Saul said. They shook hands and said their good-byes.

After the Kansas City match, their day was over. Harper was exhausted. She had been celebrating with her friends all afternoon and still had her medal proudly draped around her neck. After Autumn released the team, Bree found her family. She was finally able to congratulate Harper on her big win. She was admiring the medal when Harper took it off and wrapped it around Bree's shoulders.

"You're the best, Sis," she said.

"Thanks, Harp. How does it look on me?"

"You look like a champ," Veronica said.

As they turned to head back to the hotel, Autumn came running up to them almost out of breath. "I'm glad I caught up to you guys," she said panting.

"What's up?" Saul asked.

"I just wanted you to know I just got finished talking to a college coach and he is very interested in talking to Bree about playing for them."

"That's great," Saul said, wanting to hear more. "What school?"

"Missouri."

"Not bad" Saul said.

"It's against NCAA rules to talk to him now but I can get his info and you can call him."

"Thank you," Saul said.

"Great job today again, Bree," she said.

Autumn ran off and Bree didn't hesitate in giving Saul a glaring stare. "I'm not playing in college, Dad."

"I know that, Bree," Saul said. "I told you that you can do anything you want. But it's always good to have options."

"Mom," Bree moaned, looking at Veronica for help.

"You're not playing in college, Bree. You don't have to worry," Very assured her while reviving her dreaded death stare aimed at Saul.

They began walking towards their hotel and Saul was still in his nice and relaxed peaceful state. "Girls," he said, after taking a few steps. "There are good days and bad days in volleyball."

"And today was a very good day," Harper interjected.

"Yes, it was, Harp. Yes, it was."

Later, during the joyous ride back home to Plano, the girls were jamming to Pat Benatar's 80s' anthem, "All Fired Up." Saul didn't even have to suggest the tune. The girls did. The whole family was screaming the chorus at the top of their lungs.

Now I believe there comes a time
When everything just falls in line
We live and learn from our mistakes
The deepest cuts are healed by faith

Timely lyrics, Saul had to admit. He had never really focused on the song's simple meaning until now. He just liked the power and driving beat of the song, along with Benatar's unbelievable set of pipes.

And as he and the fired-up family of four continued north on the Dallas North Tollway singing their hearts out, for the first time in a long time, Saul's Master Athletic Plan was the furthest thing from his mind.

BREE'S DIARY
July 2
A scholarship to the University of Missouri!! WOW!! Sounds SOOOOO exciting! I better keep my options open.
 I won't tell Dad, tho.

SIDE OUT

ABOUT THE AUTHOR

R. Paul Fry is a 25-year veteran of the broadcasting industry, where he worked as an executive managing television stations and overseeing more centralized roles such as investor relations and corporate communications. After years of writing corporate non-fiction, i.e. press releases, annual reports, investor presentations and speeches, he is now writing contemporary fiction. *Days of Whine and Volleyball* is his first novel. He resides in Texas with his wife and two daughters, both veterans of the club volleyball circuit.

Made in the USA
Monee, IL
31 October 2019